Comedies & Proverbs

DATE DUE

FEB 2 0 1995	
JAN 8 2000	
MAR 8 2000	

PAJ BOOKS

Bonnie Marranca and Gautam Dasgupta,

Series Editors

ALFRED DE MUSSET
Comedies & Proverbs

INTRODUCTION

AND

TRANSLATION

BY

DAVID SICES

THE JOHNS HOPKINS UNIVERSITY PRESS
BALTIMORE AND LONDON

© 1994 The Johns Hopkins University Press
All rights reserved
Printed in the United States of America on acid-free paper

The Johns Hopkins University Press
2715 North Charles Street
Baltimore, Maryland 21218-4319
The Johns Hopkins Press Ltd., London

Library of Congress Cataloging-in-Publication Data will be found
at the end of this book.

A catalog record for this book is available from the British Library.

To J. B. S.

CONTENTS

INTRODUCTION

Although Alfred de Musset (1810–57) is traditionally anthologized, with Lamartine, Vigny, and Hugo, as one of the major French Romantic poets, he really should be considered, with Gautier, Nerval, and others, among the movement's second generation. Like many a youth, he had ambivalent feelings about the ideas and sentiments of his elders. On the one hand, his autobiographical novel, *The Confessions of a Child of the Century*, is a major model of Romantic confessional prose; on the other hand, he became identified among his peers as a major proponent of the revival of neoclassical tragedy in the theater, as well as a sarcastic, even virulent, lampooner of Romantic stylistic excesses, in his widely read and amusing *Letters of Dupuis and Cotonet*, in which he gave a well-known definition of Romanticism as "the overuse of adjectives."

Musset's primary renown in modern times has been as a dramatist. When Victor Hugo's *Hernani* and Alexandre Dumas père's *Antony* were produced around 1830, they made a considerable stir in the theater. But the "Romantic" Musset has remained perhaps the only "classic" dramatist of his time. Actually, the best of his plays were not staged during his life: of his most original works, *What Does Marianne Want?* alone was performed, in a radically altered and disfigured version, in 1851. *Lorenzaccio* had to wait until 1896, forty years after the author's death, and was then done in a "regularized" form commissioned by Sarah Bernhardt so she might add the play's hero to her list of transvestite roles — a travesty in both the usual and the etymological senses of the term.*

*See my study *Theater of Solitude: The Drama of Alfred de Musset*, Hanover, N.H., 1974, pp. 109–125. *Lorenzaccio*, which in recent years has become one of Musset's most popular stage works, has been omitted from this collection because it stands alone in Musset's dramatic production among the best of French Romantic historical tragedies and because it differs radically from the *Comedies and Proverbs* in both form and language.

The reason for which Musset's plays were not produced on stage in their own time, but saw the light of day in the pages of the *Revue des deux mondes* and the published volumes entitled *Un Spectacle dans un fauteuil ("Armchair Theater")*, has become part of French theater lore. Before his first major, and greatest, dramas — *What Does Marianne Want?*, *Fantasio*, *You Can't Trifle with Love*, and *Lorenzaccio* — Musset wrote several plays designed for specific theatrical productions. But when his *Venetian Night* was staged at the Odéon in Paris in 1830, the efforts of the notorious theater claque, in particular at the signal of an unfortunate contact between his heroine's white dress and a freshly painted green trellis, led to such an uproar that the author swore never to let his plays be staged again. This was a vow he managed to keep for about fifteen years (in the proverbial words of his own title, *Il ne faut jurer de rien*, *"You Never Can Tell"*), until the one-act play, *A Passing Fancy*, was produced without his authorization in 1847.

What makes Musset's best dramas so original and interesting is, at least in part, a result of that vow. Unconstrained by the limitations of a flourishing but convention-ridden theater (many of whose strictures, oddly enough, grand opera was then in the process of overcoming), the author was enabled to write a "theater of the mind" that did not have to take spatial or temporal unities into consideration, that was not limited by the resources of the proscenium stage, and whose prose language was imbued with a poetic spirit perhaps more genuinely lyrical than Musset's own highly considered verse.

All of Musset's plays are delightful. His best dramatic works — the four plays cited above — were written at the age of twenty-three, in a period from the spring of 1833 to the winter of 1834, during which he was carrying on an affair with the novelist George Sand (Aurore Dupin Dudevant) that led the lovers to Venice, and their love to world-wide notoriety. The extent of Musset's accomplishment — the plays' linguistic and technical mastery, their variety, and their originality (not to mention *Lorenzaccio*'s inordinate length and complexity) — bely both his youth and the rapidity of their creation. Scholars have documented the influence on his work of Shakespeare, Byron, Schiller, E. T. A. Hoffmann, Jean-Paul Richter, George Sand,

and a number of others (as well as Musset's influence on so important a dramatist as Georg Buechner). Musset himself was often accused of excessive facility: Flaubert in particular detested—or was it envied?—the ease with which he seemed to write. But there can be no denying either the significant contribution that his stage works made to French theater or their profound originality.

After these four plays, Musset continued to write drama almost until his death. His last completed stage work, *Bettine*, dates from 1851, but he left unfinished dramatic projects as well. The four later works included here—*The Candlestick, You Never Can Tell, A Passing Fancy,* and *A Door Has to Be either Open or Shut*—seem the best of them to me, a judgment that has been ratified by theater history. Like *You Can't Trifle with Love*, they owe a good deal more than their titles to the genre of the "dramatic proverb," an upper-class salon entertainment that enjoyed considerable popularity in the eighteenth and nineteenth centuries, whose most famous practitioners were Carmontelle and Leclercq. Somewhat like the game of charades, this was intended to provide an opportunity for amateurs to act out familiar expressions, though in Musset's case it became far more complex. If these later plays seem less powerful and original than those written during Musset's affair with George Sand, that has more to do with their standard upper-class themes, and their social realism, than with any faltering of theatrical mastery on the author's part. On the contrary, all four of them achieved greater popularity on stage than their predecessors, and it may indeed have been this evidence of able stagecraft that encouraged actors and producers to put on Musset's more problematic earlier ones.

Today, for a number of reasons both technical and thematic, Musset's theater production seems to be more viable, more *contemporary*, than at any point in its history. In terms of technique, the influence that cinematography has exercised over stagecraft since the early years of this century has doubtless played an important role in this. Dramas that seemed impossible to stage under the conditions of the pre-twentieth-century European stage now present no problems, thanks to advances made in lighting and machinery, not to mention the altered expectations of a theater public accustomed by cinematic scene-changes, flashbacks, and dissolves to a radically different narrative sequence.*

But these technical questions would be of little importance if Musset's work did not speak relevantly to the contemporary public—that is, if they were not thematically more contemporary, more up-to-date, than other French dramas of their period. This is reflected in the title I have chosen for Musset's *Les Caprices de Marianne*: although it is usually rendered as "Marianne's Caprices," or perhaps better "Marianne's Whims," here it is translated as *What Does Marianne Want?*, a deliberate echo of Freud's anguished question, "What do women want?"

The notion behind this choice of title is not merely a desire to be contemporary or relevant in linguistic terms. Part of what makes Musset's plays so viable on the contemporary stage is, perhaps first of all, the fact that his female characters—Marianne, Elsbeth, Camille, Jacqueline, Cecile, and Mathilde in particular—all seek to define what it is that "women want," each in her own way and according to her own needs and situation. Marianne is an ill-married woman whose sensuality craves fulfillment just as much as does Cœlio's idealistic passion, and who is trapped in the choice between "romantic" love and the physical desire aroused by Octave. Elsbeth illuminates that most modern of problems, the vexed relationship between daughter and father, even when the latter is the most loving and generous of men. Camille, like Perdican, "trifles" with love and pays the consequences; but the woman, considered as more "spiritual" than the libertine Perdican, is held to the higher, more rigorous standards represented by a choice between marriage and the convent.

Musset's later comedies reflect a greater degree of reconciliation with the society of his time; but his portrayal of women continued to be complex and empathetic. In Jacqueline we see a married woman in this more realistic context, shedding her dashing but standardized (at least by contemporary notions) garrison lover for a

---

*Bernard Masson's two major ground-breaking studies, *Musset et le théâtre intérieur* (Paris, 1974) and *Musset et son double, lecture de Lorenzaccio* (Paris, 1978), although they deal principally with the omitted *Lorenzaccio*, are excellent sources of historical information concerning the nature of Musset's stagecraft and theatrical vision.

younger, fresher, more appealing one; yet she is still the ill-married "modern" woman in a traditional society, whose elderly husband represents status but not fulfillment. The apparently ideal Cecile — ideal from the standpoint of a male libertine and of the contemporary bourgeois world — has qualities that go beyond the solid virtues that make her seem to be the realization of *My Fair Lady*'s irritated — and specious — question, "Why can't a woman be more like a man?" and its echoes of Freud's question cited above. And Mathilde, in conjunction with her witty, apparently scatterbrained, and quite feminine friend Ernestine de Léry, places the entire basis of stylish marriage in question, while she renews the traditional image and virtues of the abandoned, yet faithful wife.

Another major contemporary theme of Musset's stage works is the individual's isolation within both society and the universe. The playwright's youthful characters are as alienated as those in *Waiting for Godot* or (in a more "Romantic" vein) *Woyzek*. *Lorenzaccio* is perhaps the supreme example among his plays of this tendency, but it is evident as well in the tragic endings of *What Does Marianne Want?* and *You Can't Trifle with Love*, and expressed with great power in Fantasio's half-humorous cry, "Quelles solitudes que tous ces corps humains!" ("What solitudes all these human bodies are!"). Fantasio is obliged by his disillusionment with the world's banality — "What a fiasco that sunset is!" he says — as well as with bourgeois society, wearing an "enormous cotton nightcap," to seek asylum in the role and costume of jester in Princess Elsbeth's garden. In *What Does Marianne Want?* Musset's sense of a split between the ideal and the real is dramatically embodied by the multiplication of his hero into two separate and involuntarily interfering "lovers," the idealistic Cœlio and the rakish Octave. Both Perdican and Camille are trapped by socially defined roles — his as "man of the world," hers as virtuous young woman — in a situation that forces them to renounce their very real mutual love. If the heroes and heroines of Musset's later plays show less of a tendency to suffer from their isolation in a hostile society and universe — if, that is, the ultimate resolution of their situations and their plays is more regularly "happy" — they still bear scars of the cost of such acceptance of the way of the world: the loss of youthful ideals and illusions.

The quizzical humor that characterizes Fantasio's and Elsbeth's alienation, as well as that of Marianne, Cœlio and Octave, Perdican and Camille, Jacqueline and Fortunio, and Mathilde and Ernestine, is both typical of Musset's problematic relationship with the dominant aesthetic and ethos of his time, Romanticism (leading additionally to his being considered the best representative in France of Romantic irony), and what makes him seem so much more "modern" to today's audiences than any of his contemporaries. It is my hope that this quality comes through sufficiently in the translations in this volume so that audiences beyond Paris and the boundaries of Musset's nation may appreciate at his true worth one of France's greatest and most original dramatists.

TRANSLATOR'S NOTE

In my versions I have sought to respect the lyricism and the realism of Musset's theater language, as well as its elegance. That has involved finding a suitably aristocratic diction for his protagonists, and a suitably comic one for his "puppets": Claudio and Tibia in *What Does Marianne Want?*, the Prince of Mantua and Marinoni in *Fantasio*, the Baron, Mistress Pluche, and Masters Blazius and Bridaine in *You Can't Trifle with Love*, André and, in a different sense, Clavaroche in *The Candlestick*, and the Baroness, the Curate, and, in a still different sense, Van Buck in *You Never Can Tell* (the one-act comedies *A Passing Fancy* and *A Door Has to Be either Open or Shut* involve only aristocratic characters). I have tried throughout to avoid the use of historical or biographical annotation, beyond that of my introductions to the plays. In those few cases where simple translation of a cultural reference would have been unclear, I have tried to work an equivalent into the text (for example, in *A Door Has to Be either Open or Shut* the Count mentions Rodrigue, a character from Corneille's *Le Cid* whom Frenchmen immediately recognize). Indeed, the only places where I have found notes of any kind unavoidable are those in which the French language offers the choice between an intimate and a formal "you."

My greatest concern has been to find an English equivalent for the tone of Musset's French. The lyrical, passionate, and yet elegant diction of the youthful trio of plays gives way to a more sophisticated, aristocratic diction in the later four. Yet in all of them the sense of linguistic playfulness, of fantasy, of humor is never far away, whether it be through the irony or the satire of *What Does Marianne Want?*, *Fantasio*, and *You Can't Trifle with Love*, or through the more worldly humor in *The Candlestick, You Never Can Tell, A Passing Fancy,* and *A Door Has to Be either Open or Shut*. That is Musset's quite original type of comedy, and a good part of what gives these plays such a lively presence on the French stage today. Indeed, the choice of these seven particular works was dictated by their enduring viability as drama, their continuing importance in the French repertory.

There are a number of people to whom I am grateful for their help in this project. They will know who they are without my naming them, I am sure. But most of all, I thank my wife, Jacqueline, without whose love, encouragement, careful reading, questions, and suggestions it could never have been accomplished.

Comedies & Proverbs

What Does Marianne Want?

What Does Marianne Want? was written in early 1833 and published in the *Revue des deux mondes* of 15 May. The first of Musset's great comedies to see print, it had its première in 1851, with Madeleine Brohan making her Comédie Française debut as Marianne. *What Does Marianne Want?* was thus the only one of his major early works to be staged during his lifetime, and then only with considerable modification to make it conform better to French theater conventions. Because the changes that Musset wrought under pressure of performance tended to bowdlerize his language and to make the work less original (e.g., in order to observe the unity of time he illogically attached the final scene between Octave and Marianne to the preceding events of the evening), I have used the earlier text for my translation.

There is a great use of symmetry (e.g., between Octave and Cœlio), on both comic grounds—the two young men's exchanges in the first scene, for example—and aesthetic ones, which reflects the traditions of Italian commedia dell'arte. But this symmetry expresses a deeper theme of the play: Octave, the hedonistic rake, and Cœlio, the idealistic dreamer, are two conflicting yet complementary faces of Musset's personality, as George Sand was the first to remark (see Musset's letter to her dated 10 May 1834). In this way the interplay between artifice and personal confession so characteristic of Musset's best drama is fully realized here for the first time.

The notions of changeableness and unpredictability, assigned in this play to the character of Marianne, recur also, in differing form, in *Fantasio* and *You Can't Trifle with Love*. Although all Musset's comedies deal with "romantic" love, the author expressed his own personality (and his personal demons) in varied ways, through both male and female characters. This reflects the more essentially "Romantic" art of these early works than the later ones.

CHARACTERS

Claudio, a judge
Marianne, his wife
*Cœlio**
Octave
Tibia, Claudio's valet

Ciuta, an old woman
Hermia, Cœlio's mother
Malvolio, Hermia's steward
Servants, assassins

ACT ONE
Scene 1. *A street in front of Claudio's house.*

*(Marianne leaves her house with a prayer book in her hands.
   Ciuta accosts her.)*
Ciuta: May I have a word with you, my fair one?
Marianne: What do you want of me?
Ciuta: A young man of this city is desperately in love with you.
   For an entire month he has vainly sought an opportunity to let
   you know of it. His name is Cœlio; he is of a noble family and
   distinguished mien.
Marianne: That will do. Tell the man who sent you that he is
   wasting his time and efforts; if he has the nerve to send me
   another such message, I shall inform my husband.
   (Exit.)
Cœlio: (Entering.) Well, Ciuta, what did she say?
Ciuta: She is more proud and devout than ever. She says she will
   inform her husband if we keep on pursuing her.
Cœlio: Oh! What an unfortunate wretch I am! There is nothing
   left for me but to die. Oh! She is the cruelest of women! What
   do you advise me to do, Ciuta? What recourse is left me?
Ciuta: First of all, I advise you to move away from here, for there
   comes her husband after her.
   (Exit. Enter Claudio and Tibia.)
Claudio: Are you my faithful servant? My devoted valet? Let me
   inform you then that I must get revenge for an insult.
Tibia: You, sir?

*Pronounced "Célio."

Claudio: Yes, "me, sir"—since those impudent guitars keep on whispering beneath my wife's window. But just you wait! This isn't the end of it. Come and hear me over this way: there are people there who could overhear us. I want you to go tonight and get the assassin I spoke to you about.

Tibia: Whatever for?

Claudio: I think Marianne has taken some lovers.

Tibia: Do you think so, sir?

Claudio: Yes. There is a scent of lovers round about my house. Nobody walks past my door naturally. It keeps on raining guitars and women bearing messages.

Tibia: Can you stop people from serenading your wife?

Claudio: No. But I can post a man behind the garden gate and get rid of the first man who passes through it.

Tibia: Pshaw! Your wife doesn't have any lovers. It is as if you were to say that I have mistresses.

Claudio: Why shouldn't you, Tibia? You are very ugly, but you are quite an intelligent man.

Tibia: I agree, I agree.

Claudio: You see, Tibia, you yourself agree. There can be no doubt about it any more, my disgrace is common knowledge.

Tibia: Why common knowledge?

Claudio: I tell you it is common knowledge.

Tibia: But sir, the whole city considers your wife a dragon of virtue. She sees nobody and she never leaves the house except to go to church.

Claudio: Don't try and stop me. I am beside myself with rage, after all the presents she has gotten from me. Yes, Tibia, I am at this very moment hatching a terrible plot, and I feel ready to die of anguish.

Tibia: Oh, no, sir!

Claudio: When I tell you something, please be so kind as to believe it.
   (Exit.)

Cœlio: (Entering again.) Woe unto him who, in the midst of youth, surrenders to a hopeless love! Woe unto him who yields to a sweet, vain reverie, not knowing yet where his illusion will lead him or whether he may be requited! Lying languidly in a boat, he drifts little by little away from the shore; in the distance he spies enchanted plains, green meadows, and the dim mirage of his Eldorado. The breezes bear him on in silence, and when reality reawakens him, he is just as far from the goal he longs for as he is from the shore he left behind. He can neither pursue his journey nor return to where he started. *(The sound of musical instruments is heard.)* What is this masquerade? Isn't that Octave I see there?

(Enter Octave.)

Octave: My good sir, how fares your gracious melancholy today?

Cœlio: Octave, you fool! Your face is all caked with red! What is the meaning of this get-up? Have you no shame, in the middle of the day?

Octave: Oh Cœlio, you fool! Your face is all caked with white! What is the meaning of this great black suit? Have you no shame, in the midst of Carnival?

Cœlio: What a life you are leading! Either you are drunk, or I am.

Octave: Either you are in love, or I am.

Cœlio: More than ever, with the fair Marianne.

Octave: More than ever, on Cyprus wine.

Cœlio: I was on my way to your house when I bumped into you.

Octave: And so was I, on the way to my house. How is it doing? I haven't seen it for a week.

Cœlio: I have a favor to ask you.

Octave: Speak up, Cœlio, my dear child. Do you want money? I have none left. Do you want advice? I am drunk. Do you want my sword? Here, take this slapstick. Speak, speak, I am at your disposal.

Cœlio: How long can this go on? Not home for a week! You will kill yourself, Octave.

Octave: Never by my own hand, my friend, never! I would sooner die than take my own life.

Cœlio: Isn't the life you are leading a form of suicide?

Octave: Imagine a tightrope walker in silver slippers, with his balance pole clenched in his fists, suspended between heaven and earth; to the right and left of him little, wizened old figures, pale, emaciated phantoms, nimble creditors, relatives, and courtiers, a whole legion of monsters hang onto his coattails and tug at him from all sides, to make him lose his balance; sententious phrases, jewel-encrusted maxims gallop round him; a cloud of sinister predictions blinds him with its black wings. He sticks to his aerial course, from east to west, from dawn to setting sun. If he looks down his head spins; if he looks up he loses his footing. He runs more swiftly than the wind, and all those hands clutching at him will not make him spill a drop of the joyous cup he bears in his. That is my life, my dear friend; that is my faithful image for you to see.

Cælio: How happy you are to be mad!

Octave: How mad you are not to be happy! Just tell me, Cælio, what do you lack?

Cælio: I lack serenity, the sweet heedlessness that makes life a mirror in which everything takes form for a moment and then slips quickly away. For me a debt is a nagging remorse. Love, which for men like you is a passing fancy, stirs my life to the depths. Oh, my friend, you will never know what it means to love as I do! My study is deserted; for a month I have been wandering around this house day and night. What a magic spell I experience at moonrise, assembling my modest band of singers in the shadow of those trees across the square, directing them myself, listening as they sing the praises of Marianne's beauty! She has never appeared at her window; she has never once leaned her charming brow upon her shutter.

Octave: Who is this Marianne? Can it be my cousin?

Cælio: That is the one, the wife of old Claudio.

Octave: I have never seen her. But she definitely is my cousin. Claudio is just made for the part. Let me take care of your problem, Cælio.

Cælio: Every attempt I have made to inform her of my love has been in vain. She is fresh from the convent; she loves her husband and she respects her duties. Her door is closed to all the young men in town, and no one can get near her.

Octave: All right! Is she pretty? Oh, what an ass I am! You love her, so that doesn't matter. What might we devise?

Cælio: Shall I speak frankly with you? You won't laugh at me?

Octave: Let me laugh at you, and speak frankly anyway.

Cælio: As a relation of hers, you must sometimes be welcomed into the house.

Octave: I must be welcomed? I don't know. Let's say that I am. To tell the truth, there is one great difference between my distinguished family and a bunch of asparagus: we don't form a very close-knit unit, and our contact is mostly in writing. Marianne knows my name, though. Shall I speak to her in your behalf?

Cœlio: I have tried to approach her a dozen times; a dozen times I have felt my knees give way as I got near her. I was obliged to send old Ciuta. When I see her, my throat grows dry, and I choke as if my heart were rising up to my lips.

Octave: I have experienced that. It is like when a hunter, in the depths of the forest, sees a doe approaching little by little over the fallen leaves, and hears the branches brush against her trembling flanks, like the rustle of a flimsy gown. His heart begins to pound despite himself; he raises his gun silently, not moving an inch or taking a breath.

Cœlio: Why am I this way? Isn't it a commonplace among rakes that all women are alike? Why are there so few loves, then, that are alike? In truth, I couldn't love that woman as you would, Octave, or as I would love someone else. And yet what does it all amount to? A pair of blue eyes, a pair of ruby lips, a white dress, and two white hands. Why should what would make you gay and charming, what would draw you as a magnet draws a bit of iron, leave me sad and powerless? Who can say: this is happy or sad? Reality is just a shadow. Call what makes it immortal either phantasy or folly. Then beauty itself is folly. Every man walks along enveloped in a transparent web that covers him from head to toe. He thinks he is seeing woods and rivers, divine faces, and before his eyes all nature is tinged with the infinite shadings of his magical fabric. Octave! Octave! Please help me.

Octave: I like your love, Cœlio; it sloshes around in your brain like a bottle of Syracuse wine. Give me your hand: I'm going to help you; just wait a moment. The fresh air strikes my face, and my wits are coming back to me. I know this Marianne: she can't stand me, even though we have never met. She is a skinny doll who is always mumbling prayers.

Cœlio: Do as you like, but don't deceive me, I beg of you. I am very easily deceived, I can never suspect an action that I would not do myself.

Octave: How about climbing her wall?

Cœlio: Between the two of us there is an imaginary wall that I have not been able to climb.

Octave: Suppose you wrote to her?

Cœlio: She tears up my letters or sends them back to me.

Octave: How about loving someone else? Come on along with me to Rosalinde's.

Cœlio: My life's breath belongs to Marianne; with one word from her lips she can destroy it or set it on fire. It would be harder for me to live for someone else than to die for her; either I shall succeed or I shall kill myself. Be still! There she is, coming back around the corner.

Octave: You move off a little way, and I shall approach her.

Cœlio: What do you mean? In the outfit you have on? Wipe your face: you look like a clown.

Octave: There, it is done. My dear Cœlio, drunkenness and I are too close friends ever to quarrel; it does my will, just as I do its. Have no fear on that account; only a student on holiday, who drinks too much at a dinner party, loses his head and fights with his wine. As for me, it is in my very nature to be drunk; my way of thinking is to give in gracefully, and I would just as soon speak to the king right now as to your lady fair.

Cœlio: I don't know what it is I am feeling.—No, don't speak to her.

Octave: Why not?

Cœlio: I can't say why not; I feel you are going to betray me.

Octave: Give me your hand. I swear to you on my honor that Marianne will belong to you and to no one else in the world, as long as I can do anything about it.
(Exit Cœlio. Enter Marianne. Octave goes up to her.)

Octave: Do not turn away, oh beautiful princess! Deign to cast your eyes upon your most unworthy servant.

Marianne: Who are you?

Octave: My name is Octave; I am your husband's cousin.

Marianne: Have you come to see him? Go into the house, he will be back soon.

Octave: I have not come to see him, and I won't go into the house, for fear you will have me thrown right back out again when I have told you what brings me.

Marianne: Then you can spare yourself the trouble of telling me and detaining me any longer.

Octave: There is something that I must tell you, and I beg you to stop and listen to it. Heartless Marianne! Your eyes have done a good deal of harm, and your words are not designed to heal it. What has Cœlio done to you?

Marianne: Who are you talking about, and what harm have I done?

Octave: The cruelest of all, because it is hopeless; the most terrible, because it is an illness that cherishes itself and refuses a healing draught even from the hand of a friend; an illness that makes the lips go pale under poisons sweeter than ambrosia and makes the hardest heart dissolve into a rain of tears, like Cleopatra's pearl; an illness that all herbs and all human knowledge cannot relieve and that feeds upon the passing breeze, the aroma of a faded rose, the chorus of a song; it sips eternal nourishment of its suffering from everything around it, as a bee sucks honey from all the plants in a garden.

Marianne: Will you tell me the name of this illness?

Octave: Let him who is worthy of pronouncing it tell you. Let the dreams of your nights, these young orange trees, this cool fountain teach it to you. If you but seek it out one starry night, you will find it on your lips. Its name has no existence apart from itself.

Marianne: Is it so dangerous to say, so awful in its contagion that it frightens a tongue that pleads in its favor?

Octave: Is it so sweet to hear, cousin, that you should ask it? Yet you taught it to Cœlio.

Marianne: It must have been unintentional, since I know neither one nor the other.

Octave: The sole desire of my heart is that you should know both of them together and never separate them again.

Marianne: Is that so?

Octave: Cœlio is my best friend. If I wanted to arouse your interest, I would tell you that he is as handsome as a prince, young, noble, and I would not be lying; but I want only to arouse your pity, and so I will tell you that he has been sad unto death since the day he first saw you.

Marianne: Is it my fault if he is sad?

Octave: Is it his fault if you are beautiful? He thinks of nothing but you; day and night he wanders about your house. Have you never heard them singing under your windows? Have you never opened your shutters and your curtains at midnight?

Marianne: Anyone can sing at night, and this square belongs to everyone.

Octave: Anyone can love you, too; but no one can tell you of it. How old are you, Marianne?

Marianne: That is a fine question! Suppose I told you I was nineteen, what would you like me to make of it?

Octave: Then you still have five or six years to be loved, eight or ten to be in love yourself, and the rest to spend in prayers.

Marianne: Really? Well, to make the best use of my time, I love Claudio, your cousin and my husband.

Octave: My cousin and your husband, between the two of them, will never amount to more than a bumbling clod; you can't love Claudio.

Marianne: Nor Cœlio either, you can tell him that.

Octave: Why not?

Marianne: Why shouldn't I love Claudio? He is my husband.

Octave: Why shouldn't you love Cœlio? He is your lover.

Marianne: I wonder why I should be listening to you. Good-by, Signor Octave, this joke has gone far enough.
(*Exit.*)

Octave: My word, my word! She does have beautiful eyes.
(*Exit.*)

Scene 2. *Cœlio's house.*

(*Hermia, several servants, and Malvolio.*)

Hermia: Arrange these flowers as I ordered. Have the musicians been told to come?

A servant: Yes, madam; they will be here at suppertime.

Hermia: Those closed shutters keep it too dark in here. Let in a little daylight without letting in the sun. More flowers around this bed. Is supper good? Will we be having our beautiful neighbor, Countess Pergoli? What time did my son go out?

Malvolio: In order to have gone out he would first have had to come home. He wasn't here last night.

Hermia: You don't know what you are talking about. He had supper with me yesterday and brought me back here. Have you had the picture I bought for him this morning put in his study?

Malvolio: When his father was alive it would not have been like this. Wouldn't you think our mistress was eighteen years old again, and expecting her suitor's arrival?

Hermia: But while his mother is alive that is the way it is, Malvolio. Who put you in charge of his behavior? Remember this: I don't want Cœlio to meet with a single disapproving face; I don't want him to hear you grumbling to yourself, like a watchdog growling at a rival over a bone he wants to gnaw. Otherwise, by heaven, not one of you will spend the night under this roof.

Malvolio: I am not grumbling, and I am not trying to look disapproving: you asked me when my master left the house and I answered that he had not been home. Since he has had love on his mind we don't see him four times a week.

Hermia: Why are these books so dusty? Why is this furniture in disarray? Why must I do everything myself if I want to get anything done? It is very fine for you to look into things that don't concern you, when your work is half-done and the concerns you have been given fall on others' shoulders. Go about your business and hold your tongue.

(Enter Cœlio.)

Well, my child, what will be your pleasure today?

Cœlio: Whatever you want, mother.

(He sits down.)

Hermia: What, you will share your pleasures and not your troubles? That isn't fair, Cœlio. Keep secrets from me, my child, but not those that eat at your heart and leave you heedless of everything around you.

Cœlio: I have no secrets, and please God, if I did, that they were such as to turn me into a statue!

Hermia: When you were ten or twelve years old, all your troubles, all your little worries were tied to me; the sorrow or the joy in your eyes depended on a a harsh or indulgent look in mine that are looking at you now; your little blond head was connected by a very slender thread to your mother's heart. Now, my child, I am no more than your elder sister, unable perhaps to relieve your troubles, but not to share in them.

Cœlio: And you were once beautiful, too! Beneath the silver hair that shades your noble face, beneath the long cloak covering you, the eye can still discern the regal bearing of a queen and the graceful forms of Diana the huntress. Oh, mother, you once inspired love! The sound of guitars once whispered beneath your open window; you once walked with carefree, youthful pride through the swirling crowds on feast days in the square; you once were loved and did not requite it; a cousin of my father's died of love for you.

Hermia: Why are you reminding me of that?

Cœlio: Oh, if your heart can bear that sorrow, if it is not asking you for tears, tell me that story, mother, let me know how it all happened!

Hermia: Your father had never yet seen me then. Because of his relation to my family, he offered to convey the proposal of young Orsini, who wished to marry me. He was received by your grandfather as his condition deserved, and he was admitted into our family. Orsini was an excellent match, and yet I turned him down. Your father's pleading of Orsini's cause had snuffed out in my heart what little love he had inspired through two months' constant attentions. I hadn't suspected the depth of his passion for me. When my reply was brought to him he fell unconscious into your father's arms. Nonetheless, he went away on a long trip and increased his fortune, so it was thought that his sorrows must have abated. Your father changed roles and asked for himself what he had not obtained for Orsini. I loved him sincerely, and the esteem he had inspired in my parents left me no grounds for hesitation. Our marriage was decided that same day, and we had a church wedding a few weeks later. Orsini returned at that time. He went to see your father, showered him with reproaches, accused him of betraying his trust and causing the refusal that he had received. "But in any case," he added, "if you sought my undoing you will be satisfied." Frightened by those words, your father went and saw mine, to ask him to bear witness so Orsini might know the truth. Alas, it was too late; the poor young man was found in his bedroom, stabbed through and through with his own sword.

Scene 3. *Claudio's garden.*

(Enter Claudio and Tibia.)

Claudio: You are right, my wife is a treasure of chastity. What more can I say? She is a solid virtue.

Tibia: Do you think so, sir?

Claudio: Can she help it if people sing under her windows? The signs of impatience that she shows at home are the result of her temper. Did you notice that her mother, when I touched that cord, was immediately of the same opinion as me?

Tibia: Concerning what?

Claudio: Concerning people singing under her windows.

Tibia: There is nothing wrong with singing, I am always humming to myself, myself.

Claudio: But it is hard to sing really well.

Tibia: Hard for you and me who, not having been given a voice by nature, have never cultivated it. But just see how those stage actors manage to get along.

Claudio: They are people who spend their lives on the boards.

Tibia: How much do you suppose is given per year? . . .

Claudio: To whom? Justices of the peace?

Tibia: No, singers.

Claudio: I have no idea. A justice of the peace makes one-third of my stipend. Counselors get half.

Tibia: If I were a judge in the royal court, and my wife had lovers, I would sentence them myself.

Claudio: To how many years' hard labor?

Tibia: To death. A death sentence is a splendid thing to read aloud.

Claudio: It isn't the judge who reads it, it is the clerk of the court.

Tibia: The clerk of your court has a pretty wife.

Claudio: No, it is the chief justice who has a pretty wife; I had supper with them last night.

Tibia: So does the clerk! The assassin who is coming tonight is the lover of the clerk's wife.

Claudio: What assassin?

Tibia: The one you asked for.

Claudio: It is no use his coming, after what I just told you.

Tibia: Concerning what?

Claudio: Concerning my wife.

Tibia: Here she comes herself.

    (Enter Marianne.)

Marianne: Do you know what has been happening to me while you have been out running around? I had a visit from your cousin.

Claudio: Who might that be? Identify him by name.

Marianne: Octave; he made a declaration of love to me on behalf of his friend Cœlio. Who is this Cœlio? Do you know this man? Make sure that neither he nor Octave ever sets foot in the house.

Claudio: I know him. He is the son of Hermia, our neighbor. How did you answer that?

Marianne: It doesn't matter how I answered. Do you understand what I am saying? I want you to tell your servants not to let either Cœlio or his friend into the house. I am expecting some sort of annoyance on their part, and I would just as soon avoid it.

    (Exit.)

Claudio: What do you make of this affair, Tibia? There must be some ruse beneath all this.

Tibia: Do you think so, sir?

Claudio: Why wouldn't she tell me how she answered? The proposal is impertinent, it is true; but the answer deserves to be known. I have a suspicion that this Cœlio is the one who has arranged for all those guitars.

Tibia: The best way to keep those two men out is to bar your door to them.

Claudio: You leave that to me. I must inform my mother-in-law of this discovery. I have a feeling that my wife is betraying me, and this entire story is just an invention designed by her with the sole purpose of putting something over on me and confusing my wits completely.

(Exit.)

ACT TWO
Scene 1. *A street.*

(Enter Octave and Ciuta.)

Octave: He has given up, you say?

Ciuta: Alas, the poor young fellow is more in love than ever, but his melancholy has confused him as to the desires nourishing it! I would almost think that he distrusts you, me, and everyone around him.

Octave: No, by heaven, I won't give up! I feel as if I were another Marianne, and it is a pleasure to be stubborn. Either Cœlio will succeed or I shall know the reason why.

Ciuta: Would you go against his wishes?

Octave: Yes, to follow out mine, since they are kindred to his own. I am going to confound Signor Claudio the judge: I detest, despise, and abhor him from head to toe.

Ciuta: Then I shall bring him your reply. As for me, I shall have nothing further to do with it.

Octave: I am like a man who holds another's stakes at roulette, whose luck is running against him. He would sooner drown his best friend than give in, and his rage at losing with someone else's money arouses him a hundred times more than if he were ruining himself.

(Enter Cœlio.)

What is this I hear, Cœlio? Are you giving up?

Cœlio: What do you want me to do?

Octave: Do you distrust me? What is the matter? You look pale as a ghost. What is going on inside you?

Cœlio: Forgive me, forgive me! Do as you like. Go find Marianne. Tell her that if she betrays me she will kill me, and my life is in her eyes.

(Exit.)

Octave: By heaven, that is very strange!

Ciuta: Be still! Vespers are ringing. The garden gate has just opened; Marianne is coming out. She is slowly coming toward us.

(Ciuta withdraws. Enter Marianne.)

Octave: Fair Marianne, you may sleep in peace. Cœlio's heart belongs to another, and he will no longer give his serenades beneath *your* window.

Marianne: What a pity! And how terribly unfortunate it is I didn't have an opportunity to share in such a love! You see how fate conspires against me! Just when I was about to fall in love with him.

Octave: Is that so?

Marianne: Yes, upon my soul, tonight or tomorrow night, Sunday at the very latest, I should have been his. How could he fail with an emissary such as you? It must be that his passion for me was something like Greek or Arabic, since it needed an interpreter and could not express itself all alone.

Octave: Go ahead and jeer! We are no longer afraid of you.

Marianne: Or perhaps his love was still only a poor suckling child, and you, its good wet-nurse, dropped it on its head as you walked around town carrying it in your apron.

Octave: The good nurse had only to let it drink a certain milk that yours must certainly have given you, and most generously. You still have a drop of it on your lips, and it mingles with every word you speak.

Marianne: What is the name of that wonderful milk?

Octave: Indifference. You can neither love nor hate. You are like the roses of Bengal, Marianne — no thorns and no scent.

Marianne: Very well said. Did you prepare that simile in advance? If you don't burn the first draft of your speeches, I would deeply appreciate your letting me have them, to teach to my parrot.

Octave: What have I said that might offend you? A flower without a scent is nonetheless beautiful. On the contrary, God seems always to have made the most beautiful ones that way. And the day when, like some new sort of Galatea, you turn into a marble statue in some church corner, you will be a most charming

one, and I am certain you will find a respectable niche in some
confessional.

Marianne: My dear cousin, don't you pity the lot of us women?
Just see what is happening to me. Fate decrees that a certain
Cœlio should love me, or should think he loves me, and the
said Cœlio tells his friends, who decree in their turn that,
under penalty of death, I shall be his mistress. The gilded
youth of Naples sees fit to send a worthy representative in your
person, charged with informing me that I am to love the said
Signor Cœlio, within a week from today. Just ponder that
a moment, if you will. If I give in, what will they say of me?
Wouldn't it take a despicable woman to obey such a proposal
on the spot, at the appointed time? Won't they tear her to
shreds, point their fingers at her, and make her name into the
chorus of a drinking song? If she refuses, on the other hand, is
there any monster comparable to her? Is there a statue more
frigid than she is, and doesn't any man who speaks to her, who
dares accost her on the public square with her prayer book in
hand, have the right to say to her: "You are a rose of Bengal,
with no thorns and no scent"?

Octave: Cousin, cousin, don't be angry.

Marianne: What terribly ridiculous things virtue and fidelity are!
And a young girl's upbringing, and the pride of a heart that
imagined it had some value, that before casting the dust of its
cherished flower to the winds it should be bathed in tears,
brought to bloom by a few rays of the sun, opened gradually
by a gentle hand! Isn't all that just a dream, a soap bubble
that, at the first sigh of some dandy, should evaporate into thin
air?

Octave: You are entirely mistaken about me and about Cœlio.

Marianne: After all, what is a woman? A moment's diversion, a
fragile cup containing a drop of dew that you raise to your
lips and then toss over your shoulder. A woman is a pleasure
party! Mightn't you say when you meet one: "There goes a
beautiful night walking by"? And wouldn't a man have to be a
great schoolboy in such matters, to lower his glance before
her and tell himself: "There goes an entire life's happiness, per-
haps," and let her go on her way?
(Exit.)

Octave: (Alone.) Tra, tra, boom, boom, tra deri la la! What an odd little woman! Hey, ho! *(He knocks at the door of the inn.)* Bring me a bottle of something out here on the terrace.

Waiter: Whatever you like, Excellency. Do you want some Lacrima Cristi?

Octave: Fine, fine. And go look through the surrounding streets for Signor Cœlio, the one who wears a black cloak and even blacker breeches. Tell him one of his friends is here drinking Lacrima Cristi all by himself. After that, go to the town square and bring me a certain Rosalinde, who has red hair and is always seated at her window.

(Exit the waiter.)

I don't know what's got into my throat; I am as mournful as a funeral procession. *(He drinks.)* I may as well have dinner here; night is beginning to fall. Ding! ding! What a nuisance those vesper bells are! Is it supposed to be time to go to bed? I might as well, I feel so leaden.

(Enter Claudio and Tibia.)

Cousin Claudio, you are a fine judge. Where are you going with such judicious haste?

Claudio: What do you mean by that, Signor Octave?

Octave: I mean that you are a magistrate of the highest form.

Claudio: Of language or appearance?

Octave: Of language, of language. Your wig is crawling with eloquence, and your legs form two delightful parentheses.

Claudio: Might I say in passing, Signor Octave, that the knocker on my door really seems to me to have burned your fingers?

Octave: In what way, most learned judge?

Claudio: Whilst trying to use it, most elegant cousin.

Octave: You might as well add "most respectful" for me, judge, as far as your door knocker is concerned. You can go ahead and have it painted, for all I fear soiling my fingers.

Claudio: In what way, my most facetious cousin?

Octave: By ever knocking on it, my most caustic judge.

Claudio: And yet you did once before, since my wife has ordered her servants to shut the door in your face at the first opportunity.

Octave: Your spectacles are near-sighted, oh gracious judge: you are addressing your compliments to the wrong man.

Claudio: My spectacles are excellent, oh witty cousin: did you not make a declaration of love to my wife?

Octave: In what connection, oh subtle magistrate?

Claudio: In connection with your friend Cœlio, cousin. Unfortunately, I overheard everything.

Octave: Through whose ears, incorruptible senator?

Claudio: Through my wife's, and she has told me everything, darling ne'er-do-well.

Octave: Absolutely everything, venerable judge? Nothing at all remained hidden within that charming ear?

Claudio: Only her reply, my charming barfly, which I have been charged to deliver to you.

Octave: But I am not charged to listen to it, dear court record.

Claudio: I shall leave it up to my door in person to deliver it, then, beloved cardsharp, if you should ever decide to consult it.

Octave: I have absolutely no desire to do so, my dear death sentence: I shall live quite happily without that pleasure.

Claudio: I wish you a long and tranquil life, dear dice cup! May you have nothing but prosperity.

Octave: You may rest assured on that account, dear prison lock! I sleep as soundly as your court.

(Exit Claudio and Tibia.)

Octave: *(Alone.)* That looks to me like Cœlio coming this way. Cœlio! Cœlio! What the devil is he after?

(Enter Cœlio.)

My dear friend, do you know about the fine trick that your princess has played on us? She has told her husband everything.

Cœlio: How do you know?

Octave: From the best of all possible sources. I just this moment left Claudio. Marianne is going to have her door shut in our face if we try to bother her any more.

Cœlio: You saw her just a little while ago; what did she say to you?

Octave: Nothing to make me foresee this bit of sweet news; but nothing very encouraging, either. Listen, Cœlio, forget about that woman. Hey! Bring out another glass!

Cœlio: For whom?

Octave: For you. Marianne is a prude. I don't remember exactly what she said to me this morning; I stood there like a dummy, unable to come up with an answer. Come on, don't think about her any more! All right, that is that. May the sky fall on my head if I ever say another word to her. Buck up, Cœlio, don't think about her any more.

Cœlio: Good-by, my dear friend.

Octave: Where are you going?

Cœlio: I have some business in town this evening.

Octave: You look as if you are going somewhere to drown yourself. Come on, Cœlio, what are you thinking of? There are other Mariannes under the sun. Let's have supper together and not give a damn about that one.

Cœlio: Good-by, good-by, I can't stay any longer. I shall see you tomorrow, my friend.

(Exit.)

Octave: Cœlio! Listen to me! We shall find you a really nice Marianne, gentle as a lamb, and especially one that doesn't go to vespers! Oh, those damned bells! When will they be done digging my grave?

Waiter: *(Returning.)* Sir, the red-headed young lady isn't at her window. She can't accept your invitation.

Octave: The plague take the entire universe! Has it been ordained that I shall eat supper alone today? Night is approaching at a gallop. What the devil am I to do? All right, all right, this is what I need! *(He drinks.)* I am ready to drown my sorrow in this wine, or at least to drown this wine in my sorrow. Ah! Vespers are over; here comes Marianne back again.

(Enter Marianne.)

Marianne: Still here, Signor Octave? And already at table? It is a bit sad to get drunk all by yourself.

Octave: The entire world has forsaken me. I am trying to see double so I can keep myself company.

Marianne: What! Not a single one of your friends, not one of your mistresses to ease this terrible burden of solitude?

Octave: Must I tell you the truth? I had sent for a certain Rosalinde who normally serves as my mistress, but she is having supper in town like a lady of quality.

Marianne: That is a most sorry state of affairs indeed, and your
heart must be feeling a frightful emptiness.

Octave: An emptiness beyond my powers of expression and which
I have been trying in vain to communicate to this glass. The
vesper bells have split my skull open for the rest of the evening.

Marianne: Tell me, cousin, does that wine you are drinking cost
one franc per bottle?

Octave: Don't laugh at it; these are the tears of Christ in person.

Marianne: I am amazed you don't drink cheap, one-franc wine.
Do drink some, I beg of you.

Octave: Why should I, if I may ask?

Marianne: Try it; I am sure that there is no difference from that
wine.

Octave: There is as much difference as there is between the sun
and a lantern.

Marianne: No, I tell you, it is exactly the same thing.

Octave: God protect me! Are you making fun of me?

Marianne: You believe there is a great difference?

Octave: Absolutely.

Marianne: I always thought that with wine it was the same as
with women. Isn't a woman also a precious vessel, sealed like
this crystal flask? Doesn't she contain a coarse or heavenly
intoxication, according to her strength and her worth? And
don't you find among them the wine of the commoners and the
tears of Christ? What a miserable heart yours must be, to let
your lips teach it a lesson in taste! You wouldn't drink the wine
that commoners drink, yet you love the women they do. The
heady and poetic spirit of this golden flagon, the wonderful
juices that the lava of Vesuvius nurtured under its burning sun,
will lead you staggering and half-conscious into a harlot's
arms. You would blush to drink a coarse wine; it would make
you choke. Hah! Your lips are refined, but your heart gets
drunk cheaply. Good evening, cousin; I hope Rosalinde returns
home tonight.

Octave: Just a few words, please, fair Marianne, and my answer
will be brief. How long do you suppose one has to woo the
bottle you see here to win her favors? As you say, she is filled
with a heavenly spirit, and commoners' wine is as little like her
as a peasant is like his lord. And yet, see how she yields! I

don't imagine she has had any education, she has no morals whatsoever. See what a sweet thing she is! All it took was one word to make her leave the convent; still covered with dust, she stole out to give me a quarter-hour of forgetfulness and to die. Her maiden's crown, reddened with perfumed wax, fell immediately into dust, and, I can't hide it from you, she almost passed through my lips in one gulp, in the heat of her first kiss.

Marianne: Are you sure she is worth the more for that? And if you really are one of her true lovers, were her recipe to be lost wouldn't you go and seek out the last drop, even in the mouth of a volcano?

Octave: She is worth neither more nor less. She knows that she is good to drink and made to be drunk. God did not hide her wellspring at the summit of an inaccessible mountain, in the depths of some dark cavern: He hung her in golden bunches by the wayside; she plies the harlot's trade; she brushes the hands of passers-by; she displays the curves of her bosom in the sun's rays, and dozens of honeybees pay murmuring court around her at every hour of the day. The thirsty wayfarer can lie down under her green boughs: she never yet has let him languish, she never has denied him the sweet tears her heart is filled with. Ah! Marianne, what a tragic gift beauty is! The virtue it boasts of is a sister to miserliness, and there is more mercy in heaven for its weaknesses than for its cruelty. Good evening, cousin; I hope Cœlio forgets you!

(He goes into the inn, and Marianne goes into her house.)

Scene 2. *Another street.*

(Cœlio and Ciuta.)

Ciuta: Signor Cœlio, beware of Octave. Did he not tell you that the lovely Marianne had shut her door to him?

Cœlio: He did indeed. Why should I beware of him?

Ciuta: Just a moment ago, as I was walking down her street, I saw him talking with her on a shaded terrace.

Cœlio: What is so surprising in that? He had probably waited for her to leave the house and seized a favorable opportunity to speak to her about me.

Ciuta: I mean that they were talking very cozily, like people who have come to a good understanding.

Cœlio: Are you sure, Ciuta? If so, I am the most fortunate of men; he must have pleaded my case with great passion.

Ciuta: May heaven favor you!

(Exit.)

Cœlio: Ah! If only I had been born in the age of tourneys and battles! Had it but been granted to me to wear Marianne's colors and stain them with my blood! If only I had been given an opponent to fight against, an entire army to defy! If the sacrifice of my life might only be of use to her! I know how to act, but I cannot speak. My tongue won't serve my heart, and I shall die without making myself understood, like a mute in a dungeon cell.

(Exit.)

Scene 3. *Claudio's house.*

(Claudio and Marianne.)

Claudio: Do you think I am a dummy and that I walk over the ground to serve as a scarecrow for the birds?

Marianne: What inspires you to that elegant conceit?

Claudio: Do you think that a criminal-court judge is ignorant of the meaning of words and that people can play on his credulity as if he were an itinerant acrobat?

Marianne: What has gotten into you this evening?

Claudio: Do you think I didn't hear your very own words: "If that man or his friend comes to my door, I want it shut in their face"? And do you believe I consider it suitable for you to be seen talking freely with with him under an arbor when the sun has gone down?

Marianne: You saw me under an arbor?

Claudio: Yes, yes, with these very eyes, under the arbor of a café. The arbor of a café is no place for a magistrate's wife to have a conversation, and it is no use shutting your door, when you turn around and meet outside with so little restraint.

Marianne: Since when am I forbidden to talk with one of your relations?

Claudio: When one of my relations is one of your lovers, it is an excellent idea to avoid it.

Marianne: Octave, one of my lovers! Have you lost your mind? He never paid court to anyone in his life.

Claudio: His character is ridden with vice. He spends his life in bars and gambling dens.

Marianne: All the more reason for him not to be, as you so pleasantly state it, "one of my lovers." I happen to feel like talking with Octave under the arbor of a café.

Claudio: Don't drive me to some regrettable excess by your extravagance, and think carefully of what you are doing.

Marianne: What excess do you think I might drive you to? I am curious to know what you would do.

Claudio: I would forbid you to see him and to exchange a single word with him, either in my house, or in a third party's, or out of doors.

Marianne: Hah! Really! This is something new! Octave is related to me as much as to you. I intend to speak with him whenever I feel like it, outdoors or elsewhere, and in this house if he should wish to come here.

Claudio: Remember those last words you have just pronounced. I am reserving an exemplary punishment if you go against my wishes.

Marianne: You can rest assured that I shall follow my own, and you can reserve whatever you like. I couldn't care less.

Claudio: Marianne, enough of this chatter. Either you will realize how unsuitable it is to linger under an arbor, or you will force me to take violent measures repugnant to my cloth.
(Exit.)

Marianne: (Alone.) Hey, there! Anybody!
(Enter a servant .)
Do you see the young man seated at a table under that arbor over there? Go and tell him I want to speak to him, if he doesn't mind coming into the garden here.
(Exit the servant.)
This is something new. Who does he take me for? What can be wrong in it? How do I look today? This dress is dreadful. What does that mean? "You will force me to take violent mea-

sures." What measures? I wish my mother were here. Bah! She always agrees with him as soon as he opens his mouth. I feel like striking someone! *(She knocks the chairs over.)* I really have been pretty silly! Here comes Octave. I should like them to meet. Ah! So this is how it begins? They told me it would. I knew it. I expected it! Just wait, just wait, he is reserving some punishment for me! Whatever could that be? I should really like to know what he means!

(Enter Octave.)

Sit down, Octave, I want to speak to you.

Octave: Where do you want me to sit? All the chairs are turned upside-down. What has been going on here?

Marianne: Nothing at all.

Octave: To tell the truth, cousin, your eyes tell a different story.

Marianne: I have been thinking over what you said to me on behalf of your friend Cœlio. Tell me, why doesn't he speak for himself?

Octave: For a very simple reason. He wrote to you, and you tore up his letters. He sent you a messenger, and you didn't let her say a word. He had music played for you, and you left him standing out in the street. In the end he has said the devil take you, and to be honest it is easy to see why.

Marianne: You mean he has called upon you.

Octave: Yes.

Marianne: All right, tell me about him.

Octave: Seriously?

Marianne: Yes, yes, seriously. Here I am. I am listening.

Octave: Are you joking?

Marianne: What pitiful sort of a spokesman are you? Speak up, whether I am joking or not.

Octave: Why do you keep looking around like that? You really seem to be angry.

Marianne: I want to take a lover, Octave . . . If not a lover, at least a gallant. Who do you recommend? I shall leave the choice up to you. Cœlio or anyone else, I don't care. Tomorrow at the latest. This evening. Whoever takes it into his head to sing beneath my window will find my door ajar. Well! Won't you say something? I tell you I am going to have a lover. Here,

take my scarf as a token: whoever you choose can bring it back
to me.

Octave: Marianne! Whatever may have inspired you to this mo-
ment of kindness, since you have called me here, since you con-
sent to listen to me, in the name of heaven stay this way a
moment more, let me speak to you!

(He falls to his knees.)

Marianne: What do you want to tell me?

Octave: If ever any man in the world was worthy of understanding
you, worthy of living and dying for you, that man is Cœlio. I
have never amounted to much, and I know myself well enough
to realize that I am a miserable spokesman for the passion I
have to express. Oh, if you only knew how you are adored on
a sacred altar, like a goddess. You, so young, so beautiful, still
so pure, handed over to an old man who no longer has any
sense and who never had a heart! If you only knew what a
wealth of happiness, what a rich vein of love there is in your-
self, and in him! In this fresh dawn of youth, in this celestial
dew of life, in this first harmony of two kindred souls! I won't
speak to you of his suffering, of the sweet, sad melancholy that
has never grown tired of your harshness, and that would die
for it without a complaint. Yes, Marianne, he will die for it.
What can I say to you? What could I invent to give my words
the force they lack? I don't know the language of love. Look
into your heart: it alone can speak to you of his. Is there any
power capable of stirring you? You who know how to pray to
God, is there a prayer that can express what my heart is filled
with?

Marianne: Stand up, Octave. In truth, if someone came in here
wouldn't he believe, to hear you, that you are pleading for
yourself?

Octave: Marianne, Marianne! In heaven's name don't smile! Don't
close your heart to the first ray of light that perhaps has ever
flashed through it! This whim of kindness, this precious mo-
ment will vanish. You spoke Cœlio's name; you have thought
of him, you say. Oh, if this is a mere fancy, don't spoil it for
me! A man's happiness depends on it.

Marianne: Are you certain I shouldn't smile?

Octave: Yes, you are right; I know how much ill my friendship can do. I know who I am, I feel it; words like that in my mouth seem to be a mockery. You doubt the sincerity of what I am saying; never have I felt so bitterly as now how little confidence I may inspire.

Marianne: Why do you say that? You see I am listening. I don't like Cœlio; he is not for me. Speak to me of someone else, anyone you wish. Choose a suitor worthy of me from among your friends; send him to me, Octave. You see that I am placing myself in your hands.

Octave: Oh, daughter of Eve! You don't like Cœlio but the first man who comes along will do. A man has loved you for a month, he worships the ground you walk on, he would happily die at a word from your lips, and you don't like that man! He is young, handsome, rich, and worthy of you in every way; but you don't like him! And the first man who comes along will do!

Marianne: Do as I say or don't come back.
(Exit.)

Octave: (Alone.) Your scarf is very pretty, Marianne, and your little fit of pique is a lovely way of making peace. It wouldn't take much vanity for me to understand: a little treachery would suffice. Nevertheless, it is Cœlio who will reap the reward.
(Exit.)

Scene 4. *Cœlio's house.*

(Octave, Cœlio, a Servant.)

Cœlio: He is downstairs, you say? Tell him to come up. Why didn't you have him come up right away?
(Enter Octave.)
Well, my friend? What news do you have?

Octave: Tie this scarf to your right arm, Cœlio; take your guitar and your sword. You are Marianne's lover.

Cœlio: In the name of heaven, don't mock me.

Octave: The night is fair; the moon will soon appear on the horizon. Marianne is all alone, and her door is ajar. You are a lucky man, Cœlio!

Cœlio: Can it be true? Can it be true? Either you are my savior, Octave, or you are pitiless.

Octave: You haven't gone yet? I tell you everything is set. A song beneath her window; hide your face a bit under your cloak so that her husband's spies won't recognize you. Have no fear yourself, and they will be afraid of you; and if she resists, show her that it is a bit too late.

Cœlio: Oh, my God! I haven't the strength.

Octave: I don't either, since I haven't finished dinner.—As a reward for my efforts, tell them to bring supper up on your way out. *(He sits down.)* Do you have any Turkish tobacco? You will probably find me still here tomorrow morning. Come on, my friend, get going! You can kiss me when you come back. Get going! Get going! The night is already half over.
(Exit Cœlio.)

Octave: (Alone.) You may inscribe upon your tablets, God of justice, that this night should be counted for me in your paradise. Is it really true that you have a paradise? That woman was lovely, indeed, and her little fit of anger was very becoming. What can have caused it? How should I know? What does it matter how the ivory ball falls onto the number we have called? Stealing a mistress from a friend would be too vulgar a trick for me. Marianne or anyone else, what difference does that make to me? The real business at hand is supper; it is evident that Cœlio has gone off on an empty stomach. How you would have despised me, Marianne, if I had loved you! How you would have shut the door in my face! Your poor specimen of a husband would have seemed like an Adonis or an Apollo to you, compared to me. Where in the world is the reason for all that? Why does the smoke from my pipe drift to the right rather than the left? There is the reason for everything. A fool! You really have to be an absolute, certified fool to calculate your chances, or to try to reason things out! Heavenly justice holds a scale in her hands. The scale is perfectly balanced, but all the weights are hollow. In one there is a coin, in the other a lover's sighs, in this one a migraine headache, in that one today's weather, and all human stock rises and falls according to those arbitrary weights.

Servant: (Entering.) Sir, here is a letter addressed to you. It was so urgent that it was brought here by your servants. I was instructed to give it to you wherever you happened to be this evening.

Octave: Let's take a look at this. *(He reads it.)* "Do not come tonight. My husband has surrounded the house with assassins, and you are doomed if they find you. Marianne." What a wretch I am! What have I done! My coat! My hat! Please God there may still be time! You, follow me with all the servants who are still up at this hour. It is a matter of life or death for your master.

(Exit running.)

Scene 5. *Claudio's garden.*

(Claudio, two assassins, and Tibia.)

Claudio: Let him come in, then jump on him as soon as he has reached these trees.

Tibia: What if he comes in the other way?

Claudio: Then wait for him at the corner of the wall.

Assassin: Yes, sir.

Tibia: Here he comes. Look, sir. See how long his shadow is! He is a fine figure of a man.

Claudio: Let's move off a little way and strike when the time is right.

(Enter Cœlio.)

Cœlio: (Knocking on the shutter.) Marianne, Marianne, are you there?

Marianne: (Appearing at the window.) Run away, Octave. Didn't you get my letter?

Cœlio: Dear God! Whose name did I hear?

Marianne: The house is surrounded by assassins; my husband saw you come in this evening; he overheard our conversation, and your death is certain if you stay a minute longer.

Cœlio: Is this a dream? Am I really Cœlio?

Marianne: Octave, Octave, in heaven's name don't remain here! I hope there is still time for you to escape! Meet me tomorrow in one of the confessionals in church, I shall be there.

(The shutters close.)

Cœlio: Oh, death, since you are here, come to my aid! Octave, you traitor, my blood will be on your hands. You knew the fate that awaited me here, and you sent me in your place. Your wish will be fulfilled. Oh, death! I open my arms to you. This is the end of my torments.
(Exit. Muffled cries and a distant noise are heard in the garden.)
Octave: (Outside.) Open up or I shall break the door down!
Claudio: (Opening the door, with his sword under his arm.) What do you want?
Octave: Where is Cœlio?
Claudio: I do not believe it is his custom to sleep in this house.
Octave: If you have killed him, Claudio, watch out: I shall wring your neck with my own hands.
Claudio: Are you mad, or just sleepwalking?
Octave: How about yourself, to be wandering about so late at night with a sword under your arm!
Claudio: Search the garden if you feel like it. I have seen no one come in, and if anyone tried to, it seems to me I had a right not to open the door.
Octave: (To his servants.) Come in, and search everywhere!
Claudio: (Aside, to Tibia.) Has everything been taken care of as I ordered?
Tibia: Yes, sir. You may rest assured, they can search all they like.
(Exeunt all.)

Scene 6. *A cemetery.*

(Octave and Marianne, next to a tomb.)
Octave: I alone in all the world knew him. This alabaster urn, draped with this long mourning veil, is his perfect image. It was thus that a gentle melancholy veiled the perfection of his tender and delicate soul. For me alone his silent life was not a mystery. The long evenings we spent together are like cool oases in an arid desert; they poured upon my heart the sole drops of refreshing dew that ever fell upon it. Cœlio was the

better part of myself; now it has gone back up to heaven with him. He was a man of another time; he knew pleasure and preferred solitude; he knew how deceptive illusions are, yet he preferred illusion to reality. How happy the woman who loved him would have been!

Marianne: And wouldn't the woman who loved you be happy, Octave?

Octave: I am not capable of loving; Cœlio alone knew how. The ashes contained in this tomb are all I ever loved on earth or ever will. He alone was able to pour into another soul the wellsprings of happiness that dwelt within his own. He alone was capable of limitless devotion; he alone would have devoted his entire life to the woman he loved, as easily as he would have braved death for her. I am nothing but a heartless rake; I have no esteem for women; the love I inspire is like the love I feel, the fleeting rapture of a dream. I do not know the secrets that he knew. My gaiety is like a histrion's mask; my heart is older still, my senses have grown numb and blasé. I am just a coward: his death has gone unavenged.

Marianne: How could it have been avenged without risking your life? Claudio is too old to accept a duel, and too powerful in this city to have anything to fear from you.

Octave: Cœlio would have avenged me, had I died for him as he died for me. This grave is mine: it is I that they have laid out beneath this cold stone; it was for me they had sharpened their swords; it is me they have killed. Farewell to my joyous youth, to my heedless folly, to the gay, free life beneath the slopes of Mount Vesuvius! Farewell to the noisy feasts, the evening talks, the serenades beneath gilded balconies! Farewell, Naples and its women, the torch-light masquerades, the lengthy suppers in the shadow of the forests! Farewell to love and friendship! My place is empty here on earth.

Marianne: But not in my heart, Octave. Why do you say "farewell to love"?

Octave: I don't love you, Marianne. It was Cœlio who loved you.

THE END

Fantasio

Fantasio's plot apparently owes a good deal to the events in 1832 surrounding the marriage for political reasons of King Louis-Philippe's daughter Princess Louise to King Leopold the First of Belgium, as well as to E. T. A. Hoffmann's novella *Kater Mürr*, in which a musician, Johannes Kreisler, saves a German princess from unhappy marriage to a sinister Italian prince. But the play is Musset's hymn of praise to freedom, fantasy, and a kind of pre-Gidean *disponibilité*. The author can be found hiding behind characters of both genders in all his early plays, and Musset was fascinated by the "masks" worn by his protagonists, but the persona of Fantasio is unusual even for him: a debt-ridden young Munich burgher who assumes a deceased older man's identity—that of a deformed, more or less sexless jester—and whose closest encounter with romantic love comes when he rescues Princess Elsbeth from marriage to the sort of deadly, mechanical clown that the heroine is wedded to in *What Does Marianne Want?*.

Fantasio was written during Musset's affair with George Sand, and first published in the *Revue des deux mondes* (1 Jan. 1834) just after the lovers' departure for the South, Venice, and destiny. The play was not performed during Musset's lifetime. When it was finally mounted by the Comédie Française, in 1866, it was in a version extensively modified by the poet's brother, Paul, who created a separate third act out of the final scene in an attempt to regularize the work. Paul also sought to alter the relationship between Fantasio and the Princess so that a more conventional love interest could be found. Critics of the time, familiar with the published text, suggested that the play should have been left as it was.

CHARACTERS

The King of Bavaria	Hartman, another friend
The Prince of Mantua	Facio, another friend
Marinoni, his aide-de-camp	Elsbeth, the King of
Rutten, the King's secretary	Bavaria's daughter
Fantasio, a young man of	Elsbeth's *Governess*
the city	Officers, pages, courtiers
Spark, his friend	

Munich.

ACT ONE

Scene 1. *The court.*

(The King, surrounded by his courtiers; Rutten.)

King: My friends, it has been some time since I announced to you my dear daughter Elsbeth's engagement to the Prince of Mantua. Now I announce to you that Prince's arrival today. This evening, perhaps, tomorrow at the latest, he will be in our palace. Let this be a day of celebration for everyone. Let the prisons be opened, and the people spend the night in pleasures. Rutten, where is my daughter?

(The courtiers withdraw.)

Rutten: Sire, she is in the park with her governess.

King: Why haven't I seen her yet today? Is she sad or happy about this approaching marriage?

Rutten: It seems to me that the Princess's face was clouded with some melancholy. What girl isn't a little pensive on the eve of her marriage? Saint-John's death has upset her.

King: What do you mean: the death of my jester, a hunchbacked and nearly blind court buffoon?

Rutten: The Princess loved him.

King: Tell me, Rutten, you have seen the Prince. What kind of man is he? Alas, I am giving what I hold dearest in the world to him, and I don't know him at all.

Rutten: I stayed for only a very short while in Mantua.

King: Speak frankly. Through what eyes may I see the truth if not yours?

Rutten: In truth, sire, I could not say a thing about the noble Prince's character and intelligence.

King: So that is how it is? Even you, a courtier, hesitate! With what praise the air of this room would already be filled, with how many hyperboles and flattering metaphors, if the Prince who will be my son-in-law tomorrow had seemed worthy of the title to you! Can I have made a mistake, my friend? Can I have made a bad choice in him?

Rutten: Sire, the Prince is held to be the best of kings.

King: Politics is a delicate spider web in which many a poor, mutilated fly struggles. I shall not sacrifice my daughter's happiness to any interest.

(Exit.)

Scene 2. *A street.*

(Spark, Hartman, and Facio, sitting at a table, drinking.)

Hartman: Since this is the Princess's wedding day, let's drink, smoke, and try to make a rumpus.

Facio: It would be a good idea to mingle with all those people out in the street and douse a few lanterns on some burghers' heads.

Spark: Come, now! Let's just smoke, calmly.

Hartman: I won't do anything calmly. Even if I were to become a clapper and hang myself up in a church bell, I have to chime on a holiday. Where the devil can Fantasio be?

Spark: Let's wait for him. We can do nothing without him.

Facio: Bah, he will find us somehow! He must be getting drunk in some hole down in the lower town. Hey there, one last round! *(He raises his glass.)*

Officer: (Entering.) Gentlemen, I have come to ask you to be so good as to move off a little way, if you don't want your festivities to be disturbed.

Hartman: Why, Captain?

Officer: The Princess is up on the terrace there right now, and it is easy for you to understand that it is not fitting for your shouts to reach her ears.

(Exit.)

Facio: Why, this is intolerable!

Spark: What does it matter to us whether we laugh here or else-where?

Hartman: Who says that we shall be allowed to laugh somewhere else? You will see, some scoundrel in a green uniform will crawl out from under all the cobblestones in the city and ask us to go laugh on the moon.

(Enter Marinoni, wrapped in a cloak.)

Spark: The Princess has never acted despotically in her life, God bless her! If she doesn't want people to laugh, it is because she is sad or she is singing. Let's leave her in peace.

Facio: Humph! Here comes someone wrapped up in his cloak, who is sniffing about for news. The sucker wants to approach us.

Marinoni: (Approaching.) I am a stranger here, gentlemen. What is the occasion for this celebration?

Spark: Princess Elsbeth is getting married.

Marinoni: Ah hah! She is a beautiful woman, I presume.

Hartman: As you are a handsome man, you have said it.

Marinoni: Beloved of her people, I dare say, for it seems to me that everything is illuminated.

Hartman: You are not mistaken, my good stranger. All these lighted lanterns that you see, as you have so sagaciously observed, constitute nothing less than an illumination.

Marinoni: I meant by that to ask whether the Princess is the cause of all these signs of joy.

Hartman: The sole cause, oh powerful orator. Even if every one of us were to get married, there would not be any kind of joy in this ungrateful city.

Marinoni: Happy the Princess who makes herself beloved of her people!

Hartman: Lighted lanterns do not make a people's happiness, my dear primitive fellow. That doesn't prevent the above-mentioned Princess from being as flighty as a sparrow.

Marinoni: Is that so? "flighty," you say?

Hartman: That is what I said, mysterious stranger, that is the word I used.

(Marinoni bows and withdraws.)

Facio: What in the world can that Italian jabberer be after? There he is, after leaving us, going up to another group. He smells like a spy a mile away.

Hartman: He doesn't smell like anything at all. He is just as stupid as can be.

Spark: Here comes Fantasio.

Hartman: What is the matter with him? He is waddling along like a judicial counselor. Either I miss my guess, or there is some crazy idea ripening in his brain.

Facio: Well, my friend, what are we going to make of this fine evening?

Fantasio: (Entering.) Anything you want but a new novel.

Facio: I was saying that we ought to race through this rabble and have a bit of fun.

Fantasio: The main thing would be to get some false noses and firecrackers.

Hartman: And squeeze the girls' waists, pull the burghers' pigtails, and break street lamps. Come on, let's go, enough said.

Fantasio: Once upon a time there was a King of Persia . . .

Hartman: Come with us, Fantasio.

Fantasio: I can't be with you, I can't!

Hartman: Why not?

Fantasio: Give me a glass of that.

   (He drinks.)

Hartman: Your cheeks are as rosy as May.

Fantasio: That is true; and my heart is as cold as January. My head is like an old fireplace that has gone out: there is nothing in it but wind and ashes. Phoo! *(He sits down.)* It really irritates me, that everyone should be having such a good time! I wish this great, heavy sky were an enormous cotton nightcap, so it would wrap this stupid town and its inhabitants up to the ears. Come on, now, please tell me some worn-out joke, something really stale.

Hartman: Why?

Fantasio: So I shall laugh. I don't laugh at what people think up any more; maybe I shall laugh at something I already know.

Hartman: You seem a wee bit misanthropic and inclined to melancholy, to me.

Fantasio: Not at all. It is only that I have just come from my mistress's house.

Facio: Are you with us, yes or no?

Fantasio: I am with you, if you are with me. Let's stay here a while and talk about one thing and another, as we gaze at our new clothes.

Facio: Well, not me. You may be tired of standing up, but I am tired of sitting down. I have to stir about in the open air.

Fantasio: I really couldn't "stir about." I am going to smoke my pipe under these chestnut trees, with my good friend Spark to keep me company. All right, Spark?

Spark: As you will.

Hartman: In that case, good-by. We are going off to see the festivities.

(Exit Hartman and Facio. Fantasio sits down with Spark.)

Fantasio: What a fiasco that sunset is! Nature is pathetic this evening. Just look at that valley over there, those four or five miserable clouds climbing up that mountain. I drew landscapes like that one on the covers of my schoolbooks, when I was twelve.

Spark: This is such good tobacco! So is this beer!

Fantasio: I really must bore you, Spark.

Spark: No, why?

Fantasio: Because you bore me horribly. Doesn't it bother you to look at the same face every day? What the devil are Hartman and Facio going to do out in those festivities?

Spark: They are two active fellows. They just can't stay in one place.

Fantasio: What an admirable thing the *Arabian Nights* are! Oh, Spark, my dear Spark, if only you could transport me to China! If only I could get out of my skin for an hour or two! If I could just be that fellow walking by!

Spark: That seems rather difficult to me.

Fantasio: That fellow walking by is delightful. Look at those fine silk breeches! The beautiful red flowers on his waistcoat! His watch fob swings against his belly in syncopation with his coattails, which pirouette around the calves of his legs. I am sure that man has thousands of ideas in his head that are

completely foreign to me; his essence is peculiar to him. Alas,
everything that men say to one another is alike; the ideas they
exchange are almost always the same, in their conversation.
But inside all those isolated machines, what hidden recesses,
what secret compartments! It is an entire world that each one
carries within him, an unknown world that is born and dies in
silence! What solitudes all these human bodies are!

Spark: Just drink, you idler, instead of racking your brain.

Fantasio: There is only one thing that has tickled me for these past
three days: my creditors have gotten a judgment against me,
and if I set foot in my house four bailiffs will come and grab
me by the scruff of the neck.

Spark: That is quite jolly, indeed. Where will you sleep tonight?

Fantasio: With the first woman who comes along. Can you imag-
ine, they are selling off my furniture tomorrow! We shall buy
some of it, shan't we?

Spark: Do you need money, Henri? Do you want my purse?

Fantasio: You dolt! If I didn't have money, I wouldn't have debts. I
feel like taking a ballerina for a mistress.

Spark: That will bore you to death.

Fantasio: Not at all. My imagination will be filled with pirouettes
and white satin slippers. There will be one of my gloves on the
balcony railing from New Year's Day to New Year's Eve, and
I shall hum clarinet solos in my dreams, until I die in the arms
of my beloved from eating too many strawberries. Have you
noticed something, Spark? We have no profession, we don't
carry on a trade.

Spark: Is that what is making you sad?

Fantasio: There is no such thing as a gloomy fencing master.

Spark: To me you seem to be bored by everything in the world.

Fantasio: Ha! To be bored by everything in the world, my friend,
you have to have been to a lot of places.

Spark: Well, then?

Fantasio: Well, then, where do you want me to go? Look at this
smoky old town. There isn't a single square, a single street, a
single alleyway I haven't prowled through dozens of times.
There isn't a single cobblestone over which I haven't dragged
my worn-out heels, a single house where I don't know what

girl's or old woman's silly face is forever peeking from the window. I couldn't take a single footstep without walking in yesterday's footsteps. Well, my dear friend, this town is nothing compared with my brain. All its recesses are a hundred times more well-known; all the pathways, all the recesses of my imagination are a hundred times more worn out. I have walked around in a hundred more directions in this dilapidated brain — and I am its sole inhabitant! I have gotten drunk in all its taverns; I have driven through it like an absolute monarch in a gilded coach. I have trotted through it like a gentle burgher on a good-natured mule, and now I don't dare even steal into it like a burglar holding a covered lantern.

Spark: I just can't understand this constant struggle with yourself. As for me, for example, when I smoke my pipe my thoughts become pipe smoke; when I drink, they become Spanish wine or Flemish beer; when I kiss my mistress's hand, they go in through the tips of her tapered fingers and spread through her entire being on electric currents. It takes the mere scent of a flower to distract me, and, of all that universal nature contains, the meanest object is enough to change me into a butterfly and make me flutter to and fro with constantly renewed pleasure.

Fantasio: Let's say it outright: you are capable of sitting and fishing.

Spark: If I feel like it, I am capable of anything.

Fantasio: Even of taking the moon in your teeth?

Spark: I wouldn't feel like that.

Fantasio: Ha, ha! How do you know? Taking the moon in your teeth isn't something to be sneered at. Let's go play poker.

Spark: No, indeed.

Fantasio: Why not?

Spark: Because we would lose our money.

Fantasio: Ha! My Lord, what have you gone and dreamed up! You keep on imagining things to get yourself upset. So you see the dark side of everything, you poor fellow? Don't you have any faith in God, or hope in your heart? Are you a dreadful atheist? Why, you would be capable of hardening my heart and disillusioning me about everything, when I am still full of youth and vigor!

(He starts to dance.)

Spark: To tell the truth, there are times when I wouldn't swear you are not mad.

Fantasio: (Still dancing.) Give me a bell! A glass bell!

Spark: What do you need a bell for?

Fantasio: Didn't Jean-Paul Richter say that a man absorbed in a great idea is like a diver in his bell, in the midst of the vast ocean? I have no bell, Spark, no bell at all, and I am dancing like Jesus Christ on the vast ocean.

Spark: Become a journalist, or a man of letters, Henri. That is still the most effective means we have left, to vent our misanthropy and numb our imaginations.

Fantasio: Oh, I wish I could get excited over a lobster in mustard sauce, over a wench, over a class of minerals. Spark, let's try and build a house for the two of us!

Spark: Why don't you write down all the things you dream up? That would make a nice volume.

Fantasio: A sonnet is worth more than a long poem, and a glass of wine is worth more than a sonnet.

(He drinks.)

Spark: Why don't you travel? Go to Italy.

Fantasio: I have been there.

Spark: Well, didn't you find it a beautiful country?

Fantasio: There are swarms of flies as big as may bugs, and they bite you all night long.

Spark: Go to France.

Fantasio: There is no good Rhine wine in Paris.

Spark: Go to England.

Fantasio: I am there already. Do the English have a country of their own? I would just as soon see them here as over there.

Spark: Then go to the devil!

Fantasio: Oh, if only there was a devil in heaven! If only there was a hell, I would blow my brains out just to go and see all that! What a pitiful thing man is! He can't even jump out of his window without breaking his legs! He has to work at the violin for ten years if he wants to become a decent musician. He has to learn how to be a painter, or a groom! He has to learn how to make an omelet! You know, Spark, sometimes I just feel like sitting on a railing, watching the river flow by, and counting

one, two, three, four, five, six, seven, and so on, until the day I
die.

Spark: A lot of people would laugh at what you are saying, but it
makes me shiver. It is the story of our entire age. Eternity is a
great eagle's nest from which each new age has taken wing,
one after another, like a young fledgling, to soar across the sky
and disappear. Ours has reached the edge of the nest in its
turn, but its wings have been clipped, and it awaits death while
staring at the space into which it can't soar off.

Fantasio: (Singing.)

You call me your life, rather call me your soul,
For the soul is immortal, and life is but a day.

Do you know a more sublime song than that one, Spark? It is
Portuguese. I have never recalled it without feeling like falling
in love with someone.

Spark: With whom, for example?

Fantasio: Who? I don't know. Some pretty, buxom wench like the
women in Mieris's paintings. Something soft as the west wind;
something pale as moonbeams; something wistful like those lit-
tle serving-maids you see in Flemish paintings, who pass the
stirrup cup to some wayfarer in wide boots, sitting stiff as a
ramrod on a great white horse. What a fine thing the stirrup
cup is! A young woman on the doorstep, a glowing fire you can
glimpse inside the room, supper waiting, the children asleep;
all the serenity of the calm, contemplative life in one corner of
the picture! And here is the man, still panting but firm in the
saddle; he has traveled twenty leagues and still has thirty to go;
a swig of brandy and off he goes. The night is dark over there,
a storm is brewing, the woods are dangerous. For a moment
the good woman watches him ride off, and then as she returns
to her fire she offers up that sublime charity of the poor: "God
keep him!"

Spark : If you were in love, Henri, you would be the happiest of
men.

Fantasio: Love no longer exists, my dear friend. Religion, its nurse,
has breasts as pendulous as an old purse, in whose depths
there lies a copper penny. Love is a sacred host that must be
broken in two before an altar and swallowed jointly in a kiss.

There is no more altar, there is no more love. Long live nature!
At least there is still wine.
(He drinks.)

Spark: You are going to get drunk.

Fantasio: I am going to get drunk, as you say.

Spark: It is a bit late for that.

Fantasio: What do you call late? Is noon "late"? Is midnight
"early"? Where do you start your day? Let's stay here please,
Spark. Let's drink, let's chat, let's analyze, let's babble, let's
talk politics. Let's think up government coalitions. Let's catch
all the may bugs that fly around this candle and put them in
our pockets. Did you know that the steam-powered cannon is a
fine thing, as far as philanthropy is concerned?

Spark: What do you mean?

Fantasio: Once upon a time there was a king who was very wise,
very wise, very happy, very happy . . .

Spark: And so?

Fantasio: The only thing lacking for his happiness was to have
children. He had public prayers said in all the mosques.

Spark: What are you getting at?

Fantasio: I am thinking of my dear *Arabian Nights*. That is how
they all begin. Look, Spark, I am drunk. I must do something.
Tra la, tra la! Come on, let's stand up. *(A funeral passes by.)*
Hey there, my good fellows, who are you burying? Now isn't
the proper time for a burial.

Bearers: We are burying Saint-John.

Fantasio: Has Saint-John died? The King's jester is dead? Who has
taken his place, the Minister of Justice?

Bearers: His job is vacant; you can have it if you want.
(Exit.)

Spark: You really deserved that taunt. What were you thinking of
to stop those fellows?

Fantasio: There is nothing at all insolent about it. It is a bit of
friendly advice that man gave me, and I am going to follow
right up on it.

Spark: You are going to become court jester?

Fantasio: This very night, if they will have me. Since I can't sleep
in my house, I want to go see them perform the royal comedy

that is on tomorrow's bill, and I shall sit in the King's own box.

Spark: What a bright fellow you are! You will be recognized, and his lackeys will throw you out: aren't you the late Queen's godson?

Fantasio: What a stupid fellow you are! I shall wear a hump and a red wig, as in Saint-John's portrait, and no one will recognize me, even if I have three dozen godparents hot on my heels. *(He knocks on a shop door.)* Hey, my good man! Open up, if you haven't gone out—you, your wife, and your little dogs!

Tailor: (Opening the shop door.) What does your Lordship wish?

Fantasio: Aren't you the court tailor?

Tailor: At your service.

Fantasio: Did you make Saint-John's clothes?

Tailor: Yes, sir.

Fantasio: You knew him? You know what side his hump was on, how he curled his mustache, and what kind of wig he wore?

Tailor: Hah, hah! The gentleman is joking.

Fantasio: My good man, I am not joking at all. Go into the rear of your shop; and if you don't want to drink poison in your café au lait tomorrow, you had better be as silent as the tomb about everything that is going to happen here.

(Exit with the tailor; Spark follows him.)

Scene 3. *An inn on the road to Munich.*

(Enter the Prince of Mantua and Marinoni.)

Prince: Well, Colonel?

Marinoni: Your Highness?

Prince: Well, Marinoni?

Marinoni: Melancholy, flighty, madcap, obedient to her father, very fond of green peas.

Prince: Write that down: I don't understand anything clearly unless it is written out in a round Spenserian hand.

Marinoni: (Writing.) Melanch . . .

Prince: Write under your breath. I have been dreaming up a major plan since dinner time.

Marinoni: Here is what you wanted, your Highness.

Prince: Very good. I hereby name you my bosom friend; I know of no finer handwriting than yours in my entire kingdom. Sit down at a certain distance. *(More formally.)** Well, my friend, so you think the character of the Princess, my future bride, is secretly known to you?

Marinoni: Yes, your Highness. I have scoured the area surrounding the palace, and these ledgers contain the principal elements of the various conversations I have intruded myself into.

Prince: (Gazing at himself in the mirror.) It seems to me I have been powdered like a man of the lowest class.

Marinoni: You are dressed magnificently.

Prince: (Reverts to his earlier tone.) What would you say, Marinoni, if you were to see your master wearing a simple olive-green coat?

Marinoni: Your Highness is straining my credulity!

Prince: No, Colonel. I hereby inform you that your master is the most romantic of men.

Marinoni: Romantic, your Highness?

Prince: Yes, my friend (for I have granted you that title). The important plan that I have been pondering is unheard of in my family. I intend to arrive at the court of my father-in-law, the King, in the garb of a simple aide-de-camp. It is not sufficient to have sent someone from my household to cull public rumors about the future Princess of Mantua (and that someone, Marinoni, is yourself), I also wish to observe with my own eyes.

Marinoni: Indeed, your Highness?

Prince: Don't stand there like a statue. A man like me, at a time like this, must have no one but a vast and enterprising spirit as his bosom friend.

Marinoni: I can think of only one thing standing in the way of your Highness's plans.

Prince: What?

Marinoni: The idea of such a disguise could come only from the glorious Prince who governs us all. But if my gracious sove-

---

*The Prince passes here from the informal *tu* (used with inferiors) to a more respectful *vous*, evidently to mark Marinoni's new status as "close friend." He subsequently reverts to *tu*.

reign mingles with the staff officers, to whom will the King of
Bavaria pay the honor of the splendid banquet that is to take
place in the great hall?

Prince: You are right. If I am disguised, someone has to take my
place. That is impossible, Marinoni. I had not thought about
that.

Marinoni: Why "impossible," your Highness?

Prince: I can lower princely dignity to the rank of a colonel. But
how can you think that I could consent to raise an ordinary
man to my rank? Besides, do you think that my future father-
in-law would forgive me?

Marinoni: The King is held to be a man of great common sense
and wit, and very good-natured.

Prince: Hum! I do not give my plan up without regret. To infil-
trate this new court without pomp and fanfare, to observe
everything, to approach the Princess under an assumed name,
perhaps to make her fall in love with me! Oh, my mind is
wandering, that is impossible. Marinoni, my friend, try on
my ceremonial clothes. I just cannot resist.

Marinoni: (*Bowing.*) Your Highness!

Prince: Do you think that future centuries will forget such an
occasion?

Marinoni: Never, my gracious Prince.

Prince: Come and try on my clothes.

(*Exit.*)

ACT TWO
Scene 1. *The garden of the King of Bavaria.*

(*Enter Elsbeth and her governess.*)

Governess: My poor eyes have just wept and wept a flood of tears
for him.

Elsbeth: How kind you are! I loved Saint-John, too. He was so
witty! He was no ordinary jester.

Governess: To think that the poor man has gone off to heaven on
the eve of your engagement! He spoke of nothing but you, at
lunch and at supper, the whole day long. Such a happy fellow,

so funny he made you love his ugliness, and your eyes would be drawn to him in spite of themselves!

Elsbeth: Don't talk to me about my marriage. That is an even greater misfortune.

Governess: Don't you know that the Prince of Mantua is coming today? People say he is a real Galahad.

Elsbeth: What is that you are saying, my dear? He is awful and stupid, everyone here already knows that.

Governess: Is that so? I was told he was a Galahad.

Elsbeth: I didn't ask for a Galahad, my dear. But it is cruel sometimes to be only a King's daughter. My father is the best of men. The marriage he is arranging guarantees peace for his kingdom. In return he will receive the blessings of his people; but I, alas, shall receive his, and nothing else.

Governess: How sadly you talk!

Elsbeth: If I were to refuse the Prince, war would soon start up again. What a misfortune that these peace treaties are always signed with tears! I wish I were hard-headed and resigned to marrying whoever comes along, if that is politically necessary. Being the mother of your people may console great hearts, but not weak heads. I am just a poor dreamer. Perhaps it is the fault of those novels that you always carry in your pockets.

Governess: Oh, Lord! Don't tell anyone.

Elsbeth: I have known life so very little, and dreamed such a great deal.

Governess: If the Prince of Mantua is as you say, God won't let that business take place, I am absolutely sure.

Elsbeth: Do you think so? God lets men do as they please, my poor friend, and he takes no more account of our laments than of the bleating of sheep.

Governess: I am sure that if you turned the Prince down your father wouldn't force you.

Elsbeth: No, he certainly wouldn't force me. That is why I am sacrificing myself. Would you want me to go and tell my father to forget his promise, and to cross out his honorable name with a stroke of the pen on a contract that makes thousands of people happy? What does it matter if he makes one woman unhappy! I shall let my good father be a good King.

Governess: Boo, hoo!
(She weeps.)

Elsbeth: Don't cry over me, dear; you might make me cry, too, perhaps, and a royal fiancée must not have red eyes. Don't be distressed over it. After all, I shall be a Queen, perhaps that is fun. Perhaps I shall get to like my jewels—who knows—my carriages, my new court? Luckily there is more in a marriage for a Princess than just a husband. Perhaps I shall find happiness among my wedding presents.

Governess: You are a real sacrificial lamb.

Elsbeth: Well, my dear, let's at least start out by laughing; who knows whether we shall have to cry when the time comes? They say the Prince of Mantua is the most ridiculous thing in the world.

Governess: If only Saint-John were here!

Elsbeth: Oh, Saint-John! Saint-John!

Governess: You loved him a great deal, didn't you, my child?

Elsbeth: It is strange: his wit bound me to him with imperceptible threads that seemed to come from my heart. His constant mocking of my romantic ideas pleased me so much, whereas I can hardly bear people who agree completely with me. There was something about him, his eyes, his gestures, the way he took snuff. He was an odd man: while he spoke to me, lovely pictures would pass before my eyes. His words would give life to the strangest things, as if by magic.

Governess: He was a real Rigoletto.

Elsbeth: I don't know about that; but he was a gem of wittiness.

Governess: I see some pages over there going back and forth. I think it won't be long before the Prince appears. You ought to go back to the palace and get dressed.

Elsbeth: I beg you, let me have a few more minutes. Go prepare what I need. Alas, my dear, I haven't much time left for dreaming.

Governess: My Lord, can this marriage possibly take place if you are not happy? For a father to sacrifice his daughter! The King would be a real Jephtha to do that.

Elsbeth: Don't talk nonsense about my father. Go on, my dear, make ready what I need.
(Exit the Governess.)

(Alone.) I have the feeling there is someone behind those bushes. Is that the ghost of my poor jester I see sitting in the meadow among those cornflowers? Answer me: Who are you? What are you doing there, picking those flowers?
(She walks toward a knoll.)

Fantasio: (Seated, dressed as a jester, with a hump and a wig on.) I am just a gentle flower-picker, wishing good day to your Loveliness.

Elsbeth: What is the meaning of that getup? Who are you to come in that oversized wig and mock someone I loved? Are you an apprentice buffoon?

Fantasio: May it please your most Serene Highness, I am the King's new jester. The majordomo has greeted me with favor. I have been introduced to the King's valet. The scullery boys have taken me under their protection since yesterday evening, and I am modestly picking flowers while waiting for my wit to arrive.

Elsbeth: It seems doubtful to me you will ever pick that flower.

Fantasio: Why not? Wit can come to an old man just as well as to a young girl. It is so hard sometimes to distinguish between a witticism and utter rubbish! The important thing is to speak fast. The worst pistol shot can hit the bull's-eye if he shoots 780 shots a minute, just as well as the ablest gunman who only shoots one or two carefully aimed ones. I ask only to be fed in proportion to the size of my belly, and I shall watch my shadow in the sunlight, to see if my wig is growing.

Elsbeth: And so here you are, dressed in Saint-John's old clothes? You are right to talk of your shadow. As long as you wear that costume, I believe it will always look more like him than like you.

Fantasio: At this moment I am writing an elegy that will decide my fate once and for all.

Elsbeth: How can that be?

Fantasio: It will prove clearly that I am the foremost person in the world, or else it won't be worth a thing. I am busy turning the universe on end to fit it into an acrostic; the sun, the moon, and the stars are vying to get into my verses, like schoolboys at the stage door of a popular theater.

Elsbeth: Poor fellow! What a trade you have taken up! Being witty at so much per hour! Have you neither arms nor legs, and wouldn't you do better to furrow the soil than your own brow?

Fantasio: Poor girl! What a trade you are taking up! Marrying an idiot you have never seen! Have you neither head nor heart, and wouldn't you do better to sell your dresses than your body?

Elsbeth: That is rather bold for a newcomer!

Fantasio: What do you call that flower, please?

Elsbeth: A tulip. What are you trying to prove?

Fantasio: A red tulip, or a blue tulip?

Elsbeth: Blue, it seems to me.

Fantasio: Not at all, it is a red tulip.

Elsbeth: Are you trying to dress up an old saw? You didn't need that to say there is no arguing over taste or colors.

Fantasio: I am not arguing. I tell you, that tulip is a red tulip, and yet I admit that it is blue.

Elsbeth: How do you work that out?

Fantasio: Like your marriage contract. Who under the sun can know whether he was born blue or red? Tulips themselves don't know. Gardeners and lawyers make such extraordinary grafts that apples become pumpkins, and thistles fall from a donkey's mouth to be napped with sauce on the silver dish of a bishop. That tulip over there was indeed expecting to be red; but they married it off, and it is amazed to find itself blue. Thus is the whole world transformed by the hand of man. Poor old Mother Nature must laugh heartily at herself sometimes, when she sees her eternal masquerade in her lakes and her seas. Do you think it smelled of roses in Moses' [sic] paradise? No, it just smelled of green hay. The rose is a daughter of civilization: she is a countess, like you and me.

Elsbeth: The pale hawthorn blossom can turn into a rose, and a thistle can turn into an artichoke. But one flower cannot turn into another one. So what does it matter to Nature? She can't be changed; she can be embellished or she can be killed. The puniest violet would rather die than give in, if you tried to alter the shape of one of its stamens artificially.

Fantasio: That is why I have more respect for a violet than for a King's daughter.

Elsbeth: There are certain things that even jesters have no right to mock. Be careful. If you listened in on my conversation with my governess, mind your ears.

Fantasio: Not my ears, but my tongue. You have got the sense wrong; there is a mistaken sense in your words.

Elsbeth: Don't make puns with me if you want to earn your keep, and don't compare me with tulips unless you want to earn something else.

Fantasio: Who knows? A pun is consolation for many a sorrow. Playing on words is as good a way as any other to play with thoughts, actions, and beings. Everything here on earth is a pun, and it is just as hard to understand a four-year-old child's glance as the gibberish of three contemporary dramas.

Elsbeth: I have the impression that you look at the world through a rather changing prism.

Fantasio: Everyone has his own glasses. But no one knows for sure what color the lenses are. Who can tell me for sure whether I am happy or unhappy, good or bad, sad or gay, stupid or witty?

Elsbeth: One thing is certain, at least: you are ugly.

Fantasio: That is no more certain than your beauty is. Here comes your father with your husband-to-be. Who can tell whether you will be married?

(Exit.)

Elsbeth: Since I can't help encountering the Prince of Mantua, I may as well go and meet him.

(Enter the King, Marinoni wearing the Prince's clothes, and the Prince dressed as an aide-de-camp.)

King: Prince, this is my daughter. Please forgive her gardening clothes. You are in the house of a burgher who governs other burghers, and our etiquette is as indulgent toward us as toward them.

Marinoni: Allow me to kiss your lovely hand, Madame, if that is not too great a favor for my lips.

Elsbeth: Your Highness will excuse me if I return to the palace. I think I shall see you in a more suitable manner at this evening's presentation.

(Exit.)

Prince: The Princess is right. Her reticence is quite divine.

King: (To Marinoni.) Who in the world is this aide-de-camp following you like a shadow? I find it unbearable to hear him put in his inept comments at everything we say. Dismiss him, please.

(Marinoni speaks softly to the Prince.)

Prince: (As above.) It was very clever on your part to convince him to send me away. I am going to try and join the Princess, and drop a few subtle words to her in an offhand way.

(Exit.)

King: That aide-de-camp is an idiot, my friend. What can you be doing with a man like that?

Marinoni: Ahem! Ahem! Let us take a few more steps over this way, if your Majesty permits. I think I see a quite charming pavilion among those bushes.

(Exit.)

Scene 2. *Another part of the garden.*

(Enter the Prince.)

Prince: My disguise is working wonderfully: I observe, and I inspire love for myself. So far everything is going according to my wishes. The father seems like a great king to me, although somewhat too easygoing; I would be amazed if I haven't struck his fancy right away. I see the Princess going back to the palace; luck is favoring me singularly.

(Enter Elsbeth; the Prince approaches her.)

Your Highness, allow a faithful servant of your future husband to offer you the sincere congratulations that his humble and devoted heart cannot restrain at the sight of you. How fortunate the high and mighty are! They can marry you, and I cannot; that is quite impossible for me. I am of humble birth; my only wealth is a name feared by the enemy. A pure and spotless heart beats beneath this lowly uniform. I am a poor soldier, riddled with bullets from head to toe. I have not a ducat to my name. I am all alone and in exile from my native abode as from my heavenly homeland, that is to say, from the paradise of my dreams. I have no woman's heart to press against my own. I am accursed and silent.

Elsbeth: What do you wish of me, my good man? Are you mad, or are you asking for alms?

Prince: How hard it would be to find words to express what I feel! I saw you going by along this path all by yourself. I considered it my duty to throw myself at your feet and offer you my company as far as the gate.

Elsbeth: I am very obliged to you. Do me a favor and leave me in peace.

(Exit.)

Prince: (Alone.) Can I have been wrong to speak to her? And yet it was necessary, since I am planning to captivate her under this assumed guise. Yes, I did the right thing to accost her. And yet she answered me in a most unpleasant way. Perhaps I ought not to have spoken so vividly. Still, that was quite necessary, since her marriage is almost definite and I am supposed to be supplanting Marinoni, who is replacing me. I was right to speak animatedly. But her reply was unpleasant. Could she have a hard, disloyal heart? It might be a good idea to probe the matter skillfully.

(Exit.)

Scene 3. *An anteroom.*

(Fantasio, lying on a rug.)

Fantasio: What a delightful trade a jester's is! I may have been drunk last night when I put on this costume and appeared at the palace. But in truth, sane reason never inspired anything in me to equal that act of madness. I walk in and here I am, accepted, pampered, signed up, and, better still, forgotten. I come and go in this palace as if I had lived here all my life. I encountered the King just a while ago; he didn't even have the curiosity to look at me. Since his jester had died, he was told: "Sire, here is another one." It is amazing! Thank God, my mind is at ease now, I can talk all the nonsense I want without anyone saying anything to stop me. I am one of the King of

Bavaria's pet animals, and if I like, as long as I keep my hump and my wig on, I shall be allowed to spend the rest of my days between the spaniel and the guinea fowl. In the meantime my creditors can knock their heads against my door as much as they want. I am as safe here wearing this wig as in the West Indies.

Isn't that the Princess I see through this window in the next room? She is arranging her wedding veil; two long tears are flowing down her cheeks. There goes one, rolling down onto her breast like a pearl. Poor little thing! I overheard her conversation with her governess this morning. To tell the truth, it was by chance; I was sitting on the lawn, intending only to sleep. Now there she is, weeping and scarcely aware that I am looking at her again. Oh, if I were a student of rhetoric, how deeply I would reflect on this crowned misery, on this poor lamb around whose neck they will tie a pink ribbon, before they lead her to the slaughter! The girl is probably romantic; she finds it cruel to have to marry a man she doesn't know. And yet she sacrifices herself in silence. How arbitrary fate is! I had to go get drunk, encounter Saint-John's funeral, put on his costume, and take his place—I had to do the craziest thing in the world, in other words—in order to come and see through this window the only two tears that this child is likely to shed on her wretched wedding veil. *(Exit.)*

Scene 4. *A path in the garden.*

(The Prince and Marinoni.)
Prince: You are nothing but an ass, Colonel.
Marinoni: Your Highness is most distressingly mistaken about me.
Prince: You are an absolute lout. Couldn't you prevent this? I entrust you with the greatest plan that has been conceived for an incalculable number of years, and you, my best friend, my most loyal servant, heap one idiocy upon another. No, no, no matter what you say, it is unforgivable.
Marinoni: How could I prevent your Highness from incurring displeasures that are a necessary result of the role that you are

supposed to be playing? You order me to take your name and to act like the real Prince of Mantua. Can I keep the King of Bavaria from insulting my aide-de-camp? You were wrong to meddle in our business.

Prince: I would like to see a rogue like you take it into his head to give me orders.

Marinoni: Your Highness, please consider: I really have to be either the Prince or the aide-de-camp. I am only acting on your orders.

Prince: To tell me that I am impertinent, in the presence of the entire court, because I tried to kiss the Princess's hand! I am ready to declare war on him, return to my country, and ride at the head of my armies.

Marinoni: Your Highness, just remember that this insult was aimed at the aide-de-camp and not at the Prince. You don't expect to be respected in that disguise, do you?

Prince: That will do. Give me back my coat.

Marinoni: (*Taking off the coat.*) If my sovereign demands, I am ready to lay down my life for him.

Prince: To tell the truth, I cannot make up my mind. On the one hand, I am furious about what has happened to me. On the other, I am distressed at giving up my plans. The Princess doesn't seem to be remaining indifferent to the double entendres that I have been incessantly wooing her with. I have already managed to whisper two or three incredible things in her ear. Come, let us reflect upon all this.

Marinoni: (*Holding the coat.*) What shall I do, your Highness?

Prince: Put it back on, put it back on, and let us return to the palace.
(*Exit.*)

Scene 5. *Elsbeth and the King.*

King: My dear daughter, you must answer my question frankly: Do you object to this marriage?

Elsbeth: Sire, that is for you to answer. I am happy if you are; I am unhappy if you are.

King: The Prince seemed to me to be an ordinary man about whom it is hard to say anything. The stupidity of his aide-de-camp alone does him wrong in my eyes. As for himself, he may be a Prince, but he is not a high-minded man. Nothing in him either attracts me or repels me. What more can I tell you? Women's hearts have secrets I cannot fathom; they sometimes imagine heroes who are so strange, they seize with such single-mindedness on one or two aspects of the man who is presented to them, that it is impossible to judge for them unless one is guided by some quite unmistakable point. So tell me candidly what you think of your fiancé.

Elsbeth: I think he is the Prince of Mantua, and war will start up again between him and you tomorrow unless I marry him.

King: That is certain, my child.

Elsbeth: Then I think I shall marry him and the war will be over.

King: May the blessings of my people rain down upon you in your father's name! Oh, my darling child, I shall be glad for this alliance. But I should prefer not to see the sadness in your eyes that belies their resignation. Think about it for a few more days.

(Exit the King. Enter Fantasio.)

Elsbeth: So there you are, you poor boy. How do you like it here?

Fantasio: I feel as free as a bird.

Elsbeth: You would have answered better if you had said "like a bird in a cage." This palace is a rather beautiful one, but it is still a cage.

Fantasio: The size of a palace or a room does not make a man more or less free. The body moves wherever it can. Imagination can open wings as broad as the heavens, in a dungeon cell as tiny as one's hand.

Elsbeth: So you are a happy fool?

Fantasio: Very happy. I chat with the little dogs and the scullery boys. There is a lap dog in the kitchen, no bigger than this, who has told me some delightful things.

Elsbeth: In what language?

Fantasio: In the purest style. He would not make a single grammatical error in the space of a year.

Elsbeth: Might I hear a few words of this style?

Fantasio: To tell the truth, I wouldn't like that. It is a unique language. Not only lap dogs speak it. Trees and grains of wheat know it as well; but kings' daughters don't. When is your wedding?

Elsbeth: In a few days everything will be over.

Fantasio: You mean that everything will begin. I am planning on offering you a present myself.

Elsbeth: What present? I am curious to know.

Fantasio: I am planning on offering you a pretty little stuffed canary that sings like a nightingale.

Elsbeth: How can it sing if it is stuffed?

Fantasio: It sings perfectly.

Elsbeth: In truth, it is remarkable how relentlessly you make fun of me.

Fantasio: Not in the least. My canary has a little mechanism inside it. When you very gently push a little button under its left foot, it sings all the latest operas, exactly like Mademoiselle Grisi.

Elsbeth: That is something you have dreamed up yourself, no doubt.

Fantasio: Not at all. It is a court canary. There are a good many well-brought-up girls who act no differently than it does. They have a little button under their left arm, a pretty little one made of fine diamond, like a dandy's watch. Their tutor or their governess pushes the button, and immediately you see their lips open in the most gracious smile; a delightful cascade of honeyed words gushes forth in the sweetest murmur, and the social conventions, like airy nymphs, immediately start dancing on tiptoe around the wonderful fountain. The suitor stares in amazement, the guests whisper indulgently, and the father, filled with secret contentment, gazes down with pride at his golden shoe buckles.

Elsbeth: You seem to keep returning to certain topics. Tell me, jester, what have these poor girls done to you, that you satirize them so joyfully? Doesn't respect for any duty find favor with you?

Fantasio: I have a good deal of respect for ugliness; that is why I have such deep respect for myself.

Elsbeth: Sometimes you seem to know more than you say. Where do you come from and who are you, to have already managed within the space of one day to penetrate mysteries that princes themselves will never suspect? Are your extravagant remarks directed at me, or are you speaking at random?

Fantasio: At random. I often direct my remarks at random: it is my dearest confidant.

Elsbeth: It seems to have informed you of things you ought not to know. I might almost believe that you have been spying on my actions and my words.

Fantasio: God knows. What do you care?

Elsbeth: More than you can imagine. A little while ago, in this room, while I was putting on my veil, I suddenly heard someone walking behind the tapestry. I have a nagging feeling it was you who were walking.

Fantasio: You can rest assured that it will remain between your handkerchief and me. I am no more indiscreet than I am curious. What pleasure might your troubles give me? You are this, and I am that. You are young, and I am old; beautiful, and I am ugly; rich, and I am poor. So you can see there is no relation between us. What do you care if chance made two wheels converge that are not following the same ruts, and cannot even leave tracks in the same dust? Is it my fault if one of your tears fell on my cheek as I lay sleeping?

Elsbeth: You speak to me in the guise of a man I loved; that is why I listen to you in spite of myself. My eyes imagine they are seeing Saint-John; but what if you are only a spy?

Fantasio: What good would that do me? Even if it were true that your marriage cost you a few tears, and I learned that by chance, what could I gain by telling about that? No one would give me a penny for it, and you wouldn't be put in the cellar as punishment. I can certainly understand that it must be rather unpleasant to marry the Prince of Mantua. But after all, that is not my responsibility. Tomorrow or the day after you will have left for Mantua with your wedding dress, and I shall still be sitting on this stool in my old breeches. What could I possibly have against you? I have no reason to wish for your death: you have never lent me any money.

Elsbeth: But if chance has willed it that you saw what I wish to remain unknown, oughtn't I to have you dismissed to avoid any further accidents?

Fantasio: Are you planning to compare me with the confidant in a tragedy? Are you afraid that I shall pursue your shadow with my harangues? Please don't get me dismissed. I am having such a good time here. Look, here comes your governess with her pockets full of mysteries. The proof that I won't listen in is that I am going off to the pantry to eat a plover wing that the butler set aside for his wife.

(Exit.)

Governess: (Entering.) Do you want to hear something awful, my dear Elsbeth?

Elsbeth: What is it? You are shaking like a leaf.

Governess: The Prince isn't the Prince, and the aide-de-camp isn't, either. It is a real fairy tale.

Elsbeth: What kind of nonsense is that?

Governess: Shh! Shh! It was one of the Prince's own officers who just told me. The Prince of Mantua is a true Almaviva. He is in disguise, and hiding among the aides-de-camp. No doubt he wanted to try to see you and get to know you, as in a fairy tale. The worthy gentleman is disguised, disguised like Lindoro in the *Barber of Seville.* The one they presented to you as your future husband is just an aide-de-camp named Marinoni.

Elsbeth: That is not possible!

Governess: It is quite certain, as sure as can be. The worthy man is disguised, and it is impossible to recognize him. It is the most extraordinary thing!

Elsbeth: You say you heard this from an officer?

Governess: From one of the Prince's officers. You can ask him yourself.

Elsbeth: He didn't say which one of the aides-de-camp was the real Prince of Mantua?

Governess: Of course not, the poor fellow was trembling himself at what he was telling me. He only let me in on his secret because he wanted to make himself agreeable to you, and he knew I would tell you. As for Marinoni, it is definite; but as for the true Prince, he didn't point him out to me.

Elsbeth: That would be something for me to ponder, if it were true. Come on, bring me that officer.
(Enter a page.)
Governess: What is it, Flamel? You seem to be out of breath.
Page: Oh, madam, it is enough to make you split your sides laughing. I dare not speak of it before your Highness.
Elsbeth: Speak up. What else is new now?
Page: Just as the Prince of Mantua was riding his horse into the courtyard leading his staff officers, his wig flew up into the air and suddenly disappeared.
Elsbeth: Whatever for? What foolishness!
Page: Madam, may I die if it isn't the truth. The wig flew up in the air on a fishhook. We found it in the pantry next to a broken bottle. No one knows who played this joke. But the Duke [*sic*] is as angry as can be, and he has sworn that, if the person responsible is not put to death, he will declare war on your father the King, and will put everything to the torch and the sword.
Elsbeth: *(To the Governess.)* Let's go hear the entire story, my dear. I am having difficulty keeping a straight face. *(Enter another page.)* Well? What news?
Page: Madam, the King's jester is in prison: he is the one who removed the Prince's wig.
Elsbeth: The jester is in prison? And on the Prince's order?
Page: Yes, your Highness.
Elsbeth: Come, mother dear, I have to speak out.
(Exit with her governess.)

Scene 6. *The Prince, Marinoni.*

Prince: No, no, let me unmask myself. It is time for me to burst forth. Things cannot go on this way. Blood and thunder! A royal wig hanging on a fishhook! Are we among barbarians, in the wastes of Siberia? Is there anything left under the sun that is civilized and proper? I am frothing with rage, and my eyes are starting from my head.
Marinoni: You will spoil everything by this violence.

Prince: And this father, this King of Bavaria, this monarch vaunted
in all of last year's almanacs! This man whose appearance is
so respectable, who expresses himself in such measured terms,
and who starts laughing when he sees his son-in-law's wig fly
up in the air! For after all, Marinoni, I admit that it was your
wig that was lifted; but is it not still the Prince of Mantua's,
since it is he that people think they see in your person? When I
think that if it had been me, in flesh and blood, it was my wig
that might have been . . . Ah, there is a Providence! When God
suddenly sent me the idea of disguising myself; when that
thought flashed into my mind, "I must disguise myself," this
fated event was foreseen by destiny. That is what saved the
head that governs my people from a most intolerable affront.
But, by Heaven, all will be revealed! For too long has my
dignity been betrayed. Since divine and human majesties are
pitilessly desecrated and shattered, since men no longer possess
the notions of good and evil, since the King of several thou-
sand people bursts out laughing like a stable boy at the sight of
a wig, Marinoni—give me back my coat.

Marinoni: (Taking off his coat.) If my sovereign orders me to do
so, I am ready to suffer a thousand torments for him.

Prince: I know of your devotion. Come on, I am going to tell the
King off in no uncertain terms.

Marinoni: You are refusing the Princess's hand? And yet she ogled
you in an obvious way during the entire dinner.

Prince: You think so? I feel lost in an abyss of uncertainties. Come
on, anyway. Let's go see the King.

Marinoni: (Holding the coat.) What shall I do, your Highness?

Prince: Put it back on for now. You can give it back to me in a
while. They will be even more thunderstruck when they hear
me take my rightful tone wearing this dark-colored coat.
(Exit.)

Scene 7. *A prison cell.*

(Fantasio alone.)

Fantasio: I don't know whether or not there is a Providence, but it
is amusing to think so. Now here is a poor little Princess who,

against her will, was going to marry a filthy animal, a provincial boor on whose head chance had dropped a crown, like the tortoise that an eagle dropped on Aeschylus's. Everything was ready: the candles were lit, the suitor powdered, the poor little girl shriven. She had dried the couple of tears I saw her shed this morning. Nothing was left but two or three priestly hocus-pocuses, for her life's misfortune to be all taken care of. In all this, the future of two kingdoms, the tranquillity of two peoples were at stake. Then I had to go and disguise myself as a hunchback and get drunk all over again in our good King's pantry, and catch his dear ally's wig by the end of a fishing line! To tell the truth, when I am drunk I think I am almost superhuman. Now the wedding is off, and everything is put back in question. The Prince of Mantua has asked for my head, in exchange for his wig. The King of Bavaria found the penalty a bit too strong, so he agreed only to prison. The Prince of Mantua, thank God, is so stupid that he would sooner be drawn and quartered than change his mind. And thus the Princess will remain unmarried, at least for now. If that doesn't constitute the subject of an epic poem in twelve cantos, I miss my guess. Pope and Boileau wrote excellent verses on much less important subjects. Oh, if I were a poet, how I would depict the scene of that wig flying about in the air! But the man who has the talent to do such things disdains to write them down. And so posterity will have to do without it.

(He falls asleep. Enter Elsbeth and her governess, with a lamp in her hand.)

Elsbeth: He is sleeping. Shut the door quietly.

Governess: You see, there is no doubt about it. He has taken off his false wig, and his deformity has disappeared at the same time. There he lies as he really is, as his people see him in his triumphal chariot. It is the noble Prince of Mantua.

Elsbeth: Yes, that is him. Now my curiosity is satisfied. I wanted to see his face, and that was all. Let me see him closer up. *(She takes the lamp.)* Psyche, watch out for your drop of oil.

Governess: He is as handsome as a real Jesus.

Elsbeth: Why did you give me all those novels and fairy tales to read? Why did you sow such strange, mysterious flowers in my poor mind?

Governess: How excited you are, standing there on the tips of your toes!

Elsbeth: He is waking up. Let's go.

Fantasio: (Awakening.) Is this a dream? I am holding the hem of a white dress.

Elsbeth: Let go of me. Let me leave.

Fantasio: It is you, Princess! If it is a pardon for the King's jester that you are bringing me with such heavenly grace, let me put my hump and my wig back on. It will only take a minute.

Governess: Oh, Prince, it is so improper for you to trick us this way! Don't put that costume back on; we know the whole story.

Fantasio: Prince! Where do you see one of them?

Governess: What good does it do to pretend?

Fantasio: I am not pretending in the least. Whatever makes you call me "Prince"?

Governess: I know my duties toward your Highness.

Fantasio: Madam, I beg you to explain this good lady's words to me. Has there really been some wild misunderstanding, or am I being subjected to mockery?

Elsbeth: Why do you ask, when it is you yourself who are mocking us?

Fantasio: Might I be a Prince, by chance? Can they have conceived some suspicion concerning my mother's honor?

Elsbeth: Who are you, if you aren't the Prince of Mantua?

Fantasio: My name is Fantasio. I am a burgher of Munich.
(He shows her a letter.)

Elsbeth: A burgher of Munich! Then why are you in disguise? What are you doing here?

Fantasio: Madam, I beg your pardon.
(He falls to his knees.)

Elsbeth: What does this mean? Get up, my good man, and get out of here. I shall spare you any punishment that you might deserve. Who put you up to this action?

Fantasio: I cannot tell you what reason brought me here.

Elsbeth: You can't? But I want to know.

Fantasio: Excuse me. I don't dare confess.

Governess: Let's go, Elsbeth. You mustn't expose yourself to talk that is unworthy of you. This man is a thief, or an upstart who is going to try to make love to you.

Elsbeth: I want to know the reason why you put on this costume.

Fantasio: I beg you, spare me.

Elsbeth: No, no, speak! Or else I shall lock this door on you for ten years.

Fantasio: Madam, I am riddled with debts. My creditors have gotten a judgment against me. At this very moment my furniture has been auctioned off, and if I weren't in this prison I would be in another one. They were supposed to come and arrest me yesterday evening. Not knowing where to spend the night or how to get out of the bailiffs' clutches, I conceived the idea of putting on this costume and throwing myself at the King's feet. If you give me back my liberty, they are going to grab me by the throat. My uncle is a miser who lives on potatoes and radishes and lets me starve to death in every tavern in the kingdom. Since you want to know, I am in debt for twenty thousand *écus.*

Elsbeth: Is all that true?

Fantasio: If I am lying, I am willing to pay it all back.
(The sound of horses is heard.)

Governess: There go some horses passing by. It is the King himself; if only I could attract the attention of a page. *(She calls out the window.)* Yoo-hoo! Flamel, where in the world are you going?

Page: (Outside.) The Prince of Mantua is about to leave.

Governess: The Prince of Mantua?

Page: Yes, war has been declared. There was a horrible scene between him and the King in front of the entire court, and the Princess's marriage has been broken off.

Elsbeth: Do you hear that, Mr. Fantasio? You have made my marriage fall through.

Governess: My Lord! Can the Prince of Mantua be leaving without my ever having seen him?

Elsbeth: If war is declared, what a misfortune!

Fantasio: You call that a misfortune, your Highness? Would you rather have a husband who starts a war over his wig? Well,

Madam, if war is declared we shall know what to do with our hands. The idlers on our boulevards will put on their uniforms; I shall take up my hunting rifle myself, if it hasn't already been auctioned off. We shall go take a tour of Italy, and if ever you enter Mantua, it will be as a true Queen, with no need for any other tapers than our swords.

Elsbeth: Fantasio, do you want to remain my father's jester? I shall pay your twenty thousand *écus*.

Fantasio: I should like that with all my heart. But in truth, if I were obliged to do it, I should jump out the window and run away, one of these days.

Elsbeth: Why? You can see that Saint-John is dead. We positively must have a jester.

Fantasio: I like this trade more than all others, but I can't carry on any trade. If you think it is worth twenty thousand *écus* to be rid of the Prince of Mantua, give it to me, and don't pay my debts. A gentleman without debts would not know where to show his face. It has never occurred to me to be without debts.

Elsbeth: Well then, I shall give it to you. But take the key to my garden. Whenever you are tired of being pursued by your creditors, come and hide in the cornflowers where I found you this morning. Make sure you put your wig and your motley back on. Don't appear before me without that misshapen form and those silver bells, for that is the way I came to like you. You will become my jester again for as long as you feel like it, and then you can go about your business. Now you may leave, the door is open.

Governess: Can it be possible that the Prince of Mantua left without my seeing him!

THE END

You Can't Trifle with Love

The title of this play (in French, *On ne badine pas avec l'amour*) would seem to link it more closely than any of Musset's other "comedies" from this period with the salon genre, the proverb, illustrated by Carmontelle and Leclercq. Like *What Does Marianne Want?* and *Fantasio* (as well as the historical tragedy, *Lorenzaccio*), it was begun in 1833, during the author's love affair with George Sand. However, it seems to have been finished only after his return from the Venice adventure. According to Musset's biographer Pierre Gastinel, scene 5 of act 2 would mark the play's new beginning.

From that point on this play becomes the darkest of Musset's comedies. Perdican and Camille's "duel of vanities" costs the life of Rosette, Camille's foster sister, and the two main characters' own happiness. Whether this somber view of love may be traced to Musset's bitter experience with George Sand (her letter to Musset dated 12 May 1834 is quoted verbatim by Perdican at the end of act 2) or to his unhappy pursuit of Princess Belgioioso upon his return from Venice, there is no doubt the play expresses a great deal of personal feeling. That may explain why the notion expressed in the title, although it certainly seems proverbial, is not repeated at the end as in later works such as *You Never Can Tell* and *A Door Has to Be either Open or Shut*. Indeed, despite the title's apparently traditional proverbial form, it appears to have been coined by Musset.

The play was first published in the *Revue des deux mondes* on 1 July 1834, two months after Musset's return — alone — from Venice.

CHARACTERS

The Baron
Perdican, his son
Master Blazius, Perdican's tutor
Master Bridaine, a priest
Camille, the Baron's niece

Mistress Pluche, her governess
Rosette, Camille's foster sister
Chorus
Peasants, servants, etc.

ACT ONE
Scene 1. *A square in front of the castle.*

Chorus: Rocking along gently on his high-spirited mule, Master
Blazius wends his way through the blossoming cornflowers, in
his newest finery, with his writing case by his side. Like a baby
on a pillow, he bobs along on his bounteous belly; with half-
closed eyes he mutters Our Fathers into his triple chin. Hail to
you, Master Blazius, you arrive in time for the grape harvest,
like an ancient amphora.

Blazius: If anyone wants to hear some important news, first of all
let him bring me a cool glass of wine.

Chorus: Here is our largest beaker. Drink, Master Blazius, it is
good wine. You can talk afterward.

Blazius: My children, I hereby inform you that young Perdican,
the son of our lordship, has just reached his majority and has
been awarded his doctorate in Paris. He is returning to the
castle this very day, with his speech full of such fine, flowery
expressions that one doesn't know how to answer him three-
quarters of the time. His entire gracious person is a veritable
keepsake album; he won't see a blade of grass without tell-
ing you what it is called in Latin. When the weather is windy
or rainy, he will tell you precisely why. You would open your
eyes as wide as that door over there if you saw him unroll one
of the parchments that he has illuminated with inks of every
color, with his own hands and without telling a soul. In sum,
he is a priceless diamond from head to toe, and that is what I
am planning to announce to his lordship the Baron. You must
feel that this does me some honor, as I have been his tutor
since he was four. And so, my good friends, bring me a chair
so I can get down off this mule without breaking my neck.
The beast is just a mite balky, and I wouldn't mind taking one
more swig before I go inside.

Chorus: Drink, Master Blazius, recover your spirits. We were here
when little Perdican was born, and there was no need, since he
is coming back home, to tell us all of that. May we still find
the child in the heart of the man!

Blazius: My word, the beaker is empty. I didn't think I had drunk the whole thing. Adieu. As I was trotting along, I prepared a couple of unpretentious phrases that should please his lordship. I shall go ring the bell.

(Exit.)

Chorus: Jolting along roughly on her winded ass, Mistress Pluche is struggling up the hill. Her squire, benumbed, smites the poor beast with all his force, and it nods its head, nibbling on a thistle. Her long, skinny legs are hopping with rage as she scrapes at her rosary with bony fingers. Good day to you, Mistress Pluche. You arrive like the fever, with the wind that turns the woods yellow.

Pluche: A glass of water, you rabble, you! A glass of water, with a drop of vinegar!

Chorus: Where are you coming from, Pluche, my dear? Your wig is covered with dust. That toupee is ruined, and your chaste gown is hiked right up to your venerable garters.

Pluche: Peasants, I hereby inform you that the beauteous Camille, your master's niece, is returning to the castle today. She has left the convent on the express command of his lordship in order to come and receive in its due time and place, as is only right, the excellent inheritance that was left her by her mother. Her education is finished, thank God. Those who see her will have the joy of breathing the fragrance of this glorious flower of devoutness and propriety. There has never been anything so pure, so angelic, so lambish, and so dovelike as this dear little nun, may the Lord God in heaven guide her! Amen! Get out of my way, rabble, I think my legs have swollen.

Chorus: Smooth out your clothes, virtuous Pluche, and when you pray to God ask him for rain: our wheat is as dried out as your shinbones.

Pluche: You have brought me water in a bowl that smells of cooking. Give me your hand to get down. You are a flock of louts and boors.

(Exit.)

Chorus: Let us put on our best Sunday best and wait until the Baron summons us. Unless I miss my guess, some joyous feast is in the air today.

(Exit.)

Scene 2. *The Baron's salon.*

(Enter the Baron, Master Bridaine, and Master Blazius.)

Baron: Master Bridaine, you are my friend. Let me introduce my son's tutor, Master Blazius. Yesterday morning at precisely eight minutes past noon my son turned twenty-one years old. He has four doctoral degrees. Master Blazius, let me introduce the parish priest, Master Bridaine. He is my friend.

Blazius: (Bowing.) Four doctoral degrees, your lordship! Literature, botany, Roman law, and canon law.

Baron: Go to your room, my dear Blazius. It won't be long till my son appears. Get yourself cleaned up a bit and come back when the bell rings.

(Exit Master Blazius.)

Bridaine: Might I tell you what I think, your lordship? Your son's tutor's breath smells of wine.

Baron: That is impossible.

Bridaine: I would bet anything on it. He spoke to me close up a moment ago, and he smelled dreadfully of wine.

Baron: That will do. I tell you once again, that is impossible.
(Enter Mistress Pluche.) Here you are, my good Pluche. My niece must be with you?

Pluche: She is right behind me, your lordship. I am just a few steps ahead of her.

Baron: Master Bridaine, you are my friend. Let me introduce my niece's governess, Mistress Pluche. At precisely seven o'clock last night my niece turned eighteen years old. She has been at the best convent in France. Mistress Pluche, let me introduce the parish priest, Master Bridaine. He is my friend.

Pluche: (Curtsying.) The best convent in all France, my lord, and I can add: the best Christian in the whole convent.

Baron: Mistress Pluche, go and straighten up the disarray you are in. My niece is going to appear soon, I hope. Be ready at dinner time.

(Exit Mistress Pluche.)

Bridaine: That venerable maiden lady seems quite brimful of unction.

Baron: Of unction, and of compunction, Master Bridaine. Her virtue is unassailable.

Bridaine: But the tutor smells of wine. I am absolutely sure of it.

Baron: Master Bridaine, there are times when I doubt your friendship. Have you made it your duty to contradict me? Not a word more on that topic. I have conceived a plan to wed my son with my niece. They make a suitable couple: their education has cost me six thousand crowns.

Bridaine: It will be necessary to obtain dispensations.

Baron: I have them, Bridaine. They are on my table, in my study. Oh, my friend, be informed now that I am filled with joy! You know that I have always had the deepest fear of solitude. However, the function that I exercise and the solemnity of my office require my presence in this castle for three months each winter and three months each summer. It is impossible to guarantee the happiness of mankind in general and of one's vassals in particular without sometimes giving one's manservant strict orders not to let anyone in. How austere and difficult is a statesman's private meditation! And how much delight would I not take in tempering, by the presence of my two conjoined children, that dark sadness to which I must necessarily be prey since the king named me tax collector!

Bridaine: Will this marriage take place here or in Paris?

Baron: There I saw you coming, Bridaine. I was sure of that question. Well, my friend, what would you say if those hands there, yes, Bridaine, your very own hands—don't look at them in such a piteous fashion—were destined to give solemn benediction to the happy confirmation of my dearest dreams? Eh?

Bridaine: I cannot speak. Gratitude seals my mouth.

Baron: Look out this window. Don't you see that my servants are crowding toward the entrance gate? My two children are arriving simultaneously. That is the most fortunate of coincidences. I have arranged things in such a way as to foresee everything. My niece will be brought in by that door on the left, and my son by that door on the right. What do you think? I cannot wait to see how they will greet each other, what they will say to each other. Six thousand crowns is no paltry sum, make no mistake. Besides, the children have loved each other tenderly since the cradle. Bridaine, I just had an idea.

Bridaine: What is that?

Baron: During dinner, without really seeming to do so—you understand, my friend—as you are draining a few joyous cups . . . You do know Latin, Bridaine?

Bridaine: Ita edepol, by Jove, do I?

Baron: I would be very happy to see you try the boy out—discreetly, of course—in front of his cousin. That cannot fail to produce a good effect. Make him speak a little Latin—not precisely during dinner, that would become distasteful, and as for me, I don't understand a word of it, but during desert—do you see?

Bridaine: If you don't understand a word of it, my lord, no doubt your niece is in the same situation.

Baron: All the more reason! You don't expect a woman to admire what she understands, do you? Where in the world have you been, Bridaine? Your reasoning seems just piteous to me.

Bridaine: I do not know women very well, but it seems to me that it is hard for one to admire what one does not understand.

Baron: I know them, Bridaine. I know those charming, unfathomable creatures. You may rest assured that they love to be dazzled, and the more one dazzles them, the wider they open their eyes. *(Perdican enters from one side, Camille from the other.)* Good day, my children! Good day, my dear Camille and Perdican! Give me a kiss, and give one to each other.

Perdican: Good day, father, good day, my dearest sister! What a joy! How happy I am!

Camille: I greet you, my father and my cousin.

Perdican: How you have grown up, Camille! You are as beautiful as the day!

Baron: When did you leave Paris, Perdican?

Perdican: Wednesday, I think, or Tuesday. How you have changed; now you are a woman! So I must be a man, then! It seems only yesterday that I saw you no higher than this.

Baron: You must both be tired. The road is a long one, and it is hot today.

Perdican: Oh, no! Father, just see how pretty Camille is!

Baron: Come now, Camille, give your cousin a kiss.

Camille: Please excuse me.

Baron: A compliment calls for a kiss. Kiss her, Perdican.

Perdican: If my cousin draws back when I offer my hand, it is my turn to say, "Please excuse me." Love may steal a kiss, but not friendship.

Camille: Neither friendship nor love may accept what they cannot repay.

Baron: (To Bridaine.) Does this beginning seem to augur any good?

Bridaine: (To the Baron.) Too much modesty is a fault, no doubt. But marriage removes many a scruple.

Baron: (To Bridaine.) I am shocked—hurt.—I did not like her reply.—*Please excuse me!* Did you notice that she made as if to cross herself?—Come over here so I can talk with you.—I find this distressing to the highest degree. This moment was supposed to be such a sweet one for me, and now it is completely ruined.—I am annoyed, piqued.—The deuce! This is very bad indeed.

Bridaine: Say a few words to them. See, they have turned their backs on each other.

Baron: Well, my children, what are you thinking about? What are you doing over there by that tapestry, Camille?

Camille: (Looking at a picture.) This is a fine portrait, uncle! Isn't it one of our great-aunts?

Baron: Yes, my child, that is your great-grandmother—or rather, your great-grandmother's sister, since this dear lady never contributed, for her part, I think, otherwise than through her prayers, to the multiplication of the family. My word, she was a saintly woman.

Camille: Oh yes, a saint! That is my Great-aunt Isabelle. How well that religious habit suits her!

Baron: And what are you doing over here, Perdican, looking at this flowerpot?

Perdican: This is a charming flower, father. It is a heliotrope.

Baron: Are you joking? It is no bigger than a fly.

Perdican: This little flower, though no bigger than a fly, still has a certain worth.

Bridaine: Of course. The doctor is right. Ask him what sex and what class it belongs to; what elements it is formed of, whence it derives its sap and its color. He will enthrall you by pointing out the phenomena of this blade of grass, from the root up to the flower.

Perdican: I really don't know all that about it, Reverend. I think it smells nice, that is all.

Scene 3. *In front of the castle.*

(Enter the Chorus.)

Chorus: A number of things amuse me and excite my curiosity. Come, friends; let us sit down under this walnut tree. Two formidable eaters are confronting each other in the castle right now—Masters Bridaine and Blazius. Haven't you noticed that when two men are more or less the same, equally fat, equally doltish, having the same vices and the same passions, and they happen to meet, they will inevitably either adore or abhor each another. According to the principle that opposites attract, that a tall, skinny man will love a short, fat one, and blondes seek out brunettes, I foresee a hidden struggle between the tutor and the curate. They are both armed with equal impudence. They both have a barrel for a belly. Not only are they gluttons, but they are gourmets. At dinner they will both fight, not only over quantity but over quality. If the fish is a small one, what is to be done? In any case, a carp's tongue cannot be divided up, and a carp cannot have two tongues. *Item:* they are both jabberers; but if need be they can both talk at the same time without listening to each other. Master Bridaine has already tried to direct several pedantic questions at young Perdican, and the tutor frowned. He finds it objectionable for someone else to try and test out his pupil. *Item:* each is just as much of an ignoramus as the other. *Item:* they are both priests; one will boast of his parish, the other will take pride in his role as tutor. Master Blazius hears the son's confessions; and Master Bridaine, the father's. I can already see them, with their elbows on the table, their cheeks inflamed, their eyes bulging from their sockets, their triple chins shaking with wrath. They glare at each other from head to toe; they gradually warm up with parries and thrusts. Soon war is declared: the air is filled with a volley of pedantries of all sorts. Then, to crown it all, Mistress Pluche comes and frets between the two drunkards, driving them both back with her sharp-pointed elbows.

Now that dinner is over, the castle gate is being opened. Here comes the Baron with his guests. Let us draw to one side. (*Exit. Enter the Baron and Mistress Pluche.*)

Baron: Venerable Pluche, I am distressed.

Pluche: Is that possible, my lord?

Baron: Yes, Pluche, that *is* possible. I had been counting for a long time—I had even written it down in my notebook—that this was to be the most pleasant day of my life. Yes, my good lady, the most pleasant. You are not unaware that it was my intention to join my son and my niece in matrimony. That was decided, agreed upon; I had spoken of it with Bridaine. And yet I see, I believe I see, that these children are acting coldly toward each other. They have not spoken a word to each other.

Pluche: Here they come, my lord. Have they been informed of your plans?

Baron: I dropped a few words to them in private about it. Since they are together now, I think it would be a good thing for us to sit down under that propitious arbor and leave them alone together for a moment.

(*He withdraws with Mistress Pluche. Enter Camille and Perdican.*)

Perdican: Do you realize that it was not at all nice of you to refuse me a kiss, Camille?

Camille: That is the way I am; it is my manner.

Perdican: May I give you my arm for a walk around the village?

Camille: No, I am too tired.

Perdican: Wouldn't you enjoy seeing the meadow again? Do you remember our boat rides on the pond? Come on, we shall go down as far as the mills. I shall take the oars, and you take the tiller.

Camille: I don't feel at all like it.

Perdican: You are breaking my heart. What, not one memory, Camille; not one heartbeat for our childhood, for all that poor time past that was so good, so sweet, so full of delightful foolishness? Don't you want to come and see the path we used to take to the farm?

Camille: No, not this evening.

Perdican: Not this evening! When, then? Our whole life is there.

Camille: I am neither young enough to play with my dolls nor old enough to be fond of the past.

Perdican: What do you mean?

Camille: I mean that childhood memories are not to my taste.

Perdican: Do they bore you?

Camille: Yes, they bore me.

Perdican: My poor child! I sincerely pity you.

   (They go off separate ways.)

Baron: *(Coming back again with Mistress Pluche.)* You have seen it and you have heard it, my good Pluche. I was expecting the sweetest harmony, and I feel as if I am attending a concert in which the violin plays "My Heart Sighs for You" while the flute plays "Long Live Henry IV." Just imagine the hideous discord such a combination would produce. Yet that is what is going on inside me.

Pluche: I must confess that I find it impossible to blame Camille. There is nothing in worse taste, in my opinion, than riding in a rowboat.

Baron: Are you serious?

Pluche: My lord, a self-respecting young lady does not venture out on a millpond.

Baron: But I beg you to observe, Mistress Pluche, that her cousin is to marry her, and in that case . . .

Pluche: Propriety forbids a girl to hold a tiller, and it is unsuitable for her to leave terra firma alone with a young man.

Baron: But I repeat . . . I tell you . . .

Pluche: That is my opinion.

Baron: Are you mad? In truth, I don't know what to say . . . There are certain expressions that I do not wish . . . that I am loath . . . You make me feel like saying . . . In truth, if I didn't restrain myself . . . You are a silly goose, Pluche! I really do not know what to think of you.

   (Exit.)

Scene 4. *A square.*

(The Chorus and Perdican.)

Perdican: Hello, friends. Do you recognize me?

Chorus: Your Lordship* looks like a child we once loved a great deal.

Perdican: Wasn't it you who carried me on your backs to cross the streams in the meadows, you who bounced me on your knees, who let me ride pillion on your stout horses, who sometimes squeezed in a little room for me at your tables so that I could join you at a farm supper?

Chorus: We do remember, my lord. Indeed, your Lordship was the greatest rascal and the finest lad on earth.

Perdican: So why don't you embrace me instead of greeting me like a stranger?

Chorus: God bless you, child of our loins! Each of us would like to take you in his arms, but we are old, my lord, and you are a man.

Perdican: Yes, it has been ten years since I last saw you, and in just one day everything changes under the sun. I have grown upward a few feet toward the sky, and you have bent downward a few inches toward the grave. Your hair has turned white, your steps have gotten slower, you no longer pick your former child up. So it is my turn to be father to you, who once were mine.

Chorus: Your return is a happier day than your birth. It is sweeter to regain what you love than to embrace a newborn child.

Perdican: So here is my dear valley, my walnut trees, my green paths, my little fountain! Here are my days gone by, still full of life! Here is the mysterious world of my childhood dreams! Oh, home, home! What an unfathomable word! Is man born only for a plot of earth, to build his nest and live there just a day?

Chorus: They say that you are a learned man, my lord.

Perdican: Yes, so I have been told, too. Knowledge is a fine thing, children. These trees and meadows teach for all to hear the finest science of all: forgetting everything one knows.

---

*The Chorus uses the formal *vous* here in French, changing to the intimate *tu* only when Perdican asks why he is greeted "like a stranger." I have rendered this difference by having the Chorus address Perdican here as "your Lordship."

Chorus: There has been more than one change here durin[g]
absence. Girls have gotten married, and boys have gon[e]
the army.

Perdican: You can tell me all about that later. I do expect some
new things; but to tell the truth, I don't want them quite yet.
How small that wash house is! It used to seem enormous to
me. I had carried an ocean and forests off in my head, and I
come back and find a drop of water and a few blades of grass.
And who is that girl singing at her window, beyond those
trees?

Chorus: It is Rosette, your cousin Camille's foster sister.

Perdican: (Going toward her.) Come down quickly, Rosette, and
come over here.

Rosette: (Entering.) Yes, my lord.

Perdican: You saw me from your window and you didn't come
over, you naughty girl? Quick, give me your hand and your
cheeks so I can kiss you.

Rosette: Yes, my lord.

Perdican: Are you married, little one? I was told you were.

Rosette: Oh, no!

Perdican: Why not? There is no prettier girl in all the village. We
shall marry you off, my child.

Chorus: My lord, she wants to die a maiden.

Perdican: Is that so, Rosette?

Rosette: Oh, no!

Perdican: Your sister Camille is back. Have you seen her?

Rosette: She hasn't come over this way yet.

Perdican: Go quickly and put on your new dress, and come have
supper at the castle.

Scene 5. *A room.*

(Enter the Baron and Master Blazius.)

Blazius: My lord, I have something to say to you. The parish
priest is a drunkard.

Baron: Shame on you! That cannot be so.

Blazius: I am sure of it. At dinner he drank three bottles of wine.

Baron: That is exorbitant.

Blazius: And leaving the table he walked through the flower beds.

Baron: Through the flower beds?—I am perplexed.—That certainly is strange!—Drinking three bottles of wine at dinner! Walking through the flower beds? That is incomprehensible. And why did he not walk on the paths?

Blazius: Because he could not walk straight.

Baron: (Aside.) I am beginning to think that Bridaine was right this morning. This Blazius smells horribly of wine.

Blazius: In addition, he ate a great deal. His speech was impeded.

Baron: In truth, I noticed that, too.

Blazius: He uttered a few words in Latin, and it was nothing but solecisms. My lord, he is a depraved man.

Baron: (Aside.) Phew! This Blazius has an unbearable smell.—Let me inform you, tutor, that I have a good many other things on my mind and that I never meddle in what people eat or drink. I am not a butler.

Blazius: Please God, I would not want to displease you, Baron. Your wine is very good.

Baron: There is good wine in my cellars.

Bridaine: (Entering.) My lord, your son is out in the square, followed around by all the scamps in the village.

Baron: That is impossible.

Bridaine: I saw it with my own eyes. He was picking up stones and skipping them across the pond.

Baron: Skipping stones? My mind is boggled; all my ideas have been turned topsy-turvy. You are giving me a senseless report, Bridaine. It is unheard of for a doctor of theology to skip stones.

Bridaine: Come over to the window, my lord, and you will see him with your own eyes.

Baron: (Aside.) Heavens! Blazius is right: Bridaine is not walking straight.

Bridaine: Look, my lord, there he is by the wash house. He is holding a young peasant girl by the arm.

Baron: A young peasant girl? Has my son come here to corrupt my vassals? A peasant girl, by the arm, and all the scamps in the village around him! I feel beside myself with rage.

Bridaine: This cries out for vengeance.

Baron: All is lost!—Lost without hope!—I am lost: Bridaine is not walking straight, Blazius smells horribly of wine, and my son is seducing all the girls in the village while skipping stones across the pond.

(Exit.)

ACT TWO
Scene 1. *A garden.*

(Enter Master Blazius and Perdican.)

Blazius: My lord, your father is desperate.

Perdican: Why is that?

Blazius: You are not unaware that he had conceived the plan of uniting you with your cousin Camille.

Perdican: So?—I would be only too happy.

Blazius: The Baron thinks, however, he has observed that your tempers are not in harmony.

Perdican: That is too bad; I cannot change mine.

Blazius: Will you make this marriage impossible thereby?

Perdican: I have already told you: I ask for nothing better than to marry Camille. Go find the Baron and tell him that.

Blazius: My lord, I shall withdraw. I see your cousin coming from over that way.

(Exit. Enter Camille.)

Perdican: Already up and about, cousin? I still maintain what I said yesterday. You are as pretty as a picture.

Camille: Let's speak seriously, Perdican. Your father wants us to get married. I don't know what you think concerning that, but I feel it is my duty to let you know I have made up my mind about it.

Perdican: It is just my bad luck if you don't like me.

Camille: No more than anyone else. I just don't wish to get married. There is nothing in that to wound your pride.

Perdican: I am not much for pride. I set no great stakes either on its pleasures or on its pains.

Camille: I have come here to receive my mother's property; tomorrow I am returning to the convent.

Perdican: You are being frank and straightforward. Let's shake hands on that and be good friends.

Camille: I don't like people to touch me.

Perdican: (Taking her by the hand.) Give me your hand please, Camille. What do you fear from me? You don't want us to be married? All right, let's not get married! Is that a reason for us to hate each other? Aren't we like brother and sister? When your mother arranged in her will for us to marry, she merely wanted our friendship to be eternal, that is all. Why marry? Here is your hand and here is mine. For them to remain united to the last breath, do you think we need a priest? All we need is God.

Camille: I am so glad that my rejection is a matter of indifference to you.

Perdican: It is not a matter of indifference, Camille. Your love would have given me life, but your friendship will console me for that. Don't leave the castle tomorrow. Yesterday you refused to take a walk around the garden because you saw in me a husband that you didn't want. Stay here a few days; let me hope that our past life is not forever dead in your heart.

Camille: I am forced to leave.

Perdican: Why?

Camille: That is my secret.

Perdican: Do you love someone else?

Camille: No; but I want to leave.

Perdican: Is that irrevocable?

Camille: Yes, it is.

Perdican: Well, then, farewell! I should have liked to sit with you under the chestnut trees in the little wood, and to talk in friendship for an hour or two. But if you don't wish to, let's not speak further of it. Good-by, my child.
(Exit.)

Camille: (To Mistress Pluche, who enters.) Pluche, is everything ready? Can we leave tomorrow? Has my guardian finished his accounts?

Pluche: Yes, my dear, spotless dove. The Baron called me a silly goose last night, so I am delighted to leave.

Camille: Here, take this message and bring it to my cousin Perdican from me before dinner.

Pluche: My Lord, dear, dear! Is that possible? You are writing a
note to a man?

Camille: Am I not supposed to be his wife? I can certainly write to
my fiancé.

Pluche: His lordship Perdican has just left. What can you be writ-
ing to him? Your fiancé, for mercy's sake! Can it be true that
you are forgetting Jesus?

Camille: Do as I tell you and have everything prepared for our
departure.

(*Exit.*)

Scene 2. *The dining room. The table is being set.*

(*Enter Master Bridaine.*)

Bridaine: It is a certainty: he will be given the place of honor again
today. The seat that I have occupied for so long on the Baron's
right will fall prey to the tutor. Ah! How wretched I am! An
ignoramus, a shameless drunkard, relegates me to the foot of
the table! The butler will pour the first glass of Malaga for
him, and when the dishes arrive at my end they will be half-cold
and the best pieces will already have been gobbled up. There
will be no more cabbage or carrots left around the partridges.
Oh, holy Catholic Church! For him to have been given that
place yesterday was conceivable: he had just arrived; it was the
first time in a number of years that he had sat at that table!
My God, how he gorged himself! No, there will be nothing left
for me but bones and chicken feet. I shall not abide such an in-
sult. Farewell, venerable armchair that I have sunk into so many
times, stuffed with succulent dishes! Farewell, oh ye sealed bot-
tles, incomparable aroma of venison cooked to a turn! Farewell,
splendid table, noble dining room, I shall never again say grace!
I return to my parish; no longer shall I be seen mingling with
the throng of guests. Like Caesar, I would rather be first in the
village than second in Rome.

(*Exit.*)

Scene 3. *A field in front of a cottage.*

(Enter Rosette and Perdican.)

Perdican: Since your mother isn't home, come and take a walk around.

Rosette: Do you think all these kisses you are giving me are doing me any good?

Perdican: What can you find wrong with it? I would kiss you in front of your mother. Aren't you Camille's foster sister? Am I not your brother, just as I am hers?

Rosette: Words are words, and kisses are kisses. I am not very witty, and I notice that right away when I try to say something. Fine ladies know what is going on, according to whether you kiss their right hand or their left. Their fathers kiss them on the forehead, their brothers kiss them on the cheek, their lovers on their lips. Everyone kisses *me* on both cheeks, and that troubles me.

Perdican: You are so pretty, my child!

Rosette: You mustn't get angry about that, either. You seem so sad this morning! Is your marriage off, then?

Perdican: The peasants in your village remember they once loved me. The dogs in the barnyard and the trees in the wood remember it, too. But Camille doesn't. How about you, Rosette: When is your wedding day?

Rosette: Let's not talk about that, do you mind? Let's talk about the weather, about these flowers here, about your horses and my bonnets.

Perdican: Whatever you like, whatever can pass through your lips without making them lose that heavenly smile, which I respect more than my life.

(He kisses her.)

Rosette: You respect my smile, but you don't have much respect for my lips as far as I can see. Just look: a drop of rain just fell on my hand, and yet the sky is clear.

Perdican: Forgive me.

Rosette: What have I done to make you cry?

(Exit.)

Scene 4. *In the castle.*

(Enter Master Blazius and the Baron.)

Blazius: My lord, I have something strange to tell you. Just a
   while ago I happened to be in the pantry, I mean in the
   gallery—what would I have been in the pantry for? By chance
   I had found a bottle, I mean a pitcher of water—how could I
   have found a bottle in the gallery? Anyway, I was just taking a
   drink of wine, I mean a glass of water, to pass the time and I
   was looking out the window between two flowerpots that seem
   to me to be in a modern style, although they are Etruscan
   copies.

Baron: What an unbearable way of talking you have acquired,
   Blazius! Your speech is quite disconcerting.

Blazius: Listen to me, my lord, lend me your ears for just a
   moment. So, I was looking out the window. Please don't lose
   your temper, in heaven's name, the family honor is at stake!

Baron: The family! That is absolutely incomprehensible. The
   family honor, Blazius! Do you know that there are thirty-seven
   of us males, and almost as many females, in both Paris and
   the provinces?

Blazius: Allow me to go on. As I was taking a drink of wine, I
   mean a glass of water, to hasten a tardy digestion, just imag-
   ine: I saw Mistress Pluche passing by, out of breath, beneath
   the window.

Baron: Why out of breath, Blazius? That is not customary.

Blazius: And beside her, flushed with anger, your niece Camille.

Baron: Which one was flushed with anger, my niece or Mistress
   Pluche?

Blazius: Your niece, my lord.

Baron: My niece flushed with anger? That is unheard of. How do
   you know it was with anger? She could be flushed for any
   number of reasons. She had probably been chasing after some
   butterflies in my gardens.

Blazius: I cannot swear to anything concerning that. That may be.
   But she was shouting quite loud: "Go on, find him! Do as you
   are told! You are a fool! I want you to." And she kept striking

Mistress Pluche on the elbow with her fan, and Mistress Pluche would jump up and down in the clover at each exclamation.

Baron: In the clover? . . . So, how did the governess reply to my niece's extravagances? For her behavior deserves to be characterized as such.

Blazius: The governess answered: "I don't want to! I couldn't find him! He is wooing village girls, turkey-keepers. I am too old to start carrying love notes. I have kept my hands pure till now, thank God." And all the while she was speaking, her hands kept crumpling up a piece of paper folded in two.

Baron: I don't understand a thing. My thoughts are completely muddled. What reason could Mistress Pluche have for crumpling a piece of paper folded in two while jumping up and down in the clover? I cannot give credence to such outlandishness.

Blazius: My lord, do you not clearly understand what this means?

Baron: No, in truth, my friend, no, I absolutely do not understand a thing. It all seems like reckless behavior to me, it is true, but as much without motivation as it is without excuse.

Blazius: It means your niece is carrying on a secret correspondence.

Baron: What is that you are saying? Do you realize of whom you are speaking? Weigh your words, Father.

Blazius: Even were I to weigh them in the heavenly scales that are to weigh my soul at the Last Judgment, I should not find one word that rings false. Your niece is carrying on a secret correspondence.

Baron: But do you realize, my friend, that that is impossible?

Blazius: Why would she have given her governess a letter to deliver? Why would she have cried: "Find him!" while the other one sulked and kept refusing?

Baron: And to whom was the letter addressed?

Blazius: That is precisely the *hic,* my lord, *hic jacet lepus.* To whom was the letter addressed? To a man who is wooing a turkey-keeper. Well, now, a man who seeks out a turkey-keeper in public may be suspected of having been born to keep them himself. It is impossible for your niece, however, with the education that she has been given, to have fallen in love with such a man. That is what I say, and what makes it impossible for me to understand it any more than you do, with all due respect.

Baron: Good heavens! My niece declared to me this very morning that she was rejecting her cousin Perdican. Could she be in love with a turkey-keeper? Let us go into my study; I have been subjected to such violent shocks since yesterday that I cannot collect my thoughts.

(Exit.)

Scene 5. *A fountain in the woods.*

(Enter Perdican, reading a note.)

Perdican: "Be at the little fountain at noon." What can that mean? Such coldness, so absolute and cruel a rejection, such insensitive pride, and a rendezvous on top of it all? If it is to talk business with me, why choose a place like this? Is it flirtatiousness? This morning while walking with Rosette I heard someone moving in the bushes, and I thought it was a deer. Is this some sort of intrigue?

(Enter Camille.)

Camille: Good day, cousin. I thought I noticed, rightly or wrongly, that you were sad when you left me this morning. You took my hand against my will; now I have come to ask you to give me yours. I denied you a kiss; here it is. *(She kisses him.)* Well now, you told me you would be glad to talk in friendship with me. Sit down, and let's talk.

(She sits down.)

Perdican: Was I dreaming then, or am I dreaming now?

Camille: You found it strange to get a note from me, didn't you? My mood keeps changing. But you said something very true this morning: "Since we are parting, let us part as good friends." You don't know why I am leaving, and I have come to tell you: I am going to take the veil.

Perdican: Is this possible? Camille, is it you that I can see in this fountain, sitting on the daisies as in days gone by?

Camille: Yes, Perdican, it is me. I have come to relive a few moments of my past life. I seemed brusque and haughty to you.

It is quite simple: I have renounced the world. Before leaving it, however, I should be very glad to have your opinion. Do you think I am right to become a nun?

Perdican: Don't ask my opinion about that, because I shall never become a monk.

Camille: During the almost ten years that we have been living apart, you have begun to experience life. I know what kind of man you are, and you must have learned a lot in a short time, with a heart and a mind like yours. Tell me, have you had any mistresses?

Perdican: Why do you ask?

Camille: Please answer me without modesty or vanity.

Perdican: I have.

Camille: Did you love them?

Perdican: With all my heart.

Camille: Where are they now? Do you know?

Perdican: These are odd questions. What do you want me to tell you? I am neither their husband nor their brother; they have gone wherever they pleased.

Camille: There must undoubtedly be one of them that you preferred over the others. How long did you love the one that you loved best?

Perdican: What an odd girl you are! Are you trying to become my confessor?

Camille: I am asking you as a favor to answer me sincerely. You aren't a rake, and I believe your heart has some integrity. You must have inspired love, since you merit it, and you would not have given in to a mere whim. Answer me, please.

Perdican: Indeed, I cannot remember.

Camille: Do you know any man who has loved only one woman?

Perdican: There must certainly be some.

Camille: Was he one of your friends? Tell me his name.

Perdican: I have no name to tell you. But I believe there are men capable of loving only once.

Camille: How many times may a decent man love?

Perdican: Are you trying to make me recite a litany, or are you reciting a catechism yourself?

Camille: I should like to learn more, and to find out whether I am right or wrong to become a nun. If I were to marry you, wouldn't you have to answer all my questions frankly and bare your heart to me? I have considerable esteem for you, and I believe you are superior to many other men, by your education and your nature. I am sorry that you no longer remember what I am asking you about. Perhaps I should grow bolder if I got to know you better.

Perdican: What are you driving at? Speak: I shall answer.

Camille: Then answer my first question. Am I right to remain in the convent?

Perdican: No.

Camille: So I would do better to marry you?

Perdican: Yes.

Camille: If your parish priest blew on a glass of water and told you that it was a glass of wine, would you drink it as such?

Perdican: No.

Camille: If your parish priest blew on you, and told me that you would love me all your life, would I be right to believe him?

Perdican: Yes and no.

Camille: What would you advise me to do the day I saw that you no longer loved me?

Perdican: To take a lover.

Camille: What shall I do then the day my lover no longer loves me?

Perdican: Take another one.

Camille: How long will that go on?

Perdican: Until your hair is gray, and by then mine will be white.

Camille: Do you know what a cloister is like, Perdican? Have you ever sat for an entire day on the benches of a women's convent?

Perdican: Yes, I have.

Camille: I have, as a friend, a sister who is only thirty, and who received five hundred thousand pounds' income at the age of fifteen. She is the most beautiful and noble creature who has ever walked the earth. She was a peeress of the realm, and had one of the most distinguished men in France as a husband. None of the noble human faculties had remained uncultivated in her, and, like a plant of select breed, all her buds had grown branches. Never will love and fortune place their crown on a

more beautiful brow. Her husband deceived her. She loved
another man, and she is dying of despair.

Perdican: That is possible.

Camille: We live in the same cell, and I have spent entire nights
talking of her misfortunes. They have almost become my own:
isn't that strange? I really don't know how it can be. When
she spoke to me of her marriage, when she painted for me the
ecstasy of the first days, then the tranquillity of following ones,
and how finally everything had vanished; how she was seated
by the fire one evening with him by the window, not saying a
word; how their love had languished, and how every attempt to
draw closer ended only in quarrels; how an outsider came be-
tween them, little by little, and imperceptibly mingled in their
suffering, it was me that I saw as she spoke. When she said:
"There I was happy," my heart would leap. And when she
added: "There I wept," my tears would flow. But imagine some-
thing stranger still: I ended up by creating an imaginary life
for myself. That went on for four years. I don't need to tell you
through how many reflections, how much soul-searching, it
all came about. What I wanted to tell you as an oddity is that
all of Louise's stories, all the fictions of my dreams, bore your
resemblance.

Perdican: My resemblance?

Camille: Yes, and that is just natural: you were the only man I had
known. In truth, I did love you, Perdican.

Perdican: How old are you, Camille?

Camille: Eighteen.

Perdican: Go on, go on. I am listening.

Camille: There are two hundred women in our convent. A small
number of those women will never know life, and all the rest
are waiting for death. More than one among them left the con-
vent as I am today, virginal and full of hope. They came back
shortly afterward, old and wretched. Every day some of them
die in our dormitories, and every day new ones come to take
the place of the dead on the horsehair mattresses. Outsiders
who visit us admire the calm and order of the house. They look
attentively at the whiteness of our veils; but they wonder why
we lower them over our eyes. What do you think of these wo-
men, Perdican? Are they right or are they wrong?

Perdican: I really don't know.

Camille: There are some of them who have advised me to remain a virgin. I am very glad to consult you. Do you think those women would have done better to take a lover and advise me to do likewise?

Perdican: I really don't know.

Camille: You promised you would answer me.

Perdican: I am obviously released from my promise: I don't believe it is you talking.

Camille: That may be, there must be some quite silly things among all my ideas. It may very well be that I have been coached and that I am just a badly taught parrot. In the gallery there is a little picture representing a monk bent over a prayer book. Through the dark bars of his cell slips a dim ray of sunlight, and you can see an Italian inn, in front of which a goatherd is dancing. Which of those men do you have more esteem for?

Perdican: Neither one of them, and both. They are two flesh-and-blood men. One of them is reading, and the other is dancing. I can't see anything else in it. You are right to become a nun.

Camille: You said "no" a little while ago.

Perdican: Did I? That is possible.

Camille: So you advise me to?

Perdican: So you don't believe in anything.

Camille: Look up, Perdican! What man doesn't believe in anything?

Perdican: (Standing up.) Here is one: I don't believe in life everlasting. My dear sister, the nuns have given you their experience. But believe me, it is not your own. You won't die without knowing love.

Camille: I want to love, but I don't want to suffer. I want to love with an eternal love and make vows that are not broken. Here is my lover.

(She points to her crucifix.)

Perdican: That lover doesn't exclude others.

Camille: For me at least he shall. Don't smile, Perdican! I haven't seen you for ten years, and I am leaving tomorrow. In another ten years, if we see each other again, we shall talk about it once again. I decided not to remain like a cold statue in your memory, for lack of feeling leads to the point that I have reached. Listen to me: go back to life and as long as you remain happy,

as long as you love as one may love here on earth, forget your
sister Camille. But if you should ever forget or be forgotten,
if the angel of hope should abandon you, when you are alone
with an empty heart, think of me praying for you.

Perdican: You are filled with pride: beware.

Camille: Why?

Perdican: You are eighteen years old and you don't believe in love?

Camille: Do you who are speaking believe in it ? Here you are,
bending over beside me, with knees that have been worn out
on your mistresses' carpets, and you don't even know their
names. You have shed tears of joy and tears of despair; but you
knew that spring water was more constant than your tears, and
it would always be there to bathe your swollen eyelids. You ply
your trade as a young man, and you smile when you are told
about disconsolate women. You don't believe that people can
die of love, since you are living and you have been in love. What
is the world, then? It seems to me that you must have heartfelt
scorn for the women who take you as you are, and dismiss their
latest lovers to draw you into their arms with another's kisses
still on their lips. A little while ago I asked you whether you had
been in love, and you answered me like a tourist who is asked
whether he has been to Italy or to Germany, and who might
say: "Yes, I have been there," and then think of going to Swit-
zerland or the first country that comes along. Is your love
just a coin then that can pass from hand to hand until you die?
No, it isn't even a coin, for the thinnest gold piece is worth
more than you are, and, whatever hands it may pass through, it
keeps its stamped image.

Perdican: How beautiful you are when your eyes flash, Camille!

Camille: Yes, I am beautiful, I know it. Flatterers won't teach me
anything I don't know. The cold nun who cuts my hair will per-
haps grow pale at the sight of that mutilation. But it won't be
turned into rings and chains to go the rounds of boudoirs. My
head won't be lacking a single one when the steel passes
through my hair. I want only a single cut of the scissors, and,
when the priest who blesses me puts the gold ring of my
divine spouse on my finger, the tress that I give him will be long
enough to cover him like a cloak.

Perdican: You are angry, indeed.

Camille: I was wrong to speak. My whole life is on the tip of my
tongue. Oh, Perdican, don't mock me; all of this is deathly sad!

Perdican: My poor child, I am letting you go on, and I really
feel like saying a word in reply. You mention a nun who seems
to me to have had a harmful influence on you. You say that her
husband was unfaithful to her, and she was unfaithful in her
turn, and she is in despair. Are you sure that, if her husband or
her lover came back and reached his hand out to her through
the bars of the visiting room, she would not reach her own out
to him?

Camille: What are you saying? I don't think I have understood.

Perdican: Are you sure that if her husband or her lover came back,
and told her to suffer once again, she would say no?

Camille: I am.

Perdican: There are two hundred women in your convent, and
most of them have a deep wound in the depths of their hearts.
They have had you touch it, and they have tinged your virginal
thoughts with drops of their blood. They have lived, haven't
they? And they have shown you the way of their lives with hor-
ror. You made the sign of the cross before their scars as if it were
before Jesus' wounds. They have made a place for you in their
mournful processions, and you press against those emaciated
bodies with religious fear when you see a man go by. Are you
sure that, if the man going by was the one who was unfaithful
to them, the one for whom they are weeping and suffering, the
one they curse when they pray to God, are you sure that when
they see him they would not break their chains and run after
their past unhappiness, and press their bloody breasts against
the daggers that wounded them? Oh, my child, do you know
the dreams of these women who tell you not to dream? Do you
know what names they whisper when the sobs rising from their
lips make the holy wafer tremble at communion? They, who
sit down next to you with their shaking heads to pour their
withered old age into your ears, who sound the death knell of
their despair in the ruins of your youth and make your red
blood feel the chill of their tomb—do you know who they are?

Camille: You are frightening me. You are becoming angry, too.

Perdican: Do you know who those nuns are, you wretched girl?
They depict men's love as a lie. Do they know that there is

something worse yet, the lie of divine love? Do they know they are committing a crime, to come and whisper women's words to a virgin? Ah! How well they have taught you! How I foresaw all this when you were standing in front of our old aunt's portrait! You wanted to leave without shaking my hand. You did not want to see either these woods or this poor little fountain, which is gazing at us bathed in tears. You rejected the days of your childhood, and the plaster mask the nuns have stuck onto your cheeks denied me a brother's kiss. But your heart stirred. It forgot its lesson, since it doesn't know how to read, and you came back and sat here on the grass where we are now. Well, Camille, those women have spoken the truth. They have set you on the right path. It may cost me my life's happiness, but tell them this on my behalf: heaven is not for them.

Camille: Nor for me either, I suppose.

Perdican: Good-by, Camille. Go back to your convent, and when you are told the horrible tales that have poisoned your mind, answer this way: "All men are liars, unfaithful, false, prattling, hypocritical, vain, cowardly, despicable, and sensual. All women are fickle, scheming, vain, inquisitive, and depraved. The world is nothing but a bottomless quagmire in which the most formless creatures crawl and squirm over piles of slime. But there is one holy and sublime thing in the world: the union of two of these imperfect, horrible creatures." One is often deceived in love, often wounded and often unhappy. But one loves, and on the edge of the grave one turns around to look back, and says to oneself: "I have often suffered, I have been mistaken at times, but I have loved. It is I who have lived and not a counterfeit being, created by my boredom and my pride." *(Exit.)*

ACT THREE
Scene 1. *In front of the castle.*

(Enter the Baron and Master Blazius.)

Baron: In addition to your drunkenness, Master Blazius, you are a knave. My servants see you sneaking into the pantry furtively, and when you are convicted of stealing my bottles in the most pitiable fashion, you think you can justify yourself by accusing my niece of having a secret correspondence.

Blazius: But, my lord, please remember . . .

Baron: Leave, Reverend, and never show yourself before me again! It is irrational to behave as you have, and my dignity requires me not to pardon you for the rest of my life.

(Exit. Master Blazius follows him. Enter Perdican.)

Perdican: I really would like to know whether I am in love. On the one hand, her way of asking questions is rather cavalier for an eighteen-year-old girl; furthermore, the ideas that those nuns have put into her head will be hard to correct. Moreover, she is to leave today. The devil take it, I do love her, that is sure. After all, who knows? Maybe she was reciting a lesson, and in any case it is clear that she doesn't care for me. On the other hand, she may be pretty, but that doesn't stop her from having far too stubborn manners and too blunt a tone. I shall just have to stop thinking about her—it is clear that I don't love her. It is certain that she is pretty, but why is it that I can't get yesterday's conversation out of my head? In truth, I have spent the night raving to myself. Now where was I going? Oh, yes! I am going to the village.

(Exit.)

Scene 2. *A path.*

(Enter Master Bridaine.)

Bridaine: What are they doing now? Alas, it is noon! They are at dinner. What are they eating? What aren't they eating? I saw the cook crossing the village with a huge turkey. Her assistant was carrying the truffles, along with a basket of grapes.

(Enter Master Blazius.)

Blazius: Oh, unforeseen disgrace! Now they have thrown me out of the castle and thereby out of the dining room. I shall never again drink wine in the pantry.

Bridaine: I shall never again see the dishes steaming. I shall never again warm my broad belly by the fire of the noble fireplace.

Blazius: Why did fatal curiosity impel me to listen in on the conversation between Mistress Pluche and the Baron's niece? Why did I report everything I saw to the Baron?

Bridaine: Why has vain pride separated me from the honorable table to which I was so warmly welcomed? What did it matter to me, whether I sat on the right or on the left?

Blazius: Alas! I must confess I was drunk when I acted so stupidly.

Bridaine: Alas! The wine had gone to my head when I committed that foolishness.

Blazius: It seems to me that I see the priest over there.

Bridaine: That is the tutor in person.

Blazius: Hello! Hello, Father, what are you doing here?

Bridaine: Who, me? I am going to dinner. Aren't you coming, too?

Blazius: Not today. Alas, Master Bridaine, intervene on my behalf. The Baron has thrown me out. I falsely accused Miss Camille of carrying on a secret correspondence, and yet God is my witness that I saw or thought I saw Mistress Pluche in the clover. I am done for, Father!

Bridaine: What is this you are telling me?

Blazius: Alas, alas, only the truth! I am in total disgrace because I have stolen a bottle.

Bridaine: What do you mean, sir, about stolen bottles in connection with clover and correspondence?

Blazius: I beg you to plead my case. I am an honest man, my noble Bridaine. Oh, my worthy, noble Bridaine, I am your servant!

Bridaine: (Aside.) Oh fortune! Is this a dream? I shall be seated upon thee, then, oh blessed chair!

Blazius: I should be very grateful if you would listen to my story and be so kind as to excuse me, dear sir, my beloved priest.

Bridaine: I find that impossible, sir. Noon has rung, and I am going off to have dinner. If the Baron complains about you, that is your business. I don't intervene on behalf of a drunkard. (Aside.) Quickly, let us fly to the gate. And thou, my belly: fill thyself to the utmost!
(Exit, running.)

Blazius: (Alone.) Wretched Pluche, you are the one who will pay for all of them. Yes, you are the cause of my ruin, you shameless hussy, you base procuress; you are the one I owe my disgrace to.

Oh, Holy Sorbonne! Call me a drunkard! I am done for if I do not get hold of a letter and prove to the Baron that his niece is carrying on a correspondence. I saw her this morning writing at her desk. Aha! Here comes something new! *(Mistress Pluche goes by carrying a letter.)* Pluche, give me that letter!

Pluche: What is the meaning of this? This is a letter from my mistress that I am going to mail in the village.

Blazius: Give it to me, or you are a dead woman.

Pluche: I, a dead woman! A dead woman, Jesus and Mary, virgin and martyr!

Blazius: Yes, a dead woman, Pluche, give me that paper. *(They struggle. Enter Perdican.)*

Perdican: What is the matter? What are you doing, Blazius? Why are you attacking this woman?

Pluche: Give me back the letter. He took it from me, my lord. Justice!

Blazius: She is a procuress, my lord. This letter is a billet-doux.

Pluche: It is a letter from Camille, my lord, from your fiancée.

Blazius: It is a billet-doux to a turkey-keeper.

Pluche: You are lying, Father. You can take that from me.

Perdican: Give me that letter, I can't make head or tail of your argument. But as Camille's fiancé, I assume the right to read it. *(He reads.)* "To Sister Louise, at the **** Convent." *(Aside.)* What is this damned curiosity coming over me, in spite of myself! My heart is beating hard and I don't know what I am feeling. You may withdraw, Mistress Pluche, you are a worthy woman, and Master Blazius is a fool. Go have dinner; I take responsibility for mailing this letter.

(Exit Master Blazius and Mistress Pluche.)

Perdican: (Alone.) I know only too well that it is a crime to open a letter, so I won't do it. What can Camille have to say to that nun? Am I really in love? What power does that strange girl have over me, for the three words written in this address to make my hand tremble? How strange: Blazius broke the seal while struggling with Mistress Pluche. Is it a crime to unfold it? Well, I won't change anything in it.

(He opens the letter and reads it.)

"I am leaving today, my dear, and everything has gone as I had foreseen. It is a terrible thing, but the poor young man's heart is broken and he will never get over losing me. Yet I did everything in my power to turn him away from me. God will forgive me for reducing him to despair by my rejection. Alas, my dear, what could I do? Pray for me. We shall see each other again tomorrow, and forever. All yours, with the best of my soul, Camille."

Is it possible? Camille writes this! She is talking about *me* this way! So I am in despair at her rejection! Well, my God, if that were true it would be easy to see — what shame can there be in loving? She has done everything in her power to turn me away from her, she says, and my heart is broken. What does she have to gain by making up such a tale? Was the idea I had last night true, then? Oh, women! Poor Camille may feel deep piety, she is giving herself to God with all her heart, but she has resolved and decreed that she will leave me in despair. It was agreed on between those two good friends before she left the convent. It was decided that Camille would see her cousin again, that she would be asked to marry him, that she would refuse, and that her cousin would be wretched. It is such an interesting thing, for a girl to sacrifice her cousin's happiness to God. No, no, Camille, I am not in love with you, I am not in despair, my heart isn't broken, and I shall prove it to you. Yes, you will learn that I love another woman before you leave here. Hey, there, my good man! *(Enter a peasant.)* Go to the castle. Tell them in the kitchen to send a servant to bring this letter to Miss Camille. *(He writes.)*

Peasant: Yes, my lord. *(Exit.)*

Perdican: Now for the other one. Ha! I am in despair, am I? Hey! Rosette! Rosette! *(He knocks on a door.)*

Rosette: *(Opening.)* It is you, my lord! Come in, my mother is home.

Perdican: Put on your prettiest bonnet, Rosette, and come along with me.

Rosette: Where in the world?

Perdican: I shall tell you later. Ask your mother's permission, but hurry up.

Rosette: Yes, my lord. *(She goes into the house.)*

Perdican: I have asked Camille for another rendezvous, and I am sure she will come. But, by heaven, she won't find what she is expecting. I plan to make love to Rosette before Camille's very eyes.

Scene 3. *The wood.*

(Enter Camille and the peasant.)

Peasant: I am on my way to the castle to bring a letter for you, miss. Should I give it to you or hand it in at the kitchen as his lordship Perdican told me?

Camille: Give it to me.

Peasant: If you want me to take it to the castle, there is no need for me to linger.

Camille: I tell you to give it to me.

Peasant: As you wish. *(He gives her the letter.)*

Camille: Here, take this for your trouble.

Peasant: Many thanks. I can go now, can't I?

Camille: If you want to.

Peasant: I am going, I am going. *(Exit.)*

Camille: (Reading.) Perdican asks me to say good-by to him before I leave, near the little fountain I had him come to yesterday. What can he have to say to me? Well, here is the fountain, so I am right there. Should I grant this second rendezvous? Ha! *(She hides behind a tree.)* Here comes Perdican with Rosette, my foster sister. I suppose he is going to dismiss her. I am glad not to seem to be arriving first. *(Enter Perdican and Rosette, who sit down.)*

Camille: (Hiding, aside.) What does this mean? He is seating her down next to him? Is he asking me for a rendezvous in order to come and talk with another woman? I am curious to know what he has to tell her.

Perdican: (In a loud voice, so Camille hears him.) I love you, Rosette! You alone in all the world have not forgotten any of our beautiful days gone by. You alone recall the days of our youth. Take your share of my new life; give me your heart, my dear child. Here is a token of our love. *(He puts his chain around her neck.)*

Rosette: You are giving me your gold chain?

Perdican: Now look at this ring. Stand up and let's walk over to the fountain. Do you see the two of us in the spring, leaning against each other? Do you see your beautiful eyes next to mine, your hand in mine? See how all of that vanishes. *(He throws his ring in the water.)* See how our image has disappeared. Here it comes back again, little by little. The water that was rippled becomes calm again. It is still shimmering. Great black circles run along its surface. Just wait, we are reappearing. Already I can make out your arms twined in mine once again. One more minute, and there will no longer be a single ripple on your pretty face. Look! That was a ring that Camille had given me.

Camille: (Aside.) He threw my ring in the water.

Perdican: Do you know what love is, Rosette? Listen! The wind has fallen still; the morning dew is rolling drop by drop over the dried-out leaves warmed by the sun. I swear by the light of day, by that sun up there, that I love you! You will have me, won't you? Your youth has not been withered? Your own crimson blood has not been diluted by the dregs of a weakened blood? You don't want to become a nun. Here you are, young and beautiful, in the arms of a young man. Oh, Rosette, Rosette! Do you know what love is?

Rosette: Alas, you are a learned man, but I shall love you as best I can.

Perdican: Yes, as best you can. And you will love me better, though I am a learned man and you are a peasant girl, than those pallid statues shaped by the nuns that have their head in place of their heart, and leave the cloisters to come and spread the dank atmosphere of their cells over our lives. You have no schooling; you wouldn't read in some book the prayer that your mother taught you as she learned it from her mother. You don't even understand the meaning of the words you repeat, when you kneel down at the foot of your bed. But you do understand that you are praying, and for God that is enough.

Rosette: How you talk to me, my lord.

Perdican: You don't know how to read, but you know what these
  woods and meadows, these warm streams, these beautiful fields
  covered with their harvests, what all of nature, shining with
  youth, is saying. You recognize these thousands of brothers,
  and me as one of them. Arise, you shall be my wife, and we
  shall take root together in the heart of the almighty world.
  (Exit with Rosette.)

Scene 4.

(Enter the Chorus.)

Chorus: Something odd is certainly going on in the castle. Camille
  has refused to marry Perdican. Today she is supposed to go
  back to the convent that she came from. But I believe his lord-
  ship her cousin has found consolation with Rosette. Alas, the
  poor girl doesn't know what risk she is running, listening to a
  young, romantic nobleman's speeches.

Pluche: (Entering.) Quickly, quickly, I want my ass saddled!

Chorus: Are you going to pass by like a daydream, venerable lady?
  Are you once more and so soon going to straddle that poor
  beast, which is so unhappy to bear you?

Pluche: Thank God I won't spend the rest of my life here, rabble.

Chorus: Spend the rest of your life far away, Pluche, my love. Die
  unnoticed, in a dingy vault. We shall pray for your respectable
  resurrection.

Pluche: Here comes my mistress. *(To Camille, who enters.)* My
  dear Camille, everything is ready for our departure. The Baron
  has made his accounts, and my ass is laden.

Camille: Go to the devil, you and your ass; I am not leaving
  today.
  (Exit.)

Chorus: What does this mean? Mistress Pluche is ashen with ter-
  ror. Her hairpiece is struggling to rise up on her head, her
  chest wheezes aloud, and her fingers stretch and contort.

Pluche: Lord Jesus! Camille swore!
  (Exit.)

Scene 5.

(Enter the Baron and Master Bridaine.)

Bridaine: My lord, I must speak to you in private. Your son is courting a village girl.

Baron: That is absurd, my friend.

Bridaine: I distinctly saw him walk arm-in-arm with her on the heath. He was speaking into her ear and promising to marry her.

Baron: That is monstrous.

Bridaine: You may be sure of it. He gave her a considerable present, and the young woman has shown it to her mother.

Baron: Heavens! "Considerable," Bridaine? In what way "considerable"?

Bridaine: By its weight and by its importance. It is the chain he was wearing on his cap.

Baron: Let us go into my study. I don't know what to think.

(Exit.)

Scene 6. *Camille's room.*

(Enter Camille and Mistress Pluche.)

Camille: You say he took my letter?

Pluche: Yes, my child. He promised to put it in the mail.

Camille: Go to the drawing room, Pluche, and do me the favor of telling Perdican that I am awaiting him here.

(Exit Mistress Pluche.)

He obviously read my letter. His scene in the woods was out of revenge, like his love for Rosette. He wanted to prove to me that he loved someone else, and to act indifferent despite his rancor. Could it be that he is in love with me? *(She lifts the tapestry.)* Are you there, Rosette?

Rosette: (Entering.) Yes, may I come in?

Camille: Listen, my child: isn't his lordship Perdican courting you?

Rosette: Alas, yes!

Camille: What do you think of what he said to you this morning?

Rosette: This morning? Why, where?

Camille: Don't pretend you don't know. This morning, by the fountain in the wood.

Rosette: So you saw me?

Camille: You poor innocent thing! No, I didn't see you. He made you a fine speech, didn't he? I wager he promised he would marry you.

Rosette: How do you know that?

Camille: What does it matter how I know it? Do you believe his promises, Rosette?

Rosette: Why shouldn't I believe them? Could he be deceiving me? What for?

Camille: Perdican won't marry you, my child.

Rosette: Alas, I can't tell!

Camille: You love him, you poor girl. He won't marry you, and I shall prove it to you. Get behind this curtain, just keep your ears open, and come in when I call you.
(*Exit Rosette.*)
(*Camille, alone.*) I thought I was acting out of revenge; could it be that I am acting humanely? The poor girl's heart is caught.
(*Enter Perdican.*) Good day, cousin. Sit down.

Perdican: What a fine dress, Camille! Who is it for?

Camille: You, perhaps. I am sorry not to have been able to go to the rendezvous you asked me for. Did you have something to say to me?

Perdican: (*Aside.*) Upon my life, that is quite a big little lie for a spotless lamb. I saw her behind a tree listening to our conversation. (*Aloud.*) I have nothing but good-by to say to you, Camille. I thought you were leaving. And yet your horse is still in the stable, and you don't seem to be dressed for traveling.

Camille: I like to argue. I am not entirely sure whether I didn't feel like quarreling with you some more.

Perdican: What use is quarreling, when it is impossible for us to make up? The best part of arguments is making peace.

Camille: Are you really sure that I don't want to make peace?

Perdican: Don't mock me; I am no match for you.

Camille: I should like to be wooed. I don't know whether it is because I have a new dress on, but I feel like enjoying myself. You asked me to go to the village; let's go, I am willing. Let's go out in a boat. I feel like having a picnic on the grass or going for a walk through the forest. Might there be a full moon this evening? That is strange: you no longer have the ring I gave you on your finger.

Perdican: I lost it.

Camille: That must be why I found it. Here it is, Perdican, take it.

Perdican: Is that possible? Where did you find it?

Camille: You are looking to see whether my hands are wet, aren't you? It is true, I spoiled my convent dress pulling this little child's toy out of the fountain. That is why I changed into another one and, as I have said, that altered my mood. So put it on your finger.

Perdican: You* pulled this ring out of the water, at the risk of falling in, Camille? Is this a dream? Here it is. You are the one putting it on my finger! Oh, Camille, why are you giving me back this sad token of a happiness that is no more? Speak up, you capricious, careless girl, why are you leaving? Why are you staying? Why do you change appearances and colors from one hour to the next, like the stone in this ring, with each ray of the sun?

Camille: Do you know women's hearts, Perdican? Are you sure of their inconstancy? Do you know whether they really change their minds when at times they change their language? There are some people who say they don't. Of course we often have to play a part and often tell lies. You see I am being frank. But are you sure that everything is false in a woman when her tongue tells lies? Have you really considered the nature of this weak and violent being, the harshness with which she is judged, the behavior that is imposed on her? Who knows whether, forced by the world to deceive, the mind of this little brainless being may not take pleasure in it and tell lies sometimes as a pastime, for enjoyment, as she tells lies out of necessity.

Perdican: I don't understand any of that, and I never tell lies. I love you, Camille, that is all I know.

Camille: You say that you love me and you never tell lies?

Perdican: Never.

---

*Perdican changes here from the formal *vous* to the intimate *tu*. But Camille continues to say *vous*.

Camille: Here is one person, however, who says that you some-
times do. *(She lifts the tapestry; Rosette appears behind it in a
faint, seated in a chair.)* What will you tell that child when she
asks you for an accounting of your words, Perdican? If you
never lie, how does it happen that she fainted on hearing you
tell me that you love me? I shall leave you with her. See if
you can revive her.

(She starts to leave.)

Perdican: Just a moment, Camille. Listen* to me.

Camille: What do you want to tell me? It is Rosette you have to
speak to. I don't love you. I never went and got this unfortu-
nate child from her room, out of spite, to use her as bait, as a
plaything. I didn't unwisely repeat in front of her ardent words
that were intended for someone else. I didn't pretend, for her
sake, to throw away a memento of my cherished friendship. I
didn't put my chain on her neck. I didn't tell her that I would
marry her.

Perdican: Listen to me! Listen to me!

Camille: Didn't you smile just a moment ago when I told you that
I couldn't go to the fountain? Well, so I was there, and I did
hear everything. But God is my witness that I wouldn't want to
have spoken as you did there. What will you do with this girl
now when she comes weeping, with your burning kisses on her
lips, to show you how you have wounded her? You were trying
to take revenge on me, weren't you, and to punish me for a
letter I wrote to my convent? You were trying at any cost to
throw some dart, just so it hit me, and you counted as nothing
the fact that your poisoned arrow pierced this child, as long
as it struck me behind her. I had boasted of inspiring some love
in you, of leaving some regret. Did that wound your noble
pride? Well, you can take it from me, you love me, do you hear?
But you will marry that girl, or else you are just a coward!

Perdican: Yes, I will marry her.

Camille: You will do well to.

Perdican: Very well, even better than if I were to marry you. What
is getting you so excited, Camille? This child has fainted. We
shall bring her back to her senses; all it takes is a flask of vine-

---

*Perdican returns at this point to the formal *vous*.

gar. You tried to prove to me that I had told a lie once in my life. That is possible, but I find you too quick to decide just at what moment it was. Come, lend me a hand with Rosette. *(Exit.)*

Scene 7.

(Enter the Baron and Camille.)
Baron: If that happens, I shall go mad.
Camille: Use your authority.
Baron: I shall go mad, and I shall refuse my consent. That is completely certain.
Camille: You ought to speak to him. Make him listen to reason.
Baron: This will throw me into despair for the entire carnival season, and I shan't appear at court a single time. It is a misalliance. It is totally unheard of, to marry one's cousin's foster sister. That is going entirely too far.
Camille: Call him in and tell him in so many words that this marriage is unacceptable to you. Believe me, it is a whim and he won't resist.
Baron: I shall wear black all winter, you can rest assured.
Camille: But speak to him, in heaven's name! He was just acting on an impulse. It may already be too late. If he has talked about it, he will do it.
Baron: I am going to shut myself in, and abandon myself to grief. If he asks for me, tell him that I have shut myself in, and I am abandoning myself to grief at his marrying a nameless peasant girl. *(Exit.)*
Camille: Can't I find a man with some mettle around here? Really, when you look for one it is frightening to see how alone you are. *(Enter Perdican.)* Well, cousin, when is the wedding?
Perdican: As soon as possible. I have already spoken to the notary, the priest, and all the peasants.
Camille: So you really are intending to marry Rosette?
Perdican: Absolutely.
Camille: What will your father say?

Perdican: Whatever he wants. I like the idea of marrying that girl; I owe it to you, and I shall stick to it. Do I have to repeat to you all the banal clichés about her birth and mine? She is young and pretty, and she loves me. That is all it takes for us to be blissfully happy. Whether or not she is intelligent, I might have found worse. Let people mock and cry, I couldn't care less.

Camille: There is nothing laughable about it. You are quite right to marry her. But I am sorry about one thing for you: people will say that you have done it out of spite.

Perdican: You are sorry about that? Oh, no.

Camille: Yes, I am. I am truly sorry for you. It looks bad for a young man not to have been able to resist a fit of spite.

Perdican: Well, then, be sorry. As for me, I really don't care.

Camille: But you can't be serious. She has nothing to offer.

Perdican: Then she will have something when she is my wife.

Camille: She will bore you before the notary has put on his new suit and shoes to come here. You will feel revulsion at your wedding feast, and that same evening you will have her hands and feet cut off as in the *Arabian Nights*, because she smells of stew.

Perdican: You will see how wrong you are. You don't know me: when a woman is sweet and tender-hearted, frank, good-natured, and beautiful, I can be satisfied. Yes, truly, to the point of not caring to know whether she can speak Latin.

Camille: It is unfortunate that so much money has been spent to teach it to you. That is a waste of three thousand crowns.

Perdican: Yes, it would have been better to give them to the poor.

Camille: You may be the one to take care of that, at least for the poor in spirit.

Perdican: And they will give me the kingdom of heaven in exchange, for it is theirs.

Camille: How long will this joke go on?

Perdican: What joke?

Camille: Your marriage to Rosette.

Perdican: Not very long. God didn't make man an enduring work: thirty or forty years at most.

Camille: I look forward to dancing at your wedding!

Perdican: Listen, Camille, this mocking tone of yours is misplaced.

Camille: I like it too much to leave it.

Perdican: Then I shall have to leave you, for I have had just about enough of it now.

Camille: Are you going to your bride's house?

Perdican: Yes, I am going right now.

Camille: Let me take your arm, then. I am going, too.

(*Enter Rosette.*)

Perdican: Here you are, my child! Come, I want to present you to my father.

Rosette: (Kneeling.) My lord, I have come to ask a favor of you. All the people in the village that I talked to this morning have told me that you were in love with your cousin, and that you were only courting me so both of you could have a little fun at my expense. People mock me as I go by, and I won't ever be able to find a husband in the village now that I am everyone's laughingstock. Let me give you back the necklace that you gave me, and go live in peace with my mother.

Camille: You are a good girl, Rosette. Keep that necklace, I am giving it to you, and my cousin will take mine in its place. As for a husband, don't worry, I shall find you one myself.

Perdican: That won't be difficult, indeed. Come on, Rosette, come with me so I can present you to my father.

Camille: Why? It is pointless.

Perdican: Yes, you are right, my father would receive us badly. We ought to let the first moment of surprise pass. Come with me, we shall go back to the village square. I find it strange that people should say I don't love you, when I am marrying you. By God! We shall silence them.

(*Exit with Rosette.*)

Camille: What is going on inside me? He is walking off very calmly with her. That is strange: I feel dizzy. Can he really intend to marry her? Hey! Mistress Pluche! Mistress Pluche! Isn't there anyone here? *(Enter a servant.)* Run after his lordship Perdican. Tell him quickly to come back here, I have something to say to him. *(Exit the servant.)* But what in the world is this? I feel weak, my legs won't hold me up. *(Enter Perdican again.)*

Perdican: Did you call for me, Camille?

Camille: No,—no.
Perdican: Truthfully, you look very pale. What did you want to
say? Did you have me called back to speak to me?
Camille: No, no.—Oh, my Lord Jesus!
(*Exit.*)

Scene 8. *A chapel.*

(*Enter Camille. She throws herself down in front of the altar.*)
Camille: Oh God, have you forsaken me? You know that I had
sworn to be faithful to you when I came here. When I refused
to become the wife of anyone else but you, I thought I was
speaking sincerely, before you and my conscience. You know
that, Father; does this mean you no longer want me? Oh,
why do you let the truth itself tell lies? Why am I so weak? Oh,
I am so wretched! I can no longer pray!
(*Enter Perdican.*)
Perdican: Pride, most deadly of all human counselors, why have
you come between this girl and me? Here she is, pale and
frightened, pressing her heart and her face against the cold,
unfeeling stone. She could have loved me, we were born
for each other. Why did you have to come to our lips, pride,
when our hands were about to be joined together?
Camille: Who has followed me? Who is speaking under these
vaults? Is it you, Perdican?
Perdican: What fools we are! We love each other! What have we
been dreaming, Camille? What vain words, what senseless
madness has come between the two of us like a deadly wind?
Which one of us was trying to deceive the other? Alas, life
itself is such a painful dream; why should we go and mingle
our own dreams with it? Oh God, happiness is so rare a pearl
in this ocean down here on earth! Divine fisherman, you had
granted it to us, you had drawn this priceless jewel for us from
the depths of the sea. And we have made a plaything of it,
like the spoiled children we are. The green pathway leading us
toward each other had so gentle a slope, it was surrounded by
such flowering verdure, it went off toward so peaceful a hori-

zon! But vanity, idle chatter, and anger had to come and hurl
their formless rocks onto the celestial road that led us to you in
a kiss! We have had to hurt each other, because we are human
beings. Oh, fools, we are in love!

(He takes her in his arms.)

Camille: Yes, Perdican, we are in love. Let me feel it against your
heart. The God looking down on us won't be offended. He
does want me to love you—he has known I do for fifteen years,
now.

Perdican: My dearest, you are mine.

(He embraces her; a loud cry is heard behind the altar.)

Camille: That was my foster sister's voice.

Perdican: What is she doing here? I left her on the stairway when
you called me back. So she must have followed me without my
noticing.

Camille: Come into this gallery, that is where the cry came from.

Perdican: I don't know what it is that I am feeling. It is as if my
hands were covered with blood.

Camille: The poor child must have been spying on us. She has
fainted again. Come on, let's try and help her. Alas, this is all
so cruel!

Perdican: No, I really can't go in there. I feel a deadly coldness
paralyzing me. You go, Camille; try and bring her here. *(Exit
Camille.)* My God, I beg of you, don't let me be a murderer!
You see what is happening. We are two foolish children, and
we have been playing with life and death. But our hearts are
pure. Don't kill Rosette, God of justice! I shall find a husband
for her, I shall make up for my mistake! She is young, she
will be rich, she will be happy. Don't do this, oh God! You can
still bless four of your children. Well, Camille, what is the
matter?

(Camille comes back.)

Camille: She is dead. Farewell, Perdican!

THE END

The Candlestick

The Candlestick* appears to reflect an early amorous adventure of Musset's, recounted also in different, less light-hearted form in his autobiographical novel, *The Confessions of a Child of the Times.* Although the play dates from 1835, only a year or so after the preceding three ones, and looks back to events in the author's youth, its cynical tone and traditional "happy ending" distinguish it radically from the earlier dramatic works. Like Marianne, Jacqueline is a married woman; unlike her, she goes from one love affair to another, with some trepidation but without serious consequences.

Like the earlier plays, *The Candlestick* was published in the *Revue des deux mondes,* on 1 November 1835. It received two productions during Musset's lifetime, in 1848 at the Théâtre Historique and in 1850 at the Comédie Française. Perhaps because of its resemblance to more traditional French comedies, it was successful well before any of Musset's major comedies.

CHARACTERS

André, a notary

Jacqueline, his wife

Clavaroche, an officer of the dragoons

Fortunio, one of André's clerks

Landry, another clerk

Guillaume, another clerk

A Maid

A Gardener

---

*For the meaning of this title, see the note on page 116.

A small town.
ACT ONE
Scene 1. *A bedroom.*

(Jacqueline is in bed. Enter André, in his bathrobe.)
André: Hey, my wife! Ho, Jacqueline! Hey! Ho! Jacqueline, my
wife! The plague take her, she is sleeping so soundly! Ho, ho!
my wife, wake up! Hey, hey! Get up, Jacqueline! How deeply
she is sleeping! Hey, hey, hey! Ho, ho, ho! My wife, my wife,
my wife! It is me, André, your husband, I have to talk about
some serious matters with you. Ho, ho! Pst! Pst! Ahem! Brum!
Frum! Pst! Jacqueline, are you dead? If you don't wake up right
away, I shall pour the water pitcher over your head.
Jacqueline: What is the matter, dear?
André: Thunderation! It is about time! Will you stop stretching?
You really are a sound sleeper. Listen to me, I have to talk with
you. Yesterday evening my clerk Landry . . .
Jacqueline: My God, why it is not even light out yet! Are you out
of your mind, André, to wake me up like this for no good rea-
son? For pity's sake, go back to bed. Are you ill?
André: I am not out of my mind and I am not ill, yet. I am wak-
ing you up for a good reason. I have to talk to you now. First
try and listen to me, then answer me. Here is what happened
to my clerk Landry. You know who he is . . .
Jacqueline: What time can it be?
André: It is six o'clock. Pay attention to what I am telling you. It is
nothing to joke about, and I have no cause to laugh at it. My
honor, madam, as well as yours, and perhaps both our lives are
at stake, in the discussion the two of us are about to have. Last
night my clerk Landry saw . . .
Jacqueline: But André, if you are ill, you should have let me know
earlier. Isn't it my duty to take care of you and watch over you,
my dearest?
André: I am feeling fine, I tell you. Are you in the mood to listen
to me?
Jacqueline: Oh, my God, you are frightening me! Have we been
robbed?
André: No, we have not been robbed. Sit up over here and listen
with both your ears. My clerk Landry just woke me up to give

me a certain paper that he had undertaken to finish last night.
While he was in my office . . .

Jacqueline: Oh, holy Mother of God, I am sure you must have
had some quarrel in that café you go to.

André: No, no, I have not had any quarrel, and nothing has hap-
pened to me. Won't you listen to me? I tell you my clerk Landry
saw a man slip through your window last night.

Jacqueline: I can tell from your expression that you have lost at
cards.

André: Come now, my wife, are you deaf? You have a lover,
madam. Is that clear? You are being unfaithful to me. A man
climbed up our wall last night. What is the meaning of that?

Jacqueline: Be so kind as to open the shutters.

André: All right, they are open, you can yawn after lunch. Thank
God, you don't miss a chance for that. Look out, Jacqueline!
I am a peace-loving man, and I have taken good care of you. I
was your father's friend, and you are my daughter almost as
much as my wife. I decided as I was coming here to treat you
gently, and you can see that I am, since before I condemn you I
want to trust you and give you a chance to explain and defend
yourself categorically. If you refuse, beware. There is a garrison
in town, and you see a good number of hussars, God forgive
me! Your silence may confirm suspicions I have been harboring
for some time now.

Jacqueline: Oh, you don't love me any more, André! You can't
fool me: beneath those kind words you are concealing a
deathly coldness that has replaced all your love. There was a
time when it would not have been this way; you didn't use
to speak to me in that tone of voice. Back then you would not
have condemned me, just on a word from someone, without
hearing me out. Two years of peace, love, and happiness would
not have vanished like a shadow, just on one person's word.
Oh well! It is jealousy that is stirring you. Cold indifference has
long since found its way into your heart. What good would
proof do? Innocence itself would be wrong in your eyes. You
no longer love me, since you are accusing me.

André: Very well, Jacqueline, but that is beside the point. My
clerk Landry saw a man . . .

Jacqueline: Oh, my Lord, I heard you. Do you think I am a nitwit, to pound that into my head this way? I just can't bear this tiresome nagging.

André: What is the reason you won't answer?

Jacqueline: (Weeping.) Oh, good Lord, how wretched I am! What is to become of me? I see it all too well: you have made up your mind to kill me. You will do as you please with me; you are a man, and I am a woman. Power is on your side. I am resigned; I was expecting this. You are seizing the first excuse to justify your violence. There is nothing left for me to do but leave. I shall go off with my daughter and enter a convent, in the wilderness if possible. I shall carry off and bury in my heart the memory of times gone by.

André: My wife! My wife! For the love of God and the saints, are you mocking me?

Jacqueline: Aha! Come now, André, are you talking seriously?

André: Am I serious? Almighty God, I am losing all patience. I don't know what is keeping me from taking you to court.

Jacqueline: You, take me to court?

André: Yes, me, take you to court. It is enough to drive a man to distraction, having to deal with such a mule. I never heard a person could be so stubborn.

Jacqueline: (Jumping out of bed.) Did you see a man come in through the window? Did you see him, sir, yes or no?

André: I didn't see him with my own eyes.

Jacqueline: You didn't see him with your own eyes and you want to take me to court?

André: Yes, by God, if you don't answer!

Jacqueline: André, do you want to know something that my grandmother learned from hers? When a husband trusts his wife he keeps rumors to himself, and when he is sure of his facts he has no need to consult her. If you have doubts, clear them up; if you lack evidence, keep quiet; and if you can't prove you are right, then you are wrong. Very well, come on: let's go.

André: So this is how you take it?

Jacqueline: Yes, this is it. Forward, march; I shall go with you.

André: Where do you expect me to go so early in the morning?

Jacqueline: To court.

André: But, Jacqueline . . .

Jacqueline: Forward, march. If you threaten it had better not be in vain.

André: Come now, calm down a bit!

Jacqueline: No, you want to take me to court, and I want to go right away.

André: What will you say in your defense? You might just as well tell me now.

Jacqueline: No, I don't want to say anything here.

André: Why not?

Jacqueline: Because I want to go to court.

André: You are going to drive me crazy. I feel as if I am dreaming. God in heaven, creator of the world, I am going to be sick over this! What? How? Is this possible? I was in bed, I was asleep, and I take these four walls as witness that it was as soundly as I could. My clerk Landry, a boy of sixteen who has never maligned anyone in his life, the most innocent lad in the world, who had just spent the night copying an inventory, sees a man go in through the window. He tells me, I put on my bathrobe, I come and see you like a friend, I ask you as my sole favor to explain to me what it all means, and you insult me! You call me a madman, you even spring out of bed and grab me by the throat! No, this is going too far. I shall be incapable of doing a simple sum accurately for at least a week. Jacqueline, my little wife, is it you who are treating me this way?

Jacqueline: Come, come, you are a sorry sight!

André: But what would it cost you to answer me after all, my little darling? Do you believe I can think that you are really being unfaithful to me? My God, just a single word would do. Why won't you say it? Maybe it was some burglar slipping in through our window. This neighborhood isn't so safe any more, we ought to move. I don't much like all these soldiers, my sweetheart, my dearest jewel. When we go for a walk, to the theater or to a dance, those fellows trail after us right up to our door. I can't say a word to you without bumping into their epaulettes or without some great curved sword getting tangled in my legs. Who knows, maybe their impertinence might prompt them to climb up our windows? You know nothing, I can see. You aren't one to encourage them. Those nasty fellows are capable of anything. Come now, give me your hand. You aren't angry with me, are you, Jacqueline?

Jacqueline: Yes, indeed, I am angry with you. To threaten to take me to court! When my mother hears about that, she will really be pleased at you!

André: Oh, my child, don't tell her. What is the use of telling others about our little spats? They are just a few wispy clouds that pass quickly over, and leave the sky calmer and clearer.

Jacqueline: All right, we shall shake on that.

André: Don't I know you love me? Don't I have the most blind confidence in you? Haven't you given me every proof in the world over the past two years that you are all mine, Jacqueline? The window that Landry was speaking about doesn't open exactly into your bedroom. If you go through the gallery, it leads to the vegetable garden. I wouldn't be surprised if our neighbor Pierre came and poached on our fruit trees. All right, I am going to post our gardener as a sentinel tonight, and I shall set a wolf trap on the garden path. We shall both have a laugh tomorrow.

Jacqueline: I am ready to drop; you had no reason to awaken me.

André: Go back to bed, my little darling. I am going, I shall leave you alone. Come now, good-by, let's not think about it any more. You can see that I am not searching your apartment at all, my child. I haven't opened the wardrobe. I take your word for it. I feel as if I love you a hundred times more for having suspected you wrongly and knowing that you are innocent. I shall make up for all that. We shall go to the country, and I shall give you a present. Good-by, good-by, I shall see you later. *(Exit. Jacqueline, alone, opens the wardrobe. Clavaroche is seen in it, squatting.)*

Clavaroche: (Coming out of the wardrobe.) Whew!

Jacqueline: Quickly, get out! My husband is jealous. You were seen but not recognized. You can't come back here. What was it like for you in there?

Clavaroche: Just delightful.

Jacqueline: We have no time to lose. What are we going to do? We have to see each other, but not be seen by anyone else. What can we do? The gardener will be out tonight. I am not sure I can trust my chambermaid. There is no way to go anywhere else here: everything is conspicuous in a small town. You are covered with dust, and I thought I saw you limping.

Clavaroche: My knees and my head are broken. The handle of my sword was sticking into my ribs. Phew! You would think I had been in a flour mill.

Jacqueline: Burn my letters when you get home. If they were to be found I would be ruined, and my mother would put me in a convent. A clerk, Landry, saw you go by. He will pay for that. What should we do? What can we? Answer me. You are as pale as a ghost.

Clavaroche: I was in an awkward position when you closed the door, so I found myself sitting like a biological specimen in a jar of alcohol for a whole hour.

Jacqueline: Well, let's see, what can we do?

Clavaroche: Oh, there is nothing simpler.

Jacqueline: Well, what?

Clavaroche: I don't know, but nothing is easier. Do you think this is my first such affair? I am aching all over. Give me a glass of water.

Jacqueline: I think it would be best for us to meet at the farm.

Clavaroche: When they wake up, these husbands really are unpleasant beasts! Look at my uniform, it is in fine shape! I shall look just fine on the parade ground! *(He drinks.)* Do you have a brush here? The devil take me, with all this dust it took a hell of a lot of strength to keep from sneezing.

Jacqueline: Here is my dressing table, use what you need.

Clavaroche: *(Brushing his hair.)* Why should we go to the farm? All in all, your husband is a pretty even-tempered fellow. Are these nocturnal appearances a habit of his?

Jacqueline: No, thank God! I am still shaking. But you can be sure that with the ideas he has gotten into his head now, all suspicion is going to fall on you.

Clavaroche: Why on me?

Jacqueline: Why? Well . . . I don't know . . . It seems to me it ought to be that way. Look here, Clavaroche, truth is a strange thing. It is a little like ghosts: you feel it without being able to set your finger on it.

Clavaroche: (Straightening his uniform.) Bah! Only grandparents and justices of the peace say that the truth will out. They have one good reason: everything people aren't aware of, they don't know, and consequently it doesn't exist. That may sound a bit silly, but think about it and you will see it is true.

Jacqueline: Anything you wish. My hands are shaking, and my fear is worse than the harm done.

Clavaroche: Just wait, we shall take care of that.

Jacqueline: How? Speak up, the sun is rising.

Clavaroche: Oh, good Lord, you are such a silly thing! You are as pretty as an angel with that frightened look on your face. Let's just see; sit over there, and we shall talk about our situation. Now I am almost presentable, and the mess has been cleaned up. What a cruel closet you have there! I am glad I am not one of your frocks.

Jacqueline: Please don't laugh, you make me tremble.

Clavaroche: Well, my dear, listen to me: I shall tell you my idea. When you find the sort of evil beast that people call a jealous husband in your path . . .

Jacqueline: Oh, Clavaroche, please do have some consideration for me.

Clavaroche: Have I shocked you? *(He kisses her.)*

Jacqueline: At least speak more softly.

Clavaroche: There are three sure ways to avoid all problems. The first is to give each other up, but we certainly don't want to do that.

Jacqueline: You will frighten me to death.

Clavaroche: The second one, which is undeniably the best, is not to pay any attention and if need be . . .

Jacqueline: Well?

Clavaroche: No, that one is no good, either. You have a man of law for a husband; the sword has to remain in its sheath. So that leaves the third way: to find a *candlestick*.

Jacqueline: A "candlestick"? What do you mean?

Clavaroche: In the regiment, that's what we call a tall, nice-looking fellow who is assigned to carry a shawl or an umbrella, if need be; who, when a woman stands up to dance, goes solemnly and sits on her chair, and stares after her in the throng with a melancholy gaze, while playing with her fan; who gives her his arm to leave her box at the theater, and proudly sets the glass she has just drunk from on a nearby table; goes on walks with her; reads to her in the evening; buzzes ceaselessly around her and assaults her ears with a shower of twaddle; if someone admires his lady, he swells with pride, and if she is insulted, he fights a duel. Should the sofa lack a cushion, he's the one who runs, who dashes off, to get it, wherever it may be, for he knows the house and its layout, he is part of the furnishings and can pass through corridors without a light. In the evening he plays cards with her aunts. Since he circumvents the husband, like a clever and attentive suitor, it doesn't take long before he is resented. If there is a dance somewhere that our beauty wants to attend, he is clean-shaven at daybreak, he is out on the square or the street by noon, and he has reserved some seats with his gloves. If you should ask him why he has become a shadow of himself, he doesn't know and can't tell you. It is not as if the lady doesn't encourage him at times with a smile, and during a waltz yield her fingertips, which he presses lovingly. He is like those noblemen who have an honorary office and take part in gala occasions; but the cabinet is closed to them; that is not their business. In a word, his rewards end where the real ones begin. He has everything that you can see in women, and none of what you desire. Behind this convenient dummy hides the lucky mystery. He serves as a screen for everything that goes on under the mantelpiece. If the husband is jealous, it is of him. Do rumors spread? They are about him. He is the one who will be kicked out one fine morning when the servants have heard someone walking around madam's apartment at night. He is the one who will be spied on secretly. His letters, full of respect and tenderness, are opened by the mother-in-law. He comes and goes, he worries, they let him flounder, that is his job. And all this time the discreet lover and the very innocent woman-friend, covered by an impenetrable veil, laugh at him and the busybodies.

Jacqueline: I can't help laughing, even though I don't really feel like it. And why does this character have the strange name of *candlestick?*

Clavaroche: Why, it is because he is the one who holds the . . .*

Jacqueline: That is enough, that is enough, I understand.

Clavaroche: Now, my dear, wouldn't you have some good soul among your friends who is capable of playing this important role, which, in all good faith, is not without its charms? Keep your eyes open, observe, think about it. *(He looks at his watch.)* Seven o'clock! I have to leave you. I am on duty today.

Jacqueline: But Clavaroche, truly, I don't know anyone here. And anyway, that is a deception I wouldn't have the heart for. What, encourage a young man, attract him, raise his hopes, perhaps even make him really fall in love, and play with his suffering? That is a sly trick you are suggesting.

Clavaroche: Would you rather I lost you? In the plight we are in, can't you see that suspicion has to be deflected at all costs?

Jacqueline: Why make it fall on someone else?

Clavaroche: Hah, so that it does fall. My dear, the suspicions of a jealous husband can never float around in space. They aren't swallows; they have to perch sooner or later, and the safest thing is to build a nest for them.

Jacqueline: No, really, I can't. Wouldn't I quite really have to compromise myself?

Clavaroche: Are you joking? On the day of reckoning, won't you always be able to prove your innocence? A suitor isn't a lover.

Jacqueline: Well . . . But time is growing short. Who do you want? . . . Choose someone for me.

Clavaroche: (At the window.) Look! There are three young men sitting under a tree in your courtyard. They are your husband's clerks. I shall leave the choice up to you. When I come back, one of them should be madly in love with you.

Jacqueline: How can that be? I have never said a word to them.

Clavaroche: Aren't you a daughter of Eve? Come on, Jacqueline, say yes.

---

*In French, the familiar expression *tenir la chandelle* (to hold the candle) means "to assist another man in an amorous tryst." (This may be the distant source of the English expression "not to hold a candle to someone.")

Jacqueline: Don't count on it. I won't do it.

Clavaroche: Let's shake hands on that. Thank you. Good-by, my oh so timorous fair one. You are bright, young, and pretty, and in love . . . at least a little, aren't you, madam? Get to work, cast your net!

Jacqueline: You are bold, Clavaroche.

Clavaroche: Proud and bold: proud to be loved by you, and bold when it comes to keeping you.
(Exit.)

Scene 2. *A little garden.*

(Fortunio, Landry, and Guillaume, seated.)

Fortunio: Really, that is very odd; what a strange adventure!

Landry: Well, at least don't go and talk about it. You could get me fired.

Fortunio: So strange and so wonderful. Yes, whoever he is, he is a lucky man.

Landry: Promise me you won't say anything. André made me swear not to.

Guillaume: Never say a word about your fellow man, your king, or women.

Fortunio: It makes my heart leap to think that such things exist. Did you really see it, Landry?

Landry: All right, let's not talk about it any more.

Fortunio: You heard someone walking softly?

Landry: Stealthily, behind the wall.

Fortunio: The window made a slight noise?

Landry: Like a grain of sand underfoot.

Fortunio: Then the shadow of a man on the wall, when he came through the postern gate?

Landry: Like a ghost in its shroud.

Fortunio: And a hand behind the shutter?

Landry: Trembling like a leaf.

Fortunio: A dim light in the gallery, then a kiss, then some steps in the distance?

Landry: Then silence, the curtains were drawn, and the gleam of light vanished.

Fortunio: If I had been you I should have remained until day-break.

Guillaume: Are you in love with Jacqueline? That would have been a fine thing for you to do!

Fortunio: I swear to God, Guillaume, I have never raised my eyes in Jacqueline's presence. I wouldn't even dream of daring to fall in love with her. I met her at a dance once. My hand didn't touch hers, her lips have never spoken to me. I have never in my life known anything about what she does or thinks, except that she goes for walks here in the afternoon, and I have breathed on the windowpane so I could watch her walking along the path.

Guillaume: If you are not in love with her, why did you say that you would have stayed? There was nothing better to do than just what Landry did: go and tell the whole business to our master, the notary André.

Fortunio: Landry did as he felt best. Let Romeo possess Juliet. I wish I were the morning bird that warns them of danger.

Guillaume: You are up to your usual antics! What good does it do you if Jacqueline has a lover? It is some officer from the garrison.

Fortunio: I wish I had been in the study. I wish I had seen it all.

Guillaume: God be praised! It is our bookseller who is poisoning your mind with his novels. What do you get out of this business? You just find yourself back where you started. You are not by any chance hoping to get your turn, are you? Sure, our friend probably imagines that he will be the lucky one some day. Poor fellow! You don't know much about our beautiful small-town ladies. With our black suits, fellows like us are only small fry, good enough for seamstresses at best. They sample only the men who wear red pants, and once they have tried one of them it doesn't matter if the garrison moves on. All soldiers are alike; love one and you love them all. Only the lapels on their uniforms change, from yellow to green or white. Other-wise, don't the ladies find the same turned-up mustache, the same guardroom bearing, the same language, and the same pleasure? They are all cut from one pattern. The ladies could even get them mixed up, when it comes to that.

Fortunio: There is no talking to you. You spend your holidays and
   Sundays watching the bowlers.
Guillaume: And you spend yours all alone at your window, with
   your nose buried in your flowerpot. That is a fine difference!
   With your romantic ideas, you are going to go as mad as a hat-
   ter. Come on, let's go back inside. What are you thinking
   about? It's time for work.
Fortunio: I really wish I had been with Landry last night in the
   study.
   (Exit. Enter Jacqueline and her maid.)
Jacqueline: Our plums will be beautiful this year, and the espaliers
   are looking fine. Come over this way, and let's sit down on that
   bench.
Maid: Madam must not mind the fresh air; it is quite chilly this
   morning.
Jacqueline: To tell the truth, I don't think I have come into this
   part of the garden twice in the two years I have been living
   in this house. Just look at this honeysuckle. These trellises for
   the climbing vines are very sturdy.
Maid: And madam is not even properly dressed. She would insist
   on coming down without her hat.
Jacqueline: Tell me, as long as you are here: Who are those young
   men over there in the downstairs room? Am I wrong? I think
   they are watching us. They were here just a while ago.
Maid: Why, doesn't madam know them? They are the master's
   clerks.
Jacqueline: Oh! Do you know them, Madeleine? You seem to
   blush when you say that.
Maid: What, me, madam! Whatever for? I know them because I
   see them every day. And I can't even say every day . . . I am
   sure I have no idea whether I know them or not.
Jacqueline: Come now, admit that you blushed. As a matter of
   fact, why should you deny it? As far as I can judge from here,
   those young men aren't so bad. Let's see, which one do you
   prefer? You can confide in me. You are a pretty girl, Madeleine.
   What wrong is there for one of those young men to be court-
   ing you?

Maid: I don't say there is anything wrong with it. Those young men aren't badly off, and their families are decent enough. There is a little blond one that the shopgirls on Main Street don't look down on when he tips his hat to them.

Jacqueline: (Going toward the house.) Who, the one over there with the mustache?

Maid: Oh, no! That is Mr. Landry, a big gangling fellow who never knows what to say.

Jacqueline: It's the other one who is writing, then?

Maid: Oh, no! That is Mister Guillaume. He is a nice fellow, quite steady. But his hair isn't very curly, and he is a pitiful sight when he tries to dance, on Sundays.

Jacqueline: Then who are you talking about? I don't think there is anyone else in the office.

Maid: You don't see that well-dressed, nicely combed young man at the window? Look, now he is leaning over. It is young Fortunio.

Jacqueline: Ah, yes. I see him now. No indeed, he isn't bad looking, with his hair over his ears and that little innocent look. You had better watch out, Madeleine. Angels like that lead girls to their downfall. So the gentleman courts shopgirls, with his blue eyes? Well, Madeleine, there is no need for you to lower yours and look holier than thou. One could really do worse than that. So that one knows what to say, and he has learned how to dance?

Maid: If you will pardon my saying so, madam, if I thought he was in love here it wouldn't be with anything that lowly. If you had turned around when you were going through the hedgerow, you would have seen him more than once, with his arms crossed and his pen behind his ear, staring at you as hard as he could.

Jacqueline: Are you joking, miss? Do you realize whom you are speaking to?

Maid: A cat can look at a king, and there are some who say that the king doesn't mind being looked at by the cat. That young fellow is no dunce, and his father is a wealthy goldsmith. I don't think there is any offense in watching people go by.

Jacqueline: Who told you he looks at me? I don't suppose that he has confided any secrets about that to you.

Maid: Oh, when a young man looks around, madam, any woman can guess where his eyes are going. I have no need for him to confide his secrets, and I know what I know.

Jacqueline: I am cold. Go get me a shawl and spare me your remarks.

(Exit the maid.)

(Alone.) Unless I miss my guess, that is the gardener I saw among those trees. Oh! Pierre, listen.

Gardener: (Entering.) Did you call me, Madam?

Jacqueline: Yes, go in there and ask for a clerk named Fortunio. Tell him to come here, I have something to tell him.

(Exit the gardener. Enter Fortunio a moment later.)

Fortunio: Madam, there must be some mistake. I was just told that you were asking for me.

Jacqueline: Sit down, there is no mistake. Mister Fortunio, I am afraid you find me in a predicament, in quite some difficulty. I don't really know how to tell you what I have to ask, or why I am appealing to you.

Fortunio: I am only third clerk. If it is important business, our first clerk, Guillaume, is here. Would you like me to call him over?

Jacqueline: No, no. If it was a business matter I have my husband, don't I?

Fortunio: Can I be of some use? Please don't hesitate to speak. Although I am quite young, I would gladly die to be of service to you.

Jacqueline: That is gallantly and courteously spoken. And yet, if I am not mistaken, you don't know me.

Fortunio: A star shining on the horizon doesn't know what eyes behold it. But it is known to the meanest shepherd wending his way up the hill.

Jacqueline: I have a secret to tell you, but I am hesitating for two reasons: first, you could betray me, and second, you might judge me wrongly even if you did help me.

Fortunio: May I undergo some trial? I beg you to trust in me.

Jacqueline: But, as you say, you are quite young. You might very well have self-confidence, and yet not always be able to carry it through.

Fortunio: You are more beautiful than I am young. I can answer for what my heart feels.

Jacqueline: Necessity makes us take risks. See if anyone can hear us.

Fortunio: Nobody. This garden is empty, and I closed the door to the study.

Jacqueline: No, I am sorry, I just can't talk. Please forgive me for calling you out needlessly. Please never mention it.

Fortunio: Alas, madam, I am unfortunate indeed, but everything will be as you wish.

Jacqueline: It is just that the position I find myself in is completely senseless. What I need, if I may confess it, is not really a friend, and yet I need a friend's help. I can't decide what to do. I was strolling in the garden, looking at these shrubs, and I tell you, I don't know why, I saw you at the window, I got the idea of having you called out.

Fortunio: To whatever whim of chance I owe this favor, please let me benefit from it. I can only repeat what I said: I would gladly die for you.

Jacqueline: Don't say that too often: it would stop me from speaking further.

Fortunio: Why? I say it sincerely.

Jacqueline: Why? Why? You know nothing, and I don't even want to think about it. No. What I have to ask of you cannot have such dire results, thank God. It is nothing, a trifle. You are still quite young, aren't you? Perhaps you find me pretty, so you say a few flirtatious words to me. That is the way I take them, it is quite simple. Any man in your place could say as much.

Fortunio: Madam, I have never lied. It is quite true that I am only a child, and my words can be doubted. But, such as they are, God alone can judge them.

Jacqueline: All right. You know your part, and you won't back down. Enough of that, now. Take this chair and sit down.

Fortunio: I shall do it to obey you.

Jacqueline: Excuse me for asking a question that may seem odd to you. My chambermaid, Madeleine, told me that your father is a jeweler. He must have connections with the merchants in town.

Fortunio: Yes, madam. I can say there is hardly one of any conse-
quence who doesn't know our house.

Jacqueline: Consequently you have an opportunity to come and
go among the tradesmen, and your face is known in the shops
on Main Street.

Fortunio: Yes, madam, if you please.

Jacqueline: I have a friend whose husband is miserly and jealous.
She is not without a fortune of her own, but she cannot make
use of it. Everything is regulated and controlled: her pleasures,
her tastes, her jewelry, her whims, if you will, for no woman
lives without whims. That is not to say that at year's end she
doesn't find herself in a position to take care of considerable
expenses. But from month to month, practically from week to
week, she has to count, argue, calculate everything she buys.
As you can imagine, preaching, every possible sermon on econ-
omy, every one of a miser's arguments, never fail whenever
bills come due. And so, despite her wealth, she leads a most
parsimonious life. She is poorer than her dresser drawer, and
her money is of no use to her. You know that for a woman
clothes are paramount. So she has positively been forced to re-
sort to a few stratagems. Her tradesmen's bills mention only
those everyday purchases that her husband calls "absolutely
necessary." Such things are paid openly. But at certain agreed-
on times, certain other secret bills mention a few trifles that
this woman, in turn, calls "almost as necessary." Those are the
true necessities, though spiteful tongues might call them "lux-
uries." In this way, it all works out perfectly. Everyone gains by
it, and her husband, who is sure of his receipts, doesn't know
enough about frocks to guess that he has not paid for every-
thing he sees his wife wearing.

Fortunio: I can't see much wrong with that.

Jacqueline: Well now, here is what has happened. Her husband,
who is a bit suspicious, has finally begun to notice, not the
extra frocks, but the missing money. He has threatened the ser-
vants, rapped on his money box, and scolded the merchants.
The poor, forsaken woman has not lost a franc that way; but
she finds herself, as tormented as Tantalus, thirsting for her
frocks from morning till night. No more confidants, no more

secret bills, no more hidden expenses. And yet her thirst tortures her, and she tries every way she can to quench it. What she needs is a clever young man, discreet especially, and of high enough status in town not to awaken any suspicion, who might go and visit the shops and buy, as if for himself, whatever she might feel she needs. First of all, he would have to have easy access to the house; be able to go in and out with assurance; have good taste, of course, and know how to choose correctly. It might perhaps be a fortunate coincidence if there were some pretty, appealing girl in town that he was known to be courting. I don't suppose you might happen to be in that situation, would you? That coincidence would excuse everything. Then the purchases would supposedly be made for the girl. That is what we have to find.

Fortunio: Tell your friend that I am ready, and I shall serve her as best I can.

Jacqueline: But if things should happen to work out that way, you realize, don't you, that in order to have the free access to the house I have spoken about, the confidant would have to appear elsewhere than just in the downstairs room? You realize that he would have to be welcome at table and in the salon? You realize that discretion is too arduous a virtue for him not to be the object of gratitude, but that in addition to good will, a certain amount of tact would not be out of place? He would have to be able one evening, say, for instance, this evening, to find the door ajar and bring a jewel in stealthily, like a daring smuggler. No air of mystery must ever reveal his dexterity. He must be careful, deft, and clever. He must remember a Spanish proverb that can take those who obey it very far: "The Lord helps those who help themselves."

Fortunio: I beg you, rely on me.

Jacqueline: Once all those conditions were fulfilled, if only one could be sure of his discretion, the confidant could be told the name of his new lady friend. He would then, like a young maidservant, receive without compunction a purse that he would know how to use. Careful! I see Madeleine coming to bring me my cloak. Be careful and discreet. Good-by! The friend is me; the confidant is you; the purse is there under the chair.

(Exit Jacqueline. Guillaume and Landry call from the doorway.)

Guillaume: Hey! Fortunio! The master is calling you there.

Landry: There is work to be done on your desk, what are you doing there outside the office?

Fortunio: What? Excuse me? What do you want?

Guillaume: We are telling you that the master is asking for you.

Landry: Come in, we need you here. What can that dreamer be thinking about?

Fortunio: In truth, this is quite odd, and it is a strange adventure. *(Exit.)*

ACT TWO
Scene 1. *A salon.*

(Clavaroche, standing in front of a mirror.)

Clavaroche: Upon my honor, if we were really to fall in love with these beautiful ladies it would be a poor business. Being a ladies' man is, all in all, a ruinous affair. Sometimes, right in the middle of the best part, a valet scratching on the door compels you to slip away. The woman who is ruining her reputation for you keeps her ears open as she surrenders: in the midst of the sweetest ecstasy you get pushed into a wardrobe. Sometimes when you are lying on a couch at home, worn out from maneuvers, a messenger sent in haste comes to remind you that you are adored two miles away. Quick, a shave and my valet! You run, you fly, it is too late, the husband has come home, it is raining. You have to stand watch for an hour on end. If you should take it into your head to be sick, or even in a bad mood! No: heat, cold, storms, uncertainty, danger, all *that* is there only to make you more hardy. Ever since there have been proverbs, obstacles have had the privilege of increasing pleasure, and the north wind would be sorry if it didn't think it was giving you more courage by freezing your face. In truth, love is represented with a quiver and arrows. It would

be better to depict him as a wild duck hunter, with a water-
proof coat and a curly woolen wig to shield his pate. What stu-
pid beasts men are to give up a life of pleasure in order to run
after—after what, just tell me?—after the shadow of their van-
ity! But you are stationed in a town for six months. You cannot
always be going to the café. Provincial actors are boring, you
look at yourself in the mirror and you don't want to be hand-
some for nought. Jacqueline is nice and slim; so you are pa-
tient, you adjust to everything without making too much fuss.
(Enter Jacqueline.) Well, my dear, what have you done? Did
you follow my advice, and are we out of danger?

Jacqueline: Yes.

Clavaroche: How did you manage it? You must tell me all about
it. Is it one of André's clerks that has taken charge of our
safety?

Jacqueline: Yes.

Clavaroche: You are an exceptional woman. No one is more
intelligent than you are. You have had the young man come to
your boudoir, haven't you? I can just see him with his hands
clasped, turning his hat around with his fingers. But what story
did you tell him to succeed so quickly?

Jacqueline: Whatever came into my mind, I don't know.

Clavaroche: Now you see what we are like when we let you be-
witch us, poor devils! And how does our husband look at this
affair? Has the lightning that was threatening us already felt
the magnetized needle? Is it beginning to turn away?

Jacqueline: Yes.

Clavaroche: By Jove, we shall have some fun! I am really looking
forward to studying this comedy, observing its mechanisms and
action, and playing my own role in it. And please tell me, has
the humble slave fallen in love with you since I left you? I'll bet
he was the one I met on my way upstairs: he had a busy ex-
pression, and he looks cut out for the role. Has he already
started playing his part? Does he manage the necessary atten-
tions with ease? Is he already wearing your colors? Does he
put the screen in front of the fire? Has he ventured a few words
of timid love and respectful tenderness? Are you satisfied with
him?

Jacqueline: Yes.

Clavaroche: And as an advance on his future services, have your beautiful, sparkling dark eyes already given him some hint that he may sigh for them? Has he already received some slight favor? Come on, be frank, how far along have you gotten? Have your glances met? Have you crossed swords? You have to give him at least some encouragement in return for the favor he is doing us.

Jacqueline: Yes.

Clavaroche: Whatever is the matter with you? You are distracted, and you hardly answer me.

Jacqueline: I have done what you told me to.

Clavaroche: Are you sorry about it?

Jacqueline: No.

Clavaroche: But you seem preoccupied, and there is something troubling you.

Jacqueline: No.

Clavaroche: You wouldn't find anything serious in such a prank? Forget it, there is nothing to it.

Jacqueline: If people knew what has happened, why would they blame me, and perhaps commend you?

Clavaroche: Come, now! It is just a game, it is really a trifle. Don't you love me, Jacqueline?

Jacqueline: Yes.

Clavaroche: Well, then, who can trouble you? Wasn't it to save our love that you did all this?

Jacqueline: Yes.

Clavaroche: I assure you, I find it amusing and won't let it bother me.

Jacqueline: Quiet, it is getting toward dinner time, and here comes André.

Clavaroche: Is that our man with him?

Jacqueline: That is the one. My husband asked him, and he is spending the evening here.

(Enter André and Fortunio.)

André: No, I don't want to hear anything about business today. I want people to work only at dancing and having fun. I am delighted, I am up to my neck in joy, and I intend only to have a good dinner.

Clavaroche: The deuce take it! You are in a wonderful mood, André, as far as I can see.

André: I have to tell all of you what happened to me yesterday. I unjustly suspected my wife; I had a trap set in front of my garden gate, and I found my cat in it this morning. It serves me right, I deserved it. But I want to be fair to Jacqueline and to let you know that we have made up and she has pardoned me.

Jacqueline: All right, all right, I don't have any hard feelings. You would be doing me a favor not to talk about it any more.

André: No, I want everyone to know. I have spoken about it all over town, and I brought home a little sugar napoleon in my pocket. I want to put it on the mantelpiece as a token of reconciliation, and every time I look at it, I shall love my wife a hundred times better. That will protect me against any distrust in the future.

Clavaroche: That is what I call acting like a worthy husband. That is André all over.

André: Captain, greetings. Will you have dinner with us? We are having a sort of little celebration at our house today, and you are welcome to join in.

Clavaroche: You are doing me too much honor.

André: Let me introduce a new guest: he is one of my clerks, Captain. Ha, ha! *Cedant arma togæ.* There is no intent to offend you: the little rascal is very clever; he has come to court my wife.

Clavaroche: Sir, may one ask your name? I am delighted to make your acquaintance.

(Fortunio bows.)

André: Fortunio. It is a lucky name. To tell you the truth, he has been working in my office for almost a year now, and I hadn't noticed how deserving he is. As a matter of fact I would never have thought of it if it weren't for Jacqueline. His handwriting isn't very good, and his brackets are not always faultless; but my wife needs him for a few little errands, and she has nothing but praise for his diligence. That is their secret: we husbands have no business poking our noses into it. An amiable guest in a small town is no small prize. So please God he finds it to his liking; we shall welcome him as best we can.

Fortunio: I shall do everything in my power to be worthy of it.

André: (To Clavaroche.) As you well know, my work keeps me home during the week. I am not sorry to see Jacqueline enjoy herself however she wishes, without me. She has sometimes needed a man's arm to take a stroll through town. The doctor wants her to walk, and the fresh air is good for her. This young man knows what is going on, he reads aloud very well. He comes from a good family, moreover, and his parents have brought him up right. He is an escort for my wife, and I ask you to extend your friendship to him.

Clavaroche: My friendship is entirely at his service, my worthy André. It is something that you have won and that is at your disposal.

Fortunio: The Captain is too kind, and I don't know how to thank him.

Clavaroche: Shake on it! The honor is all mine, if you count me as a friend.

André: Fine, that is just wonderful! Long live joy! The tablecloth is spread for us; give Jacqueline your arm, and come taste my wine.

Clavaroche: (Softly, to Jacqueline.) André doesn't seem to me to be taking things exactly as I had expected.

Jacqueline: (Softly.) His confidence and his jealousy depend on a word and the way the wind is blowing.

Clavaroche: (As above.) But this is not what we require. If things take that turn, we won't need your clerk.

Jacqueline: (As above.) I have done as you told me.
   (Exit.)

Scene 2. *In the study.*

(Guillaume and Landry, working.)

Guillaume: It seems to me that Fortunio didn't remain in the office long.

Landry: There is a gala party at the house this evening, and André has invited him.

Guillaume: Yes, and so the work remains for us to do. My right hand is paralyzed.

Landry: And yet he is only third clerk. They could have invited us, too.

Guillaume: Well, after all, he is a nice fellow. There is nothing wrong in that.

Landry: No. There wouldn't have been anything wrong, either, if they had included us in the party.

Guillaume: Hmm! Just smell the cooking! With all the noise they are making up there, you can't hear yourself think.

Landry: I think they must be dancing. I saw some fiddlers.

Guillaume: To hell with these wretched papers! I can't write any more today.

Landry: Do you want to know something? I have the feeling there is some mystery going on here.

Guillaume: Bah! What do you mean?

Landry: Yes, yes. It isn't all very clear, and if I wanted to tell a thing or two . . .

Guillaume: Don't be afraid, I won't talk.

Landry: Do you remember I saw a man climb through the window the other day? Nobody ever knew who it was. But today, only this evening, I saw something with my own eyes, and I do know what it was.

Guillaume: What was it? Tell me all about it.

Landry: I saw Jacqueline, in the twilight, opening the garden gate. There was a man behind her who slipped along the wall and kissed her hand. After that, he took off, and I heard him say, "Don't worry, I shall be back in a little while."

Guillaume: Really? It just is not possible.

Landry: I saw him just as I am seeing you.

Guillaume: Well, if it was like that, I know what I would do if I were you. I would let André know, just like last time.

Landry: I shall have to think about that. With a man like André, it would be running a risk. He changes his mind every morning.

Guillaume: Do you hear the rumpus they are making? Bang, there go the doors! Clink clink, the plates, the dishes, the forks, the bottles! I believe I hear them singing.

Landry: Yes, that is the voice of André himself. The poor old fellow, they really are poking fun at him!

Guillaume: Come on out for a little walk. We shall be able to chatter at ease. After all, when the master is having a good time, it is only right for his clerks to rest.
(Exit.)

Scene 3. *The dining room.*

(André, Clavaroche, Fortunio, and Jacqueline seated at table. Dessert has been served.)

Clavaroche: Come on, Mr. Fortunio. Pour some wine for madam.

Fortunio: With all my heart, Captain. I drink to your health.

Clavaroche: Shame on you, that is not very gallant on your part. To the health of the lady sitting next to you.

André: That is right, to my wife's health. I am delighted that you find this wine to your taste, Captain. *(He sings.)*
    Come, friends, let's raise our glasses . . .

Clavaroche: That song is too old. Why don't you sing something, Mr. Fortunio?

Fortunio: If madam deigns to request it.

André: Ha, ha! The lad knows his manners.

Jacqueline: All right, go ahead and sing, please.

Clavaroche: Just a moment. Before you sing, eat a little of this cake. It will open up your throat and give you some volume.

André: The Captain is always ready with a jest.

Fortunio: Thank you, but it would make me choke.

Clavaroche: All right, then. Ask madam to give you a piece of it. I am sure it will seem light if it comes from her lily-white hands. *(Looking under the table.)* Heavens! What do I see? Your feet are on the floor! Madam, suffer a cushion to be brought.

Fortunio: (*Standing up.*) Here is one under this chair.
    (He puts it under Jacqueline's feet.)

Clavaroche: Very good, Mr. Fortunio. I thought you would let me do it. A young man who is paying court must not let anyone steal a march on him.

André: Oh, this lad will go far. You only have to say the word and he is there.

Clavaroche: So now, sing, please. We are all ears.

Fortunio: I don't dare in front of connoisseurs. I don't know any drinking songs.

Clavaroche: Since madam has requested it, you cannot escape.

Fortunio: Then I shall do the best I can.

Clavaroche: Mr. Fortunio, haven't you written any poetry to madam yet? This is a fine opportunity.

André: Quiet, please. Let him sing.

Clavaroche: Make it a love song. Isn't that right, Mr. Fortunio? Nothing else, I beseech you. Madam, please beg him to sing a love song for us. We couldn't live without it.

Jacqueline: Please, Fortunio.

Fortunio: (Singing.)

> If you think that I will tell
>   Whom I dare love,
> I couldn't speak her name
>   For Heav'n above.

> Let us all sing in turn
>   As once of old
> That I adore her hair
>   Of purest gold.

> I'll do whate'er her fancy
>   Deigns to command.
> Indeed, my very life
>   Is in her hand.

> My soul is torn in two
>   By such an ill
> That unrequited love
>   Will one day kill.

> And yet I love too well
>   Whom I dare love;
> I'll die and keep her name
>   For Heav'n above.

André: In truth the little rascal is in love, just as he says. He even has tears in his eyes. Come, now, my lad, have a drink and pull yourself together. It must be some shopgirl in town who has given you that nasty gift.

Clavaroche: I don't believe that Mr. Fortunio has such low-class ambitions. His song is worthy of more than a shopgirl. What does madam have to say, and what is her opinion?

Jacqueline: Very nice. Give me your arm, and we shall go have coffee.

Clavaroche: Quick, Mr. Fortunio. Offer your arm to madam.

Jacqueline: (*She takes Fortunio's arm; softly, on the way out:*) Did you take care of my errand?

Fortunio: Yes, madam, it is all in the office.

Jacqueline: Go wait for me in my room. I shall join you there in a moment.

(*Exit.*)

Scene 4. *Jacqueline's bedroom.*

(*Enter Fortunio.*)

Fortunio: Is any man more fortunate than I? I am sure that Jacqueline loves me, there is no mistaking all the signs she gives me. I am already welcomed, entertained, pampered in her house. She had me seated next to her at table. If she goes out, I shall go with her. How sweet she is! What a voice, what a smile! When she looks at me, an unknown feeling runs through my body. I feel choked up with joy. If I didn't restrain myself, I would throw my arms around her. No, the more I think about it, the more I reflect, the least signs, the slightest favors, it is all quite sure. She loves me, she loves me, and I would have to be an utter fool to pretend not to see it. When I sang just a while ago, I could see how her eyes shone! Come on, let's not lose any time. Let's put this box containing a few jewels here. It is a secret errand, and Jacqueline will certainly be here before long.

(*Enter Jacqueline.*)

Jacqueline: Are you here, Fortunio?

Fortunio: Yes. Here is your jewel box, Madam, and what you asked for.

Jacqueline: You are a man of your word, and I am pleased with you.

Fortunio: How can I tell you what I feel? A glance from your eyes changed my fate, and I live only to serve you.

Jacqueline: That was a pretty song you sang for us at table a while ago. Who was it for? Would you write it down for me?

Fortunio: It was written for you, Madam. I am dying of love, and my life is yours.

(He falls to his knees.)

Jacqueline: Really! I thought that your refrain forbade saying who the loved one is.

Fortunio: Oh, Jacqueline, take pity on me. It is not just since yesterday that I have been suffering. For two years now I have been following your footsteps along these garden paths. For two years, perhaps without your ever knowing of my existence, you have not gone in or out, your light, flickering shadow has not appeared behind your curtains, you have not opened your window, you have not stirred through the air without my being there, without my seeing you. I could not come near you, but your beauty belonged to me, thank God, as the sun belongs to everyone. I sought it out, I breathed it in, I lived on the shadow of your life. You went through the doorway every morning; I would come back and weep there every night. A few words from your lips had reached me, and I would repeat them all the day long. You grew flowers, so my room would be full of them. You sang at your piano in the evening, and I knew your songs by heart. Everything that you loved, I would love. I was intoxicated with what had come through your lips and from your heart. Alas, I see that you are smiling! God knows my pain is real, and that I love you enough to die for it.

Jacqueline: I am laughing, not at hearing you say that you have loved me for two years, but because I think that tomorrow will make two days.

Fortunio: May I lose you if the truth is not as dear to me as my love! May I lose you if I have not lived for you alone, for two years!

Jacqueline: Please get up; how would I look if someone came along?

Fortunio: No, I won't get up, I won't leave this spot if you don't believe my words. If you reject my love, at least you won't doubt it.

Jacqueline: Are you making advances?

Fortunio: Advances, but fearful ones, unhappy and yet hopeful ones. I don't know whether I am living or dead; I cannot imagine how I have dared speak to you. I have lost my reason. I love, I suffer; you must know it, you must see it, you must have pity on me for it.

Jacqueline: Why, this naughty, stubborn child is capable of remaining like this for an hour! Come now, get up, I want you to.

Fortunio: So you believe in my love?

Jacqueline: No, I don't. I prefer not to.

Fortunio: That is impossible! You cannot doubt it.

Jacqueline: Hah! I cannot be taken in so quickly by a few gallant remarks.

Fortunio: I beseech you, just look at me! Who could have taught me how to deceive? I am only a child, born yesterday, and I have never loved anyone but you, and you didn't know it.

Jacqueline: You court shopgirls, I know that as well as if I had seen it.

Fortunio: You are joking. Who can have told you that?

Jacqueline: Yes, yes, you go dancing, and to picnics on the grass.

Fortunio: With my friends, on Sundays. What is wrong with that?

Jacqueline: I told you yesterday already; it is perfectly normal; you are young, at an age when one's heart is rich and one's lips are not stingy.

Fortunio: What must I do to convince you? I beg of you, tell me.

Jacqueline: You are asking for a nice piece of advice. Well, you would have to prove it!

Fortunio: My Lord, I have nothing but my tears. Do tears prove that one loves? What, here I am on my knees before you; at each beat my heart would like to leap up to your lips; here I am, cast down at your feet by a pain that crushes me, that I have fought against for two years, that I can no longer restrain, and you remain cold and unbelieving? I cannot make a single spark of the fire consuming me pass into you? You even deny what I am suffering, when I am ready to die before you? Oh, that is harsher than rejection! That is more terrible than scorn! Even indifference can believe, and I haven't deserved that.

Jacqueline: Get up! Someone is coming. I believe you, I love you. Go out by the back staircase, come back downstairs, I shall be there.

(Exit.)

Fortunio: (Alone.) She loves me! Jacqueline loves me! There she goes, leaving me like this! No, I can't go down yet! Quiet! Someone is approaching. Somebody stopped her. Someone is coming in. Quick, I have to leave! *(He raises the tapestry.)* Oh, the door is locked from the outside, I can't get out! What can I do? If I go down the other way, I shall meet whoever is coming.

Clavaroche: (Outside the door.) Come on, just come on now!

Fortunio: That is the Captain coming up with her. Quick, I had better hide and wait a while. I mustn't be seen here.

(He hides behind the bed. Enter Clavaroche and Jacqueline.)

Clavaroche: (Falling onto the sofa.) My word, madam, I looked everywhere for you! What were you doing all alone?

Jacqueline: (Aside.) Thank God Fortunio is gone!

Clavaroche: You left me in really unbearable company. What am I supposed to do with André, I ask you? And you leave us together just when the husband's tippling ought to make the wife's pleasant conversation all the more desirable.

Fortunio: (Hiding.) That's strange. What can it mean?

Clavaroche: (Opening the jewel box on the table.) Now, let's see. Are these rings? Tell me, what do you want with them? Are you giving someone a present?

Jacqueline: You know very well that is our story.

Clavaroche: But, upon my honor, this is gold! If you are going to use the same stratagem every morning, our game soon won't be worth . . . By the way, that dinner really amused me! What a curious expression our young accomplice had!

Fortunio: (Hiding.) Accomplice! In what? . . . Does he mean me?

Clavaroche: The chain is a fine one. It is a valuable piece of jewelry. What a strange idea you had.

Fortunio: (As above.) Oh, he seems to be in Jacqueline's confidence, too.

Clavaroche: How the poor lad trembled as he raised his glass! I couldn't help laughing at his cushions! He was a fine sight to see!

Fortunio: (As above.) He most certainly is talking about me and referring to the dinner just now.

Clavaroche: I suppose you will return this to the jeweler who provided it.

Fortunio: (As above.) Return the chain! Why should she?

Clavaroche: I particularly enjoyed his song, and André appreciated it, too. God forgive me, he actually had tears in his eyes.

Fortunio: (As above.) I don't dare believe this now or understand it. Am I dreaming? Am I awake? Who is this Clavaroche, anyhow?

Clavaroche: In any case, it is becoming useless to pursue this any further. What good is an inconvenient third party if no more suspicion is forthcoming? Husbands never fail to adore their wives' suitors. Just see what has happened! Now that you are trusted, we can snuff out the candle.

Jacqueline: Who knows what will happen? With his temper nothing is ever sure, so we should keep whatever we need to get out of trouble ready at hand.

Fortunio: (As above.) If they are using me as their pawn, there must be some reason for it. All this talk puzzles me.

Clavaroche: In my opinion, we should dismiss him.

Jacqueline: As you wish. I am not following my own idea in all this. If it were a necessary evil, do you think it would be my choice? But who knows whether a storm might not brew tomorrow, this evening, within an hour? We mustn't count on the calm with too much certainty.

Clavaroche: You think so, dear?*

Fortunio: (As above.) Christ, he is her lover!

Clavaroche: Well, then, do as you like with him. Without ousting the young man completely, he can be kept on a leash; but at some distance, on the fringes. If André's suspicions should ever come back to his mind, why then, we would have your Mr.

*Clavaroche passes here from a formal *vous* to an intimate *tu,* thus revealing to Fortunio his relationship with Jacqueline. In my translation I have rendered this change through use of the term of endearment.

Fortunio on hand to deflect them once again! I consider him a fresh-water fish: he loves the hook.

Jacqueline: I thought someone moved.

Clavaroche: Yes, I thought I heard a sigh.

Jacqueline: It must be Madeleine. She is putting things away in the closet.

ACT THREE
Scene 1. *The garden.*

(Enter Jacqueline and the maid.)

Maid: Madam, there is a danger threatening you. A moment ago, while I was in the hall, I heard the master speaking with one of his clerks. As far as I could tell, it was about an ambush that is to take place tonight.

Jacqueline: An ambush? Where? What for?

Maid: In the office; the clerk claimed that he had seen madam and a man with her in the garden. The master swore to God that he wanted to catch you and he would sue you.

Jacqueline: You are not mistaken, Madeleine?

Maid: Madam may do as she pleases. I am not honored with her secrets, but that doesn't keep a person from doing someone a favor. I have my sewing to do.

Jacqueline: Very well. You can be certain that I won't be ungrateful. Have you seen Fortunio this morning? Where is he? I have to talk to him.

Maid: He didn't come to the office. I believe the gardener saw him. But he is badly needed, and they were looking all over the garden for him a while ago. Look, there is the head clerk, Mr. Guillaume, who is still looking for him. Do you see him going by over there?

Guillaume: (Backstage.) Hey! Fortunio! Fortunio! Hey! Where are you?

Jacqueline: Go on, Madeleine; try and find him.

(Exit Madeleine. Enter Clavaroche.)

Clavaroche: What the deuce is going on here? I should think that I have some claim on André's friendship, but when I just ran into him he didn't even say hello to me. The clerks are giving me funny looks, and I had the feeling that even the dog was going to snap at my heels. Please tell me, what has come up? What is the reason for mistreating people this way?

Jacqueline: There is nothing for us to laugh at. What I had foreseen has happened, and this time it is serious. We have gotten beyond words; it is time for action.

Clavaroche: Action? What do you mean?

Jacqueline: Those damned clerks are behaving like spies. We have been seen, and André knows it; he intends to hide in the office, and we are running the gravest risks.

Clavaroche: Is that all that is worrying you?

Jacqueline: Of course, what worse could you ask for? The hardest thing is not for us to avoid them today, since we are forewarned. But since André is acting without saying a word, we have everything to fear from him.

Clavaroche: Really, is that all there is to the business; there is no more harm than that?

Jacqueline: Are you mad? How is it possible for you to joke about it?

Clavaroche: It is just that there is nothing simpler than getting us out of this trouble. You say that André is in a rage? Well, let him yell, what is the problem? He wants to lie in ambush? Let him do it, nothing could be better. The clerks have been let in on it? Let the whole town join in if it amuses them. They want to catch the beautiful Jacqueline and her most humble servant? Ha! Let them catch all they want, I won't stop them. What do you see in that to bother us?

Jacqueline: I don't understand a word you are saying.

Clavaroche: Bring me Fortunio. Where has that fellow gone off to? What, we are in danger and the scoundrel leaves us in the lurch? Come, quickly, let him know!

Jacqueline: I have thought of that. No one knows where he is; he hasn't shown up this morning.

Clavaroche: Pshaw! That is impossible. He must be somewhere around under your skirts, you have left him in some wardrobe, and your maid must have put him on a hanger without thinking.

Jacqueline: But I ask you again, how can he help us? I have asked where he is without really knowing why myself. When I think about it I don't see what good he can do us.

Clavaroche: Ho, ho! Don't you see that I am ready to make the greatest of sacrifices for him! Nothing less than giving up all the privileges of love to him for this evening.

Jacqueline: For this evening? Whatever for?

Clavaroche: For the definite and formal purpose of making sure our worthy André doesn't have to spend a night out in the cold fruitlessly. You wouldn't want those poor clerks, who are going to go to such great pains, not to find anyone home, would you? Shame on you! We can't let those fine fellows come back empty-handed. We have to provide them with someone.

Jacqueline: That can't be. Find something else. What an awful idea! I cannot consent to it.

Clavaroche: Why "awful"? Nothing could be more innocent. You write a note to Fortunio, if you can't find him yourself; for a tiny note is worth more in this world than the greatest piece of writing. You tell him to come this evening on the pretext of a rendezvous. He comes in; the clerks apprehend him, and André nabs him on the spot. What do you think can happen to him? You go downstairs in your nightcap and ask, just as naturally as can be, why they are making all the noise. They explain. André in turn asks you furiously why his young clerk has slipped into his garden. You blush a bit at first, then you confess sincerely whatever you want to confess: that the lad is visiting your tradesmen, that he is bringing you jewelry in secret; in other words, the plain truth. What is so frightening about that?

Jacqueline: They won't believe me. Does it seem plausible that I would give someone a rendezvous to pay bills?

Clavaroche: People always believe what is true. Truth has a sound that it is impossible not to recognize, and well-born souls are never mistaken about it. After all, aren't you really using the young man for your errands?

Jacqueline: Yes.

Clavaroche: Well, then, since you are doing that, say so and they will see it is the truth. Make sure he has evidence in his pockets, a jewel box like yesterday, whatever; that will be enough. Just remember: if we don't use that means we shall be in trouble for an entire year. André is setting an ambush today, he will set another one tomorrow and so on until he catches us. The less he finds the more he will search. But if he finds someone once and for all, we shall be in the clear.

Jacqueline: It is not possible! We mustn't think of doing that.

Clavaroche: A rendezvous in a garden isn't such a great sin, in any case. If for one reason or other you don't like the night air, you needn't even come downstairs. They will find just the young man, and he will always find some way out. It would be a strange thing if a woman couldn't prove she is innocent when she is. Come now, take out your note pad and write with this pencil.

Jacqueline: You can't be serious, Clavaroche. This is a trap you are setting.

Clavaroche: (Handing her a pencil and some paper.) Now, please write: "At midnight this evening in the garden."

Jacqueline: It is sending the child into a trap, handing him over to the enemy.

Clavaroche: Don't sign your name, it is not necessary. *(He takes the paper.)* Frankly, my dear, the night will be chilly, and you will do better to stay in your room. Let this young man walk around by himself and enjoy the weather. I believe as you do that they will find it hard to believe he is coming about your tradesmen. You will do better, if they ask you, to say you don't know anything, and you have nothing to do with the business.

Jacqueline: This note will be evidence.

Clavaroche: Shame on you! Do you think that tender-hearted people like us would show a husband his wife's handwriting? What could we gain by it, anyway? Would we be any the less guilty for the crime's having been shared? Anyway, you can see that your hand must have been trembling a bit, and these letters are almost unrecognizable. Well now, I am going to give this letter to the gardener so Fortunio will get it right away. Come now, the vultures have their prey, and the bird of Venus, the pale turtledove, can sleep in its nest in peace. *(Exit.)*

Scene 2. *A grove.*

(Fortunio, alone, sitting on the grass.)
Fortunio: To make a young man fall in love with you solely to
deflect onto him the suspicions falling on someone else; to let
him believe you love him, to tell him so, if need be; perhaps
to disturb many a tranquil night; to fill a young heart, prone to
suffer, with hope and doubt; to throw a stone into a lake that
has never yet had a single ripple on its surface; to expose a
man to suspicion, to every danger of a requited love, and yet
not grant him anything; to remain motionless and cold in
a matter of life and death; to deceive, to lie, to lie from the
depths of your heart; to use your body as bait; to toy with
everything that is sacred under the heavens, like a thief with
loaded dice: that is what makes a woman smile! That is
what she does with a little, heedless air. *(He stands up.)*

This is your first step in learning the ways of the world, For-
tunio. Think, reflect, compare, examine, don't jump to conclu-
sions. The woman has a lover, and she loves him. She is sus-
pected, tormented, threatened; she takes fright, she is going to
lose the man who fulfills her life, who means more to her than
the entire world. Her husband arises with a start, warned by
a spy. He wakes her up, he wants to drag her before a court of
justice. Her family is going to renounce her, an entire town is
going to curse her. She is ruined and dishonored, and yet she is
in love and cannot help it. She must save the sole object of her
worry, her anguish, and her pain at all costs; she must love in
order to go on living, and deceive in order to love. She leans
out her window, she sees a young man downstairs. Who is he?
She doesn't know him at all, she has never seen his face. Is he
good or bad, discreet or faithless, sensitive or carefree? She has
no idea; she needs him, she calls him over, she beckons to him,
she adds a flower to her attire, she speaks, she has wagered her
life's happiness on a card, and she plays the red or the black.
If she had turned to Guillaume rather than to me what would
have come of all this? Guillaume is a fine fellow, but he has
never noticed that his heart serves any other purpose than
breathing. Guillaume would have been delighted to go have

dinner with his boss, to sit next to Jacqueline at table, just as I
was delighted myself. But he wouldn't have seen anything else
in it; he wouldn't have fallen in love with anything but André's
wine cellar. He wouldn't have knelt down. He wouldn't have
listened in at the door. It would have been pure profit for him.
What would have been wrong with using him to deflect a
husband's suspicions without his knowledge, then? Nothing at
all. He would have peacefully carried out the duties required
of him; he would have lived happily, calmly, for ten years with-
out noticing a thing. Jacqueline would have been happy and
calm, too, for ten years, and not said a word to him. She
would have flirted with him, and he would have responded,
but it would never have led anywhere. Everything would have
gone perfectly, and nobody would have been able to com-
plain, the day when the truth came out. *(He sits down again.)*

Why did she turn to me? Did she know that I loved her,
then? Why me rather than Guillaume? Was it by chance, or
planned? Perhaps she suspected deep down that I wasn't
indifferent. Had she seen me at that window? Had she ever
turned around in the evening when I would watch her in
the garden? But if she knew I loved her, why then? Because
my love facilitated her plans, and as soon as she spoke I would
fall into the trap she was setting for me. My love was just a
lucky accident; she saw nothing but an opportunity in it.

Is that really sure? Isn't there anything else? What, she sees I
am going to suffer, and she thinks of nothing but to take ad-
vantage of it! She finds me in her path, with love in my heart
and desire in my eyes, young and passionate, ready to die for
her, and when she smiles at me and tells me she loves me, see-
ing me at her feet, it is only a ruse and nothing else! Nothing,
nothing true in her smile, in her hand brushing against mine,
in her voice that thrills me? God of justice, if that is the way it
is, what kind of monster am I dealing with, and what pit have
I sunk into? *(He gets up.)*

No, so much horror is not possible! No, a woman couldn't
be a malevolent statue made both of flesh and of stone! No,
even if I saw it with my own eyes, even if I heard it from her
own lips, I wouldn't believe she was capable of that. No, when

she smiled at me, it didn't mean she loved me, she was smiling to see that I loved her. When she reached out her hand to me, she wasn't giving me her heart, she was letting mine give itself. When she said, "I love you," she meant, "Love me." No, Jacqueline isn't evil, there is neither ruse nor coldness in all that. She lies, she deceives, she is a woman. She flirts, she mocks, she is gay, bold, but not vile, not unfeeling. Oh, you fool, you are in love with her! You love her, you pray, you weep, and she is laughing at you!

(Enter Madeleine.)

Madeleine: Ah, thank God, I have found you at last! Madam has been asking for you. She is in her room. Come quickly, she is waiting for you.

Fortunio: Do you know what she wants to tell me? I can't go there right now.

Madeleine: Do you have some business with the trees? Come on, she is very worried, the whole house is in an uproar.

Gardener: (Entering.) So here you are, sir! They are looking for you everywhere. Here is a note for you that our mistress gave me just now.

Fortunio: (Reading.) "At midnight this evening in the garden." *(Aloud.)* Is this from Jacqueline?

Gardener: Yes, sir. Is there a reply?

Guillaume: (Entering.) Whatever are you doing, Fortunio? They are looking for you in the office.

Fortunio: All right, I am going. *(Softly, to Madeleine.)* What were you saying just now? What is your mistress worried about?

Madeleine: (Softly.) It is a secret. The master is angry.

Fortunio: (As above.) He is angry? Whatever for?

Madeleine: (As above.) He has gotten it into his head that Madam has been seeing somebody in secret. Don't say anything about it, all right? He is planning to hide in the office tonight. I am the one who found it out, and, if I am telling you, well, it is because I think that you are concerned to some extent.

Fortunio: Why should he hide in the office?

Madeleine: To catch everything in the act and get a court case.

Fortunio: Really? Is that possible?

Gardener: Is there any reply, sir?

Fortunio: I shall go myself. Come on, let's go.
(*Exit.*)

Scene 3. *A bedroom.*

(*Jacqueline, alone.*)

Jacqueline: No, it just can't be done. Who knows what a man like
André may think up for revenge once he is pushed to the point
of violence? I won't send this young man into such terrible dan-
ger. Clavaroche is pitiless; for him everything is a battlefield,
and he has no feelings whatever. Why expose Fortunio when
there is nothing simpler than exposing neither oneself nor any-
one else? It might be that all suspicion would evaporate by
that means, but the means itself is evil, and I don't want to use
it. No, it upsets me and I don't like it. I don't want the boy
to be mistreated. Since he says he loves me, well then, so be it!
I don't return evil for good. (*Enter Fortunio.*) You must have
been given a letter from me. Did you read it?

Fortunio: I was given it and I read it. I am at your disposition.

Jacqueline: It is no use, I have changed my mind. Tear it up, and
let's not speak of it any more.

Fortunio: Can I be of any other use to you?

Jacqueline: (*Aside.*) That is odd, he doesn't insist. (*Aloud.*) Why
no, I don't need you. I had asked you for your song.

Fortunio: Here it is. Is that all you wished?

Jacqueline: Yes, I think so. What is the matter? You look pale to
me.

Fortunio: If you have no further need of me, allow me to with-
draw.

Jacqueline: I like this song a great deal. It seems a little naïve, just
like your hairdo; it suits you perfectly.

Fortunio: You are much too kind.

Jacqueline: Yes, you see, at first I thought I would send for you.
But then I thought it over, and it made no sense. I listened to
you too quickly. So sit down at the piano and sing me your
song.

Fortunio: Excuse me, I couldn't, now.

Jacqueline: Why not? Are you ill, or is this just a naughty whim? I almost feel like making you sing, whether you want to or not. Don't I have some rights over that piece of paper?

(She sets the song on the piano.)

Fortunio: It is not ill will. I just can't stay any longer, André needs me.

Jacqueline: I should be quite happy for you to be scolded. Sit down and sing.

Fortunio: If you order me to, I shall obey.

(He sits down.)

Jacqueline: Well, now, what are you thinking of now? Are you waiting for someone to come?

Fortunio: I am suffering. Don't make me stay.

Jacqueline: Sing first, and then we shall see whether you are suffering and I am making you stay. Sing, I tell you, I want you to. You are not singing? Well, now, what is he doing? Come, come, if you sing I shall give you the tip of my mitten.

Fortunio: Listen to me, Jacqueline. You would have done better to tell me; I would have gone along with the whole thing.

Jacqueline: What is that you are saying? What are you talking about?

Fortunio: Yes, you would have done better to tell me. Yes, as God is my witness, I would have done everything for you.

Jacqueline: Done everything for me? What do you mean by that?

Fortunio: Oh, Jacqueline, Jacqueline! You must really love him. It must be hard for you to lie and to mock me so pitilessly.

Jacqueline: Me, mock you? Who told you that?

Fortunio: I beg of you, don't tell more lies. That is enough now, I know everything.

Jacqueline: Why, what do you know?

Fortunio: I was in your room yesterday when Clavaroche was there.

Jacqueline: Is that possible? You were behind the bed?

Fortunio: Yes, I was. In the name of heaven, don't say another word about it.

(A moment's silence.)

Jacqueline: Well, sir, since you know everything, all I can do now is to ask you to remain silent. I am aware enough of the wrong I have done you, not to try and lessen it in your eyes. What necessity dictates and what it can lead to might perhaps be understood by someone else than you, and he might, if not pardon, at least excuse my conduct. But unfortunately you are too interested a party to judge it with indulgence. I am resigned and waiting.

Fortunio: You needn't be afraid. Rather than do anything to hurt you, I shall cut this hand off.

Jacqueline: Your word is enough, I haven't any right to doubt it. I must even say that if you were to forget it, I would still have no right to complain. My recklessness deserves punishment. I turned to you, sir, without knowing who you were. If that circumstance lessens my guilt, it made my danger all the greater. Since I have laid myself open to it, you should treat me as you feel entitled. Some of the things that were said yesterday perhaps call for an explanation; but since I can't justify everything, I prefer to remain silent about everything. I prefer to believe that it is only your pride that has been hurt. If that is so, let these past two days be forgotten. Later on, we can speak about them again.

Fortunio: Never: that is my heart's wish.

Jacqueline: As you will. I must obey. However, if I must no longer see you, I would like to add one word. Between the two of us I have no fear, since you promise to remain silent. But there is another person whose presence in this house may have unfortunate consequences.

Fortunio: I have nothing to say on that subject.

Jacqueline: I am asking you to listen to me. Any clash between you and him, you must realize, is bound to ruin me. I shall do everything I can to prevent it. I shall submit unquestioningly to whatever you may demand. Don't leave me without reflecting on that. Dictate your own conditions. Must the person I am speaking of stay away for some time? Must he apologize to you? Whatever you judge proper will be accepted by me as a favor, and by him as a duty. The memory of a few joking

remarks obliges me to question you on that point. What do
you want? Answer me.

Fortunio: I don't demand anything. You love him; be in peace as
long as he loves you.

Jacqueline: I thank you for both promises. If you should come to
regret them, I repeat that any condition you impose will be
accepted. You may count on my gratitude. Is there anything
else I can do now to make up for my wrongs? Is there any
means in my power of obliging you? Even if you should not
believe me, I confess that I would do anything in the world to
leave you a less unflattering memory. What can I do? I am at
your orders.

Fortunio: Nothing. Good-by, madam. Have no fear; you will
never have reason to complain of me.

(He turns to leave and takes his song.)

Jacqueline: Oh, Fortunio, leave that for me.

Fortunio: And what will you do with it, you heartless woman?
You have been talking to me for a quarter-hour, and nothing
has come out of your lips from your heart. What do I care for
your excuses, your sacrifices, and your reparations! What do I
care for your Clavaroche and his stupid vanity! What do I
care about my pride! So you think you wounded it? You think
what troubles me is that I was played for a fool, and teased at
that dinner? I don't even remember it. When I tell you I love
you, do you really think I don't feel a thing? When I speak to
you of two years' suffering, do you really think that I am like
you? What, you break my heart, you claim you are sorry for it,
and this is the way you leave me! You say it was necessity that
made you do wrong, and you feel regret for it. You blush, you
look away; you pity me for my suffering. You see me, you
understand what you have done; and this is the way you heal
the wound you have opened in me! Ah, it is in my heart,
Jacqueline, and all you had to do was reach out your hand. I
swear to you, if you had wished, however shameful it may be
to say it, even if you yourself should smile at it, I was capable
of accepting anything. Oh God, I feel faint, I can't go out now.
(He leans against the furniture.)

Jacqueline: My poor child! I am so guilty. Here, take a breath from this flask.

Fortunio: Oh, keep it for him; keep these attentions I don't deserve for him! They aren't made for the likes of me. I don't have an inventive mind, I am neither lucky nor clever. I wouldn't know how to devise a cunning plan when it is needed! What a fool! I thought I was loved! Yes, because you smiled at me, because your hand trembled in mine, because your eyes seemed to seek out my eyes and, like two angels, invite me to a feast of joy and life; because your lips had parted and a hollow sound had come forth from them, yes, I confess, I had dreamed, I had believed that love was like that! What poor nonsense! Was it at a parade, and your smile congratulated me on the beauty of my horse? Was it the sun striking my helmet that dazzled your eyes? I came out of a dark room, from which I had been watching you walk along the path for two years. I was a poor third clerk who just managed to weep in silence. That was all there was to love.

Jacqueline: Poor child!

Fortunio: Yes, poor child! You can say that again, because I don't know whether I am awake or dreaming and, in spite of everything, whether or not you love me. I have been sitting on the ground since yesterday, pounding my heart and my head. I keep remembering what my eyes have seen, what my ears have heard, and wondering if it is possible. Right now you tell me, I feel it, I am suffering from it, I am dying from it, and I don't believe it or understand it. What had I done to you, Jacqueline? How can you, for no reason, feeling neither love nor hate for me, not knowing me, never having seen me, how can you, whom everyone loves, whom I have seen giving alms and watering those flowers, who are good, who believe in God, whom I never . . . Oh, I am accusing you, you that I love more than my life! Oh God, have I reproached you? Jacqueline, forgive me.

Jacqueline: Please, please calm yourself.

Fortunio: My God, what good am I, except to lay down my life for you, except for the meanest use you want to make of me, except to follow you, to protect you, to push a thorn away from your footstep? I dare to complain, and you had chosen me! I had my place at your table, I was going to matter in your existence. You were going to tell all of nature, these gardens, these meadows, to smile at me as you did. Your beautiful, radiant image was beginning to walk before me, and I was following it. I was going to live . . . Am I losing you, Jacqueline? Have I done anything for you to send me away? Why won't you go on pretending to love me?

(He falls in a faint.)

Jacqueline: (Running over to him.) Lord God, what have I done? Fortunio, wake up.

Fortunio: Who are you? Let me go.

Jacqueline: Lean on me, come over to the window. Please, lean on me. Put your arm around my shoulder, I beg you, Fortunio.

Fortunio: It is nothing. I am feeling better already.

Jacqueline: How pale he is, and how fast his heart is beating! Do you want to moisten your temples? Take this cushion, take this handkerchief. Am I so hateful to you that you would reject my help?

Fortunio: I feel better. Thank you.

Jacqueline: How cold your hands are! Where are you going? You can't go out. At least wait a moment. Since I have hurt you so, at least let me take care of you.

Fortunio: There is no need, I have to go downstairs. Forgive anything I may have said. I lost control of my tongue.

Jacqueline: What do you want me to forgive you for? Alas, you are the one who won't forgive. But what is your hurry? Why leave me? You keep looking for something. Don't you recognize me? I beg you, please stay still. For my sake, Fortunio, you can't go out yet.

Fortunio: No, good-by, I can't stay!

Jacqueline: Oh, I have hurt you so badly!

Fortunio: They were calling for me when I came upstairs. Good-by, madam, you can count on me.

Jacqueline: Will I see you again?

Fortunio: If you want.

Jacqueline: Will you come upstairs to the salon this evening?

Fortunio: If that is what you want.

Jacqueline: So you are leaving? Just a moment more.

Fortunio: Good-by, good-by! I can't stay.

(*Exit.*)

Jacqueline: (*She calls.*) Fortunio, listen to me!

Fortunio: (*Coming back.*) What do you want of me, Jacqueline?

Jacqueline: Listen, I have to talk to you. I don't want to ask your
forgiveness; I don't want to take anything back; I don't want to
justify myself. You are good, brave, and sincere. I have been
treacherous and disloyal. We can't part this way.

Fortunio: I forgive you with all my heart.

Jacqueline: No, you are suffering, the harm is done. Where are
you going? What are you going to do? How can you have come
back here when you knew everything?

Fortunio: You sent for me.

Jacqueline: But you were coming to tell me that I would see you at
that rendezvous. Would you have come?

Fortunio: Yes, if it could be of use to you, and I confess that I
thought it might.

Jacqueline: Why would it be of use to me?

Fortunio: Madeleine said a few words to me . . .

Jacqueline: You knew about it, poor thing, and you were going to
come to the garden!

Fortunio: The first thing I ever told you in my life was that I
would gladly die for you, and the second was that I never told
a lie.

Jacqueline: You knew about it, and you were going to come? Do
you realize what you are saying? It was a trap.

Fortunio: I knew everything.

Jacqueline: You were going to be caught, killed perhaps, dragged
off to prison, who knows? It is horrible to talk about.

Fortunio: I knew everything.

Jacqueline: You knew everything? You knew everything? You were
hiding here yesterday, behind the bed curtains. You were listen-
ing, weren't you? You knew the whole thing, didn't you?

Fortunio: Yes.

Jacqueline: You knew that I am a liar, that I deceive, I laugh at
you, and I could get you killed? You knew I love Clavaroche
and that he makes me do anything he wants? That I play a

role? That I used you as a dupe yesterday? That I am weak and despicable? That I can expose you to death for my pleasure? You knew everything, you were certain of it? Well, well, what do you know now?

Fortunio: Why, Jacqueline, I think . . . I know . . .

Jacqueline: Do you know that I love you, child that you are? That you have to forgive me or I shall die? That I am asking you to on bended knee?

Scene 4. *The dining-room.*

(André, Clavaroche, Fortunio, and Jacqueline at table.)

André: Thanks be to God, here we are, all happy together again and friends. If ever I should have any doubts about my wife, may my wine poison me!

Jacqueline: Pour some wine for me, Mr. Fortunio.

Clavaroche: (Softly.) I tell you once again that your clerk is a nuisance. Please be so kind as to send him packing.

Jacqueline: (Softly.) I am doing as you told me.

André: When I think that I spent all last night in the office, fretting over a cursed suspicion, I don't know what to call myself.

Jacqueline: Mr. Fortunio, give me that cushion.

Clavaroche: (Softly.) Do you take me for another André? If your clerk doesn't leave this house, I shall soon leave myself.

Jacqueline: I am doing as you told me.

André: But I have told everyone about it. Justice must be served here on earth. The whole town will know who I am. Henceforth, as penance, I shall never have the slightest suspicion.

Jacqueline: Mr. Fortunio, here is a toast, to your loves.

Clavaroche: (Softly.) That will do, Jacqueline. I know what this means. That is not what I told you.

André: Yes, to Fortunio's loves!

(He sings.)

Come, friends, let's raise our glasses . . .

Fortunio: That song is such an old one. Why don't you sing, Mr. Clavaroche!

THE END

You Never Can Tell

First published in the 1 July 1836 issue of the *Revue des deux mondes*, *You Never Can Tell* was successfully produced at the Comédie Française on 22 June 1848. However, the political events of the time — the Revolution of 1848, which had such profound repercussions throughout Europe, broke out in Paris that day—prevented it from holding the boards after its première; and it was not staged again until 1864, a half-dozen years after Musset's death.

Here, as in its salon models, the proverb that gives the work its title is cited at the end by the protagonist, Valentin, who has learned his lesson: that is, not even a devil-may-care "dropout" from the upper middle class, like him, can escape marriage when he is confronted with a suitable and attractive match, having a handsome dowry to cap it all.

The play is a paean to middle-class values—fortune, marriage, fidelity, charity, goodness, common sense (in Mlle. de Mantes' differential imagery, Ceres versus Venus)—and it is therefore profoundly anti-"Romantic." That represents an evident departure from Musset's aristocratic, Romantic, and essentially tragic (or at least pathetic) viewpoint in the earlier comedies. And yet in the way that the play mocks Valentin's superficial adherence to Romantic fashion—his beard, his long hair, his dissolute lifestyle, his radical social views—it is typical of some of the ambiguities that characterized Musset himself. As much as *Fantasio, You Never Can Tell* can be taken as an excellent example of the Romantic irony, characteristic of E. T. A. Hoffmann and Jean-Paul Richter in Germany, that some critics see Musset best embodying in France.

CHARACTERS

Van Buck, a merchant	A curate
Valentin Van Buck, his	A dancing master
nephew	An innkeeper
The Baroness of Mantes	A waiter
Cecile, her daughter	

The scene is Paris.*
ACT ONE
Scene 1. *Valentin's bedroom.*

(Valentin is seated. Enter Van Buck.)

Van Buck: My dear nephew, I wish you a good day.

Valentin: My dear uncle, the same to you.

Van Buck: Remain seated. I have to talk with you.

Valentin: Sit down. I suppose I have to listen to you. Please take that armchair and put your hat down here.

Van Buck: (Sitting down.) My dear nephew, the most stubborn patience, and the most patient obstinacy, must sooner or later come to an end. What has been tolerated becomes intolerable, what has not been corrected becomes incorrigible; and the man who, time after time, has thrown out a line to a madman bent on drowning himself can one day be forced to abandon him, or perish with him.

Valentin: Oh, oh! That is quite a beginning. Your metaphors are up very early this morning.

Van Buck: Please remain silent, sir, and don't indulge in fun at my expense. In vain has the wisest advice sought to gain some hold on you for the past three years. Either lack of concern or blind rage, ineffectual resolutions, a thousand pretexts you delight in inventing, your damned condescension, everything I have done or may yet do (but, by Jove, I shall not do anything further! . . .). Where in the world are you dragging me? You are as stubborn . . .

---

*Actually, only the first scene takes place in Paris; the rest of the play is set in and around a castle not far from Paris, no doubt in the environs of Mantes-la-Jolie, some thirty-five miles from the capital.

Valentin: Uncle Van Buck, you are angry.

Van Buck: No, sir, do not interrupt. You are just as stubborn as I
have shown myself patient and credulous, to my misfortune.
I ask you, is it credible that a young man of twenty-five should
spend his time as you do? What good have my admonitions
done, and when will you take up some trade? You are poor
since, when all is said and done, you have no other fortune
than my own. But I am not on my deathbed, you know, and
my digestion is still as hearty as a younger man's. What are
you planning to do from now until I die?

Valentin: Uncle Van Buck, you are angry, and you are about to
lose your temper.

Van Buck: No, sir, I know what I am doing. If I am the only one
in the family who entered trade, it is thanks to me, and don't
you forget it, that the remains of a dilapidated fortune have
nonetheless been restored. It is just fine for you to sit there and
smirk while I talk: if I hadn't sold gingham in Antwerp you
would be in the poor house today, with your paisley robe. But,
merciful God, your damned poker games . . .

Valentin: Uncle Van Buck, here comes the trivial. You are chang-
ing tone. You are losing your temper. You started out better
than this.

Van Buck: Confound it, are you making fun of me? Apparently I
am only good for paying your IOU's. I received one this morn-
ing: sixty *louis!* Who do you think you are fooling? It is very
fine for you to dress like Beau Brummell (the devil take these
English expressions!) when you can't pay your tailor! It is one
thing to dismount from a fine horse and go home to a good,
wealthy family on the main floor of a town house, and quite
another to jump out of a rented carriage and climb up two
or three flights. For all your satin vests, you ask your door-
keeper for a candle when you come home from the ball, and
he grumbles if he hasn't gotten his Christmas tip. Lord knows
if you even give him one every year! Running around with a
circle of friends that is richer than you, you are learning from
them to look down on your own kind. You wear your beard
trimmed in a Vandyke, and your hair down to your shoulders,
as if you didn't have money for a ribbon to tie it up. You

scribble in newspapers. You are capable of becoming a Saint Simonian Socialist when you no longer have a penny to your name, and that day will come, believe me. Come now, a public scribe is worth more than you are. I shall end up by cutting you off, and you will die in a garret.

Valentin: My dear uncle Van Buck, I love and respect you. Please do me a favor and listen to me. You paid one of my IOU's for me this morning. When you came, I was at the window and I saw you arriving. You were pondering a sermon exactly as long as from here to your house. Spare your breath, please. I know just what you are thinking. You don't always mean what you say. For what you do, I thank you. It is quite possible that I have debts and that I am good for nothing, but what can you do about that? You have an income of sixty thousand pounds.

Van Buck: Fifty.

Valentin: Sixty, uncle. You have no children, and you are very good to me. If I take advantage of that, what harm is there? With sixty thousand pounds' income . . .

Van Buck: Fifty, fifty and not a cent more.

Valentin: Sixty: you told me so yourself.

Van Buck: Never. Where did you get that idea?

Valentin: Let's say fifty. You are young, still in sound health, and you enjoy life. Do you think that troubles me, and that I am thirsting after your fortune? You wouldn't insult me that way, and you know that headstrong young men don't always have the hardest hearts. You take issue with my bathrobe, but you have worn plenty of them yourself. My pointed beard doesn't mean that I am a Socialist: I have too much respect for inheritance. You complain about my vests: you don't want me to go out in my shirt-sleeves, do you? You tell me that I am poor and my friends are not: hurrah for them, it is not my fault. You imagine that they are spoiling me and that their example is making me disdainful: I disdain only what bores me; and since you pay my debts you can see that I don't owe any money. You rebuke me for taking cabs; that is just because I don't have a carriage. You say that I take my candle from my doorkeeper when I get home: that is just so I won't go upstairs without any light; would you have me break my neck? You would like to

see me take up a trade: have me named prime minister and you
will see how well I make my way. But if I was an extra clerk
in some attorney's office, I ask you what I would learn from
that, except that all is vanity. You say I play poker: that is only
because I win when I have three of a kind; but you can be sure
that as soon as I lose I regret my stupidity. It would be differ-
ent, you say, if I dismounted from a fine horse and went into a
good town house: I am sure of that; it is easy enough for you
to say. You add that you are proud, despite having sold ging-
ham. Would to God that I sold it; at least that would prove I
could buy it! As for my nobility, it is as dear to me as it can be
to you yourself. But that is why I don't put on a harness, any
more than one does on purebred horses. Look, Uncle, if I am
not mistaken you haven't had breakfast yet. You have gone
without eating, over that damned IOU. Let's swallow it to-
gether; I shall order some hot chocolate.
   (He rings. Breakfast is brought in.)
Van Buck: What a breakfast! Devil take me, you live like a prince!
Valentin: Well, what can I do, when you are starving you have to
   try and while the time away.
   (They sit down to table.)
Van Buck: I am sure you imagine I have forgiven you because I am
   sitting down here.
Valentin: What, me? Not at all. What saddens me when you are
   irritated is that you sometimes use shoptalk without realizing
   it. Yes, without knowing it you stray from that flower of
   courtesy that particularly distinguishes you. But if it isn't in the
   presence of others, you understand that I won't mention it.
Van Buck: All right, all right. I know very well what I am saying.
   But enough of that, let's talk about something else. You really
   ought to get married.
Valentin: My Lord, what is that you are saying?
Van Buck: Give me something to drink. I said you are getting on
   in years, and you ought to get married.
Valentin: But Uncle, what have I done to you?
Van Buck: You have done IOU's. But even if you hadn't done any-
   thing, what is so dreadful about marriage? Come now, let's
   talk seriously. You certainly would be an object of pity if you

should have some pretty, well-brought-up girl put in your arms
this evening, with fifty thousand crowns on the table to cheer
you up when you wake up tomorrow morning! That would be
quite a misfortune; no wonder you are so touchy about it!
You have debts, but I shall pay them; once you are married you
will settle down. Mademoiselle de Mantes has everything it
takes . . .

Valentin: Mademoiselle de Mantes! You are joking!

Van Buck: Since I have let her name slip, no, I am not joking. She
is the one I am talking about, and if you are willing . . .

Valentin: And if she is willing. It is as the song goes:

> I know that it would only depend on me
> To marry her, if she was willing.

Van Buck: No, it all depends on you. You have been accepted, she
likes you.

Valentin: I never saw her in my life.

Van Buck: That doesn't matter. I tell you she likes you.

Valentin: Is that true?

Van Buck: I give you my word.

Valentin: Well, then, I don't like her.

Van Buck: Why not?

Valentin: For the same reason that she likes me.

Van Buck: It doesn't make any sense to say that we don't like peo-
ple when we don't even know them.

Valentin: Any more than to say we like them. Please, let's not talk
of this any more.

Van Buck: But my boy, when you think of it (give me something
to drink) you have to settle down some time.

Valentin: Certainly, just as you have to die once in your life.

Van Buck: I mean that you have to make up your mind and find
your place in life. What will become of you? I warn you, one
day or another I shall just drop you in spite of myself. I won't
have you driving me to ruin, and if you want to be my heir
you still have to be in a position to wait. Your wedding would
cost me money, it is true; but once and for all, and less than
your extravagances. Anyway, I prefer to get rid of you. Think
of this: Do you want a pretty wife, your debts paid, and a
life of peace and quiet?

Valentin: Since you insist on it, Uncle, and you are talking seriously, seriously I shall answer you. Have some pâté and listen to me.

Van Buck: Tell me, how do you feel about it?

Valentin: Without wanting to go back very far, or tire you with too many preambles, I shall begin with ancient times. Need I remind you how a man who hadn't deserved it in any way was treated; a man who was mild-mannered all his life, to the extent that, even after her transgression, he took back the woman who had been so outrageously unfaithful to him? Moreover, as the brother of a powerful monarch and crowned in the worst possible way . . .

Van Buck: Who the deuce are you talking about?

Valentin: Menelaus, Uncle.

Van Buck: The devil take you and me with you! I am a fool to be listening to you.

Valentin: Why? It seems quite obvious to me . . .

Van Buck: You damned rascal! You crackpot! There is no way to make you talk sense. *(He stands up.)* All right, let's forget it, that is enough! Today's youth respects nothing.

Valentin: Uncle Van Buck, you are going to lose your temper.

Van Buck: No, sir. But to tell you the truth, it is just inconceivable. Can you imagine a man of my age being used as a child's plaything? Do you take me for your playfellow? Do I have to tell you again . . .

Valentin: What? Is it possible that you have never read Homer, Uncle?

Van Buck: (Sitting down again.) Well, what if I have?

Valentin: You are talking to me of marriage. It is quite normal for me to cite the most famous husband of ancient times.

Van Buck: I couldn't care less about your maxims. Will you answer me seriously?

Valentin: All right. Let's drink to that, sincerely. I won't be understood by you unless you are willing not to interrupt me. I didn't cite Menelaus to you just to display my erudition, but in order not to name a good many worthy men. Do I have to tell you exactly what I mean?

Van Buck: Yes, right away or I am leaving.

Valentin: When I was sixteen, just out of school, a fine lady whom we both know first took notice of me. At that age, who knows what is innocent or illicit? One evening I was at my mistress's house, by the fireside, with her husband present. The husband stands up and says that he is going out. At that, a quick glance between my love and me makes my heart leap with joy. We were going to be alone! I turn around and see the poor man putting on his gloves. They were suede, greenish in color, too big and with a hole in the thumb. While he was plunging his hands into them, standing in the middle of the room, an imperceptible smile passed over the corner of the woman's mouth and traced the dimples of her cheeks like a faint shadow. A lover's eye alone sees such smiles, for they are felt more than they can be seen. That one went right to my heart, and I swallowed it like a sherbet. But by some strange quirk, the memory of that delicious moment became invincibly linked in my mind to that of the two big, red hands struggling into greenish gloves. I can't say just why those hands, in their trust-ing activity, looked sad and pitiable, but I have never thought of them since without the womanly smile coming to tickle the corners of my mouth, and I swore that no woman in the world would ever make me wear gloves like that.

Van Buck: What you mean is that as a true rake you have doubts about women's virtue, and you are afraid that others will pay you back for the ill you have done them.

Valentin: That is exactly it. I am afraid of the devil, and I don't want to wear those gloves.

Van Buck: Hah! That is a young man's notion.

Valentin: As you wish. It is mine, in any case. In thirty years or so, if I am still around, it will be an old man's notion, for I shall never get married.

Van Buck: Do you claim that all women are fickle and all hus-bands are cuckolds?

Valentin: I don't "claim" anything, and I have no idea. I "claim" that when I walk down the street, I won't throw myself down under carriage wheels. When I dine, I won't eat whiting. When I am thirsty, I won't drink from a broken glass. And when I see a woman, I won't marry her. And I still am not sure that I

won't get run over, choke on a bone, become gap-toothed,
or . . .

Van Buck: Shame on you! Mademoiselle de Mantes is virtuous
and well-brought-up; she is a fine young girl.

Valentin: God forbid I should speak ill of her! I am sure she is the
best in the world. She is well-brought-up, you say? What kind
of education has she had? Have they taken her to the ball, to
the theater, to the races? Does she go out alone in a cab at
noon and come back at six? Does she have a clever chamber-
maid, a hidden staircase? Has she seen *La Tour de Nesle*,
and does she read Balzac novels? Is she taken on summer even-
ings, after a good dinner, to see ten or twelve naked brutes
with muscular shoulders wrestle on the Champs-Elysées? Is her
dancing master a handsome waltzer, a solemn, well-curled fel-
low with solid Prussian legs, who presses her fingers when she
has drunk some punch? Does she receive visitors alone in the
afternoon, sitting on a springy sofa in the shade of a pink cur-
tain? Does she have a gilded bolt on her door that she can slide
with her little finger while turning her head away, as a thick,
muffled tapestry falls softly over it? Does she put her glove in
her glass when they start to pour the champagne? Does she
pretend to go to the Opera ball, and then disappear for half an
hour, run over to Musard's, then come back and yawn? Has
she been taught to show only the whites of her eyes, like an
amorous dove, when Rubini sings? Does she spend summers at
the country home of an experienced woman friend who
vouches for her to her family, and leaves her playing the piano
while she goes for a stroll through the woods, whispering
with some cavalry officer? Does she go to spas? Does she have
migraine headaches?

Van Buck: Goodness gracious! What is this you are talking about?

Valentin: It is just that if she knows nothing about all that she
hasn't been taught much. For, as soon as she is married she
will know it all, and then who can tell what will happen?

Van Buck: You have some odd ideas about women's education.
Would you want people to follow them?

Valentin: No, but I should like a young girl to be a blade of grass
in the woods, and not a hothouse plant. Come on, Uncle, let's
go to the Tuileries and not talk any further about all this.

Van Buck: So you reject Mademoiselle de Mantes?

Valentin: No more than any other girl; but neither more nor less.

Van Buck: You will drive me crazy; you are incorrigible. I had such high hopes: the girl will be quite rich some day. You will be my ruin and you will go to the devil, that is what will happen. What is the matter? What do you want?

Valentin: To give you your walking stick and your hat and go out for some fresh air, if you are willing.

Van Buck: I couldn't care less about fresh air! I shall disown you, if you refuse to get married.

Valentin: You will disown me, Uncle?

Van Buck: Yes, by heaven! I swear it! I shall be just as stubborn as you, and we shall see which one of us gives in.

Valentin: Will you disown me in writing, or just orally?

Van Buck: In writing, you impudent rascal!

Valentin: Then who will you leave your property to? Will you found a prize for virtue, or a Latin grammar contest?

Van Buck: Rather than let myself be ruined at your hands I shall go to ruin all by myself, and at my own pleasure . . .

Valentin: There is no lottery or gambling any longer. You will never be able to drink it all away.

Van Buck: I shall leave Paris and go back to Antwerp. Maybe I shall get married myself, if need be, and give you six first cousins.

Valentin: Then I shall go to Algiers. I shall become a trumpeter in the dragoons, I shall marry an Ethiopian and give you twenty-four grand-nephews, black as ink and dumb as dogs.

Van Buck: My Lord! If I take my stick . . .

Valentin: Watch out, Uncle. Be careful, if you strike, that you don't break the staff of your old age.

Van Buck: *(Embracing him.)* Oh, you rascal, you are taking advantage of me!

Valentin: Listen to me: I detest marriage; but for you, my good Uncle, I am ready for anything. No matter how strange what I am about to propose may seem, promise me you will accept it without reservation and, in turn, I give you my solemn word.

Van Buck: What do you mean? Be quick.

Valentin: Promise first, I shall talk afterward.

Van Buck: I can't without knowing anything.

Valentin: You have to, Uncle. It is essential.

Van Buck: All right, so be it, I promise.

Valentin: If you want me to marry Mademoiselle de Mantes, there is only one way to do it. I have to be absolutely certain that she will never put the pair of gloves we were talking about on my hands.

Van Buck: How can you expect me to know that?

Valentin: There are odds on it that can be easily calculated. Will you agree that if I was sure she could be seduced within a week, I would be very wrong to marry her?

Van Buck: Certainly. What likelihood? . . .

Valentin: I am not asking you for any longer than that. The Baroness has never seen me, neither has her daughter. You are going to have your carriage hitched, and you will go pay them a visit. You will tell them that, to your great regret, your nephew is going to remain a bachelor. I shall arrive at the castle an hour after you, and you will be careful not to recognize me. That is all I ask of you; the rest is up to me alone.

Van Buck: You frighten me. What are you planning to do? How are you going to introduce yourself?

Valentin: That is my business. Don't recognize me, that is all I ask of you. I shall spend a week at the castle. I need some fresh air, so it will do me good. You can stay, too, if you want.

Van Buck: Have you gone mad? What do you think you are going to do? Seduce a girl in one week? Play the suitor under an assumed name? What a fine invention! There isn't a fairy tale in which that kind of nonsense hasn't been worked to death. Do you want me to turn into a Dutch uncle?

Valentin: It is two o'clock; let's go to your place.

(*Exit.*)

Scene 2. *In the castle.*

(*The Baroness, Cecile, a curate, and a dancing master.*)
(*The Baroness, seated, is chatting with the curate and doing needlework. Cecile is taking a dancing lesson.*)

Baroness: It is such an odd thing that I can't find my blue yarn.

Curate: You were holding it a few minutes ago. It must have rolled off somewhere.

Master: If Mademoiselle would just step through the *poule* with me once more, we can rest after that.

Cecile: I should like to learn the quick waltz.

Master: The Baroness is quite opposed to that. Please be so kind as to turn your head toward me and move in opposition.

Curate: Madam, what do you think of the latest sermon? You heard it, didn't you?

Baroness: It is green and pink on a black background, just like the little chair upstairs.

Curate: Excuse me?

Baroness: Oh, pardon me, I was miles away.

Curate: But I thought I saw you there.

Baroness: Where in the world?

Curate: At Saint-Roch's, last Sunday.

Baroness: Why yes, of course. Everyone was in tears. The Baron just kept on blowing his nose. I left in the middle because the lady next to me had the vapors, and right now I am under the care of homeopaths.

Master: Mademoiselle, no matter how often I ask you to, you just won't move in opposition. Turn your head away slightly now and round your arms for me.

Cecile: But if I don't want to fall, sir, I really have to look in front of myself.

Master: For shame! That is just terrible. Look here, could anything be simpler? Look at me; am I falling? You move to the right, you look to the left; you move to the left, you look to the right. Nothing could be more natural.

Baroness: I just don't understand why I can't find my blue yarn.

Cecile: Mother, why don't you* want me to learn the quick waltz?

Baroness: Because it is indecent. Have you read *Jocelyn*?

*Cecile and her mother, the Baroness, address each other with the formal *vous*, as was the custom in many noble and upper-class families. That makes Valentin's facile use of the intimate *tu* with her in act 3, scene 4 seem even more striking to Cecile.

Curate: Yes, madam, there are some beautiful verses in it; but I
have to admit that the material . . .

Baroness: The material is black; the entire little chair is. You will
see how pretty it is against rosewood.

Cecile: But Mother, Miss Clary waltzes, and so do the Misses de
Raimbaut.

Baroness: Miss Clary is English, young lady. Father, I am sure you
are sitting on them.

Curate: What, me, madam, on the young ladies?

Baroness: Why, no, on my skeins of yarn. There is one. No, it is
the red. Where did the blue go?

Curate: I found the scene with the bishop quite beautiful. It has
real genius, a good deal of talent, and . . . polish.

Cecile: But Mother, why is it decent for an Englishwoman to
waltz?

Baroness: There is also a novel I have read that they sent me from
Mongie's. I don't remember its title or its author. Have you
read it? It is quite well written.

Curate: Yes, madam. I think there is someone opening the gate.
Were you expecting a visitor?

Baroness: Oh, yes, that is right. Cecile, listen to me.

Master: The Baroness wishes to speak to you, mademoiselle.

Curate: I don't see any carriage entering. It is some horses about
to leave.

Cecile: (Coming up to her.) Did you call me, Mother?

Baroness: No. Oh, yes. There is someone coming. Bend down so I
can speak in your ear. It is a possible match. Has your hair
been done?

Cecile: A match?

Baroness: Yes, very suitable. Between twenty-five and thirty, or
younger. No, I have no idea. Very well, go and dance.

Cecile: But Mother, I wanted to tell you . . .

Baroness: I just can't imagine where that yarn went. I have only
one skein of the blue, and it has to go and vanish.
(Enter Van Buck.)

Van Buck: Baroness, I wish you a good day. My nephew couldn't
come with me. He asked me to express his regrets and to
excuse him for not keeping his word.

Baroness: Hah! Really, he is not coming? That is my daughter, taking her lesson. Do you mind if she continues? I had her come downstairs because her room is too small.

Van Buck: I hope I am not disturbing anyone. If my harebrained nephew . . .

Baroness: Won't you have something to drink? Come, sit down. How are you?

Van Buck: My nephew is very sorry, madam . . .

Baroness: Just let me tell you. Father, you are staying with us, aren't you? Well, Cecile, what is the matter with you?

Master: Mademoiselle is tired, madam.

Baroness: Poppycock! If she were at the ball at four in the morning, she wouldn't be tired, that is as plain as day. You, tell me now: *(Softly to Van Buck)* Is it off?

Van Buck: I am afraid so. If I must speak frankly . . .

Baroness: Hah, he refuses? Well, that is a fine thing!

Van Buck: My Lord, madam, please don't believe that it is in any way my fault. I swear to you by my late father . . .

Baroness: Well, he refuses, is that it? It is off?

Van Buck: Why, madam, if I could truthfully say . . .
 (Noises are heard outside.)

Baroness: What is that? Please have a look, Father.

Curate: Madam, it is a carriage that has overturned outside the castle gate. They are bringing in a young man who seems to have lost consciousness.

Baroness: Oh, my Lord, there is a dead man coming! Have the green room tidied up quickly. Come, Van Buck, let me take your arm.
 (Exit.)

ACT TWO
Scene 1. *A pathway through a grove.*

(Enter Van Buck with Valentin, whose arm is in a sling.)

Van Buck: You poor wretch, is it possible that you really dislocated your arm?

Valentin: Nothing is more possible. It is even probable, and what is worse, quite painfully true.

Van Buck: I don't know which of us is more worthy of blame in this matter. Has anything quite so preposterous ever been seen?

Valentin: I had to find some pretext to be admitted properly. What other reason do you want me to find for getting introduced to a respectable family, incognito, this way? I had given my coachman a *louis* and made him promise to overturn me in front of the castle. He is an honest man, I can't say anything against him, and his money is perfectly well-earned. He caught his wheel in the ditch with the most heroic loyalty. I dislocated my arm, that is my own fault, but I did overturn, so I can't complain. On the contrary, I am delighted: it lends things an air of truth that attracts sympathy toward me.

Van Buck: What are you going to do? What is your plan?

Valentin: I haven't come here at all to marry Mademoiselle de Mantes, but only to prove to you that I would be wrong to marry her. My plan is made up, my cannons are aimed, and up to now everything has gone perfectly. You have kept your promise, like Regulus or Hernani. You haven't called me your nephew, that is the principal and the most difficult thing. Here I am, welcomed, lodged, put up in a fine green room, with orange blossoms on my night table and white curtains on my bed. I have to give your Baroness credit, she has received me just as well as my coachman overturned me. Now we have to see whether the rest will go off the same way. I intend to declare my love first of all, then write a note . . .

Van Buck: Never mind, I won't allow this damned joke to go any further.

Valentin: Would you go back on your promise? Well, as you wish. I shall take back my promise right away, too.

Van Buck: But, nephew . . .

Valentin: If you say one word, I shall take the mail coach right back to Paris. No more promise, no more marriage. You can disown me if you like.

Van Buck: What an unbelievable hornet's nest! I don't know how I got into this. But at least explain yourself!

Valentin: Uncle, just think about our agreement. You said and you agreed that, if my fiancée was going to glove me with certain gloves, I would be crazy to make her my wife. Consequently, since the test has been accepted, you will find it only right, just, and proper that it should be as complete as possible. What I say will be well-said, what I attempt will be well-attempted, and anything I do will be well-done. You are not going to split hairs with me, and in any case I have carte blanche.

Van Buck: But my dear sir, there are still certain limits, certain things . . . I shall have you know that if you think you will take advantage . . . Mercy me, you are impossible!

Valentin: If our bride-to-be is as you think, and as you represented her to me, there isn't the slightest danger, and she will be shown to be all the more worthy. Just imagine that I am the first man to come along; I am in love with Mademoiselle de Mantes, the virtuous wife of Valentin Van Buck. Just think how bold and enterprising today's youth is! And besides, when one is in love, isn't one capable of anything? Clambering up through windows, writing four-page letters, shedding torrents of tears, sending boxes of candy: Will a lover stop at anything? Can he be held to any account? What harm does he do? How can anyone be offended? He is in love. Oh, Uncle Van Buck, remember when you were in love!

Van Buck: I have always been a proper man, and I hope you will be, too; otherwise I shall tell the Baroness everything.

Valentin: I am not planning to do anything that could shock anyone. First I plan to make my declaration; second, write several letters; third, bribe the chambermaid; fourth, skulk about in the shadows; fifth, take a print of the locks with sealing wax; sixth, make a rope ladder and cut the windowpanes with my ring; seventh, fall down on my knees and recite Rousseau; and eighth, if I am not successful, go and drown myself in the pond. But I swear to you that I shall be proper, and I shan't utter a single swearword or anything that goes against the proprieties.

Van Buck: You are a rake and a scoundrel. I won't stand for anything of the sort.

Valentin: But just think: everything that I have been telling you is what someone else will be doing four years from now, if I marry Mademoiselle de Mantes. How do you expect me to find out how much resistance she is capable of if I haven't tried it myself? Someone else will try a lot harder, and will have a lot more time at his disposal. When I asked you for only a week, I was performing an act of deep humility.

Van Buck: You set a trap for me. I had never foreseen all this.

Valentin: What did you think would happen when you accepted the wager?

Van Buck: Why, my friend, I thought, I believed—I believed you were going to court the young woman . . . but politely . . . like, for example . . . like saying to her . . . Or if, by chance . . . indeed, I haven't any idea . . . But, deuce take it, you are frightening!

Valentin: Look! Here comes the fair Cecile, walking toward us with dainty steps. Do you hear the twigs cracking? Her mother is doing needlework with her curate. Quick, jump into the bushes. You can witness the first skirmish and give me your opinion.

Van Buck: You will marry her if she acts unpleasant?
(He hides in the bushes.)

Valentin: Just leave it to me and don't move. I am delighted to have you as a spectator, and the enemy is turning down our path. Since you said I was crazy, I am going to show you that when it comes to preposterous behavior, the more the better. With a little skill I shall show you what honorably received wounds can contribute to attracting the fair sex. Admire this pensive walk and be so kind as to tell me if this crippled arm doesn't become me. What do you expect? If you are pale, there is nothing like it in the world:

A young convalescent, with measured step . . .

Be sure not to make any noise. This is the critical moment. Remember that you have sworn an oath. I am going to go sit under a tree, like a shepherd of olden times.
(Enter Cecile with a book in her hand.)

Valentin: Are you up already, Mademoiselle? All alone in the woods so early?

Cecile: Oh, is that you, sir? I didn't recognize you. How is your sprain doing?

Valentin: (Aside.) Sprain! What an ugly word! *(Aloud.)* It is so good of you to ask. There are certain wounds that one hardly feels at all.

Cecile: Has breakfast been brought you?

Valentin: You are too kind. Of all your sex's virtues, hospitality is the least common, and it is nowhere to be found so sweet and so precious as in you. If the concern that I am being shown . . .

Cecile: I shall go tell them to bring some broth to your room. *(Exit.)*

Van Buck: (Coming back.) You will marry her! You will marry her! Confess that she was absolutely perfect. What naïveté! What heavenly modesty! You couldn't make a better choice.

Valentin: Just a minute, Uncle, just a minute. You are jumping to conclusions.

Van Buck: Why not? That is all it takes. You can see quite clearly who you are dealing with; it will always be that way. How happy you will be with that woman! Let us go tell everything to the Baroness. I shall take responsibility for calming her down.

Valentin: Broth! How can a young lady pronounce a word like that? I don't like her. She is ugly and stupid. Good-by, uncle, I am going back to Paris.

Van Buck: Are you joking? What about your promise? How can you deceive me this way? What is the meaning of these lowered eyes, this stricken countenance? Does it mean you take me for a reprobate of your ilk, that you are profiting from my misguided good will as a cloak for your own evil designs? Is it really only seduction that you came here to attempt under the guise of a test? Good heavens, if I thought so! . . .

Valentin: I don't like her, it isn't my fault, I couldn't vouch for that.

Van Buck: What is there about her you don't like? She is pretty, if I know anything at all. She has long, well-shaped eyes, marvelous hair, not a bad figure. She is perfectly well-brought-up; she knows English and Italian; she will have an income of thirty thousand pounds and, in the meanwhile, a very fine dowry. What can you reproach her with, and why won't you have her?

Valentin: There is never any reason to give, why you like people or not. One thing is certain: I don't like either her, her sprain, or her broth.

Van Buck: It is your self-esteem that is hurt. If I hadn't been there you would have come and told me a hundred stories about your first conversation and boasted of your high hopes. You had imagined that you would make her conquest in a flash, and that smarts. You liked her yesterday evening when you had barely seen her, and she was scurrying around with her mother taking care of you after your foolish accident. Now you find her ugly because she scarcely paid attention to you. I know you better than you think, and I won't give up so quickly. I forbid you to leave.

Valentin: As you wish. I don't want anything to do with her. I repeat that I find her ugly, and she has a silly air that is revolting. She has large eyes, it is true, but they don't express a thing. She has beautiful hair, but she has a low forehead. As for her figure, that is probably her best point, even though you find it only "not bad." I congratulate her on knowing Italian, she may seem more intelligent in it than in French. As for her dowry, let her keep it; I don't want it, any more than her broth.

Van Buck: Can you imagine such a stubborn mule? Who could have expected anything like this? Go on, what I was saying yesterday is the pure truth: all you can do is dream of twaddle. I am not going to trouble with you any more. Go ahead and marry a washerwoman. Since you turn down your fortune when it is right in your hands, let chance decide the remainder. Look for it in your dice cups. God is my witness, I have been so patient these past three years that perhaps no one else, in my place . . .

Valentin: Am I mistaken? Look there, Uncle, I think she is coming back this way. Yes, I can see her through the trees. She is going to walk around the grove again.

Van Buck: Where? What is that you are saying?

Valentin: Don't you see a white dress beyond those clumps of lilacs? I am not mistaken, it really is her. Quickly, Uncle, go back into the bushes, we mustn't be caught together.

Van Buck: What is the use, since you don't like her?

Valentin: It doesn't matter, I want to talk to her again so you won't say I judged her too hastily.

Van Buck: You will marry her if she persists?

  (He hides again.)

Valentin: Shh! Not a sound, here she comes.

Cecile: (Entering.) Sir, my mother sent me to ask you if you were planning on leaving today.

Valentin: Yes, mademoiselle, that is my intention. I have asked for some horses.

Cecile: It is just that we are going to play whist in the salon, and my mother would be obliged to you if you would be a fourth.

Valentin: I am very sorry, but I don't know how to play.

Cecile: If you stay for dinner we are having pheasant with truffles.

Valentin: Thank you, but I never eat pheasant.

Cecile: After dinner some people are coming over, and we shall dance the mazurka.

Valentin: Excuse me, but I never dance.

Cecile: That is really too bad. Good-by, sir.

  (Exit.)

Van Buck: (Coming back.) Well now, let's see. Will you marry her? What does all this mean? You say you have asked for some horses. Is that so, or are you fooling me?

Valentin: You were right, she is nice. I found her better than the first time. She has a little mark at the corner of her mouth that I hadn't noticed.

Van Buck: Where are you going? What is going on? Will you answer me seriously?

Valentin: I am not going anywhere, I am going for a walk with you. Do you think she is bad-looking?

Van Buck: Who, me? God forbid! I think she is perfectly fine.

Valentin: It seems to me rather early to be playing whist. Do you play, Uncle? You ought to be going back to the castle.

Van Buck: Of course I ought to be going back. I am waiting for you to be so kind as to answer me. Are you staying here or not?

Valentin: If I stay it is because of our wager. I wouldn't want to be the one to back down. But don't count on anything for now. The pain in my arm is torturing me.

Van Buck: Come back in, you will get some rest.

Valentin: Yes, I feel like having some of that broth upstairs. I have to write a letter. I shall see you at dinner.

Van Buck: Write a letter! I hope you are not writing to her.

Valentin: If I write to her, it is because of our wager. You know that is what we agreed upon.

Van Buck: I am categorically opposed to it unless you show me the letter.

Valentin: Just as you wish. I have already told you, and I repeat, that I don't like her all that much.

Van Buck: What need is there for you to write to her? Why didn't you make your declaration orally just now, as you had decided?

Valentin: Why not?

Van Buck: Yes, why not? What was stopping you? You had all the courage in the world.

Valentin: It is just that my arm was hurting me. Look! Here she comes a third time. Do you see her over there on the path?

Van Buck: She is going around the flower bed, and the grove is circular. There is nothing at all improper in that.

Valentin: Ha! The little flirt! She is flitting around the flame like a dazzled moth. I am going to toss this coin heads or tails to see whether I shall love her.

Van Buck: Try to get her to love you first. The rest is easier.

Valentin: All right. Let's both take a good look at her. She is going to pass between those two clumps of trees. If she turns her head our way I love her. Otherwise I shall go back to Paris.

Van Buck: I bet she won't turn around.

Valentin: Oh, yes she will! Let's not lose sight of her.

Van Buck: You are right. No, not yet. She seems to be absorbed in her reading.

Valentin: I am sure she is going to turn around.

Van Buck: No, she is going on. She is getting close to the clump of trees. I am convinced she won't.

Valentin: But she must see us. There is nothing hiding us. I tell you she will turn around.

Van Buck: She has passed by. You lose.

Valentin: I am going to write her, or may the sky fall on my head! I have to know what to think. It is incredible for a young girl to treat people so lightly. It is sheer hypocrisy, just a subterfuge! I am going to send her a real letter: I shall tell her that I am dying of love for her, that I broke my arm just to see her, that if she rejects me I shall blow my brains out, and that, if she will have me, I shall carry her off tomorrow morning. Come on, let's go back in, I want to write in your presence.

Van Buck: Just a minute, nephew, what has gotten into you? You will play us some bad turn here.

Valentin: Do you really think that a few words in passing can mean anything? Did I say anything unusual to her, and did she answer me differently? It is quite normal for her not to turn around. She doesn't know anything, and I haven't managed to say anything to her. I am just an ass, if you will. It is possible that my pride has been hurt, and that my self-esteem is at stake. I don't much care whether she is beautiful or ugly; I just want to get a glimpse into her heart. There is some ruse, some bias underneath all this that we aren't aware of. Leave it to me and the whole matter will be cleared up.

Van Buck: The devil take me if you are not talking like a lover! You wouldn't by some chance be in love, would you?

Valentin: No. I told you I don't like her. Do I have to say the same thing over and over, a hundred times? Hurry up, let's go back to the castle.

Van Buck: I have told you I don't want any letters, especially not the kind you are talking of.

Valentin: Come on anyway, we shall make our minds up.

(*Exit.*)

Scene 2. *The salon.*

(*The Baroness and the curate are seated at a card table.*)

Baroness: Say what you want, it is distressing to play with a dummy. I hate being in the country because of that.

Curate: So, where is Mr. Van Buck? Hasn't he come downstairs yet?

Baroness: I saw him in the park a little while ago with that gentleman from the carriage. Parenthetically, I don't find him very polite to refuse to stay with us for dinner.

Curate: Well, if he has pressing business . . .

Baroness: Ha! Everyone has "business." A fine excuse! If people thought only of business, we would never get anywhere. Come on, Father, let's play cards; I am in the mood to make a killing.

Curate: (Shuffling the cards.) It is certain that young people, today, take no pride in being polite.

Baroness: Polite! I should think so! Do they have the slightest idea? And what would that mean, to be polite? My coachman is polite. In my day, Father, people were gallant!

Curate: Those were the days, Baroness. I wish to heaven I had been born then!

Baroness: I should just like to have seen my brother, who was one of the future king's courtiers, fall from a carriage in front of a castle, and he had been kept there overnight. He would rather have lost his fortune than refuse to play a fourth hand. Well, let's not talk about such things. It is your pick; aren't you going to throw anything out?

Curate: I don't have an ace. Here is Mr. Van Buck.
     (Enter Van Buck.)

Baroness: Let's keep going. It is your bid.

Van Buck: (Softly, to the Baroness.) Madam, I must say a few words of the greatest importance.

Baroness: All right, after the scoring.

Curate: Five cards, worth forty-five points.

Baroness: That is not enough. *(To Van Buck.)* What is it?

Van Buck: I beg you to give me a moment of your time. I can't speak in front of a third party, and what I have to tell you can't wait.

Baroness: (Standing up.) You frighten me. What is the matter?

Van Buck: Madam, it is a very serious business, and perhaps you will be angry with me. I am forced by necessity to break a promise that I made unwisely. The young man to whom you offered your hospitality last night is my nephew.

Baroness: Ha! Why in the world!?

Van Buck: He wanted to approach you without being recognized. I thought it wouldn't be wrong of me to go along with a scheme that is far from new in such situations.

Baroness: Oh, my goodness, I have seen much worse!

Van Buck: But I have to warn you that at this very moment he has written to Mademoiselle de Mantes, and in the most extravagant terms. Neither my threats nor my prayers could dissuade him from his lunacy. One of your servants, I regret to say, agreed to deliver the letter to its addressee. It is a declaration of love, and I must say, a most extravagant one.

Baroness: Really? Well, that is not so bad. That little nephew of yours has a mind of his own.

Van Buck: Good Lord, I shall vouch for that! I have known it for a long time. Still, madam, it is up to you to find a way to prevent this business from going too far. You are in your own house. As for me, I must tell you that I can't get my breath and I am about to collapse. Oof!
(He falls into a chair.)

Baroness: Heavens, what in the world is the matter with you? You are as pale as a ghost! Quickly, tell me everything that has happened, and don't keep anything secret.

Van Buck: I have told you the entire thing. I have nothing more to add.

Baroness: Hah, is that all? You have nothing to fear. If your nephew has written to Cecile, the girl will show me the letter.

Van Buck: Are you sure, Baroness? That is dangerous.

Baroness: A fine question! Things will have come to a pretty pass if a daughter doesn't show her mother a letter she has received.

Van Buck: Hum, I wouldn't swear to it.

Baroness: What are you saying, Mr. Van Buck? Do you know whom you are speaking to? What kind of society have you been living in, to utter such a doubt? I don't much know how things are done today, nor what your bourgeoisie is up to. But, upon my life, that is about enough! It just so happens that I see my daughter; you will see that she brings me her letter. Come on, Father, let us play some more.
(She starts playing again. Enter Cecile, who goes to the window, takes up her needlework, and sits down a little way off.)

Curate: Forty-five isn't enough?

Baroness: No, you have nothing. Fourteen for the ace, six and fifteen, that makes ninety-five. It is your turn to play.

Curate: Clubs. I think I am out.

Van Buck: (Softly, to the Baroness.) I don't see Mademoiselle Cecile letting you in, so far . . .

Baroness: (Softly, to Van Buck.) You don't know what you are talking about. She is embarrassed because of the curate. I am as sure of her as I am of myself. I shall just draw once more. One hundred seventeen left over. It is your deal.

Servant: (Entering.) Father, you are being asked for. It is the sacristan and the beadle, from the village.

Curate: What do they want of me? I am busy.

Baroness: Give your cards to Van Buck. He will play this hand for you.

(Exit the curate. Van Buck takes his place.)

Baroness: It is your deal, I have cut. It is easy to see that you are holding some cards. What do you have in your hand?

Van Buck: (Softly.) I confess I am uneasy. Your daughter hasn't said a word, and I don't see my nephew.

Baroness: I tell you I shall vouch for her. You are the one who is embarrassing her. I can see her signaling me from here.

Van Buck: Do you think so? I can't see a thing.

Baroness: Cecile, come over here for a moment. You are a mile away. *(Cecile draws her chair closer.)* Don't you have something to tell me, darling?

Cecile: I? No, Mother.

Baroness: Humph! I have only four cards, Van Buck. It is your point. I have three jacks.

Van Buck: Do you want me to leave you alone?

Baroness: No, please stay, it doesn't matter. Cecile, you can speak up in front of this gentleman.

Cecile: Me, Mother? I have no secrets to tell.

Baroness: You don't have to talk to me?

Cecile: No, Mother.

Baroness: This is unbelievable. What kind of stories have you been telling me, Van Buck?

Van Buck: Madam, I told you the truth.

Baroness: That just can't be. Cecile has nothing to tell me. It is clear that she hasn't received a thing.

Van Buck: (Standing up.) Well, by golly, I saw it with my own
eyes.

Baroness: (Standing up, also.) Daughter, what does this mean?
Stand up straight and look at me. What do you have in your
pocket?

Cecile: (Weeping.) But, Mother, it isn't my fault. It is that gentle-
man who wrote to me.

Baroness: Let's see it. *(Cecile gives her the letter.)* I am curious to
see the style of "that gentleman," as you call him. *(She reads.)*
"Mademoiselle, I am dying of love for you. I saw you last win-
ter and, knowing you were in the country, I resolved to see you
again or die. I gave a *louis* to my coachman . . ." Would he
like us to reimburse him? Why do we have to know that?
" . . . to my coachman, so he would overturn me in front of
your gate. I met you twice this morning, but I couldn't say any-
thing to you, your presence troubled me so. Nevertheless, my
fear of losing you and my obligation to leave the castle . . . " I
like that! Who was asking him to leave? He is the one who
refuses to stay for dinner. " . . . require that I ask you to grant
me a rendezvous. I know that I have no claim on your
trust . . . " A fine remark, and very true. " . . . but love can
excuse everything. This evening at nine, during the ball, I shall
be hiding in the woods. Everyone here will think I have left, for
I shall leave the castle in a carriage before dinner; but I shall
only go a short way and get out . . . " A short way! A short
way! My driveway is a long one. You would think it was only a
couple of steps! " . . . and get out. If you can get away during
the evening, I shall be waiting for you. Otherwise I shall blow
my brains out." Good. " . . . my brains out. I don't think your
mother . . . " Ha, your mother? Let us have a look at this.
" . . . will pay much attention to you. She is a scatterbr . . . "
Mr. Van Buck, what is the meaning of this?

Van Buck: I didn't hear, Madam.

Baroness: Read it yourself, and do me the favor of telling your
nephew to leave my house at once and never set foot in it
again.

Van Buck: It does say "scatterbrain," that is definite. I hadn't
noticed it. And yet, he read me his letter before he sealed it.

Baroness: He read you this letter, and you let him give it to my ser-
vants! Well, you are an old fool, and I never want to see you
again in my life.
(Exit. The sound of a carriage is heard.)

Van Buck: What is that? Is my nephew leaving without me? How
does he expect me to go? I have sent my horses away. I shall
have to run after him.
(Exit, running.)

Cecile: (Alone.) That is odd. Why should he write me, when
everyone is willing for him to marry me?

ACT THREE
Scene 1. *A road.*

*(Enter Van Buck with Valentin, who knocks at the door of an
inn.)*

Valentin: Hey! Ho! Is there anyone here who can run an errand
for me?

Waiter: (Coming out.) Yes, sir, if it isn't too far. You can see that it
is pouring out.

Van Buck: I am opposed to it, with all my authority and in the
name of the laws of the kingdom.

Valentin: Do you know the castle of Mantes nearby?

Waiter: Of course, sir, we go there every day. It is on the left; you
can see it from here.

Van Buck: My friend, I forbid you to go there if you have any
notion of right and wrong.

Valentin: You can earn two *louis.* Here is a letter for Mademoiselle
de Mantes: give it to her chambermaid and no one else, and
secretly. Hurry and come back.

Waiter: Oh, have no fear, sir.

Van Buck: Here are four *louis* if you refuse.

Waiter: Oh, there is no danger, your lordship.

Valentin: Here are ten *louis.* And if you don't go I shall give you a
beating with my stick.

Waiter: Oh, you can rest assured, my prince. I shall be right back.
(Exit.)

Valentin: Now, uncle, let's find shelter. If you take my advice, we shall have a glass of beer. All that running must have tired you out.

(He sits down on a bench.)

Van Buck: You can be certain that I won't leave you, I swear by my late brother's soul and the light of the sun. As long as my feet can carry me, as long as I have a head on my shoulders, I shall be opposed to this despicable act and its horrible consequences.

Valentin: You can be sure that I won't give up, I swear by my just anger and by the night that will protect me. As long as I have paper and ink and there remains a *louis* in my pocket, I shall pursue and attain my end, whatever may come of it.

Van Buck: Have you neither morals nor honor left? Can you really be of my flesh and blood? What, neither respect for innocence, nor a sense of propriety, nor the certainty that you will make me run a temperature, nothing is capable of moving you!

Valentin: Have you neither pride nor shame? Can you really be my uncle? What, neither the insult that has been done us, nor the way in which we have been thrown out, nor the insults that have been flung in your face, nothing is capable of instilling some courage in you!

Van Buck: At least if you were in love! If I could believe that such extravagance comes from a motive that had something human about it! But instead you are just a Lovelace, you exude sheer treachery, and loathsome revenge is your only desire and your only love.

Valentin: At least if I saw you curse! If I could tell myself that at the bottom of your heart you don't give a damn for that Baroness and her crowd! But instead you are just afraid of the rain, you are thinking of nothing but the bad weather, and concern for your silk stockings is your only fear and your only torment.

Van Buck: Ah, people are so right when they say that the first sin leads to a precipice! Who could have told me this morning, when the barber had shaved me and I had put on my new coat, that this evening I would be in a barn, caked with mud and soaked to the skin! What, is this me! Good Lord, at my age, to have to leave my post chaise, which we were settled in so comfortably; to have to run across the fields out in the country, after a madman! To have to drag myself at his heels like a confidant in some tragedy, and the result of all this perspiration will be my family's dishonor!

Valentin: On the contrary, we could only dishonor ourselves by retreat, but not by a glorious campaign from which we can only emerge victorious. You may blush, Uncle Van Buck, but let it be with a noble indignation! You call me Lovelace: yes, by heaven, that name suits me! Just like him, I have had a door surmounted by a proud escutcheon slammed in my face; like him, an odious family thinks it can crush me with an insult; like him, like a sparrow hawk, I rove and I soar about the country; but, like him, I shall seize my prey and, like Clarissa, my sublime prude, my beloved, will be mine.

Van Buck: Oh, heavens, why am I not back in Antwerp, seated before my counter in my leather armchair, rolling out my taffeta! Why didn't my brother die a bachelor, rather than get married when he was over forty! Or rather, why didn't I die myself, the first day the Baroness of Mantes invited me to lunch!

Valentin: You should regret only the moment when, through a fatal weakness, you revealed the secret of our agreement to that woman. You are the one who caused the commotion. Stop insulting me, I shall set everything right again. Can you doubt that a young girl who hides love letters so well in her apron pockets would come to a rendezvous? Yes, she would certainly have come. So she is even more certain to come this time. By my patron saint, I look forward to seeing her come downstairs in her nightgown, her nightcap, and her little slippers, from that great rusty-brick barracks! I don't love her, but even if I did, revenge would be stronger and would stifle love in my heart. I swear that she will be my mistress, but will never be my wife. There is no longer any test, or promise, or alternative. I want this family to remember forever the day they threw me out.

Innkeeper: (*Coming out of the house.*) Gentlemen, the sun is starting to go down. Won't you do me the honor of dining at my place?

Valentin: Why, yes. Bring us the menu, and have a fire lit for us. As soon as your waiter comes back tell him to give me the reply. Come on, Uncle, chin up. Come and order dinner.

Van Buck: They probably have appalling wine, I know the region. It is a horrid vinegar.

Innkeeper: Excuse me. We have champagne, chambertin, or anything you may desire.

Van Buck: Really? In a hole like this? It is not possible, you are joking.

Innkeeper: The mail coach stops here. You will see if we lack anything.

Van Buck: Come on, then, let's try and have dinner. I feel that my death is imminent; in a little while I shan't be dining any more. *(Exit.)*

Scene 2. *At the castle. A salon.*

(Enter the Baroness and the curate.)

Baroness: God be praised, my daughter is locked in. I think I shall be ill from all this.

Curate: Madam, if I may be permitted to give you some advice, I must tell you that I am deeply worried. As I went across the courtyard, I thought I saw a quite nasty-looking man, wearing a smock, with a letter in his hand.

Baroness: The door is locked; there is nothing to fear. Help me with this ball a little, I don't have the strength to deal with it.

Curate: In such grave circumstances, couldn't you postpone your plans?

Baroness: Are you mad? Do you want me to have all of Saint-Germain come out from Paris, only to say "No, thank you" and shut my door in their faces? Just think for a moment about what you are saying!

Curate: I thought that on such an occasion one might, without hurting anyone's feelings . . .

Baroness: And in the midst of everything else, I am all out of candles! Please go see if Dupré is here.

Curate: I think he is doing the syrups.

Baroness: You are right. Those damned syrups, that is another thing that will drive me to my grave. I wrote myself, a week ago, and they just arrived an hour ago. I ask you, can people drink such a thing!

Curate: Baroness, that man in the smock is some sort of emissary, you can be sure of it. It seems to me, as far as I can remember, that one of your women was chatting with him. That young man from yesterday is a troublemaker, and you can be sure that the sharp manner in which you got rid of him . . .

Baroness: Hah! Van Bucks? Cloth merchants? What do you think people like that can do? Even if they shouted, would anyone hear them? I have to move the furniture out of the little salon. I shall never have enough seats for everyone I have invited.

Curate: Is your daughter locked in her bedroom, Madam?

Baroness: Ten plus ten make twenty. The Raimbaults are four; ten, thirty. What did you say, Father?

Curate: I just asked whether Mademoiselle Cecile is locked up in her beautiful yellow bedroom, Baroness?

Baroness: No, she is there in the library. It is even better, I can keep track of her. I don't know what she is doing or whether she is being dressed, and now my migraine is coming on.

Curate: Would you like me to speak with her?

Baroness: I told you the door is locked. What is done is done. There is nothing we can do.

Curate: I think it was her chambermaid who was chatting with that oaf. Please believe me, I beg you: there is some snake in the grass here that you mustn't ignore.

Baroness: I absolutely have to go to the pantry. This is the last time I shall entertain here.
(Exit.)

Curate: *(Alone.)* I thought I heard a noise in the room adjoining this salon. Might it not be the girl? Dear me, this is unexpected!

Cecile: *(Outside.)* Father, will you open the door for me?

Curate: I can't, Mademoiselle, not without previous authorization.

Cecile: *(As above.)* The key is there under the sofa cushion. All you have to do is get it and open the door.

Curate: (Getting the key.) You are right, Mademoiselle, the key is indeed where you said. But I cannot in any way use it, despite all my personal feelings.

Cecile: (As above.) Oh, my Lord, I am going to faint!

Curate: Good Lord! Pull yourself together. I shall go and summon the Baroness. Can a grievous accident have stricken you so suddenly? In heaven's name, Mademoiselle, answer me, what is the matter?

Cecile: (As above.) I am going to faint! I am going to faint!

Curate: I just can't let such a charming person expire this way. Goodness, I shall have to take it upon myself to open the door, whatever people may say.
(He opens the door.)

Cecile: Goodness, Father, I shall take it upon myself to run away, whatever people may say.
(She runs off.)

Scene 3. *In the woods.*

(Enter Van Buck and Valentin.)

Valentin: The moon is rising, and the storm is passing. Look at these beads of water on the leaves; how this warm wind rolls them off! The sand hardly shows our tracks; the gravel is dry and has already absorbed the rain.

Van Buck: For a chance inn we didn't dine badly at all. I needed that blazing fire; my old legs are perked up again. Well, my boy, are we getting there?

Valentin: This is where we stop. But if you take my advice, you will keep on now as far as that farm over there with the light in its windows. Sit by the fire and order us a big bowl of hot wine with sugar and cinnamon.

Van Buck: You won't be long, will you? How long are you going to stay here? At least remember your promises and try to be ready when the horses are.

Valentin: I swear to you that I won't undertake any more or any less than we agreed to. You see how I am yielding to you in everything, Uncle, and how I am following your wishes. As a matter of fact, now that I have eaten on it, I do feel that anger can be a bad companion. Both sides have given in. You allow me a quarter-hour of flirting, and I shall give up all claim to revenge. The girl will go back home, we shall go back to Paris, and that will be that. As for the hated Baroness, I shall forgive and forget her.

Van Buck: That is wonderful! And don't be afraid you will lack for women on that account. Let no one say that a crazy old woman can harm decent people who have amassed a considerable fortune and who aren't bad-looking. By God, there is a fine moon shining; it reminds me of my youth.

Valentin: The letter I just received isn't all that silly, do you know? The girl has wit and even something better. Yes, there is feeling in those few lines, something tender and yet bold, chaste and yet at the same time courageous. The rendezvous she is granting me is like her letter, moreover. Look at this thicket, this sky, this bit of greenery in such a wild place. Ah, the heart is a great teacher! No one can ever invent what it finds, and it alone chooses all.

Van Buck: I remember when I was in The Hague and I had an adventure of this sort. My goodness, she was a fine-looking girl, five feet some inches tall, with a lusty pair of . . . What Venuses those Flemish women are! You can't tell what a woman is like now. With all those Parisian beauties, it is half flesh and half cotton.

Valentin: I think I see lights moving around over there in the woods. What could that mean? Can they be searching for us now?

Van Buck: It is probably that they are getting ready for the ball. There is a party at the castle this evening.

Valentin: Let's each go our separate way for safety: I shall see you in half an hour at the farm.

Van Buck: As you say. Good luck, my boy. You will tell me all about your affair and we shall make up a song about it. That was the way we used to do things: no escapade without some verse.

(He sings.)

> Ah, yes indeed, Mademoiselle,
> Ah, yes indeed, we shall be three!
> *(Exit Valentin. Men bearing torches are seen roaming through the forest. Enter the Baroness and the curate.)*

Baroness: It is as clear as can be, she is mad. She was seized by a dizzy spell.

Curate: She called out to me, "I feel ill," so you can imagine my situation.

Van Buck: (Singing.)
> And so it is true,
> My charming Colette,
> And so it is true
> That for your fête
> Colin gave you . . .
> Those flowers blue.*

Baroness: And just at that moment I see a carriage arrive. I barely had time to call Dupré. Dupré wasn't there. People were coming in, so I went downstairs. It was the Countess of Hicksvale and the Baron of Dungburg.

Curate: The first time I heard her call, I hesitated. But what can you do? I could just see her there, lying on the ground, unconscious. She was shouting at the top of her lungs, and the key was near at hand.

Van Buck: (Singing.)
> When he gave it to you,
> My charming brunette,
> When he gave it to you,
> My dainty Colette,
> They say you were taken . . .
> By a fit of shakin'.

Baroness: Can you imagine that? I ask you: my daughter running off across the fields, and thirty carriages arriving at the same time! I shall never recover from a moment like that.

---

*This "risqué" drinking song, evidently from Van Buck's youth, is translated freely. Its effect depends primarily on the innuendo suggested by the ellipses in the next-to-last line of each stanza. The main reason for its presence is to illustrate Van Buck's inebriation.

Curate: If only I had had time, I might perhaps have held her back
by her scarf . . . or at least . . . well, by my prayers, by my
well-chosen remarks.

Van Buck: Now just try to swear
> By heaven above,
> Now just try to swear
> That you really don't love
> A faithful young man . . .
> To give you a fan.

Baroness: Is that you, Van Buck? Oh, my dear friend, we are lost.
What does all this mean? My daughter is mad, she is running
across the fields! Can you imagine such a thing? I have forty
people at my house, and here I am out on foot in weather like
this. You didn't see her in the woods? She has run away, it is all
like a bad dream. Her hair was combed and powdered on one
side, or so her chambermaid told me. She went out wearing
white satin slippers. She knocked the curate down as he stood
there, and ran right over him. I am going to die! My servants
can't find a thing; there are no two ways about it, I must go
back. It isn't by any chance your nephew playing a trick like
this on us, is it? I was abrupt with you; let's not talk about it
any more. Here, come help me and let's make up. You are my
old friend, aren't you? I am a mother, Van Buck. Oh, cruel for-
tune, cruel fate! What have I done to deserve this?
(She starts to cry.)

Van Buck: Is it possible, Baroness? You, alone, on foot, looking
for your daughter! Good Lord, you are crying! Oh, what a
wretch I am!

Curate: Could you know anything about it, sir? I beg you, illumi-
nate this for us.

Van Buck: Come, Baroness, take my arm and, God willing, we
shall find them! I shall tell you everything. Don't be afraid. My
nephew is a man of honor, and everything can still be mended.

Baroness: Ah, so it was a rendezvous? The little minx! Whom can
one trust now?
(Exit.)

Scene 4. *A clearing in the woods.*

(Enter Cecile and Valentin.)

Valentin: Who is there? Cecile, is it you?

Cecile: It is me. What is the meaning of those torches and lights in the woods?

Valentin: I don't know. What does it matter? It isn't for us.

Cecile: Come over here where the moon is shining. Over here, where you see this rock.

Valentin: No, come over here where it is dark. Over here, in the shadow of these birches. They may be looking for you, and we must not be seen.

Cecile: I wouldn't see your face. Come on, Valentin, be good.

Valentin: Wherever you want, charming girl.* Wherever you go, I shall follow you. Don't take that trembling hand away from me, let my lips reassure it.

Cecile: I couldn't come sooner. Have you been waiting for me long?

Valentin: Since the moon has been up. See how this letter is moistened with tears. It is the note that you sent me, my darling.

Cecile: Liar, it is the wind and the rain that have wept on this paper.

Valentin: No, my Cecile, it is joy and love, it is happiness and desire. What is worrying you, my dearest? Why are you glancing about? What are you looking for?

Cecile: That is strange, I think I am lost. Where is your uncle? I thought I saw him here.

Valentin: My uncle is drunk on burgundy. Your mother is far away, darling, and all is still. This place is the one you chose, and that your letter indicated to me.

Cecile: Your uncle is drunk? Why did he hide in the bushes this morning?

Valentin: This morning? Where, darling? What do you mean? I was walking by myself in the garden.

*Valentin begins to address Cecile with the intimate *tu* here (see the note on act 1, scene 2). Cecile, however, continues to use the formal *vous* in reply. I have rendered this difference in English by Valentin's frequent use of terms of endearment.

Cecile: This morning when I spoke to you your uncle was behind a tree. Didn't you know? I saw him when I turned down the path.

Valentin: You must have been mistaken, my sweet. I didn't notice a thing.

Cecile: Oh, I saw him all right. He was peeping through the branches; perhaps it was to spy on us.

Valentin: What nonsense, you must have dreamed it! Let's not talk of that any more. Give me a kiss.

Cecile: Yes, my love, with all my heart. Sit down here next to me. Why in the world did you speak ill of my mother in your letter yesterday?

Valentin: Forgive me, it was a moment of delirium; I wasn't in control of myself.

Cecile: She asked me for that letter, and I didn't dare show it to her. I knew what was going to happen. But who had told her? She couldn't have guessed anything, the letter was right there in my pocket.

Valentin: My poor child! You have been mistreated. It must be your chambermaid who gave you away. Who can you trust at a time like that?

Cecile: Oh, no! My chambermaid is sure. There was no need for you to give her money. But when you were disrespectful to my mother, you must have realized that you were to me, as well.

Valentin: Let's not talk about it any more, since you have forgiven me. Let's not spoil such a precious moment. Oh, my Cecile, how beautiful you are, and what happiness lies within you! By what oaths, by what treasures can I repay your sweet caresses? Oh, a lifetime would not be long enough. Come to my bosom, let your heart feel mine beating, and let this clear sky carry them both off to God!

Cecile: Yes, Valentin, my heart is sincere. Just feel how soft my hair is. I have iris powder on that side, but I didn't have time to put it on the other. Why in the world did you hide your name when you came to our house?

Valentin: I can't tell you. It was a whim, a wager that I had made.

Cecile: A wager? With whom?

Valentin: I have no idea now. What does such nonsense matter?

Cecile: Perhaps it was your uncle. Was it?

Valentin: Yes. I loved you, and I wanted to get to know you without anyone coming between us.

Cecile: You are right. If I had been you, I would have wanted to do the same.

Valentin: Why are you so curious, darling? What is the use of all these questions? Don't you love me, my beautiful Cecile? Just say yes and forget all the rest.

Cecile: Yes, dear, yes, Cecile loves you, and she wishes she were more worthy of being loved. But it is enough for her to be loved by you. Put your hands in mine. Why did you say no before, when I invited you to dinner?

Valentin: I wanted to leave. I had business this evening.

Cecile: Not such important business, or so distant, as far as I can tell; for you got out at the end of the driveway.

Valentin: You saw me? How do you know?

Cecile: Oh, I was watching. Why did you tell me you don't dance the mazurka? I saw you dance it last winter.

Valentin: Where? I don't remember that.

Cecile: At Madame de Gesvres's masked ball. How come you don't remember? You told me in your letter yesterday that you had seen me last winter. That was where it was.

Valentin: You are right, darling. I remember. Just see how pure this night is! How the breeze lifts from your shoulders the jealous filmy cloth that cloaks them! Just listen! It is the voice of the night, the song of a bird calling us to happiness. Behind this towering boulder no glance can discover us. All is asleep except for those in love. Let my hand take off this veil and my two arms replace it.

Cecile: Yes, dear. I hope I seem beautiful to you! But don't take your hand away from me. I feel that my heart is in mine, and it goes to yours that way. Why did you want to leave, and pretend to be going to Paris?

Valentin: I had to. It was for my uncle. Anyhow, could I dare foresee that you would come to this rendezvous? Oh, how I trembled as I wrote that letter, and how I suffered as I waited for you.

Cecile: Why wouldn't I have come, since I know that you are going to marry me? *(Valentin stands up and takes a few steps.)*

What is the matter? Is something troubling you? Come back
and sit down beside me.

Valentin: It is nothing; I thought . . . I thought I heard . . . I
thought I saw someone over there.

Cecile: We are alone; don't be afraid. Come on. Should I get up?
Did I say something that hurt you? Your face is no longer the
same as it was. Is it because I kept my shawl on although you
wanted me to take it off? It is just that it is cold and I am wear-
ing my ball gown. Just look at my satin slippers. What is poor
Henriette going to think? What is the matter? You don't an-
swer, and you are sad. What in the world can I have said to
you? It is my fault, I can see.

Valentin: No, I swear to you, Cecile,* you are wrong. It was an
involuntary thought that just went through my mind.

Cecile: Just a while ago you kept saying "darling" to me, and even
a little bit carelessly, I think. What was the disagreeable
thought that suddenly struck you? Did I do something you
don't like? I am very sorry if I did. But I don't think I said any-
thing wrong. Still, if you prefer to walk I won't stay seated.
(She stands up.) Give me your arm and let's walk around. Do
you know something? This morning I had some good broth
that Henriette made brought up to your room. When I met you
I told you so. I thought you didn't want to drink it and you
didn't like it. I went back along the path three times; did you
see me? Then you went upstairs; I went and stood at the edge
of the lawn, and I saw you through your window. You were
holding the cup in both hands, and you drank it down in one
gulp. Is that true? Did you like it?

Valentin: Yes, my dear child, it was the best in the world, as good
as your heart and yourself.†

Cecile: Oh, when we are husband and wife I shall take better care
of you than that. But tell me, what in the world does it mean
for you to go and throw yourself into the ditch? You could
have gotten killed, and what for? You knew you would be wel-

*Valentin uses *vous* here.
†He reverts to *tu* at this point, but the tone intended is different—protective and
perhaps somewhat paternalistic.

come in our house. I can understand your wanting to arrive all alone; but what good was the rest? Do you like novels?

Valentin: Sometimes. Let's go sit down again.

(They sit down again.)

Cecile: I confess that I don't much like them. The ones I have read are meaningless. It seems to me they are just a pack of lies, and everything in them is made up. All they talk of is seduction, ruses, intrigues, a thousand impossible things. The only thing that interests me is the scenery: I like the landscapes but not the descriptions. Take this evening, for example; when I got your letter and saw that it was about a rendezvous in the woods, it is true that I gave in to a desire to come here that is a little like in a novel. But it is just that I also found something to my advantage in real life. If my mother knew, and she will, you understand that they will have to let us get married. Whether or not your uncle is on bad terms with her, they will have to make up. I was ashamed of being locked in. As a matter of fact, why should I have been? The curate came, I played dead, he opened the door for me, and I ran off. That was my trick; I shall give it to you for what it is worth.

Valentin: (Aside.) Am I a fox caught in his own trap, or a fool who has recovered his reason?

Cecile: Well, you haven't answered me. Is this sadness going to last forever?

Valentin: You seem to me very wise for your age, and at the same time just as dizzy as I am, and I am as mad as a March hare.

Cecile: As for dizzy, I have to admit it. But it is because I love you, dear. Shall I tell you? I knew you loved me, and it is not just since yesterday that I have suspected it. I saw you only three times at that ball, but I am sentimental and I remember. You waltzed with Mademoiselle de Gesvres, and going through the doorway her Italian hairpin struck the panel, and her hair came undone over her shoulders. Do you remember now? Thoughtless man! The first words of your letter said that you remembered. So how my heart beat! Why, that is what proves you are in love, believe me, and that is why I am here now.

Valentin: (Aside.) Either I have my arm around the trickiest demon that hell ever vomited forth, or the voice talking to me is an angel's, and is opening the way to paradise for me.

Cecile: As for wise, that is another question, but I want to answer, since you won't say anything. Look, do you know what that is?

Valentin: What? That star to the right of the tree?

Cecile: No, the one that you can scarcely see, and is shining like a tear.

Valentin: You have read Madame de Staël?

Cecile: Yes, and I like that word, *tear,* I don't know why, like the stars. A beautiful, clear sky makes me feel like weeping.

Valentin: And me like loving you, like telling you about it and living for you. Cecile, do you know who you are speaking to, and what kind of man it is who dares to kiss you?

Cecile: First tell me the name of my star. You can't get off so easily.

Valentin: All right; it is Venus, the star of love, the finest pearl in the ocean of night.

Cecile: No, it isn't. It is a chaster one, and more worthy of respect. You will learn to love it some day, when you live on the farm and have your own poor people. Admire it, and be sure not to laugh: it is Ceres, the goddess of bread.

Valentin: My sweet child, I am beginning to understand your heart. You do charitable works, don't you?

Cecile: It is my mother who taught me. There isn't a better woman in the world.

Valentin: Really? I should never have guessed.

Cecile: Oh, neither you nor many others realize how good she is, dear. People who have seen my mother for a little while think they can judge her by a few random words. She spends the day playing cards and the evening doing needlework. She wouldn't leave her card game for a prince; but if Dupré comes and whispers to her, you will see her get up from the table if there is a beggar waiting. So many times we have gone together in silk dresses, as I am here, along the paths in the valley, bringing soup and boiled beef, shoes and linen to poor people! So many times I have seen the eyes of the unfortunate brimming with tears in church, when my mother looked at them! You know, she has a right to be proud, and I have often been proud of her.

Valentin: You are still looking at the celestial tear. I am, too, but in your blue eyes.

Cecile: How great the sky is! How happy this world is! How calm and benevolent nature is!

Valentin: So, do you want me to teach you science, and talk to you of astronomy? Tell me: In that cloud of worlds up there is there one that doesn't know its path, that hasn't received its mission together with its life, and is not destined to die fulfilling it? Why isn't this immense sky motionless? Tell me: If there ever was a moment in which everything was created, by dint of what force were these endlessly moving worlds set in motion?

Cecile: By eternal thought.

Valentin: By eternal love. The hand that has suspended them in space wrote just one word, in letters of flame. They live because they attract one another, and the suns would fall to dust if one of them stopped loving.

Cecile: Oh, all of life is in that!

Valentin: Yes, all of life—from the ocean rising under the pale kisses of Diana down to the scarab beetle falling asleep in its jealously guarded flower. Ask the woods and the rocks what they would say if they could speak. They have love in their hearts and can't express it. I love you, that is all I know, my dear. That is what the flower will tell you, as it chooses in the heart of the earth the juices that can feed it, as it refuses and rejects the impure elements that might tarnish its purity! It knows that it must be beautiful by daylight, and it must die in its wedding dress under the sun that created it. I know less than it does about astronomy. Give me your hand; you know more about love.

Cecile: I hope at least that my wedding dress won't be fatally beautiful. It seems to me someone is prowling around us.

Valentin: No, all is still. Aren't you afraid? Did you come here without trembling?

Cecile: Why? What should I have been afraid of? Was it you, or the night?

Valentin: Why not me? What assurance do you have? I am young, you are beautiful, and we are alone.

Cecile: Well, what harm is there in that?

Valentin: You are right, there is no harm. Listen to me, and let me kneel down.

Cecile: What is the matter? You are trembling.

Valentin: I am shivering with fear and joy, for I am going to open my heart to you. I am a fool of the worst sort, even though what I am going to confess to you is just something to shrug at. I have done nothing but gamble, drink, and smoke ever since I got my wisdom teeth. You have told me that novels shock you. I have read a lot of them, and the worst ones, too. There is one entitled *Clarissa Harlowe*; I shall give it to you to read when you are my wife. The hero loves a beautiful girl like you, my dear, and he wants to marry her. But first he wants to test her. He abducts her and carries her off to London; after that, since she resists, Bedford arrives . . . I mean Tomlinson, a captain . . . I mean Morden . . . no, I am mistaken . . . Well, to make a long story short . . . Lovelace is a fool and so am I, to have wanted to follow his example . . . Praise God, you didn't understand! . . . I love you, I am marrying you. Nothing else in the world matters but babbling of love.

(Enter Van Buck, the Baroness, the curate, and several servants carrying torches.)

Baroness: I don't believe a word you are saying. He is too young for such a black deed.

Van Buck: Alas, madam, it is the truth!

Baroness: Seduce my daughter! Deceive a child! Dishonor an entire family! Nonsense! I tell you it is balderdash. People don't do things like that any more. Look, there they are, kissing! Good evening, son-in-law. Where the devil have you been hiding?

Curate: It is too bad that it has taken so long for us to discover them. All your guests must have left by now.

Van Buck: Well, nephew, I certainly hope that with your foolish wager . . .

Valentin: Uncle, you never can tell. And what is more, you should never wager on anything, with anyone.

THE END

A Passing Fancy

A Passing Fancy was written in May 1837, published in the *Revue des deux mondes* of 15 June, performed in Saint Petersburg in December 1843 (by the Russian actress Karatyghina, who had it translated for herself), and played for the first time in French, at the Comédie Française, by her friend Madame Allan-Despréaux on 27 November 1847. This production marked the first success of Musset's plays in the Paris theater; it also led to an unhappy love affair between the author and his Madame de Léry.

Despite the play's nonproverbial title (*Un Caprice,* in French), its closing line, pronounced by the husband, Monsieur de Chavigny (*"un jeune curé fait les meilleurs sermons,"* "a young preacher gives the best sermons"), links this work quite clearly to the proverb genre, as with *You Never Can Tell* and *A Door Has to Be either Open or Shut.* Here, only a few years after Musset's major plays, we can see a worldly, rather cynical notion of love—conjugal love—characteristic of the author's "maturity."

CHARACTERS

Monsieur de Chavigny	*Madame de Léry*
Mathilde, his wife	A servant

The scene is Mathilde's bedroom.
Scene 1.

(Mathilde is alone, tatting.)
Mathilde: One more stitch and it is done. *(She rings; a servant enters.)* Has anyone come from Janisset's?
Servant: No, madam, not yet.
Mathilde: That is intolerable. I want someone to go back there; hurry up. *(Exit servant.)* I ought to have taken any old tassels. It is

196

eight o'clock; he is getting dressed, and I am sure he will come in before everything is ready. Then it will get done one day later. *(She stands up.)* Making a purse in secret for one's husband would seem more than a bit romantic to a lot of of people. After a year of marriage! What would Madame de Léry, for example, say about this if she knew of it? And what will he think of it himself? Well, perhaps he will laugh at all the mystery, but he won't laugh at the present. Why so much mystery, in any case? I don't know. I don't think I could have worked with such enthusiasm in front of him. It would have seemed like saying: "You see how I am thinking of you." It would be like a reproach, whereas when I show him my little task all done, he is the one who will say to himself that I have been thinking of him.

Servant: (Coming back in.) This has come for madam from the jeweler's. *(He gives a little package to Mathilde.)*

Mathilde: At last! *(She sits back down.)* Let me know when Monsieur de Chavigny is coming. *(Exit servant.)* So, my dear little purse, we are going to give you the finishing touches. Let's see, will you be attractive with these tassels? Not bad. Now, how will you be received? Will you tell how much pleasure was felt in making you, how much care was taken in dressing you up? You are unexpected, young lady. We didn't want to show you without all your frills. Will you get a kiss for your trouble? *(She kisses her purse, then stops.)* Poor little thing! You aren't worth much, you wouldn't sell for two *louis*. Why should I find it sad to part with you? Weren't you meant to be finished as quickly as possible? Oh, you were begun more joyfully than I am completing you. And yet it's been only two weeks; only two weeks, is it possible? No, no more than that; and so much has occurred in two weeks! Are we arriving too late, little one? . . . Why should I have such ideas? I think someone is coming. It is him! He still loves me!

Servant: (Entering.) The Count is coming, madam.

Mathilde: Oh, my Lord! I have put only one tassel on, and I forgot the other one. What a silly goose! I shan't be able to give it to him again today! Let him wait a moment, a minute, in the salon. Quick, before he comes in . . .

Servant: Here he comes, madam. *(Exit. Mathilde hides her purse.)*

Scene 2.

(Mathilde and Chavigny.)

Chavigny: Good evening, my dear. Am I disturbing you?*

Mathilde: Me, Henri? What a question!

Chavigny: You look troubled, preoccupied. I always forget I am your husband, when I come into your room, and so I open the door too quickly.

Mathilde: There is a bit of naughtiness in that, but since there is a bit of love, too, I shall give you a kiss nonetheless. *(She kisses him.)* Who do you think you are, my dear sir, when you forget you are my husband?

Chavigny: Your lover, my fair one. Am I wrong?

Mathilde: Lover and friend, you are not wrong. *(Aside.)* I feel like giving him the purse just as it is.

Chavigny: What is this dress you have on? Aren't you going out?

Mathilde: No, I wanted . . . I was hoping that perhaps . . .

Chavigny: You were hoping? . . . What in the world is it?

Mathilde: Are you going to the ball? You are so elegant.

Chavigny: Not that much. I don't know whether it is my fault or my tailor's, but I don't cut the same figure I did in the regiment.

Mathilde: You fickle man! You aren't thinking of me when you look at yourself in the mirror.

Chavigny: Hah! Who else? Am I going to the ball to dance? I swear to you that it is a chore, and I don't know why I drag myself there.

Mathilde: Well, then, stay home, I beg you. We shall be alone, and I shall tell you . . .

Chavigny: I think your clock must be fast. It can't be that late.

Mathilde: No one goes to the ball at this hour, whatever the clock says. We have just gotten up from dinner.

Chavigny: I told them to get the carriage ready. I have to stop off on the way.

Mathilde: Oh, that is different. I . . . I didn't know . . . I had thought . . .

---

*Chavigny and Mathilde use the formal, aristocratic *vous* in speaking with each other.

Chavigny: Well?

Mathilde: I had supposed . . . from what you were saying . . . But the clock is right; it is only eight o'clock. Grant me just a moment. I have a little surprise for you.

Chavigny: (Standing up.) You know, my dear, that I leave you free, and you go out when you feel like it. It is only fair for it to be reciprocal, don't you think? What is the surprise?

Mathilde: Nothing. I don't think I used that word.

Chavigny: I must be mistaken, then, I thought I had heard it. Do you have those Strauss waltzes here? Lend them to me if you don't need them.

Mathilde: Here they are. Do you want them now?

Chavigny: Why, yes, if that isn't any trouble. Someone asked to borrow them for a day or two. I won't deprive you of them for very long.

Mathilde: Are they for Madame de Blainville?

Chavigny: (Taking the waltzes.) Excuse me? Were you speaking of Madame de Blainville?

Mathilde: Me? No! I didn't speak of her.

Chavigny: This time I heard you right. *(He sits down again.)* What are you saying about Madame de Blainville?

Mathilde: I thought that my waltzes were for her.

Chavigny: And why did you think that?

Mathilde: Why, because . . . because she likes them.

Chavigny: Yes, and so do I. You too, don't you? There is one of them, especially; what is it like? I have forgotten . . . How does it go?

Mathilde: I don't know whether I shall remember. *(She sits down at the piano and plays.)*

Chavigny: That is the one! It is charming, heavenly, and you play it like an angel or, to put it better, like a true waltzer.

Mathilde: As well as she does, Henri?

Chavigny: Whom do you mean? Madame de Blainville? You just can't seem to get her out of your mind.

Mathilde: Oh, not really. If I were a man, she is not the one who would turn my head.

Chavigny: And you would be right, madam. A man must never let either a woman or a waltz turn his head.

Mathilde: Are you planning to gamble this evening, dear?

Chavigny: Oh, my dear, what sort of an idea is that? People gamble, but they don't "plan to gamble."

Mathilde: Do you have any gold pieces in your pockets?

Chavigny: Perhaps I do. Do you want some?

Mathilde: What, me? Heavens! Whatever could I do with it?

Chavigny: Why not? I may open your door too quickly, but at least I don't open your desk drawers, in which I am perhaps doubly wrong.

Mathilde: You are lying, sir. Not long ago I noticed that you had opened them, and you leave me far too much.

Chavigny: Not at all, my dear, not as long as there are poor people. I know how you use your fortune, and I ask you to let me give charity through your hands.

Mathilde: My dearest Henri! How noble and kind you* are! Tell me, do you remember one day when you had a little debt to pay, and you complained that you didn't have a purse?

Chavigny: When was that? Oh, that is right. The fact is that, when you go out, it is unbearable to have to trust pockets that barely hold on . . .

Mathilde: Would you like a red purse with a black net?

Chavigny: No, I don't like red. My word! You remind me, it just so happens I have a brand new purse I got yesterday. It is a gift. What do you† think of it? *(He draws a purse from his pocket.)* Is it in good taste?

Mathilde: Let's see. Will you show it to me?

Chavigny: Here. *(He hands it to her; she looks at it, then gives it back to him.)*

Mathilde: It is very pretty. What color is it?

Chavigny: (Laughing.) What color? That is a wonderful question.

Mathilde: I am mistaken . . . I mean . . . Who gave it to you?

Chavigny: Oh, that is just too funny! My word, your absent-mindedness is adorable.

---

*Mathilde changes here to the intimate *tu,* expressing her sentiment for her husband; he replies in kind.

†Henri's return at this point to the formal *vous* seems to reflect his distraction from thinking about his wife, or perhaps his sense of guilt. The couple, as well as Madame de Léry, use this form throughout the remainder of the play.

Servant: (*Announcing.*) Madame de Léry.

Mathilde: I said not to open my door.

Chavigny: No, no, let her come in. Why not receive her?

Mathilde: Well, at long last, sir, may I know the name of that purse's maker?

Scene 3.

(*Mathilde, Chavigny, and Madame de Léry dressed in her ball gown.*)

Chavigny: Come in, madam, come in, please do. You couldn't have come at a better time. Mathilde has just made a slip of the tongue that is truly worth its weight in gold. Just imagine: I showed her this purse . . .

Léry: Well! That is quite nice. Let me see it.

Chavigny: I showed her this purse, she looked at it, felt it, turned it over, and as she gave it back to me, do you know what she said? She asked me what color it was!

Léry: Why, it is blue!

Chavigny: Yes, it is blue! . . . That is quite obvious . . . That is precisely what is so funny. Can you imagine anyone asking?

Léry: How delightful. Good evening, my dear Mathilde. Are you coming to the ambassador's this evening?

Mathilde: No, I am planning to stay home.

Chavigny: But you are not laughing at my story?

Léry: Of course I am. And who made this purse? Oh, I recognize it, it is Madame de Blainville's. What, you are really not going out?

Chavigny: (*Brusquely.*) What do you recognize it by, if you don't mind?

Léry: Precisely the fact that it is blue. I have seen it dragging about for ages. It took seven years to make, so you can imagine whether it changed beneficiaries during all that time. It has belonged provisionally to three people I know. You have a treasure there, Monsieur de Chavigny. That is quite a legacy you have come into.

Chavigny: You would think there was only one purse in all the world.

Léry: No, but there is only one blue one. First of all, I find blue
hideous. It doesn't mean a thing, it is a stupid color. I can't
mistake something like that, I only have to see it once. As
much as I adore lilac, I detest blue.

Mathilde: It is the color of constancy.

Léry: Humph! It is the color of hairdressers. I am just passing by,
as you can see, I am in full regalia. You have to arrive early in
this country. It is so crowded you could break your ribs in
the crush. So, why aren't you coming? I wouldn't miss it for the
world.

Mathilde: I didn't think of it, and now it is too late.

Léry: Not at all, you have all the time in the world. Well, my dear,
I am going to ring. Ask for a dress. We shall put Monsieur de
Chavigny out the door with his little article. I shall do your
hair, I shall pin two sprigs of flowers on you, and I shall carry
you off in my carriage. Come now, that will take care of the
whole business.

Mathilde: Not this evening. I am definitely staying home.

Léry: Definitely! Have you made up your mind? Monsieur de Cha-
vigny, please bring Mathilde.

Chavigny: (With irritation.) I don't meddle in anyone's business.

Léry: Oh, oh! Apparently you like blue. Well, listen. Do you know
what I am going to do? Give me some tea and I shall stay here.

Mathilde: You are so sweet, my dear Ernestine! No, I don't want
to deprive the ball of its queen. Go have a waltz for me, and
come back at eleven o'clock, if you think of it. We shall have a
nice chat by the fireside, since Monsieur de Chavigny is desert-
ing us.

Chavigny: What, me? Not at all. I don't know whether I shall go
out.

Léry: All right, it is agreed, I shall leave you. By the way, have you
heard about my misfortune? I have been robbed, just like on
the highway.

Mathilde: Robbed? What do you mean?

Léry: Four dresses, my dear, four darling dresses that I had coming
from London, lost to customs. If you had only seen them, it is
enough to make you cry. One was turquoise, and one was puce;
they will never make anything else like them.

Mathilde: I pity you quite sincerely. Were they confiscated, then?

Léry: Oh, no. If it were only that I would shout so loud that they would give them back to me, because it is absolute murder. Now I shall be naked for the entire summer. Just imagine, they poked holes in my dresses. They stuck their probes through my packing case somehow or other. They made holes big enough to stick your finger through. That is what they brought me at lunch yesterday.

Chavigny: There weren't any blue ones, by chance?

Léry: No, sir, not a single one. Good-by, darling. I shall just put in an appearance. I think I am up to my twelfth case of flu this winter. I shall catch my thirteenth. As soon as that is done, I shall come right back and sink into one of your armchairs. We shall chat about customs, frocks, all right? No, I am quite sad; we shall be sentimental. Well, it doesn't matter! Good evening, my azure sir . . . If you see me out, I shan't come back. *(Exit.)*

Scene 4.

(Chavigny and Mathilde.)

Chavigny: What an addlepate that woman is! You choose your friends well.

Mathilde: You are the one who wanted her to come upstairs.

Chavigny: I would bet you think it was Madame de Blainville who made my purse.

Mathilde: No, since you have said it wasn't.

Chavigny: I am sure you think she did.

Mathilde: Why are you so sure of that?

Chavigny: Because I know you. Madame de Léry is your oracle. It is an idea that makes no sense.

Mathilde: That is a fine compliment I scarcely deserve.

Chavigny: Oh, my Lord, yes you do! And I had just as soon see you be frank as be secretive about it.

Mathilde: But if I don't think she did, I can't pretend to think so in order to seem sincere to you.

Chavigny: I tell you you think she did. It is written all over your face.

Mathilde: If I have to say so to please you, all right, I agree, I think she did.

Chavigny: You do? And if it were true, what would be wrong about that?

Mathilde: Nothing at all, and that is why I can't see why you should deny it.

Chavigny: I am not denying it. She did make it. *(He stands up.)* Good evening. Perhaps I shall come back in a while and have tea with your friend.

Mathilde: Henri, don't leave me this way!

Chavigny: What do you mean by "this way"? Are we angry with each other? It seems perfectly simple to me: someone made a purse for me, and I am using it. You ask me who, and I tell you. That doesn't seem at all like a quarrel to me.

Mathilde: If I asked you for that purse, would you give it up for me?

Chaigny: Perhaps. What use would it be to you?

Mathilde: That doesn't matter. I am asking you for it.

Chavigny: I don't suppose it is in order to carry it. I want to know what you would do with it.

Mathilde: I want to carry it.

Chavigny: What a joke! You would carry a purse made by Madame de Blainville?

Mathilde: Why not? You are carrying it.

Chavigny: A fine reason! I am not a woman.

Mathilde: Well, if I don't use it, I shall throw it in the fire.

Chavigny: Aha! Now you are finally being sincere. Well, I shall be quite sincere, too, and keep it, if you don't mind.

Mathilde: You are certainly free to do so. But I confess that it hurts me to think that everyone knows who made it for you, and you are going to show it everywhere.

Chavigny: Show it everywhere! You would think it was a trophy!

Mathilde: Listen to me, please. Leave your hand in mine. *(She kisses him.)* Do you love me, Henri? Answer me.

Chavigny: I love you, and I am listening to you.

Mathilde: I swear to you I am not jealous. But if you give me that purse as a friend, I shall thank you from the bottom my heart. It is a little exchange I am offering you, and I think, or at least I hope, that you won't find yourself on the losing end.

Chavigny: May I see what you are offering in exchange?

Mathilde: I shall tell you, if you insist. But if you let me have the purse first, I give you my word that you would be making me very happy.

Chavigny: I don't give anything on anyone's word.

Mathilde: Please do, Henri.

Chavigny: No.

Mathilde: Well, then, I beg you on bended knee.

Chavigny: Get up, Mathilde, it is my turn to beseech you. You know I don't like such manners. I can't bear to see anyone lower himself, and I understand it even less in this case. You are making too much of a trifle. If you were to request it seriously, I would throw this purse in the fire myself, and I would have no need of anything in exchange. Come now, get up and let us not speak about it any more. Good-by. I shall see you this evening when I get back.

Scene 5.

(Mathilde, alone.)

Mathilde: Since it is not that one, I shall burn the other. *(She goes to her desk and takes out the purse she has made.)* Poor little thing, I kissed you a while ago. Do you remember what I said to you? We are too late, as you see. He doesn't want you, and he no longer wants me. *(She goes toward the fireplace.)* It is so foolish to have dreams! They never come true. What is the attraction, the irresistible charm that makes us cling to an idea? Why do we take so much pleasure in pursuing it, carrying it out in secret? What good is all that? Just for tears, afterward. What does merciless chance require? It takes so many precautions, so many prayers to attain the simplest wish, the most modest hope! You were telling the truth, Count, I am insisting on a trifle, but it was so sweet to insist on it. As for you, so proud or so faithless, it would not have cost you much to go along with my whim. Oh, he no longer loves me, no, he doesn't! He loves you, Madame de Blainville! *(She weeps.)* Come now, I mustn't think about it any more. Let's throw this child's toy in the fire, since it didn't arrive in time. If I had given it to him this evening, he might perhaps have lost it tomorrow. Oh, I am sure he would have. He would leave my purse lying around on his table, who knows where, among his castoffs, whereas the other one will go around with him everywhere, and as he gambles, at this very moment, he is pulling it out proudly. I see him laying it on the gaming table and jingling the gold in it. I am so wretched and jealous! *(She goes to throw her purse in the fire, then stops.)* But what have you done? Why destroy you, my poor handiwork? It is none of your fault. You were waiting, you were hoping, too! Your bright colors didn't grow pale during that cruel conversation. I like you, I feel that I love you. In this little, delicate mesh there are two weeks of my life. Oh, no, no, the hand that made you won't destroy you. I want to keep you, I want to finish you. For me you will be a relic, and I shall wear you next to my heart. You will do me good and harm at the same time; you will remind me of my love for him, his forgetfulness, his whims. Who knows, if I hide you there, perhaps he will come back and get you? *(She sits down and attaches the missing tassel.)*

Scene 6.

(Mathilde and Madame de Léry.)

Léry: (Offstage.) There is no one anywhere! What does this mean? The door is wide open to everyone. *(She opens the door and calls, laughing.)* Madame de Léry! *(She comes in, and Mathilde stands up.)* Hello again, my dear. Not a servant in the house. I have been running all over trying to find someone. Oh, I am worn out! *(She sits down.)*

Mathilde: Take off your furs.

Léry: In a moment; I am frozen. Do you like this fox? It is supposed to be Ethiopian marten or something of the sort. Monsieur de Léry brought it from Holland for me. Frankly, I think it is ugly. I shall wear it three times to be polite, then I shall give it to Ursule.

Mathilde: A chambermaid can't wear that.

Léry: That is true. I shall have a little rug made of it.

Mathilde: Well, was the ball really beautiful?

Léry: Oh, my Lord, the ball! Why, I am not coming from there. You will never believe what happened to me.

Mathilde: So you didn't go?

Léry: Oh, yes, I did; but I didn't go in. You will die laughing. Just imagine, the line . . . the line . . . *(She bursts out laughing.)* Do things like that frighten you?

Mathilde: Why, yes. I don't like traffic jams.

Léry: It is distressing when you are alone. No matter how I shouted at the driver to keep moving, he wouldn't budge. I was so angry. I felt like climbing up on his seat. I assure you, I would have cut through their line. But it is so stupid to be there in your ball gown, staring out a dripping window—for on top of everything it was pouring. I amused myself for half an hour watching the passers-by wading about, and then I asked to return. So that was my ball. This fire is so good! I feel as if I am being reborn! *(She takes off her furs. Mathilde rings and a servant comes in.)*

Mathilde: Tea. *(Exit servant.)*

Léry: So Monsieur de Chavigny has gone out?

Mathilde: Yes. I think he is going to the ball, and he will be more persistent than you.

Léry: I don't think he likes me very much, between the two of us.

Mathilde: I assure you, you are wrong. He has told me a hundred times that, in his eyes, you are one of the prettiest women in Paris.

Léry: Really? That is very polite of him. But I deserve it, for I think he is quite handsome. Will you lend me a pin?

Mathilde: There is one next to you.

Léry: That Palmire makes dresses that you can't feel on your shoulders. You keep thinking that the whole thing is going to fall down. Is she the one who makes those sleeves for you?

Mathilde: Yes.

Léry: Very pretty, very nice, very pretty. There is really nothing like straight sleeves. But I have taken so long getting used to them. Besides, I think one really mustn't be too fat to wear them, because otherwise you look like a grasshopper, with a thick body and skinny arms.

Mathilde: I like that simile very much. *(Tea is brought in.)*

Léry: Isn't it true? Look at Mademoiselle Saint-Ange. But one mustn't be too skinny, either, because then there is nothing left. People rave about the Marquise d'Ermont, but I think she looks like a gallows. Granted, she has a beautiful face; but it is like a Madonna on a stick.

Mathilde: (Laughing.) Can I pour for you, dear?

Léry: Nothing but hot water, with just a hint of tea and a drop of milk.

Mathilde: (Serving the tea.) Are you going to Madame Egly's tomorrow? I shall take you, if you want.

Léry: Oh, Madame Egly! There is another one! With her curls and her legs, she looks to me like one of those mops they use to dust spiderwebs. *(She drinks.)* Why certainly, I shall go tomorrow. No, I can't. I am going to the concert.

Mathilde: It is true that she is a little odd.

Léry: Now look at me, please.

Mathilde: Why?

Léry: Look me straight in the face, now.

Mathilde: Do you think I look so unusual?

Léry: Ha, you certainly do have red eyes! You have just been crying, it is as plain as day. What ever is going on, my dear Mathilde?

Mathilde: Nothing, I swear. What do you think could be going on?

Léry: I don't know a thing, but you have just been crying. I am disturbing you; I shall go now.

Mathilde: Not at all, dear. I beg you, stay.

Léry: Is that really sincere? I shall stay if you like, but you must tell me your troubles. *(Mathilde shakes her head no.)* No? Then I shall go; you must understand: if I can't be of any use, I can only do harm without meaning to.

Mathilde: Stay, I am very glad to have you here, your wit amuses me, and if it were true that I had some problem, your gaiety would make me forget it.

Léry: Well, I do love you. Perhaps you think I am flighty, but no one is more serious than I am when it comes to serious matters. I can't understand how anyone can trifle with the heart, and that is why I seem not to have one. I know what it is like to suffer, I was taught that when I was still quite young. I also know what it is like to tell someone your troubles. If what is bothering you can be shared, speak freely. I am not asking just out of curiosity.

Mathilde: I believe you are kind and, especially, quite sincere. But please excuse me for not obeying you.

Léry: Oh, my Lord, now I have it! It is the blue purse. I made a frightful blunder when I named Madame de Blainville. I thought of that as I left you. Is Monsieur de Chavigny courting her? *(Mathilde stands up, since she cannot answer, turns away, and wipes her eyes with her handkerchief.)*

Léry: Can it be possible? *(A long silence. Mathilde walks around for a while, then sits down at the other end of the room. Madame de Léry appears to reflect. She stands up and goes toward Mathilde, who reaches out her hand to her.)*

Léry: You know, my dear: dentists tell you to scream when they hurt you. Now I shall tell you to cry! Bitter or sweet, tears are always a relief.

Mathilde: Oh, my Lord!

Léry: Why, such a thing is incredible! No one can be in love with Madame de Blainville. She is a half-forgotten coquette, she is neither witty nor beautiful. She isn't worth your little finger. No one leaves an angel for a devil.

Mathilde: (Sobbing.) I am sure he is in love with her, I am sure he is!

Léry: No, my child, that is not possible. It is a passing fancy, a whim. I know Monsieur de Chavigny better than he thinks. He is naughty, but he is not mean. He must have acted on an impulse. Did you cry in front of him?

Mathilde: Oh, no, never!

Léry: That is good. I wouldn't be surprised if it should make him happy.

Mathilde: Happy? Happy to see me cry?

Léry: Oh, my Lord, yes! It is only yesterday that I was twenty-five, but I know what is what about a lot of things. How did it all come about?

Mathilde: Why . . . I don't know . . .

Léry: Speak up. Are you afraid of me? I shall reassure you right away. If I have to make a commitment myself to put you at your ease, I shall prove to you that I trust you and force you to trust me. Do I have to? I shall do it. What would you like to know about me?

Mathilde: You are my best friend. I shall tell you everything, I trust you. It is nothing very serious, but I was carried away by my imagination. I had made a little purse in secret for Monsieur de Chavigny, and I was intending to offer it to him today. I have scarcely seen him the last two weeks; he spends his days at Madame de Blainville's. If I offered him this little present, it was to be like a mild reproach for his absence, and to show him that he was leaving me by myself. Just when I was about to give him my purse, he pulled out the other one.

Léry: That is not worth crying about.

Mathilde: Oh, yes it is something to cry about, because I did a terribly foolish thing. I asked him for the other purse.

Léry: Ouch! That wasn't diplomatic.

Mathilde: No, Ernestine; and he refused . . . And then . . . Oh, I am ashamed . . .

Léry: Well?

Mathilde: Well, I asked him on bended knee. I wanted him to make that little sacrifice for me, and I would have given him my purse in exchange for his. I begged him . . . I pleaded with him . . .

Léry: And he wouldn't, that goes without saying. Poor, innocent girl! He doesn't deserve you.

Mathilde: Oh, in spite of it all, I shall never believe that!

Léry: You are right, I am expressing myself badly. He deserves you and he loves you. But he is a man and he is vain. What a pity! So where is your purse?

Mathilde: Here it is, on the table.

Léry: (Taking the purse.) This purse? Well, my dear, it is four times prettier than hers. First of all, it isn't blue, and in addition, it is exquisite. Lend it to me, I know how to make him find it to his taste.

Mathilde: Please try. You will restore me to life.

Léry: To have come to this after one year of marriage; it is un-
heard of. There must be some evil spell behind it. That Blain-
ville, with her indigo! I dislike her from head to toe. Her eyes
have rings around them down to her chin. Mathilde, will you
do one thing for me? It won't cost us anything to try. Is your
husband coming back this evening?

Mathilde: I really don't know, but he said he would.

Léry: What were you like when he went out?

Mathilde: Oh, I was very sad, and he was very stern!

Léry: He will come. Are you brave? I warn you, when I have an
idea, I have to catch myself as I go by. I know myself, I shall
succeed.

Mathilde: Just tell me what to do and I shall obey.

Léry: Go into the dressing room, get ready quickly, and run down
to my carriage. I don't want to send you to the ball, but you
will have to look as if you have been there when you get back.
Have my coachman take you wherever you want, to the Inva-
lides or the Bastille. It won't be much fun, but you will be just
as well off there as here, as long as you are not sleeping. Is that
agreed? Now, take your purse and wrap it in this paper. I shall
write the address. Good, that is done. When you get to the cor-
ner, stop the carriage and tell my groom to bring this little
package back here, give it to the first servant he encounters,
and leave without any other explanation.

Mathilde: At least tell me what you are going to do.

Léry: My child, what I'm going to do is impossible to say, and I
shall see whether it is possible to do. Once and for all, do you
trust me?

Mathilde: Yes, anything in the world for love of him.

Léry: Come now, quickly, here comes a carriage!

Mathilde: It is him. I hear his voice in the courtyard.

Léry: Run! Is there a back staircase that way?

Mathilde: Yes, fortunately. But my hair isn't done. How will any-
one think I have been to the ball?

Léry: (*Taking off the flowers she has in her hair and giving them
to Mathilde.*) Here, you can arrange this as you go. (*Exit
Mathilde.*)

Scene 7.

(Madame de Léry, alone.)

Léry: On her knees! A woman like that on her knees! And that man refuses her! A woman twenty years old, as beautiful as an angel, and as faithful as a hound! The poor child, she asks as a favor to have a purse that she has made accepted, in exchange for a present from Madame de Blainville! Why, what an abyss men's hearts must be! Oh, my word, we are better than they are! *(She sits down and picks up a pamphlet on the table. A moment later a knock is heard at the door.)* Come in.

Scene 8.

(Madame de Léry and Chavigny.)

Léry (Reading distractedly.) Good evening, Count. Do you want some tea?

Chavigny: No, thank you. I never drink any. *(He sits down and looks around him.)*

Léry: Was the ball amusing?

Chavigny: So-so. Weren't you there?

Léry: That is not a very gallant question. No, I wasn't there. But I sent Mathilde, whom you seem to be looking around for.

Chavigny: You are joking, I see.

Léry: Excuse me? Please forgive me, this article in the *Revue* interests me a great deal. *(Silence. Chavigny, worriedly, stands up and walks around.)*

Chavigny: Is Mathilde really at the ball?

Léry: Of course. You can see I am waiting for her.

Chavigny: That is odd. She didn't want to go out when you suggested it to her.

Léry: Evidently she changed her mind.

Chavigny: Why didn't she go with you?

Léry: Because I didn't bother about it any more.

Chavigny: So she went out without a carriage?

Léry: No, I lent her mine. Have you read this, Monsieur de Chavigny?

Chavigny: What?

Léry: It's the *Revue des deux mondes.* There is a very nice article by Madame Sand about orang-utans.

Chavigny: About? . . .

Léry: About orang-utans. Oh, I am wrong! It is not by her, it is the one after. That is very amusing.

Chavigny: I don't at all understand this idea of going to the ball without telling me first. At least I could have brought her back.

Léry: Do you like Madame Sand's novels?

Chavigny: No, not at all. But if she is there, how come I didn't see her?

Léry: Who, George Sand? She is right here.

Chavigny: Are you making fun of me, madam?

Léry: Perhaps. It depends on what about.

Chavigny: I am talking to you about my wife.

Léry: Did you ask me to keep an eye on her?

Chavigny: You are right. I am being quite ridiculous. I shall go and get her right away.

Léry: Humph! You will get caught in the crowd.

Chavigny: That is true. I may as well wait, so I shall do that. *(He goes to the fire and sits down.)*

Léry: (Putting down her reading.) Do you know, Monsieur de Chavigny, you really astonish me? I thought I heard you say you left Mathilde completely free, and she could go wherever she wanted?

Chavigny: Certainly. You can see that with your own eyes.

Léry: Not all that well. You look furious.

Chavigny: Me! Why, not in the least.

Léry: You can't stay in your seat. I thought you were a quite different sort of man, I shall confess. Seriously speaking, I wouldn't have lent my carriage to Mathilde if I had known this.

Chavigny: But I assure you this seems perfectly simple to me, and I am grateful to you for doing it.

Léry: No, no, you are not grateful at all. I assure you that you are angry. To tell the truth, I think she went out at least in part to meet you.

Chavigny: Well, I like that. Why didn't she go with me?

Léry: Why, yes, that is what I said! But that is the way we women are: first we don't feel like it, then we do. You really won't take some tea?

Chavigny: No, it doesn't agree with me.

Léry: Well, then, pour me some.

Chavigny: Excuse me, madam?

Léry: Pour me some. *(Chavigny stands up and fills a cup, which he offers to Madame de Léry.)*

Léry: That is fine, put it down there. Do we have a cabinet this evening?

Chavigny: I haven't any idea.

Léry: What strange shops those cabinets are. People walk in and out without knowing why. It is a parade of marionettes.

Chavigny: Drink your tea, now; it is already half cold.

Léry: You didn't put enough sugar in it. Put in a lump or two for me.

Chavigny: As you wish; it won't be any good.

Léry: Fine. Now, a little more milk.

Chavigny: Are you satisfied?

Léry: And now just a drop of hot water. Is that it? Give me the cup.

Chavigny: (Handing her the cup.) Here it is, but it won't be any good.

Léry: Do you think so? Are you sure?

Chavigny: Without the slightest doubt.

Léry: And why won't it be any good?

Chavigny: Because it is cold, and too sweet.

Léry: Well, if the tea is no good, just pour it out. *(Chavigny stands holding the cup. Madame de Léry looks at him and laughs.)*

Léry: Oh, my Lord, you do amuse me! I have never seen anything so grouchy.

Chavigny: (Annoyed, he empties the cup into the fire, then strides back and forth, and says with irritation:) My word, that is true, I am acting like a fool.

Léry: I had never seen you jealous, but you are as jealous as Othello.

Chavigny: Not in the least. I can't bear people being put out or putting others out in any way. Why should you think I am jealous?

Léry: Out of vanity, like all husbands.

Chavigny: Humph, spoken like a woman. People say, "Jealous, out of vanity" because it is a cliché, as they say, "I am your devoted servant." They are terribly hard on poor husbands.

Léry: Not as hard as on poor wives.

Chavigny: Oh, my Lord, yes they are. Everything is relative. Can women be allowed to live on the same footing as us? That is patently absurd. There are thousands of things that are quite momentous to them and that have no importance whatever to a man.

Léry: Yes. Passing fancies, for example.

Chavigny: Why not? Why, yes, passing fancies! It is certain that a man can have them, but a woman . . .

Léry: Does, too, sometimes. Do you think a dress is a talisman that protects you from them?

Chavigny: It is a barrier that ought to stop them.

Léry: Unless it is a veil that covers them up. I hear footsteps. It is Mathilde coming back.

Chavigny: Oh, no, it is not midnight! *(A servant enters and gives a little package to Monsieur de Chavigny.)*

Chavigny: What is this? What do they want of me?

Servant: This was just brought for your lordship. *(Exit. Chavigny unwraps the package, which contains Mathilde's purse.)*

Léry: Is it another present for you? That is a bit too much at such an hour.

Chavigny: What the devil does this mean? Hey, François, hey! Who brought this package?

Servant: (Coming back in.) Sir?

Chavigny: Who brought this package?

Servant: It was the doorman who just came upstairs, sir.

Chavigny: There is nothing with it? No letter?

Servant: No, sir.

Chavigny: Did the doorman have this for long?

Servant: No, sir. It was just given to him.

Chavigny: Who gave it to him?

Servant: He doesn't know, sir.

Chavigny: He doesn't know! Have you lost your mind? Was it a man or a woman?

Servant: It was a servant in livery, but he didn't know him.

Chavigny: Is this servant still downstairs?

Servant: No, sir. He left right away.

Chavigny: He didn't say anything?

Servant: No, sir.

Chavigny: That will do. *(Exit servant.)*

Léry: I think you are being spoiled, Monsieur de Chavigny. If you drop your money, it won't be the ladies' fault.

Chavigny: I'll be hanged if I understand any of this.

Léry: Come now, you are acting like a child!

Chavigny: No, I give you my word of honor that I can't guess. It must be a mistake.

Léry: Isn't there an address on it?

Chavigny: My word, yes, you are right. That is odd; I recognize the handwriting.

Léry: May I have a look?

Chavigny: It is perhaps indiscreet of me to show it to you. Well, too bad for whoever took the risk. Here. I am sure I have seen this handwriting somewhere.

Léry: So have I, I am quite sure.

Chavigny: Wait a moment . . . No, I am mistaken. What kind of writing is it, block letters?

Léry: Shame on you; it is a purebred English hand! Just see how fine these letters are. Oh, this lady is well-bred!

Chavigny: You seem to know her.

Léry: *(Feigning embarrassment.)* What, me? Not in the least. *(Chavigny, who is surprised, looks at her, then continues walking back and forth.)* So, where were we? Ah, yes, I think we were talking about passing fancies. This little red love note arrives just at the right time.

Chavigny: You are in on the secret, admit it.

Léry: Some people just don't know how to do anything. If I were you, I would already have guessed.

Chavigny: Come on, be frank! Tell me who it is.

Léry: I am fairly sure it is Madame de Blainville.

Chavigny: You are merciless, madam. Do you know, we are going to quarrel!

Léry: I really hope so, but not this time.

Chavigny: You won't help me solve this puzzle?

Léry: A fine activity! Just forget about it. You want me to think you are not used to it. You can mull this over when you are in bed, if only out of courtesy.

Chavigny: Isn't there any more tea? I feel like having some.

Léry: I shall make you some. Now just say that I am not kind. *(Silence.)*

Chavigny: *(Still walking back and forth.)* The more I try, the less I see.

Léry: Oh, come now, have you made up your mind not to think of anything but that purse? I am going to leave you to your day-dreams.

Chavigny: It is just that I am completely in the dark.

Léry: I tell you it is Madame de Blainville. She thought it over about the purse's color, and she is sending you another one out of remorse. Or better still, she wants to tempt you, and see whether you will carry this one or hers.

Chavigny: I shall definitely carry this one. It is the only way to find out who made it.

Léry: I don't understand. That is too deep for me.

Chavigny: Suppose the person who sent it to me sees it in my hands tomorrow. Do you think I could make any mistake?

Léry: *(Laughing.)* Ha, that is too much! I can't bear it.

Chavigny: Would it be you, by any chance? *(Silence.)*

Léry: Here is your tea, made with my own lily-white hands, and it will be better than what you concocted for me a while ago. Now please stop looking at me that way. Do you take me for an anonymous letter?

Chavigny: It is you; it is some sort of joke. There is a plot beneath all this.

Léry: It is a pretty well-knit plot.

Chavigny: So admit that you are in on it.

Léry: No.

Chavigny: Please.

Léry: Still no.

Chavigny: I beg you!

Léry: Ask me on bended knee and I shall tell you.

Chavigny: On bended knee? As you wish.

Léry: Come on, then.

Chavigny: Are you serious? *(He gets down on his knees, laughing, at Madame de Léry's feet.)*

Léry: (Curtly.) I like that posture, it suits you perfectly well. But I advise you to get up, so I won't be too moved to pity.

Chavigny: (He rises.) So you won't say anything, will you?

Léry: Do you have your blue purse with you?

Chavigny: I don't really know, I think so.

Léry: I think so, too. Give it to me, and I shall tell you who made the other one.

Chavigny: So you do know.

Léry: Yes, I do.

Chavigny: Is it a woman?

Léry: Unless it is a man, I don't really see . . .

Chavigny: I mean, is it a pretty woman?

Léry: It is a woman who, to your eyes, is one of the prettiest women in Paris.

Chavigny: Dark or fair?

Léry: Blue.

Chavigny: What letter does her name begin with?

Léry: You won't accept my deal? Give me Madame de Blainville's purse.

Chavigny: Is she tall or short?

Léry: Give me the purse.

Chavigny: Just tell me whether she has small feet.

Léry: Your purse or your life!

Chavigny: Will you tell me her name if I give you the purse?

Léry: Yes.

Chavigny: (Taking out the blue purse.) Your word of honor?

Léry: My word of honor.

Chavigny: (He seems to hesitate; Madame de Léry reaches out her hand; he stares at her. Suddenly, he sits down next to her and says, gaily:) Let's talk about passing fancies. So you agree that a woman can have them?

Léry: Have you reached the point of asking that?

Chavigny: Not entirely. But a married man can happen to have two different ways of talking and, up to a certain point, of acting.

Léry: Well, has our deal vanished? I thought we had made one.

Chavigny: A man who is married is no less a man. The wedding blessing doesn't transform him, but it sometimes requires him to play a role and speak its lines. It is merely a question of knowing, in our world, whom people are talking to when they speak to you, whether it is the real "you" or the assumed "you," the person or the actor.

Léry: I understand. That is a choice one can make. But how can the audience tell?

Chavigny: I don't think it is very lengthy or difficult for an intelligent audience.

Léry: So you are giving up on that name? Come on, now, give me the purse.

Chavigny: An intelligent woman, for example (an intelligent woman knows so many things!), to my mind ought not to be mistaken as to the true nature of people. She ought to see at first glance . . .

Léry: You are definitely keeping the purse?

Chavigny: You seem to care a great deal about it. An intelligent woman ought, therefore, to be able to distinguish between the husband and the man, ought she not, madam? What has happened to your hairdo? You were wearing all those flowers this afternoon.

Léry: Yes. They were bothering me, so I made myself comfortable. Oh, my goodness, my hair has come undone on one side. *(She gets up and fixes her hair before the mirror.)*

Chavigny: You have the prettiest figure one may see. An intelligent woman like you . . .

Léry: An intelligent woman like me says the devil take her when she is dealing with an intelligent man like you.

Chavigny: That doesn't matter. I am a good-hearted devil.

Léry: Not good for me, at least as far as I can tell.

Chavigny: Apparently someone else must be hurting my cause.

Léry: What is that supposed to mean?

Chavigny: It means that if you don't like me, it is because someone else is preventing it.

Léry: That is modest and polite. But you are wrong. I don't like anyone, and I don't want anyone to like me.

Chavigny: At your age, and with eyes like those, I dare you.

Léry: And yet it is the absolute truth.

Chavigny: If I believed that, you would give me a very bad opinion of men.

Léry: I shall make you believe it quite easily. My vanity won't stand for a master.

Chavigny: Can't it accept a servant?

Léry: Hah! Servants or masters, you are all just tyrants.

Chavigny: (Rising.) That is quite true. I shall confess that I have always detested men's behavior in that domain. I don't know what makes them so obsessed with imposing themselves. It only ends up getting them disliked.

Léry: Is that your sincere opinion?

Chavigny: Very sincere. I can't conceive how anyone can imagine that, if someone likes you this evening, you are entitled to take advantage of it tomorrow.

Léry: And yet that is the very first chapter of world history.

Chavigny: Yes; but if men had a little common sense, women wouldn't be so cautious.

Léry: That is possible. Love affairs are marriages in our times; when it comes to the wedding day, that is worth thinking about.

Chavigny: You couldn't be more right. So, tell me, why is it so? Why so much playacting and so little sincerity? Can't a pretty woman who trusts in a gentleman tell the difference? There aren't only fools here on earth.

Léry: That is a good question.

Chavigny: But just suppose that, by chance, there should be a man who doesn't go along with the fools on that point; suppose that an opportunity should arise when one may be frank without danger, without second thoughts, without fear of indiscretion. *(He takes her hand.)* Suppose one should say to a woman: "We are alone, you are young and beautiful, and I prize your intelligence and your heart as they deserve. A thousand barriers separate us, a thousand troubles await us if we try to see each other again tomorrow. Your pride will accept no yoke, and your caution will accept no ties. You need fear neither one nor the other. You are not being asked for a declaration, or a commitment, or a sacrifice, nothing but a smile from those rosy lips and a glance from those beautiful eyes.

Smile as long as that door is shut; your freedom lies at the door-step, you will regain it when you leave this room. What is being offered you is not pleasure without love, it is love without pain or bitterness. It is a passing fancy, since that is what we are talk-ing about; not a blind, sensual fancy, but one from the heart, which is born in a moment and whose memory is eternal."

Léry: You talked about playacting; it seems that you do it rather dangerously at times. I do feel somewhat like allowing myself a passing fancy before I answer that speech. It seems to me that now is the time, since you are pleading its cause. Do you have a deck of cards here?

Chavigny: Yes, in this table. What do you want to do with it?

Léry: Give it to me, I have my whims, and you are obliged to obey, if you don't want to contradict yourself. *(She takes a card from the deck.)* All right, Count, say red or black.

Chavigny: Will you tell me what is at stake?

Léry: It is winner take all.

Chavigny: All right, I shall call red.

Léry: It is the jack of spades. You lose. Give me that blue purse.

Chavigny: With all my heart, but I shall keep the red one; and even though its color made me lose, I shall never hold that against it, because I know as well as you do whose hand made it for me.

Léry: Is that hand small or large?

Chavigny: It is charming, and soft as velvet.

Léry: Will you allow it to give way to a little fit of jealousy? *(She throws the blue purse into the fire.)*

Chavigny: Ernestine, I adore you!

Léry: *(She watches the purse burning. She goes toward Chavigny and says to him, tenderly:)* So you no longer love Madame de Blainville?

Chavigny: Oh, my God, I never loved her!

Léry: Neither did I, Monsieur de Chavigny.

Chavigny: But who can have told you I was thinking of that woman? Oh, it is not her I would ask for a moment of happi-ness; she is not the one who will give it to me.

Léry: Nor will I, Monsieur de Chavigny. You have just made me a little sacrifice, and that is very gallant of you. But I don't want to deceive you: the red purse wasn't made by me.

Chavigny: Is that possible? Then who did make it?

Léry: A more beautiful hand than mine. Do me a favor: just reflect for a moment and solve this riddle for me, now. You made me a very nice proposal, in the purest style. You got down on bended knee, and you will note there isn't even a carpet. I asked you for your blue purse, and you let me burn it. Now, tell me, who am I to deserve all that? What makes me so extraordinary to you? I am not bad, it is true; I am young; it is certain that my feet are small. But that is not so rare, after all. When we have proven to each other that I am a flirt and you are a rake, for no other reason than that it is midnight and we are alone together, what a fine skirmish that will make to write down in our diaries! And yet isn't that all there is to it? And what you have granted me with a smile, and doesn't even cause you any regret, this insignificant sacrifice that you make for an even more insignificant passing fancy, you would refuse to the only woman who loves you, the only woman you once loved! *(The sound of a carriage is heard.)*

Chavigny: Madam, who can have told you? . . .

Léry: Speak more softly, sir, she is coming back, and that carriage has come to get me. I don't have time to finish my lesson. You are a man of heart, so your heart will finish for me. If you find that Mathilde's eyes are red, wipe them with this little purse that her tears will recognize, for it was your good, kind, faithful wife who spent two weeks making it. Good-by. You will be angry with me today, but tomorrow you will feel friendlier toward me and, believe me, that is better than a passing fancy. But if you absolutely need one, well, here is Mathilde, you can have a fine one tonight. I hope it will make you forget another one that nobody in the world, not even she, will ever know about. *(Mathilde comes in, and Madame de Léry goes to meet her and kisses her.)*

Chavigny: *(He watches them, goes toward them, takes Madame de Léry's wreath of flowers from his wife's head, and says to Madame de Léry as he gives them back to her:)* I beg your pardon, madam; she shall know about it; and I shall never forget that a young preacher gives the best sermons.

THE END

A Door Has to Be either
Open or Shut

One of the best of Musset's one-act proverbs (a group that could include *You Can't Think of Everything* [*On ne saurait penser à tout*]* as well as this volume's *A Passing Fancy*), *A Door Has to Be either Open or Shut* was written in 1845, was published in the 1 November issue of the *Revue des deux mondes*, and premièred at the Comédie Française on 7 April 1848, starring the excellent actors Brindeau and Mme. Allan-Despréaux. Chronologically, it is the last of Musset's completely successful plays.

The work's light, worldly tone distinguishes it from the comedies of Musset's youth, despite the Count's praise of romantic love in the face of the Marquise's apparent mocking insensibility. The earlier plays' linguistic elegance seems to be all that remains here of Musset's poetic vision. But the characters of this comedy are so well developed, within their psychological and social limits, that it has remained one of Musset's most popular plays in France, often serving as a curtain raiser for longer, more serious works at the Comédie Française.

Although it would be more correct to render the French *marquise* as "marchioness," I find that title too cumbersome and unfamiliar, so I have kept "marquise," which is frequently used, in American English at least.

---

*That play is absent from this collection because it owes enough to Carmontelle's *Le Distrait* ("The Absent-minded Man") to disqualify it as an authentic Musset work.

CHARACTERS

The Count   *The Marquise*

The scene is Paris.
A little salon.

(The Count and the Marquise. The latter, sitting on a sofa by the fire, is doing needlework. The Count enters and bows to her.)

Count: I don't know when I shall get over my absent-mindedness, but it treats me cruelly. I can't seem to get myself to remember on what day you receive, and every time I feel like seeing you it never fails to be a Tuesday.

Marq.: Do you have something to say to me?

Count: No, but even if I did I couldn't, since it is only by chance you are alone, and in a few minutes you are going to have a swarm of your close friends here, so, I warn you, I shall have to run.

Marq.: It is true that today is my day, though I really can't say why I have one. Still, it is a fashion that does have some purpose. Our mothers kept open house; there weren't so many people in good society, and in each circle they were limited to a handful of tiresome people one more or less had to stomach. Now if you open your doors, you open them to all of Paris. And "all of Paris," in times like ours, is really and truly the entire city and its suburbs. When you are at home, you are out in the street. Some remedy had to be found; that is why everyone has a day. It is the only way to see each other as seldom as possible, and when you say, "I am at home on Tuesdays," it is clearly as if you had said, "Leave me alone the rest of the time."

Count: It is all the worse for me to come today, since you let me see you during the week.

Marq.: You may as well sit down here. If you are in a good mood, you can talk. Otherwise, just get warm. I am not expecting many people today, you can watch my little magic lantern show parade by. What is the matter, though? You seem . . .

Count: What?

Marq.: For my own self-respect, I don't want to say.

Count: Oh, dear, I must confess I was, a bit, before I came in.

Marq.: What? Now it is my turn to ask.

Count: Will you be angry if I tell you?

Marq.: I am going to a ball this evening and I want to look pretty, so I won't get angry the entire day.

Count: Well, I was a little bored. I don't know what is wrong with me. It is an illness that is in fashion, like your receptions. I have been wretched since noon. I have made four visits and didn't find anyone home. I was supposed to dine out somewhere, but I sent my excuses for no good reason. There isn't a single show this evening. I went out in freezing weather; I have seen nothing but red noses and purple cheeks. I don't know what to do, I feel like an absolute fool.

Marq.: I can't offer you any better. I am bored to tears. It is the weather, no doubt.

Count: It is a fact that cold weather is ghastly. Winter is a disease. Idlers, seeing the streets clean, the sky clear, and a good stiff wind biting their ears, call it a beautiful frost. It is as if you should say a beautiful inflammation of the lungs. They can keep beauties of that kind!

Marq.: I couldn't agree with you more. It seems to me that my boredom comes less from the outside air, as cold as it may be, than from what other people breathe. Perhaps we are just getting old. I shall be thirty soon, and I am losing my zest for life.

Count: I have never had that zest, and what frightens me is that I am catching it. As one gets on in years, one grows either dull or mad. I have a dreadful fear of dying a wise man.

Marq.: Ring to have a log put on the fire. Your idea makes me shiver.

(A bell is heard ringing outside.)

Count: There is no need. The doorbell has rung, and your parade is arriving.

Marq.: Let's see what flag they are flying; please try to stay.

Count: No, really, I am leaving.

Marq.: Where are you going?

Count: I have no idea. *(He stands up, bows, and opens the door.)* Good-by, madam. I shall see you Thursday evening.

Marq.: Why Thursday?

Count: (Standing, holding the doorknob.) Isn't that your day at the Opéra Comique? I shall come pay you a little visit.

Marq.: I don't want anything to do with you. You are too glum. Moreover, I am taking Mr. Camus.

Count: Mr. Camus, your neighbor from the country?

Marq.: Yes. He sold me some apples and hay in a most gallant manner, and I want to return the courtesy.

Count: Well, isn't that just like you! The most boring person! He ought to be paid back in kind. By the way, do you know what people are saying?

Marq.: No. But nobody is coming. Whoever rang the bell?

Count: (Looking out the window.) No one. A little girl with a carton, something or other, a laundress, I think. She is there in the courtyard, talking with your servants.

Marq.: You call that "something or other." How polite: that is my bonnet. So, what are people saying about me and Mr. Camus? Please close that door . . . There is an awful draft coming in.

Count: (Closing the door.) They are saying that you are thinking of getting married again, that Mr. Camus is a millionaire, and that he comes to your place quite often.

Marq.: You don't say! Is that all? And you say that right to my face?

Count: I am telling you because that is what people are saying.

Marq.: That is a fine reason. Do I repeat to you everything people say about you, too?

Count: About me, madam? What can they say that can't be repeated, if you don't mind?

Marq.: Why, you see, anything can be repeated, since you inform me that I am on the verge of being introduced as Mrs. Camus. What people are saying about you is at least as serious, since unfortunately it appears to be true.

Count: And what can that be? You are almost frightening me.

Marq.: Further proof that people are not mistaken.

Count: I beg you, please tell me what you mean.

Marq.: Ha! Not at all. That is your business.

Count: (Sitting back down.) I beseech you, Marquise, I ask you as a special favor. You are the person whose opinion counts the most for me in all the world.

Marq.: One of the persons, you mean.

Count: No, Madam, I say, "the person," the one whose esteem, whose feelings, whose . . .

Marq.: Heavens, you are about to make a speech!

Count: Not at all. If you don't see anything, it is apparently because you don't want to.

Marq.: See what?

Count: It is understandable, in any case.

Marq.: I understand only what I hear, and even then I have to be really listening.

Count: You laugh at everything. But sincerely, can it be possible that, seeing you practically every day for two years, with the kind of person you are, your wit, your grace, and your beauty . . .

Marq.: Why, my goodness, it is even worse than a speech, it is a declaration of love you are making! At least give some warning: Is it a declaration or a New Year's compliment?

Count: Suppose it was a declaration?

Marq.: Oh, in that case I don't want one this morning. I told you I was going to the ball, and I am likely to hear some this evening. My health doesn't allow me such things twice in one day.

Count: Really, you are discouraging, and I shall rejoice heartily when you are caught in your turn.

Marq.: I shall, too. I swear there are times when I would give anything just to feel some slight distress. Why, I felt that way, as my hair was being done, only a little while ago. I was sighing great, deep sighs, out of desperation at my lack of worry.

Count: That is it, laugh at me! You will come around.

Marq.: That is quite possible. We are all mortal. If I am reasonable, whose fault is it? I assure you I am not defending myself.

Count: Don't you want to be courted?

Marq.: No. I am a very good-natured person, but as for that, it is just too stupid. You have some common sense. Now, just tell me, what does it mean "to pay court to a woman"?

Count: It means you like that woman, and you are happy to tell her so.

Marq.: Fine. But does the woman like you to like her? You think I am pretty, I suppose, and it amuses you to let me know it.

Well, so what? What does that prove? Is that any reason for me to love you? I imagine that if I like someone, it is not because I am pretty. What does he gain by these compliments? A fine way to make someone love you: you come and plant yourself in front of a woman with your lorgnette, you look her up and down, like a doll in a store window, and you say to her, quite pleasantly: "Madam, I find you charming!" Add a few insipid phrases, a waltz, and a bouquet, and that is what they call "paying court"? For shame! How can an intelligent man acquire a taste for nonsense of that sort? It makes me angry just to think of it.

Count: But there is nothing to get annoyed at.

Marq.: Why yes, there is. One must suppose a woman has a really empty head and a great amount of stupidity, to imagine one charms her with merchandise like that. Do you think it is very amusing to spend one's life in the midst of a flood of balderdash and to have one's ears filled with twaddle from morning to night? It seems to me, in truth, that if I were a man and I saw a pretty woman, I would say to myself, "There is an unfortunate creature, who must really be bored to death with compliments." I would spare her, I would take pity on her and, if I wanted to try and make her like me, I would do her the honor of talking about something other than her wretched face. But no, it is always "You are pretty," then, "You are pretty," and again, "pretty." My Lord, one knows that quite well! Shall I tell you? You men of fashion are nothing but confectioners in disguise.

Count: Well, madam, you are charming, take that any way you like. *(The bell is heard.)* Someone is ringing again. Good-by, I have to run. *(He stands up and opens the door.)*

Marq.: Wait a moment, I wanted to say . . . I can't remember what it was . . . Oh, are you by any chance going past Fossin's along your way?

Count: It won't be by chance, madam, if I can be of use to you in any way.

Marq.: Another compliment! Good Lord, how you bore me! It is a ring that I have broken. I could really just send it to them, only I have to explain to you . . . *(She takes the ring off her finger.)*

Here, you see, it is the setting. There is a little point here; you can see it, can't you? It opened up on the side, this way. I knocked it against something or other this morning, and the spring was forced open.

Count: Tell me, Marquise, if it is not indiscreet: Was there a lock of hair inside?

Marq.: Perhaps there was. What are you laughing at?

Count: I am not laughing in the least.

Marq.: You are an impudent rogue. It was my husband's hair. But I don't hear anybody. Who was it ringing this time?

Count: (Looking out the window.) Another little girl, with another carton. One more bonnet, I suppose. By the way, I might add, you still haven't let me in on a secret.

Marq.: Please close that door, I am freezing.

Count: I am leaving. But you promise you will tell me what they have told you about me, won't you, Marquise?

Marq.: Come to the ball this evening and we shall talk.

Count: Oh, of course, talk at a ball! A fine place to have a conversation, with trombone accompaniment and the tinkling of glasses of sugar water! This one steps on your feet, that one bumps your elbow, while a sticky waiter dumps an ice into your pocket. I ask you, do you think that is where . . .

Marq.: Are you staying or leaving? I tell you once again, you are giving me a head cold. Since no one is coming, what makes you rush off?

Count: (Shutting the door and coming to sit down again.) It is just that, in spite of myself, I feel in such a bad mood that I am really afraid of irritating you. I definitely must stop coming to see you.

Marq.: That is very polite. Whatever for?

Count: I don't know, but I bore you, you said so yourself a moment ago, and I can feel it, it is only natural. It is just those wretched lodgings I have across the street. I can't go out without seeing your windows, and I come in here automatically, without thinking of what I am doing here.

Marq.: If I said you were boring me this morning, it is because it is not your custom. Seriously, I would be distressed. I am very glad to see you.

Count: You? Not at all. Do you know what I am going to do? I am going to go back to Italy.

Marq.: Oh! I wonder, what would Miss . . .

Count: What Miss, if you please?

Marq.: Miss something or other, your protégée Miss what's-her-name. How should I know the names of your ballet dancers?

Count: Aha, so that is the fine thing people have been telling you about me?

Marq.: Exactly. Do you deny it?

Count: That is just a cock-and-bull story.

Marq.: It is unfortunate that you were seen quite distinctly at the theater, with a certain pink hat with flowers, of a kind that grow only at the opera. You are into the chorus line, my good neighbor, everyone knows that.

Count: Like your marriage with Mr. Camus.

Marq.: You are back to that? Well, why not? Mr. Camus is a very decent man; he is a millionaire several times over. Although he is of fairly respectable age, that is just right for a husband. I am a widow, and he is a bachelor. He is quite presentable, when he wears gloves.

Count: And a nightcap, too. That must suit him.

Marq.: Will you please be still? Is it possible to talk about such things?

Count: Indeed, to someone who might see them.

Marq.: It is evidently your young ladies who have been teaching you such fine manners.

Count: (*Standing up and taking his hat.*) Well, Marquise, I shall say good-by. I might say something foolish.

Marq.: What exquisite tact!

Count: No, really, you are too cruel. It is bad enough for you to forbid men to love you without accusing me of loving someone else.

Marq.: Better and better. What a tragic tone! Did I forbid you to love me?

Count: Certainly—at least to talk to you about it.

Marq.: All right, I shall let you. Let's hear your eloquence.

Count: If you were saying that seriously . . .

Marq.: What does it matter, as long as I say so?

Count: It is just that there might be someone here who was running a risk, all laughter aside.

Marq.: Ha, ha! Great dangers, sir?

Count: Perhaps, madam. But unfortunately, the danger would be only for me.

Marq.: If you are afraid, you shouldn't act the hero. Well, let's hear it. You have nothing to say? You threaten me, I throw myself open, and you don't budge? I was expecting to see you at least cast yourself at my feet like Rodrigue in *The Cid*, or Mr. Camus himself. He would already have done it if he was you.

Count: Does it really amuse you to make fun of a poor fellow like me?

Marq.: And does it really surprise you to have someone challenge you to your face?

Count: Beware, if you challenge me! I used to be a cavalryman, I don't mind telling you, madam, and not so very long ago.

Marq.: Really! Well, that is fine. A cavalryman's proposal must be unusual. I have never seen one, in all my life. Do you want me to call my chambermaid? I suppose she will know how to answer you. You can put on a performance for me. *(The bell is heard ringing.)*

Count: That bell again! Well, good-by, Marquise. But we are not yet even, as far as I am concerned.
(He opens the door.)

Marq.: I shall still see you this evening, shall I not? But what in the world is that noise I hear?

Count: (Looking out the window.) It is a sudden change in the weather. It is raining and hailing cats and dogs. Someone is bringing you a third bonnet, and I am quite afraid it has a cold in it.

Marq.: But is that racket thunder? In the middle of January? What use are the almanacs?

Count: No, it is just a windstorm, some sort of cloudburst passing by.

Marq.: It is frightening. Please do close the door; you can't go out in weather like this. Whatever could be causing such a thing?

Count: (Closing the door.) Madam, it is divine wrath punishing the windowpanes, umbrellas, ladies' ankles, and chimney pots.

Marq.: And my horses are out!

Count: There is no danger, unless something falls on their heads.

Marq.: That is it, it is your turn to joke! I prize cleanliness, sir; I don't like my horses to get dirty. It is incredible! A little while ago the sky was as clear as could be.

Count: With this hailstorm, you can be sure that nobody will come. That is one less day for your salon.

Marq.: Not at all, since you are here. Please put down your hat, it is making me nervous.

Count: A compliment, madam! Beware. Since you profess to hate them, yours could be taken for the truth.

Marq.: I tell you so, and it is quite true. Your coming to see me gives me a good deal of pleasure.

Count: (Sitting down again next to the Marquise.) Then let me love you.

Marq.: But I have told you that, too; I am quite willing. It doesn't bother me in the least.

Count: Then let me talk to you about it.

Marq.: Cavalry-style?

Count: No, madam, you may rest assured that, though I don't have the heart, I have enough sense to respect you. But it seems to me one really is entitled, without offending a person one respects . . .

Marq.: To wait for the rain to pass? You came in here a while ago, not knowing why, you said so yourself. You were bored, you didn't know what to do, you might even be considered rather grumpy. If you had found three persons, anyone at all, here by the fire, by now you would be talking of literature or the railroads, after which you would go out to dinner. So it is because I am alone that you suddenly imagine yourself to be honorbound—yes, honor-bound—to pay me that same court, that everlasting, unbearable court, which is such a useless, ridiculous, banal thing. Why, whatever have I done to you? If some visitor happens to arrive, perhaps you will become witty. But I am alone, so you are as trite as an old music-hall song. Presto, you start up your theme and, if I were willing to listen to you, you would present me with a declaration, you would recite your love to me. Do you know what men seem like in such cases? Like those poor, unsuccessful authors who always have a manuscript in their pockets, some unpublished, unplayable tragedy that they pull out to bore you to death with as soon as you are alone with them for a few minutes.

Count: So you tell me you don't dislike me, I answer that I love you, and that is that, in your opinion?

Marq.: You don't love me any more than the Sultan of Turkey.

Count: Oh, my word, that is going too far. Listen to me for just a moment, and if you don't think I am sincere . . .

Marq.: No, no, and no! Good Lord, do you think I don't know what you might say to me? I have a good deal of respect for your learning but, just because you have been educated, do you think I haven't read anything? Listen, I once knew an intelligent man who had bought a collection somewhere or other, of fifty rather well-done letters, very correctly written, love letters of course. These fifty letters were arranged so as to form a sort of short novel in which every situation was foreseen. There were letters for proposals, for frustrations, for hopes, for the moments of hypocrisy when you fall back on friendship, for quarrels, for despair, for moments of jealousy, for bad moods, even for rainy days like today. I have read those letters. The author claimed in a sort of preface to have used them for himself, and never to have found a woman who could hold out longer than number thirty-three. Well, I held out for the entire collection! I ask you, do I know literature? Can you flatter yourself you could teach me something new?

Count: You are so blasé, Marquise.

Marq.: Insults, now? I prefer that; it is less insipid than all that sweet talk.

Count: Yes, it is true. You are so blasé.

Marq.: Do you think so? Well, I am not at all.

Count: Like an old Englishwoman who is the mother of fourteen children.

Marq.: Like the feather that dances on my hat. You must imagine that it takes quite profound wisdom to know you men by heart. But there is no need for study to learn; we only have to leave it to you. Just think: it is quite easy to figure out. Men kind enough to respect our poor ears and not sink to sugary

talk are extremely rare. On the other hand, there is no denying
that, at those sad moments when you try and lie in order to
please us, you look as alike as peas in a pod. Fortunately for
us, divine justice didn't put a terribly varied vocabulary at your
disposal. As the saying goes, you all sing the same song, so
the mere fact of hearing the same phrases, the mere repetition
of the same words, the same ready-made gestures, the same
tender glances, the mere spectacle of those various faces, which
may be quite all right in themselves, but which all take on the
same humbly conquering expression in those fatal moments,
all that saves us, thanks to our desire to laugh, or at least sim-
ple boredom. If I had a daughter and I wanted to protect her
from those approaches people call "dangerous," I would make
sure not to forbid her to listen to her dancing partners' love
poems. I would say to her: "Don't listen to just one, listen to
them all. Don't close the book, and don't mark the page; leave
it open, let these gentlemen recite their little pleasantries to
you. If, unfortunately, there should be one you like, don't re-
sist, just wait a while. Another one will come along just like
him, and he will make you sick of them both. You are fifteen
years old, I suppose. Well, my child, it will be like this till
you are thirty, and it will always be the same thing." That is
my story and my wisdom. Do you call that being blasé?
Count: Horribly, if what you say is true. But it seems so unnatural
that some doubt might be permitted.
Marq.: What does it matter to me whether you believe me or not?
Count: Better and better. Can it be true? What, you disdain love
at your age? The words of a man who loves you strike you like
a bad novel? His glances, his gestures, his feelings seem like
playacting to you? You take pride in speaking the truth, and
yet you see nothing but lies in others? Why, what in the world
have you been through, Marquise? What has given you maxims
like these?
Marq.: I have been through a good deal, neighbor.
Count: Yes, through what your nanny told you. Women imagine
they know everything there is to know, and they don't know a
thing. I ask you, yourself: What experience can you have had?
It is like the traveler who saw a red-haired woman at an inn,
and wrote in his diary: "Women have red hair in this country."

Marq.: I asked you to put a log on the fire.

Count: (Putting the log on it.) To be a prude is understandable. To say no, to stop up one's ears, to hate love is possible. But to deny it is ridiculous! You discourage a poor fellow when you say to him, "I know what you are going to say to me." But wouldn't he be right to answer you, "Yes, madam, perhaps you do; and I, too, know what people say when they are in love, but I forget it when I am speaking to you! There is nothing new under the sun; but I say in my turn, 'What does that prove?'"

Marq.: That is fine, at least you speak quite well! It is as close as one can get to a book.

Count: Yes, I speak. And I assure you that if you are the way you wish to appear, I sincerely pity you.

Marq.: Go ahead. Make yourself right at home.

Count: There is nothing in that to hurt your feelings. If you have the right to attack us, don't we have the right to defend ourselves? When you compare us to unsuccessful authors, what do you think you are accusing us of with that? Ha, my Lord, if love is just a stage play . . .

Marq.: The fire is dying. The log is askew.

Count: (Fixing the fire.) If love is a play, this play, as old as the world, fiasco or not, is, all in all, the least bad thing that has so far been found. The roles are trite, I admit, but if the play had no value the whole universe wouldn't know it by heart. And I am wrong to say it is old. Is to be immortal to be old?

Marq.: Sir, that is poetry.

Count: No, madam. But this twaddle, this nonsense that bores you, these compliments, these proposals, all this drivel, are quite good old things, conventional if you will, tiresome, silly at times; but they go with something else that is always young.

Marq.: You are getting mixed up. What is always old, and what is always young?

Count: Love.

Marq.: Sir, that is eloquence.

Count: No, madam. I mean just this: that love is immortally young, and the ways to express it are and will remain eternally old. The worn-out formulas, the repetitions, those bits of

novels that issue from one's heart for some reason or other, all
this backdrop, all this paraphernalia is a parade of old cham-
berlains, old diplomats, old ministers, it is the chatter of a
king's antechamber. It all passes, but the king never dies. Love
is dead, long live love!

Marq.: Love?

Count: Love. And even if one were only to imagine . . .

Marq.: Give me that screen over there.

Count: This one?

Marq.: No, the taffeta one. Your fire is blinding me now.

Count: (Giving the screen to the Marquise.) Even if one were only
to imagine one was in love, isn't it still a delightful thing?

Marq.: But I tell you it is always the same thing.

Count: And always new, as the song goes. What do you want peo-
ple to invent? Apparently you have to be made love to in
Greek. The Venus on your clock over there is also forever the
same thing. I ask you, does that make her any less beautiful?
If you look like your grandmother, does that make you any less
pretty?

Marq.: Fine, there is that refrain again: "pretty." Give me the
cushion over by you.

Count: (Picking the cushion up and holding it in his hand.) That
Venus was made to be beautiful, to be loved and admired, and
it doesn't bother her in the least. If the beautiful torso found in
Milo ever had a living model, you can be sure the wench had
more lovers than she needed, and she let them love her like any
other woman, like her cousin Astarte, like Aspasia and Manon
Lescaut.

Marq.: Sir, that is mythology.

Count: (Still holding the cushion.) No, madam. I cannot tell you
how much it pains me to see this fashionable indifference, this
railing and disdainful coldness, this air of experience that
reduces everything to nothing, in a young woman. You are not
the first one to show the symptoms of this illness that is
spreading through the salons. Young women turn away and
yawn, as you are doing right now, they say they don't want to
hear any talk of love. Then why do you wear lace? What is
that pompom doing on your head?

Marq.: And what is that cushion doing in your hands? I asked you for it so I could put it under my feet.

Count: Well, then, here it is, and me as well. And I shall make you a proposal whether you want it or not, as old as the hills and as silly as a goose, because I am absolutely furious with you. *(He sets the cushion on the ground before the Marquise and kneels on it.)*

Marq.: Will you please do me a favor, and get up from there?

Count: No. You have to listen to me first.

Marq.: You won't get up?

Count: No, no, and no, as you said a moment ago. Not unless you consent to listen to me.

Marq.: Then I am afraid I must say good-by.

(She stands up.)

Count: (Still on his knees.) Marquise, in heaven's name, this is too cruel! You will drive me mad, you are making me desperate.

Marq.: You will get over it at the Café de Paris.

Count: (As above.) No, on my honor, I am speaking from the depths of my heart. I agree all you like that I came in here with no purpose. I was intending only to see you for a moment, as you can see by that door, which I have opened to leave three times already . The conversation we have just had, your mockery, your very coldness, perhaps have made me go farther than I should have. But it is not just today, it is since the first day I saw you that I have loved you, I have adored you . . . I am not exaggerating when I say that . . . Yes, for more than a year I have adored you, I have thought of nothing . . .

Marq.: Good-by.

(The Marquise goes out, leaving the door open.)

Count: (Left alone, stays on his knees for a moment longer, then stands up and says:) It is true, that door is freezing. *(He starts to leave and sees the Marquise.)* Oh, Marquise, you are teasing me.

Marq.: (Leaning on the half-open door.) Are you standing up again?

Count: Yes, and I am leaving, and I won't ever see you again.

Marq.: Come to the ball this evening, I shall reserve a waltz for you.

Count: Never, never shall I see you again! I am in despair, I am finished.

Marq.: What is the matter?

Count: I am finished, I love you like a baby. I swear to you on all that is most holy . . .

Marq.: Good-by.

(*She starts to leave.*)

Count: I am the one who is leaving, madam. Stay, I beg of you. Oh! I know how much I am going to suffer!

Marq.: (In a serious tone.) Sir, what is it that you want of me, finally?

Count: Why, madam, I want . . . I should like . . .

Marq.: What? You are trying my patience. Do you imagine that I shall be your mistress, and inherit your pink hats? I warn you, I find such an idea more than unpleasant, I find it revolting.

Count: You, Marquise! Good Lord, if it were possible, I would place my entire life at your feet. I would like to grant you my name, my property, my very honor. Do you think I would confuse you even for a moment, not just with those creatures you mention only to annoy me, but with any woman in the world! Can you really have thought that? Do you think me so bereft of sense? Has my blundering or my senselessness gone so far as to make you doubt my respect? You were telling me a while ago that you took some pleasure in seeing me, that you perhaps felt some affection for me (isn't that so, Marquise?); could you imagine that a man thus singled out by you, whom you could deem worthy of such a precious, such a sweet indulgence, could possibly not realize your worth? Am I blind or mad, then? You, my mistress! No, no: my wife!

Marq.: Oh. Well, if you had told me that when you came in, we wouldn't have argued. So, you want to marry me?

Count: Why, certainly, I am dying to, I have never dared tell you so, but I have thought of nothing else for a year. I would give my life's blood to be permitted the slightest hope.

Marq.: Just a moment. You are wealthier than I am.

Count: Oh, my Lord, I don't think so, and what does that matter? I beg of you, let us not talk of such things! Your smile, at this moment, makes me tremble with hope and fear. Please, just one word, my life is in your hands!

Marq.: I am going to quote you two proverbs. The first is: "He who understands amiss, answers worse." Therefore we shall talk further about this.

Count: So you are not angry over what I have dared say to you?

Marq.: Of course not. Here is my second proverb: "A door has to be either open or shut." Now, for the past three-quarters of an hour this door, thanks to you, has been neither one nor the other, and this room is absolutely freezing. Therefore, once more, you are going to give me your arm, to go have dinner at my mother's house. After that you will go to Fossin's.

Count: To Fossin's, madam? Whatever for?

Marq.: My ring.

Count: Oh, that is right, I had forgotten. Well, then, what about your ring, Marquise?

Marq.: You said "Marquise"? Well, it just so happens that there is a small marquise's crown on the setting. And since it might be used as a seal . . . Tell me, Count, what do you think of that? Perhaps the crown will have to be removed? Come, I am going to put my hat on.

Count: I am overjoyed! . . . How can I express? . . .

Marq.: Why, shut that wretched door! This room won't be fit to stay in any more.

THE END

SELECT BIBLIOGRAPHY

Affron, Charles. *A Stage for Poets: Studies in the Theater of Hugo and Musset*. Princeton, 1971.

Bailey, Helen Phelps. *Hamlet in France: From Voltaire to Laforgue*. Geneva, 1964.

Gamble, Donald R. "The Image of Italy and the Creative Imagination of Alfred de Musset." In *Proceedings of the XIIth Congress of the International Comparative Literature Association, II, Space and Boundaries in Literature*, edited by Roger Bauer et al. Munich, 1988.

Gastinel, Pierre. *Le Romantisme d'Alfred de Musset*. Rouen, 1933.

Gochberg, Herbert. *Stage of Dreams*. Geneva, 1967.

Haldane, Charlotte F. *Alfred; The Passionate Life of Alfred de Musset*. New York, 1960.

Howarth, W. D. "Drama." In *The French Romantics*, edited by D. G. Charlton. Cambridge, 1984.

Lafoscade, Léon. *Le Théâtre d'Alfred de Musset*. Paris, 1901.

Lefebvre, Henri. *Alfred de Musset dramaturge*. Paris, 1955.

Masson, Bernard. *Musset et le théâtre intérieur*. Paris, 1974.

———. *Musset et son double, lecture de Lorenzaccio*. Paris, 1978.

Musset, Paul de. *Alfred de Musset, sa vie, son oeuvre*. Paris, 1877.

Rees, Margaret A. *Alfred de Musset*. London, 1971.

Shroder, Maurice Z. *Icarus: The Image of the Artist in French Romanticism*. Cambridge, Mass., 1961.

Sices, David. *Theater of Solitude: The Drama of Alfred de Musset*. Hanover, N.H., 1974.

Siegel, Patricia J. *Alfred de Musset: A Reference Guide*. Boston, 1982.

Thomas, Merlin. "Alfred de Musset: Don Juan on the Boulevard de Gand." In *Myth and Its Making in the French Theater*, edited by E. Freeman et al. Cambridge, 1988.

Library of Congress Cataloging-in-Publication Data

Musset, Alfred de, 1810–1857.
[Selections. English. 1994]
Comedies and proverbs / Introduction and translation by David Sices.
p.   cm.
Includes bibliographical references.
ISBN 0-8018-4682-X. — ISBN 0-8018-4683-8 (pbk.)
1. Musset, Alfred de, 1810–1857 — Translations into English.
I. Sices, David.   II. Title.
PQ2369.A28   1994
841′.7 — dc20   93-4371